PRAISE FOR THE NOVELS OF STACEY BALLIS

"With lively humor, Ballis pulls together a diverse cast, evocative renovation details, and delicious food descriptions in this well-seasoned novel. Fans of Mary Kay Andrews will enjoy this."

—*Booklist*

"Ballis's heroine is a perfect blend of tough and vulnerable as she struggles to straighten out her messy life."

—Heroes and Heartbreakers (A Best Read of the Month)

"A sparkling, heartwarming novel with all the elements of a can't-put-it-down read—a heroine you'll root for, unexpected plot twists, and dangerously good descriptions of food!"

—Sarah Pekkanen, author of *Things You Won't Say*

"A funny and heartfelt tale . . . This is Stacey Ballis at her witty and chef-tastic best."

—Amy Hatvany, author of *Safe with Me* and *Heart Like Mine*

"Readers hungry for cleverly written contemporary romances will definitely want to order *Off the Menu*."   —*Chicago Tribune*

"Insightful and hilarious."   —*Today's Chicago Woman*

"With the perfect blend of humor and heart, Ballis's writing is powerfully honest and genuinely hilarious."

—Jen Lancaster, *New York Times* bestselling author of
The Best of Enemies and *I Regret Nothing*

"Witty and tender, brash and seriously clever . . . Her storytelling will have you alternately turning pages and calling your friends urging them to come along for the ride."

—Elizabeth Flock, *New York Times* bestselling author of
What Happened to My Sister

BERKLEY BOOKS BY STACEY BALLIS

Room for Improvement

The Spinster Sisters

Good Enough to Eat

Off the Menu

Out to Lunch

Recipe for Disaster

Wedding Girl

Big Delicious Life
(Intermix)

Wedding Girl

STACEY BALLIS

BERKLEY BOOKS, NEW YORK

BERKLEY

An imprint of Penguin Random House LLC
375 Hudson Street, New York, New York 10014

Library of Congress Cataloging-in-Publication Data

Names: Ballis, Stacey, author.
Title: Wedding girl / Stacey Ballis.
Description: Berkley trade paperback edition. I New York : Berkley Books,
2015. I Description based on print version record and CIP data provided by
publisher; resource not viewed.
Identifiers: LCCN 2016005760 (print) I LCCN 2015050518 (ebook) I ISBN
9780698171251 () I ISBN 9780425276617 (paperback)
Subjects: LCSH: Single women—Fiction. I Bakers—Fiction. I
Weddings—Planning—Fiction. I BISAC: FICTION / Contemporary Women. I
FICTION / Humorous.
Classification: LCC PS3602.A624 (print) I LCC PS3602.A624 W43 2015 (ebook) I
DDC 813/.6—dc23
LC record available at http://lccn.loc.gov/2016005760

PUBLISHING HISTORY
Berkley trade paperback edition / May 2016

PRINTED IN THE UNITED STATES OF AMERICA

10 9 8 7 6 5 4 3 2 1

Penguin
Random
House

For Bill, in honor of our fifth wedding anniversary, who shows me every day that marriage is the most amazing, joyous, exhilarating adventure, and that it is fueled by laughter, great food, spectacular wine, and deep deep love. Thank you for being my real husband. I STILL love you more than Pamplemousse. Happy anniversary!

ACKNOWLEDGMENTS

This book would not be possible without my loving family, thank you all for showing me the best of marriage every day: Stephen and Elizabeth Ballis, Deborah and Andy Hirt, Jamie and Steve Surratt, and Jim and Shirley Thurmond.

Some other couples whom I find incredibly inspiring on the marriage front: Amy and Wayne Gould, Rick and Rachel Boultinghouse, Susan Kaip and Jeremy Kay, Kevin and Anna Ardito, Frank and Marnee Ardito, Karen and Mark Boerner, Jen Lancaster and John Fletcher, and most especially my other sets of parents: Susan and Henry Gault, Andi and Michael Srulovitz, Susan and George Heisler, and Carol and Larry Adelman. . . . Larry, you are much missed, and always in our hearts.

As always, whatever skill I have in cooking started with my grandmother, Jonnie Ballis. Thank you for teaching me to be fearless in the kitchen!

My agent and friend, Scott Mendel, who is invaluable professionally and so much fun personally.

For Wendy McCurdy, without whom this book literally would not exist, thank you so much for being on the ride, and making me a better writer.

For Danielle Perez, for getting me over the finish line. So blessed to be working with you, and looking forward to all that we have in front of us.

For Leslie Gelbman, Craig Burke, Brian Wilson, and the rest of the amazing team at Penguin Random House, thank you all for all you do.

For Penny, always.

My ever expanding circle of friends, especially my fellow writers, you know who you are and what you mean to me. Thanks for always being here, and being hungry!

Wedding Girl

Every Girl Should Be Married

(1948)

I may not meet the right man today. Or even this
week. Or even this year. But believe me, when I
see him, I'll know it.

• BETSY DRAKE AS ANABEL SIMS •

Nine months ago . . .

"You look gorgeous, Sunshine. A vision of loveliness." My dad
seems horribly uncomfortable in his tuxedo. He's tugging a bit
at the bow tie, which is crooked, but at least is black and real, as
opposed to what he showed up with this morning: a purple
clip-on covered in multihued Grateful Dead bears. His cum-
merbund is upside down, and he's wearing scuffed black Dr.
Martens, which are making his pants look short. But today I'm
so happy I don't even correct him on using the wrong name.

"Look what we made, Robert, just look." My mother glides
across the room in what can only be described as a fringed lavender muumuu, her waist-length graying curls twisted up in an
elaborate braided bun, like a black-and-white Greek Easter
bread attached to the back of her head. She tucks her short,
round form into the long expanse of my dad's embrace, and he
pulls her close and rests his head atop hers, both of them looking at me with a combination of deep love and concern.

"I know, Diane, I know. We did good." She beams up at him, and he kisses her deeply. With tongue. Gack.

"Hey, parents, could we please keep the making out to a minimum, at least until after dinner?" Don't get me wrong; it's fantastic that after over forty years together my folks are still hot for each other. I just really don't need to see it in shiny Technicolor.

They pull apart with a sickeningly slurpy squelch and look over at me.

"Poor Sunshine, she's still embarrassed of us," my dad teases.

"Bobby, you know she prefers Sophie; today of all days, give her a break," says Bubbles from her perch across the room in a comfortable chair. Thank god for the voice of reason.

"Of course, Mom, you're right; have to respect the bride's wishes." My dad walks over and kisses my grandmother on her soft, powdery cheek.

"Good boy." Bubbles pats the hand he has placed on her shoulder.

I was born Sunshine Sophie Summer Karma Bernstein. The Sophie was in honor of my dad's dad, Solomon, Bubbles's husband, who died only a month before I was born. I was Sunshine until I got to kindergarten, but when the whole class burst out in cruel laughter when the teacher called my name, I quickly replied, "My name is Sophie," and so I have been to everyone in my life except my dad ever since. My mom, as a clinical psychologist, is very much committed to honoring people's choices, so she made the switch immediately and with great purpose, correcting family friends and colleagues swiftly and firmly if they slipped. On my thirtieth birthday I gave myself a gift and had my name legally changed to Sophie Rosalind Bernstein. Bubbles's middle name is Rosalind, and Rosalind Russell is our favorite actress, so it seemed like a good choice. I still haven't gotten up the nerve to tell my parents. Bubbles says there's no need to cause trouble where there is none, so it is our secret. I once asked her if she minded being called Bubbles, and she laughed.

"You named me, and I wouldn't want to be called anything else."

When I was just learning to talk, at the precocious age of ten months, my parents kept trying to get me to call her Bubbe—Yiddish for "grandmother"—but I kept saying Bubbles, and it stuck. I've often felt bad about dumping such a frivolous name on someone so elegant and sophisticated, but she swears she loves it.

"You are a vision, Sophie, truly," she says, and I turn back to the full-length mirror that has been set up in our little lounge. And I have to admit, I look like Katharine Hepburn. Well, actually I look like I *ate* Katharine Hepburn, if you want to know the truth, but I look as glamorous and radiant as a girl could corseted within an inch of her life and stuffed into her custom size-twenty Vera Wang gown. Because you know what's fun, designers? That when us bigger girls go wedding-dress shopping, already a horror show of "sample" sizes we have to be shoehorned into to get a "sense" of how a dress "might" look, we discover your sizing is scaled for Lilliputians and completely unrelated to every other size chart on the planet. I'm a solid size sixteen almost everywhere, an eighteen in some of the more luxury brands, and a glorious, if rare, size fourteen in some lower-end brands. But only in Wangland am I a twenty. Oh, and the upcharge for bigger sizes is also a real treat; nothing like paying a fat tax for your special day. Thanks for that.

None of it matters today. The dress is a perfect rich off-white, the color of the cream of grass-fed cows; made of the heaviest matte silk; and in a simple strapless style that's fitted at the waist and then drapes over a subtle crinoline to just above my ankle. The gauzy organza overdress has wide, fluttery lapels and long, loose balloon sleeves cuffed at the wrist, which help to mask my not-exactly-Michelle-Obama-esque upper arms, and it buttons tightly on either side of my waist before extending over the skirt, which moves around me with a languorous swoosh. The dress was inspired by Katharine Hepburn's wedding dress in *The Philadelphia Story*, adjusted appropriately for my ample curves and made a bit more modern, but the feel is the same. I think Kate would approve, frankly. My thick, dark, often-unruly curls have been tamed into sleek, shiny waves, held back over my left ear with a jeweled clip, and my makeup is simple, highlighting my fair skin and hiding the spray of freckles across the bridge of my nose. A little silver shimmer on my eyelids makes my blue-gray eyes sparkle, and there's just a swipe of pale pink on my lips. The Dior pumps were probably a splurge I should have done without, considering the total cost of this day, but I couldn't resist. The opaline silver was just the perfect color, and while I'll probably be crippled for the rest of the week, they look fantastic. Heels are the bane of anyone who spends long workdays on her feet in supportive clogs.

Candace, the event manager here at the Ryan Mansion, comes flying in. "Sophie? Do you have time for a quick walk-through before we open the doors?"

"Of course."

My mom starts to walk toward us, but Bubbles catches the look on my face.

"Diane, dear, would you get me some more of that sparkling water, please? You go ahead, Sophie; the three of us will wait here for you." Thank god for Bubbles. She knows how much work went into planning this day. And she also knows that I don't want anything to mar it. Like another lecture from my happily unmarried parents about why a piece of paper doesn't mean anything, and about how many wells could be dug in Africa for what I'm spending on my top-shelf open bar, or how many cleft palate surgeries could be performed in South America for a fraction of what the flowers cost.

I follow Candace out of the lounge and down the hall to the elevator.

"You look gorgeous," she says as we ride down to the main floor. "How do you feel? Nervous at all?"

"Actually, no. I feel great. Never felt better!"

And I do. No jitters, no sweaty palms, no butterflies. This is the day I was destined for. The man I was destined for. Dexter Kelley IV—DK to his friends, and Dex to me—is literally my every dream come true. After a lifetime of listening to my mother proudly announce her "Ms." status when correcting people who referred to her as "Mrs.," I'm ready to happily check the "Mrs." box. After endlessly explaining why my last name is different from both my parents'—Dad's is Bernard, Mom's is Goldstein, so I got to be Bernstein, a combination of the two, invented in no small part because of Carl Bernstein and the fact that my folks met at an anti-Nixon rally in 1973—I'm ecstatic to become simply Sophie Kelley.

And who wouldn't be? In Dex, I've found my perfect partner in all things. We work together at Salé et Sucré, the two-Michelin-starred restaurant from Alexandre Leroux and Georg Zimmer. I'm the senior pastry sous chef and heir apparent to Georg, and Dexter is the head sommelier. We've been working together for six years and have been a couple for nearly three. We've landed an angel investor for a soon-to-be restaurant of our own. Local socialite Colleen "Cookie" Carlisle has agreed to terms on funding the purchase and build-out of our first place, including finding us a stunning location on Fulton in a huge warehouse space and hiring the superhot Palmer Square Development team to do the design/build.

I have to say, as much as I love my Dexter . . . our general contractor, Liam, is insanely gorgeous. I don't know how his wife, Anneke, ever lets him out of her sight. Of course, since she's the lead architect, I guess she doesn't really have to, but when those babies drop, she's not going to have much of a choice; I would imagine twins are going to trump just about everything. Our project manager, Jag, promises that it'll be smooth sailing, and both Cookie and Dexter have total confidence, so I'm following along. After all, it's Cookie's money, and some of Dexter's. The agreement is that I will cover the wedding and he will cover the restaurant, and that seems more than fair as we begin our lives together. My dad, ever the lawyer, thought we should both equally fund two separate accounts to pay for things so that it was all even, but I didn't even broach the idea with Dex. To be honest, I don't really want him to know what I'm spending on this event. Despite keeping the guest list down to under a hundred and calling in major at-cost favor pricing from chef pals and vendors who work with the restaurant, the event was still coming in at nearly seventy grand, which has pretty much emptied my savings and maxed out all my credit cards, including three brand-new ones. Gone are the gifts from my family: five grand from Mom and Dad and two from Bubbles. Not to mention the bat mitzvah bonds I cashed in. But a girl only gets one shot at her dream wedding, and besides, Dexter's trust fund will come entirely under his own control in a few weeks, which is why he said we should both stay in our apartments and wait before looking for a new place for the two of us, and postpone planning our honeymoon.

"When the trust turns over, we'll be able to find the perfect house, and when we officially quit, we can take a few weeks off to travel before jumping into the restaurant full bore. Everything will be so much easier then. Do you really want to go through the hassle of combining households in one of our places now and then having to repack and reorganize in a few months?"

I'm sure that when his trust kicks in, my newly minted

hubby will have no problem helping me pay off this minor debt I've accrued. After all, while the trust isn't billions, it certainly has enough zeroes that we should be able to do everything we want house- and honeymoon-wise, with plenty of cushion for the future, and I know he'll see the value of starting our life together debt-free. Especially with the lifelong memories of this glorious day.

Candace and I step off the wood-paneled elevator and into the wide entry room of the mansion. This place is my win-the-lottery dream house: twelve thousand square feet of late-1800s graystone on elegant Astor Street. And we are using all of it. The first-floor dining room will have the ceremony; the adjoining living room will house our cocktail hour. Then everyone will go up to the second level for the sit-down five-course dinner and dancing in the massive formal ballroom, with the anterooms set up for cozy conversation, and a smoking room for the cigar crowd. At midnight everyone will be shuttled back to the first floor to the library for a breakfast/late-night-snack-food buffet, and then out through the foyer, where silver gift bags will be magically waiting. Then Dexter and I will head up to the third-floor suite for our wedding night before meeting our out-of-town guests and closest friends and family tomorrow at Manny's for a brunch generously hosted by Bubbles.

As Candace walks me through all the spaces, I'm blown away. The flowers—arranged by Cornelia McNamara, who does all the special events at the restaurant—feature Cornelia's signature effortlessly elegant style, all in shades of white and cream with plenty of greenery, and displayed in crystal vases and silver bowls on every surface. The ceremony chairs are swagged in sheer tulle, and the gossamer chuppah is wound with ivy and fairy lights, the canopy gathered in perfect folds to create a small tent. Georg and Alexandre both got Internet-ordained so that they can jointly do the ceremony for us, Georg

covering the Jewish parts and Alexandre taking care of the secular stuff.

The round dining tables, small six-tops to keep conversation
flowing, are set with white linen cloths with deep-magenta
linen napkins, centerpieces that are a riot of magentas and
oranges, candles in silver candlesticks, bone china, and Riedel
crystal glasses lined up for the exquisite wine pairings Dexter
has planned for every course. The stage is set up for the jazz
orchestra, and there, in the center of the dance floor, is the cake.

Three square tiers of hazelnut cake filled with caramel
mousse and sliced poached pears, sealed with vanilla buttercream scented with pear eau-de-vie. It's covered in a smooth
expanse of ivory fondant decorated with what appear to be natural branches of pale green dogwood but are actually gum paste
and chocolate, and with almost-haphazard sheer spheres of silvery blown sugar, as if a child came by with a bottle of bubbles
and they landed on the cake. On the top, in lieu of the traditional
bride and groom, is a bottle of Dexter's favorite Riesling in a bow
tie and a small three-tier traditional wedding cake sporting a
veil, both made out of marzipan. It took me the better part of the
last three weeks to make this cake. Not to mention the loaves of
banana bread, the cellophane bags of pine nut shortbread cookies, and the little silver boxes of champagne truffles in the gift
bags. And the vanilla buttermilk panna cottas we're serving
with balsamic-macerated berries as the pre-dessert before the
cake. And the hand-wrapped caramels and shards of toffee and
dark-chocolate-covered candied ginger slices that will be served
with the coffee.

There's no point to being a pastry chef if you can't get your
own wedding sweets perfect.

"It's, just, *everything*," I whisper.

Candace puts an arm around my waist and squeezes. At least
I think she's squeezing; who can feel anything through this cor-

set? "It's one of my most favorite weddings we've ever had here. You should be a wedding planner."

"Not me. I only want to plan one wedding in my life, and this one is it. The rest of the brides are on their own."

"Well, maybe for a daughter someday?"

"Maybe." I say this, but I don't really mean it. The restaurant business, even under the best of circumstances, is a hard row to hoe for parents. Kids don't care that the James Beard Award people are in the house and lingering over their luncheon coffee when you are supposed to be watching your special snowflake play a carrot in the school show. And *Saveur* magazine doesn't care that your kids were up at two a.m. projectile pooping in your bed the night before your big photo shoot. But the health department cares very much if you have been exposed to chicken pox or strep throat or lice, and wants you not to come within a hundred yards of your own premises. None of this bodes well for being either a fantastic restaurateur or a perfect mommy, so I'm reasonably certain parenting isn't in the cards. Dexter seems fine with the idea that there won't be a Dexter V; after all, he says, he's got two older sisters popping out heirs, and a younger brother to carry on the family name, so he's off the hook in the breeding department.

I have to admit, seeing Anneke all preggers out to there, and the way Liam watches her and smiles and gently touches her belly when he walks by her, does give the old ovaries a twinge. Hopefully, if the new place gets up and running well, and we have some success, maybe in a couple of years we can revisit, see if maybe just one child might be a possibility. I would really love to see Bubbles become a great-grandbubbles, and unlike Dex, I have no siblings to rely on for that.

"Well, if everything looks good to you, I'd say we could open the doors and get ready to welcome your guests," Candace says.

"Can I check in on the kitchen?" I ask.

She looks me up and down. "Yes, but hold on a second." She disappears down the hallway and returns with a large men's trench coat. "Lost-and-found treasure," she says as I eye the garment. "Put this on; I'm not sending you into that kitchen with this dress exposed. And promise you'll stand in the doorway. I'll bring everyone to you." I laugh and slide the coat over myself, grateful that it buttons, albeit tightly, over my hips.

We walk over to a swinging door, and she holds it open while I stand just inside. "Bride in the house!" she calls out, and immediately three people come walking over.

"Hello, Chef, congrats to you," says my friend Erick, who has taken a night off from both of his restaurants to man the kitchen.

"You congratulate the groom, silly, and wish the bride luck." I accept his kiss on my cheek.

"You don't need luck; you're a rock star," says Gino, who is serving as Erick's sous chef today and running the line.

"We're gonna ruin these people," says Megan, who is doing all the appetizers and covering the midnight buffet.

The menu is spectacular. Passed hors d'oeuvres include caramelized shallot tartlets topped with Gorgonzola, cubes of crispy pork belly skewered with fresh fig, espresso cups of chilled corn soup topped with spicy popcorn, mini arepas filled with rare skirt steak and chimichurri and pickled onions, and prawn dumplings with a mango serrano salsa. There is a raw bar set up with three kinds of oysters, and a raclette station where we have a whole wheel of the nutty cheese being melted to order, with baby potatoes, chunks of garlic sausage, spears of fresh fennel, lightly pickled Brussels sprouts, and hunks of sourdough bread to pour it over. When we head up for dinner, we will start with a classic Dover sole amandine with a featherlight spinach flan, followed by a choice of seared veal chops or duck breast, both served with creamy polenta, roasted mushrooms, and lacinato kale. Next is a light salad of butter lettuce with a sharp lemon Dijon vinaigrette, then a cheese course with each table receiving a platter of five cheeses with dried fruits and nuts and three kinds of bread, followed by the panna cottas. Then the cake, and coffee and sweets. And at midnight, chorizo tamales served with scrambled eggs, waffle sticks with chicken fingers and spicy maple butter, candied bacon strips, sausage biscuit sandwiches, and vanilla Greek yogurt parfaits with granola and berries on the "breakfast" buffet, plus cheeseburger sliders, mini Chicago hot dogs, little Chinese take-out containers of pork fried rice and spicy sesame noodles, a macaroni-and-cheese bar, and little stuffed pizzas on the "snack food" buffet. There will also be tiny four-ounce milk bottles filled with either vanilla malted milk shakes, root beer floats made with hard root beer, Bloody Marys, or mimosas. As Megan said, we plan on ruining these people. The initial sticker shock on just the food bill almost made me pass out, and I thought long and hard about nixing the whole midnight-buffet idea. But I figure, if Dex and I are about to open a restaurant, especially a restaurant we hope will be hosting special events, these are the people we are going to need in our corner to help us promote it, so it's important to let them see how we bring an event together. Plus, if I'm to be honest, having been to a zillion boring, disappointing weddings, I think there is something to be said for being the person who pulls off the amazing one that people remember.

I look at these dear friends who are practically working for free to make our day perfect, and grin at them.

"We expected nothing less, and we cannot thank you all enough for all of this. You know that I owe every one of you wedding or birthday cakes when the time comes!"

"We're going to hold you to that. Have the day you deserve, and don't worry, we got this!" Erick says, winking at me. "Let's go, everyone; we've got mouths in ninety minutes."

Candace shuttles me out of the kitchen, relieves me of my borrowed trench coat, and hustles me back to the elevator. "We're opening the doors, and I know you said you weren't doing the whole surprise thing, but I just want to check that you are still planning on mixing and mingling pre-ceremony?"

"We're not superstitious, and the more people we have face time with before the ceremony and during the cocktail hour, the more we will be able to just sit and enjoy our dinner." We have a cozy table for two up in the ballroom, close to the dance floor, but still just a little quiet space for ourselves.

"Okay, then I would do one last lip gloss and hair spray check, and send your family down, and then join them in about ten minutes."

"Will do."

I head back upstairs to my lounge. The door is slightly ajar, and I can hear my parents talking.

"It isn't that I don't like him; I just don't like him for her. He seems just a little too slick for my taste," my dad says.

My mother pipes up. "I know, I agree, but what can we do? She loves him. We have to support her fully in that."

"Does she?" my dad says. "Or does she love what he represents? Does she love the idea of him? Does she love that he isn't me?"

"Pish, Robert, it isn't about you," my mom says. "She wants everything that isn't us, that isn't what we chose, and we can't choose for her. All we can do is help her have her perfect day the way she wants it, and hope for the best."

"What the two of you can do is stop worrying and let the smart, beautiful, capable girl you raised make her own life the way she wants it. She's not some child; she's thirty-four years old. And who she is and what she chooses and what she may or may not think of you and your choices is officially none of your business." Go Bubbles.

I move a few steps back from the door and stomp loudly, calling out, "You guys ready to get your party on in there?" and fly into the room in a swirl of silk, with a big smile. Nothing can ruin today, not even my parents' concerns. It isn't like I don't know what they think of me, of the life I've pursued. With his brain, his mouth, and his Ivy League degrees, Dad could have been a powerful litigator and partner at a big firm but chose the life of a public defender with pro bono exoneration work instead. My mother, equally smart and accomplished and accredited, could have been the ultimate therapist to the rich and famous, but she chose a position in which she's effectively a social worker, as a psychologist attached to local public hospitals, schools in terrible neighborhoods, group homes, and juvenile detention centers. She does a lot of work with my dad's clients when they get court-ordered therapy. When I went to culinary school after college, they were thrilled. Right up until I decided on a life of cooking in high-end fine-dining restaurants, and not running a soup kitchen staffed by reformed convicts, or teaching cooking classes to welfare moms. They don't even like me cooking for the 1 percent; marrying one of them was never going to go over terribly well.

"We're ready if you are!" Lucky for me, my mom is adept at putting a good face on it, and for today, that is enough.

"I'm ready. Dad, if you will please escort these lovely ladies downstairs, I will be down in two shakes to join you. Bubbles, there is a cozy corner in the library if you need to sit."

"I'm not infirm, child. I'll be perfectly fine with the rest of them, thank you very much." Bubbles claims eighty-two, though I suspect that may be slightly underestimating things. But she is reasonably fit, if occasionally forgetful, so I leave it to her to decide when she needs to sit.

My dad looks me deep in my eyes and leans over to kiss the tip of my nose like he used to when I was little. "See you down there, Sunshi . . . um, Sophie."

I walk over to the mirror and check myself one last time. Everything is in place. And my future is waiting. I turn and head out of the room, closing the door behind me. When I get off the elevator, well-wishers immediately surround me. Holding the wedding on a Monday helped keep the costs down a bit, but more important, it meant that our friends from work were all able to come, since we are closed Monday nights. And a lot of our friends from other restaurants are here as well. All the local restaurant critics and food bloggers we've befriended over the years are here. The hum of people is warm and welcoming, and as I move through the crowd, I accept the compliments and congratulations graciously.

Dexter should be around here somewhere, but I don't see his brother yet, so maybe they are still on their way. Dexter's parents are on an exclusive safari in South Africa, which apparently was booked over a year ago and which we didn't know about until I had already plunked down the substantial nonrefundable deposit on the space. I thought perhaps they would offer to cover the costs of changing the date, but instead they said they would throw us an East Coast reception at the family home in Connecticut this summer. His sisters just couldn't make the trip what with all the kids and the Monday date, so it is just his little brother, Dave, who is here to represent the family. Except "here" is not exactly correct. Dexter said he was picking him up at the airport yesterday morning, and that the two of them were doing bachelor stuff, and then golfing today, but it is nearly five o'clock, so they must be close. I left my phone off and upstairs in the safe in the lounge—this is not the time for text messages from vendors about produce orders, or Facebook updates about dog videos. I'll take one more pass around, and if I don't see Dexter, I'll just zip upstairs and check my phone in case they are stuck in traffic.

"This is amazing, and you are spec-freaking-tacular." I turn to see the beaming face of my best friend, Ruth. Ruth and I grew up on the same block and have been friends since we were five. Just seeing her grinning face immediately makes me forget my momentary worry. I hug her.

"Thank you."

"I can't believe the whole thing. Are you ready?"

"Ready as anything. Where is Jean?" Jean was Ruth's first girlfriend in college, part of Ruth's transition from "bi-curious" to "full-time power lesbian," and while the romance fizzled quickly, the friendship was forever. Jean quickly became one of my dearest friends as well, and the pair of them keep me sane. Ruth is an investment banker, all badass in her fabulous Armani suits, and Jean is a freelance costume designer for theater, all kinds of funky and artsy and creative. Between the two of them, I get the best possible advice on everything under the sun.

"You know Jean; she had a meeting this afternoon that she swore would be done by three, but those theater people take two hours to just say good-bye. She texted me that she is en route."

I hear the doors open and peek over Ruth's head to see who is coming in, and it is Jean, but her face is ashen. I wave and she makes a beeline over to me. I notice that the hum in the room has softened a bit, and it seems that suddenly a lot of people are reaching for their cell phones, and the loud chatter is now a lot of whispering.

"Hey, honey," Jean says, grabbing me in a deep and powerful hug.

"Don't wrinkle the bride!" Ruth tries to pry Jean away, but Jean won't let go.

"Jean. Have corset. Can't breathe." I lean back and Jean finally breaks her embrace.

"Baby girl, we are here for you and with you, and this is all going to be okay."

My stomach drops.

"What the fuck are you talking about, Jean?" Ruth is snippy.

"I heard it on the radio on my way over. Dexter . . ."

Oh no. This cannot be happening. There's been a horrible accident. He cannot be gone. I make a little yelping noise as my eyes fill with tears. "Is he . . . ?"

Jean shakes her head, her eyes reflexively filling with sympathy tears. "He's not coming, dearheart. He's in St. Barths."

My heart drops back into my chest. My tears dry up. "I'm sorry, what?"

"Jean, you are making no fucking sense whatsoever. Spit it out, woman." Ruth shakes her shoulders a bit.

"I was listening to the news on WGN radio on my way over. They congratulated local girl Cookie Carlisle and her new husband, hotshot sommelier Dexter Kelley, on their elopement today in St. Barths."

All the air flies out of my lungs.

"That bastard," Ruth mutters.

I look up and see that everyone in the room is looking over at me with shocked faces or still staring at their phones, which I presume are blowing up with the news, and my parents and Bubbles are elbowing their way purposefully through the crowd. This isn't possible. This is a night-before-the-wedding nightmare. I'm going to wake up any minute in my cozy bed and get ready to start my wedding day.

But then Bubbles holds her arms out to me and says, "Here, *shayna maidela*, here," and I know that it is real as soon as I sink into her embrace.

My dad is rubbing my shoulders and saying all the things one would imagine a pissed-off dad would say, and my mom has joined the hug with Bubbles and me and is telling me into my hair that it is all going to be okay. Ruth and Jean are whispering behind me, and everything is soft-focus, and numb.

I stand up straight and shake them all off. "Okay, then," I say.

"What do you need?" my dad asks.

"What do you want?" my mom asks.

"Who can I kill?" Ruth asks.

"I have this," I say. Because if Dexter Kelley the fucking Fourth is going to steal my happiness and my future and my hopes and dreams, he sure as shit is not going to steal my dignity. I'm going to do what Rosalind Russell would do. Fake it till I make it.

I take a deep breath and try to keep the waver out of my voice as I call out, "Can I have everyone's attention, please?" The already-quiet crowd shifts immediately to dead silent.

Ruth takes my hand and squeezes. Which gives me just enough power to continue. "I take it that what I am about to say is not going to come as a surprise to many of you, but it appears that this wedding was rescheduled, unbeknownst to us all, at a different location. And apparently with a different bride. This is obviously not how we all thought things were going to go today, but I know one thing. I have some of the best chefs in the city in that kitchen making a meal that is going to knock your socks off. I have a lot of wine and liquor that has already been paid for, and a really great band warming up, and none of us are going to let any of that, or this beautiful venue, go to waste. So I'm going to ask your indulgence as I take a few moments to myself, and hope that when I return, you will all join me in having a spectacular party. We're going to think of this as my official Dodged a Bullet celebration, and I expect you all to eat and drink copiously, and dance with abandon, and please not offer me any condolences. Only happy talk tonight. If you know a joke or two, get them ready; we're going to do open mike instead of toasts. I'll be back soon, but please get the party started. My wonderful parents and

grandmother are going to show you all to the living room, where
you can get cocktails, and the food will be out soon." The crowd
bursts into applause and hoots and hollers and shouts of "You go,
girl!" and "You rock, Sophie!" and my parents wink at me, and
Bubbles squeezes my arm, and they head over to wrangle the
crowd on my behalf.

I head for the elevator, Ruth and Jean in tow, and we make
our way upstairs. In the lounge, the two of them begin a long
string of expletives and threats on Dexter's manhood, and I go
to the safe and get my phone and turn it on. No messages from
Dexter. No texts from him. No emails from him, just those
offering support from people who heard the bad news. And noti-
fications that my Facebook and Twitter feeds are going crazy. I
shut it down.

"Are you . . . ?" Ruth starts, and I hold my hand up.

"Not now. I cannot do anything right now. Right now I
would just like for the two of you to agree to spend the night
here with me tonight after the party, when I'm reasonably sure
I will be ready for a total meltdown. But for the moment, there
is one quick thing I need to do, and then we are going down
there, and I mean it, not one word about him or this insane situation or anything unhappy. We are going to get through this
night with our best faces on, and have a slumber party, and then
tomorrow we can figure it all out. Deal?"

"Deal," Jean says. "I'm so proud of you."

"You are the most amazing woman I know," Ruth says.

They follow me out, and we head back downstairs, stopping
at the second floor. "Hold the elevator for me, would you? I'll be
right back."

I walk up the hallway to the ballroom and open the door.
The room is just as perfect as before. The band is beginning to
do a sound check. A busboy is leaning against a wall, and I wave
him over.

"Hi, you see that small table for two near the dance floor? Can you please make it disappear before we come back up?" He nods, heads right over, and starts removing the dishes. I cross the room and go to the cake table. Gently, so as not to mar the top surface, I remove the whimsical toppers. I look for a place to set them down or throw them away, and not finding one in my line of sight, slowly and deliberately, bit by bit, I eat them.

The Awful Truth

(1937)

No, things are the way you think I made them. I didn't make them that way at all. Things are just the same as they always were, only, you're the same as you were too, so I guess things will never be the same again.

· IRENE DUNNE AS LUCY WARRINER ·

Today . . .

I grab the last box out of my battered Honda, lock the doors, and carry it up the wide stoop and through the front door.

"My goodness, now that is a very stinky Snatch!" I hear Bubbles in the other room, and I shake my head and suppress my giggles. A fat, elderly pug comes barreling down the hallway in my direction, in a custom sweater with black-and-yellow bumblebee stripes. Bubbles is on his heels with what looks like a dryer sheet in each hand.

"Snatch. You stop right there, young man," she says to the dog, who halts and plops down on his wide ass. If he weren't a boy, I'd say Snatch has childbearing hips, in addition to his desperately horrible moniker. Bubbles, completely unaware of any alternate meaning, named the pup thusly because he has a habit of snatching anything in his reach and running away with it, a favorite game. So Snatch he became, much to my amusement and my parents' mortification.

"He rolled in something dead in the backyard," Bubbles says, by way of explanation, removing the offending garment and rubbing his rolls down with the dryer sheet in an effort to deodorize him. "Silly Snatch," she says lovingly to him, and I head upstairs before I burst out laughing.

Straight up the narrow staircase and left at the top, into the second room on the right. Boxes are stacked floor to nearly ceiling on three of the four walls; there are piles of clothes on the bed, tote bags of all shapes and sizes on the floor and on the desk. I drop the last box on the floor in the far corner and sink into the battered blue velvet chair with shiny patches on the arms where the velvet has been rubbed away from years of use. The room, with an antique four-poster bed that had belonged to my great-grandparents, periwinkle walls, and a sparkly chandelier, had felt spacious and warm before I filled it with all my crap.

"Is that everything?" Bubbles asks from the doorway.

"That's it." I wave my arm around the room. "The sum total of my worldly possessions."

She crosses the space delicately, weaving around the obstacles on the floor with fluid grace. She perches on the wide arm of the chair and takes my chin in her hands. "Your worldly possessions are in here and here." She points her finger at my heart and kisses my forehead. "Everything else is just stuff."

"Well, here is all my stuff."

"I forgot to ask; maybe we should have painted the room? You picked this color when you were six. I know your taste has changed."

My room. Growing up, I spent a lot of time here at Bubbles's house. She insisted on taking me after school one day a week and one weekend a month. It gave my parents a break and gave us quality time together. I always stayed in the room that had been my dad's when he was a boy. When I was six, I told Bubbles that I loved coming over but that the Cubs-blue walls and boyish décor were not really my style, and the next time I came for the weekend, we decorated the room. We picked out the pale color at the hardware store and painted the walls ourselves. I agonized at Vogue Fabrics, finally settling on deep-eggplant-purple linen, and Bubbles whipped up some drapes on her trusty Singer in a flash. She took me into her attic of treasures and let me pick out the bed and desk from the stash of family antiques that no one wanted but she couldn't bear to give away. We found the velvet chair at a thrift store. And the next time I came over, she had installed the chandelier over the bed, all the shiny crystals making a dance of light on the ceiling when the sunlight caught them. It was my magical princess room, and over the years the walls sported posters first of unicorns and kittens and then of boy bands and then grunge bands, and then, in college, came the ubiquitous poster of Klimt's *The Kiss.* Now they are bare, with teeny holes visible here and there where pushpins used to be. The desk where I did all sorts of homework and sticker-collection management, and wrote in little diaries with tiny locks and keys, is empty, the top clear except for a picture of my granddad in a silver frame, looking dapper in a suit and jaunty fedora, winking at the camera and, by proxy, at me, the namesake he never met.

"It's still my favorite room. I wouldn't change a thing," I say, smiling at her as best I can.

"Well, if you change your mind, we'll redecorate. Now, all of this stuff will wait. I've got treats downstairs. We'll have some Nook time."

In my grandmother's kitchen is a small bay window where there is a tiny café table with two chairs that she and my grandfather brought back from their honeymoon in Paris. They got the set for a song from a little bistro that was going out of business near their hotel, and then schlepped all three pieces back with them as luggage. The story of taking it all on the Métro is a family classic. But the creamy white marble top is shot with blue green like really good Roquefort, and has been worn matte and smooth like a river rock with years of use. The chairs with their scrolled iron frames and worn wooden seats are shockingly comfortable. We have always called the charming tableau in the window "the Nook," and all of our most important conversations have happened there, with cups of cocoa or hot tea or champagne or bourbon, and always with some sort of sweet little nibble: My decision to go to culinary school, right at that table with a mouth full of apricot coffee cake. The John Hughes—esque choice to say yes to the nervous, bespectacled boy from my English class who'd never uttered a word in my direction until he asked me to prom, and who did not become a wild romance but did become an unexpectedly good friend. The decision to legally change my name, and the equally important decision not to tell my parents.

"I'll be down in ten minutes, I promise."

"I'll put the kettle on. You hear that whistle; you get your tushy downstairs."

"Deal."

Bubbles heads to the kitchen, and I take stock of my shame. I am thirty-four years old. Nine months ago, I was left at the altar by my perfect-on-paper fiancé in favor of a tanorexic new-money skeleton of a socialite, resulting in my being over fifty grand in debt on my dream wedding and one hundred percent screwed on my dream life. My wedding photographer, unbeknownst to me, did not capture my "riot grrrl" moment of announcing Dexter's departure from my life and telling my nearest and dearest that the show would go on and to drink up. But he did quite adequately capture my consumption of my own wedding-cake toppers, and my drunken rendition of Quarter-flash's quintessential breakup ballad "Harden My Heart" with the band. He got great shots of my epic wipeout on the dance floor when Jean tried to spin me, a real flattering ass-up, crinoline-over-the-head, Spanx-akimbo classic. And my personal favorite: the picture of me alone, sitting on the stairs, one Dior pump with a broken-off heel lying next to me, with an enormous piece of wedding cake that I am eating out of my hand as crumbs scatter down the front of my dress. Fat Cinderella wannabe after the ball, with no prince chasing her, just a broken shoe and a broken heart, eating her feelings. These lovely memories he sold to everyone who would buy them, and I spent the better part of a month confronted with photo arrays of my own embarrassment all over the local Chicago papers and the national online gossip magazines. The mortifying images were usually accompanied by a picture of Dexter and Cookie on a beach at sunset kissing passionately, the official wedding picture their publicist sent out. I even got a sympathetic mention from Hoda and Kathie Lee, and if I hadn't been so completely horrified, I probably would have eventually gotten around to sending them the cupcakes I meant to bake for them: Cabernet cupcakes with mascarpone frosting—wine and cheese.

I decided it was best to still take the week off after the wedding. Dexter and I had planned on a little staycation honeymoon, and so I wasn't expected at work. I spent the week in a daze, holed up in my apartment, ignoring calls and well-wishers and interview requests. The night before I was scheduled to return to work, my boss, Georg, called to see if I needed more time, but also informed me that Dexter had quit, making it safe for me to come back if I was ready. I thought that work would be my refuge. I wouldn't have to see his lying, cheating face every day or work with him. And for nearly six weeks, I just put my head down and channeled all my anger and mortification and thwarted passions into my work. I didn't even blink when a large box containing all the belongings I'd left at Dexter's apartment arrived by messenger without so much as an apology note. The fact that when I went to do the same I was confronted with the realization that the only things of his at my place were a toothbrush and a stick of deodorant made me wonder if I had been delusional about the entire relationship, but I shook it off. His apartment had been so much more comfortable than mine and was walking distance from work, I had liked staying there as much as Dexter did, and I wasn't ever one of those girls who needed him to nest at my place just because it was mine. He had the good TV, the better wine, the bigger bed, the nicer tub.

I threw away the toothbrush and deodorant, and washed my hands of it. The mistake hadn't been mine; it had been his. And I was grateful he had shown his true colors before we made things legal. I was strong. I was tough. I was impressive.

Right up until the entire staff got invited to the soft opening of Abondance, the "new restaurant venture from Dexter and Cookie Kelley."

They'd kept the name I had come up with, the French word for "abundance"; my concept, French-influenced comfort foods elevated to fine-dining quality; and the glorious space I had helped conceive. I looked at the invitation, everything it represented, and I officially lost my shit.

I started phoning it in at work, taking shortcuts, losing my perfectionist's edge. I sent out desserts that were overbaked, breads that were lackluster, chocolates that hadn't been properly tempered and had no shine or snap. I was short and snippy with everyone I worked with, and downright insubordinate with Georg, who had been my mentor as well as my boss since I got out of culinary school. He was patient for a couple of weeks and then terse for another month, and then he stopped giving me a break and simply gave me enough rope to hang myself. I skated by for a couple more months, my work getting shoddier by the day and my attitude getting worse. I systematically alienated every person at the restaurant from the dishwashers to the front-of-house staff, people I had once thought of as friends, who now could barely be civil to me. Abondance opened to rave reviews and plenty of press, which caused an unfortunate resurgence in coverage of my sad little tale of romantic woe and the accompanying pictures. I drowned my feelings in food and gin until every piece of clothing I owned was tight as a tourniquet, and I only backed off my binging because I couldn't afford to buy new ones. After I came in hours late for the fourth day in a row, Georg demoted me from senior pastry sous chef to pastry assistant, and when I told him in no uncertain terms that every original idea that had come out of the pastry kitchen in the last four years had been mine, and that he had better not expect me to give up the goods if I was just a lowly assistant, he fired me.

Boy, did I ever deserve it. The news of my career fall from grace only served to flip the script on my victimhood in the whole Dexter debacle, making everyone think that he bailed on the wedding because I'm insane and difficult, and that Cookie saved him from marrying a horrible person. What few friends I had left in the local industry dried up and became Team Dexter.

Ruth and Jean abducted me to Canyon Ranch spa, where one of Ruth's clients owned a home she had always offered to Ruth, and the three of us spent a week detoxing and exercising. I had several sessions with one of the counselors where I cried a lot and mourned what was supposed to be, and I returned home somewhat more myself and with something of a plan. I would sell my condo and my engagement ring, and use the profits to pay off my credit card debt. I'd move in with Bubbles temporarily while I got my shit together, and think about my next professional move. The Chicago restaurant scene will be pretty closed to me for the foreseeable future—I now have enough of a rep as a problem-child diva to have ensured that—but I might be able to do something in catering or hotel work.

The plan started great. My folks had been toying with trying to convince Bubbles to explore assisted-living communities—some recent bits of forgetfulness were giving them concern about her living alone—but Bubbles was having none of it, so my offer to go live with her came off as a generous granddaughter move, and everyone was delighted. But then my Realtor informed me that while we should be able to sell the condo fast, I would be lucky to break even. I had bought at close to the height of the market, put only 5 percent down, and then literally two months later, the economy tanked. The place, despite the recent bounce-back in values, needed upgrading I had never gotten around to, and there was a large special assessment in the offing to get a new roof on the building. The engagement ring turned out to have been chosen more for size than quality—leave it to Dexter to be more concerned about the surface appearance of things than the deep-down reality—so between them, I made enough money to put about twelve grand in the bank for a cushion to get me through till I find another job, but nothing at all extra to send to the credit cards. So much for wiping out my debt.

I can hear the kettle squeal downstairs.

"Come sit." Bubbles gestures to the Nook, where a plate of golden mandel bread, sort of a Jewish biscotti, awaits, crispy and studded with walnuts and mini chocolate chips. I crunch the end off one in an explosion of crumbs. It's a good one, plenty of texture but not rock hard, solid enough that I know it will stand up to a dunk in the hot sweet tea Bubbles has placed in front of me. She sits across from me, and Snatch plumps down at her feet.

"So. How are you, really?"

I take a sip of the tea, some exotic Russian blend she keeps loose in a battered red tin. I can taste the comforting flavors of vanilla and chocolate and the barest hint of cinnamon. "I'm a little bit adrift. But trying to figure everything out."

"Leaving the job, I'm going to guess, was less under your control than you would have your parents believe?"

I look sheepishly at my cookie. The official press release said that I had resigned to pursue other opportunities, saving me what little face I had left and saving the restaurant from my filing for unemployment. My parents had assumed that the memories were just too much there and that I needed a clean break. I had not exactly disabused them of that notion. "Something like that."

"But you're better now? Coming out of the fog?"

"I'm trying, Bubbles. I'm really trying."

"Good. That is all you can do. So while you are trying, we will do what we do. After all, the movies never let us down."

Bubbles and I have one thing that is our deep, shared passion, beyond sweets. Old black-and-white movies from the thirties and forties. Anything with Cary Grant or Katharine Hepburn or Myrna Loy or William Powell, or our favorite, Rosalind Russell. Romantic comedies especially. Even the bad ones, we love. The ones that are so dated and absurd in their overall message that it makes them ridiculous. We love the clothes and the homes and the elegance. The bottomless bottles of champagne. The quippy banter. We can watch them over and over.

"That sounds like good medicine to me," I say, thinking about losing myself in a world long past, where getting left at the altar would be a funny device used to get the heroine into the arms of her true love and not the beginning of the unraveling of her mental health and ability to support herself financially.

"TCM is running a marathon today, all of the Thin Man movies in order. I think it starts in about an hour. We'll watch all six in a row, and only pause to make martinis and order Chinese food." This is not an offer or a request; it is a statement of fact, and every bit of it sounds like the perfect thing.

"Well, then I will do a little unpacking, and meet you in the den, and we will hunker down for some serious screen time."

I finish my tea, grab another piece of mandel bread, and get up from my chair. Bubbles grabs my wrist in a firm grip. "Darling girl, it will all be okay. All of the most successful people with the most exciting lives start over at least once. Your grandfather did it twice. You mark my words, sooner than you think, this will all officially become the best thing that ever happened to you."

I lean over and kiss the top of her silvery head, breathing in the scent of the Arpège perfume she has always worn. "I'm gonna take your word for that."

I spend the next hour putting clothes away in the closet that Bubbles emptied out for me and in the small dresser. My wardrobe isn't exactly expansive, consisting mostly of chef's gear for work, jeans and sweaters for when I'm not at work, and a couple of go-to dresses for evenings out. And, of course, my wedding dress, freshly cleaned and in its special garment bag. I hang it way in the back of the closet. Ruth and Jean wanted me to have some sort of defacing ceremony, splattering it with paint or burning it in effigy, but I just couldn't bring myself to ruin it. It wasn't the dress's fault. A part of me thinks I should be smart and try to sell it; after all, it's worth a bloody fortune, only worn once, and there has to be another voluptuous bride who would want it, but I'm not quite ready for that yet.

I manage to clear off the bed and arrange all my boxes so that I know what is in them—mostly cookbooks and cooking equipment. I sold my condo fully furnished; the guy who bought it was a bachelor and a first-year associate at a law firm who was happy not to have to make any decisions and paid a bit extra for me to leave everything behind. None of it had any particular sentimental value, and I was glad to just be out clean. Plus I didn't want to waste money on a mover or a storage unit.

"Just in time." Bubbles pats the couch next to her when I get to the den, and I snuggle in. She hands me one of the crocheted throw blankets that she made as a young bride when they were all the rage, and I tuck it around me. The television, a fancy flat-screen we bought her for her eightieth birthday a couple of years ago to replace her ancient tube television, has all the bells and whistles: a Comcast Xfinity X1 DVR, a Blu-ray, a DVD player, Apple TV. I'm in charge of her technology lessons, and she has become very adept at managing Netflix and Hulu and Amazon Prime, in addition to On Demand programming and all the shows she records and the large DVD collection she has amassed over the years. Snatch succeeds in hauling his lumpy carcass up onto the couch, in a fresh sweater that looks like a tuxedo jacket with a jaunty felt gardenia sewed into the buttonhole, and burrows in next to Bubbles, who scratches his head and makes him wiggle and grunt happily.

Then she takes my hand in hers, and as soon as the MGM lion roars, I can feel my shoulders unclench just a little bit, and my breath is slightly less tight in my chest, and before long, for the first time in I can't remember when, I'm feeling at ease in the world and thinking that, if nothing else, I'm home.

If You Could Only Cook

(1935)

The worst thing in the world is to get where you close your mind to a new idea. Any man who is up against it and just sits back and does nothing and is afraid to try something new—well, he is better off dead! He is dead! He doesn't know enough to lie down!

· JEAN ARTHUR AS JOAN HAWTHORNE ·

"Sophie . . ." Bubbles calls up to me from the bottom of the stairs.

"Coming!" I check my watch. Nearly eleven thirty. Must be time to organize lunch. One of the things I've learned in my few weeks of living here is that daily life with an older person has a certain amount of scheduling attached. Bubbles likes to breakfast promptly at seven thirty, and while she doesn't expect me to join her, she nevertheless manages to make enough noise organizing her tea and toast and soft-boiled eggs or her oatmeal and coffee that it's impossible to sleep, no matter how many earplugs I go through. And I go through earplugs like nobody's business.

I've always been a notoriously light sleeper; the smallest bit of unexpected light or noise can rouse me fully. Bubbles gave me a satin sleep mask when I was eight or nine. I loved how the soft fabric felt against my eyelids, and the blissful dark it provided, and have slept with one ever since. In college, a brief fling with a musician left me with a stash of squishy foam earplugs that he had me use when going to see his band play—they were louder than they were talented—and I discovered that the plugs did wonders for my sleeping. Unfortunately, I have weirdly little ears, and I'm something of a sleep flopper, so as I move from side to side, they pop out and get lost in the bedding. I buy them in bulk and keep them in a large silver bowl on my nightstand, and have mastered the art of reaching for them in the dark and replacing the missing plugs, usually without even fully breaking my hold on sleep. My morning routine includes a round of "find the plugs," which are usually under the pillows or trapped in the folds of a blanket or sheet, or, worse, stuck to parts of me that have nothing to do with my ears. They are so small and so smooshy that they are barely noticeable when they migrate, and I'm always finding them on me in the shower, nestled snugly under a boob, tucked into my hair, stuck in my armpit, and occasionally in more delicate and embarrassing places. Let's just say that the day my gynecologist discovered one during an exam was not my proudest moment.

I get up from the desk, where I've been scanning the job boards for something, *anything* in my industry that won't require an extensive reference. The job hunt is going beyond badly. I can't bring myself to go hat in hand to Georg to ask him to provide references, and since I landed in his kitchen right out of culinary school, without him I'm screwed. I feel a little bit the way convicted felons must feel, just wanting to get a job but having that small background problem that makes every application a gut-wrenching nightmare. Luckily, my overhead is almost nothing while I'm here at Bubbles's: My car is paid off, and I'm not paying rent or utilities. But even making only the minimum payments on my credit cards, I've only got enough in the bank to survive another six months or so if I don't get some income coming in.

Snatch is waiting for me at the foot of the stairs, wheezing and grunting in his little piglike way, and I lean down and give him a good head scratch, getting right into his neck rolls the way he likes, before heading for the kitchen. Bubbles is up to her elbows in meat and steamed cabbage leaves.

"It seemed like a day for stuffed cabbage rolls," she says, tilting her head at the window, which shows the kind of day that is quintessential March in Chicago: gray and overcast, the last of the winter ice and snowpack filthy and not melting, depressing and with the kind of damp cold that gets into the bones.

"It does indeed," I say, smelling the spicy-sweet aroma of the sweet-and-sour tomato sauce simmering on the stove, ready to have the rolls full of seasoned ground beef and rice dropped in to braise slowly.

"Figured it would make the house smell good, and since your folks are coming over for dinner, it will feed us all and still leave some leftovers for the weekend."

"A good plan. You should have called me; I would have helped."

"I did call you, and you are going to help. I need you to go to Langer's."

"Is that place still there?" Formerly *the* place for the Chicago Jewish elite to order their holiday sweets trays, and birthday cakes, and especially wedding cakes from the fifties through the early nineties, Langer's Bakery was once a cornerstone of the little community where Bubbles lives. Shabbat challahs, Passover macaroons, honey cakes to make the New Year sweet, and strangely blandly satisfying butter cookies for any occasion. Langer's was particularly famous for their simple birthday cakes, decorated with one's choice of balloons or flowers, and their wedding cakes, towering white columned confections with buttercream swags and fondant flowers that looked perfect on tulle-draped tables. Completely old-school. I haven't been in there since college and presumed it had gone the way of the dodo in this economy and with the new bakery reality. But maybe old Langer had a kid come in and take over, update the model.

"Of course Langer's is still there; where would it be?" Bubbles shakes her head like I've taken complete leave of my senses. "We'll want a rye bread to go with the cabbage rolls, and your dad will want onion kuchen, and maybe some cookies or something for dessert."

"Anything else you want or need while I'm out? Should I pick up something for lunch since you've turned the kitchen into a disaster area?"

Bubbles looks at her watch perched delicately on the counter, away from the mess. "Goodness, it's nearly noon! Yes, you had better pick something up for us. I had no idea the time had gotten away from me." There's that schedule again; if lunch doesn't happen before noon thirty, the earth might spin right off its axis.

"I'll grab a chicken at Kolmar's; that way we can have chicken salad for lunch tomorrow." Kolmar's is the butcher up the block from Langer's, and they do a great rotisserie chicken, complete with baby potatoes that cook in the chicken fat and drippings on the bottom of the rotisserie.

"Perfect. My credit card is in my purse on the front table."

"I've got it."

"No arguing with me, young lady. Take the card."

"Fine." Luckily, when I moved in, my dad slipped me a MasterCard and told me that when she insisted on paying for stuff, I should pay on his card and give her the receipt. The numbers are too small for her to see, so she never knows that we do a switcheroo on her. "I'll take Snatch too; he could use the exercise."

"Good idea. See you soon."

I get Snatch leashed up, putting him in one of his sweaters for good measure. You'd think a dog this fat wouldn't get cold, but he is a delicate flower and shivers in the tiniest breeze. This one is a hand-knitted navy-blue number with an orange Chicago Bears logo on the front. Bubbles has lovingly sewn or knitted his many sweaters, from his velvet smoking jacket to his preppy argyle vest, and one for every Chicago sports team. My granddad was a hopeless fan, and now Bubbles follows all the teams as well. She talks to my granddad during the games, often shaking her finger at the sky when they lose, blaming him for not helping them out enough. "Solly! Stop flirting with dead movie stars and pay attention to your poor Blackhawks!" She fully credits him for the Stanley Cup win and fully blames him for the Super Bowl loss. Always makes me smile.

Snatch and I walk out into the day, which is more brisk than bone-chilling, and head up the block. The little commercial stretch where Langer's and Kolmar's reside is only four blocks from the house, and Snatch prances proudly beside me, snuffling at each tree and marking his territory every ten feet or so. The street has barely changed at all, tucked away on the border between what used to be a conservative Eastern European Jewish community and what used to be a Polish Catholic community. The connection between them naturally was food, so the bakery and the butcher and the small grocery were perfectly located to join the two groups. Of course, now there are few holdouts like Bubbles, and the neighborhoods have merged into one amorphous group, initially with a large influx of Koreans and Filipinos, and, more recently, with some hipsters and young families. The classic transitional Chicago neighborhood. Where the grocer used to be is now a small coffeehouse, and the barbershop on the corner, where my grandfather used to go to have Al give him a trim and a shave and a manicure once a week, is now a full-service salon. But there in the center of the block is Langer's, just as it always was, and I push open the door, which is fogged over on the inside, grateful for these cozy, family-owned neighborhood storefronts where dogs are welcome. I always feel bad when I see pups tied up outside less hospitable places. Snatch has obviously been here before and snorts happily as we head inside.

And walk right into 1990. By way of 1950.

With the heady scent of yeast in the air, it quickly becomes clear that Langer's hasn't changed *at all*. The black-and-white-checked linoleum floor, the tin ceiling, the heavy brass cash register, all still here. The curved-front glass cases with their wood counter, filled with the same offerings: the butter cookies of various shapes and toppings, four kinds of rugelach, mandel bread, black-and-white cookies, and brilliant-yellow smiley face cookies. Cupcakes, chocolate or vanilla, with either chocolate or vanilla frosting piled on thick. Brownies, with or without nuts. Cheesecake squares. Coconut macaroons. Four kinds of Danish. The foil loaf pans of the bread pudding made from the day-old challahs. And on the glass shelves behind the counter, the breads: Challahs, round with raisins and braided either plain or with sesame. Rye, with and without caraway seeds. Onion kuchen, sort of strange almost-pizza-like bread that my dad loves, and the smaller, puffier onion rolls that I prefer. Cloverleaf rolls. Babkas. The wood-topped café tables with their white chairs, still filled with the little gossipy ladies from the neighborhood, who come in for their mandel bread and rugelach, for their Friday challah and Sunday babka, and take a moment to share a Danish or apple dumpling and brag about grandchildren.

On the walls, the faded framed photographs of wedding

cakes gone by, elegant and coveted in their day, looking sad and dated and dumpy by today's standards. Behind the counter, Herman Langer, as round and jolly as I remember him, slightly rounder perhaps, with much less hair on his head and much more in his eyebrows, but still with the powerful arms, well muscled from years of wrangling mountains of dough into submission.

"It can't be little Sophie?" he says when he sees me.

"Hello, Mr. Langer, how are you?"

"Well, well, well, I'm fine! Just fine!" He reaches into the case and hands me a black-and-white cookie, the way he always used to, knowing that I'm a girl who loves chocolate and vanilla so equally that I could never choose between them. I suddenly remember that he always teased me about *Sophie's Choice*, which cracked Bubbles up. He winks as I take the cookie from him, and grabs a dog biscuit from the jar on the counter.

"Hello, young man," he says, tossing the treat to Snatch, who accepts it gratefully with a yip, and reduces it to crumbs in an instant. "What can I get you, Sophie who is all grown up?"

"I need a rye bread with seeds, an onion kuchen, and a pound of rugelach."

"Sounds like family dinner; if you need a kuchen, Robert must be coming."

"You guessed it."

He slides a crusty rye bread into a paper bag, the top of the loaf a deep mahogany, the bottom speckled in cornmeal. He carefully chooses the kuchen with the most onion on it and wraps it in parchment paper, twisting the ends deftly. "Chocolate, walnut, poppy seed, or apricot rugelach?"

"Mixed, please."

"Good choice. You always knew how to order," he says with a wink.

He fills a white box with at least two pounds of rugelach, and I wonder how on earth he is managing to stay in business. Besides the horribly outdated offerings, nostalgic though they may be, if he's selling me a pound of rugelach and gifting me an additional pound, the bottom line must be suffering.

"How much?" I ask around a mouthful of black-and-white cookie.

"On the house, little Sophie; it's good to see you back."

"Oh, no, Mr. Langer, I insist. Please let me pay. Us bakers have to stick together. I can't let you give the goods away."

"I'll hear none of it. Besides, I have an ulterior motive."

"Hmm, very mysterious. I'll warn you, Mr. Langer; I'm off the dating market for the moment."

He laughs his deep laugh. "As am I, young lady, as am I. No, I'm hoping you'll assist me. I thought with all of your contacts, you might have someone to recommend to me?" He gestures behind him, and there, on the lowest shelf, is a dusty hand-lettered sign: "Part-Time Baker Wanted." My stomach drops. "I know your colleagues are all fancy schmancy, but maybe someone could use something part-time on the side?" He wrings his hands together and winces. "The arthritis is kicking in more and more these days, and I'm afraid some of the heavy lifting is getting a little too heavy, if you know what I mean. I need someone maybe four days a week. Well, I probably need someone six days a week, but I can afford someone four days a week. Maybe thirty hours total. Twelve dollars an hour and all of yesterday's product they care to carry. Know anyone?"

Do I?

On the one hand, the money is so low it makes my stomach clench. On the other, what he is making here is stuff I can knock out in my sleep; it's all first-year-cooking-school level, nothing complicated or fussy, nothing challenging. Close to home, so the walkable commute will keep me out of my car and save gas money. And while my pride aches a bit at the thought of working in this dusty run-down relic of a neighborhood bakery, it would be the perfect place to hide out temporarily while I find something better. And goodness knows Mr. Langer couldn't be a sweeter guy, so if I have to work for someone, he'd be a soft place to land. He can think of it as part-time, but if I think of it as a baking temp job, then maybe . . . just to get some cash flow. I take a deep breath and consider what the counselor at Canyon Ranch said about my ego, my vanity. That my constant awareness of what other people think of me and my decisions was ultimately a huge part of my downfall. That I was far too concerned about public perception. That perhaps if I hadn't had some insane picture in my head of a type of life that I was trying so desperately to attain, as if it was my destiny, maybe I would have had a clearer eye about Dexter, or would have planned a wedding I could afford, or would have been able to shrug off the humiliation and not derail my job and relationships. I hated how much of that landed. So even though every fiber of my being is screaming out that everything about this situation is beneath me, I have to face that turning down an opportunity for honest paid work in my field is more beneath me. Pride is a lot harder to swallow than a black-and-white cookie.

"Mr. Langer, I believe I do know someone for you."

⌒⟋⟍⌒

"That was delicious, Mom; thanks for dinner," my dad says, wiping the sauce off his plate with a piece of the onion kuchen.

"Thank you, dear; glad you liked it. I'll pack some up for you to take home to Diane; that girl just works too hard."

"What can you do? She's committed," my dad says, reaching

for the last spoonful of buttered carrots. My mom was called away last minute to counsel a young woman who had just joined a group home and had had some sort of episode that worried the staff. "And how's my girl?" He turns to me. We've kept the conversation light and lively: television and movies and current events and the weather. This isn't terribly different from how things were when I was growing up. I love my parents, and I respect the impetus for the choices they've made in their lives, though I don't always understand or fully agree with them. I've always been of the personal opinion that there is just as much value in providing funding for good works as there is in doing the good works oneself, much to their ongoing chagrin. I know that the differences in our worldviews keep something of a chasm between us, but it is a chasm filled with genuine love and affection, if not understanding, and we bridge it easily. They've never said one word about being relieved that Dexter did his runner, even though I know they never liked him and didn't approve of my marrying him. They've been supportive and kind and blissfully non-probing about all of it, which makes things manageable. I don't know how they are going to take the news of my latest adventure, and I was hoping to do this with the whole family here, but I guess that won't be possible with my mom off saving the world yet again.

"I took a job." Bubbles winks at me and begins clearing the table. She was thrilled when I came home and told her about my conversation with Mr. Langer. We talked it over during our lunch of roasted chicken and potatoes, splitting the brownie and the macaroon Mr. Langer had added to my bag when I told him I would come work with him. I was very clear that the situation is just temporary to help him out and keep me busy while we both look for a more long-term solution. He agreed to keep the sign up—I didn't want him to lose out on someone who might actually want the job permanently—and I agreed to give him at least a month's notice when I find my next job.

"*That's fantastic!* I'm so excited for you, sweetheart. Tell me all about it! Is it the perfect opportunity you've been holding out for?" My parents, since they believe I left S&S of my own accord because I felt awkward about the Dexter juju all over the place, have no idea that I have eight years of spectacular work experience and no references. They just assumed that I wasn't going to settle for anything less than a step up or at least a lateral step somewhere comparable. And since no one knows about my debt but me, no one has been pushing me to get a job at a faster pace.

"It's actually just a temporary thing; I still haven't found the perfect fit yet, but in the meantime, I need to be doing something, so I'm going to help out Mr. Langer for a bit. Just while we both look for the right full-time thing." This comes out in one breath, and I hope the air of justification is just in my head and that my dad doesn't notice.

"Well, that will be fun, won't it?" I can tell he is a little bit shocked, but he's covering well. "Couldn't be more convenient, what with you living here. It's nice of you to help him out; I'm always amazed the man is still in business. Good for you, sweetie. Wait till your mom hears. You'd better get the secret chocolate babka recipe; she's wanted it since we met!"

Whew. "I promise. I'll master the babka for her."

"Speaking of Langer's . . ." Bubbles enters with a plate overflowing with rugelach.

The three of us fall silent as we indulge in the small snail-shaped pastries of tender cream-cheese-infused dough wrapped around various fillings: one with walnuts and cinnamon, one bursting with chocolate, one with a thick, sweet poppy seed paste, and one with apricot jam that has been bumped up with some chewy bits of diced dried apricots. I examine each one before I eat it, wondering if I will still find them so charming and delicious when I'm making six dozen of each four days a week.

And worse, wondering what would happen if anyone from my former life ever found out.

His Girl Friday

(1940)

You're wonderful, in a loathsome sort of way.
· ROSALIND RUSSELL AS HILDY JOHNSON ·

"If you're good here, I'm going to take a little break," Herman says to me, and I check my watch. Noon on the dot.

"Of course, go have your lunch. I'm going to prep tomorrow's rye." Herman uses a basic starter from leftover dough for his rye breads, giving them a little bit of a sourdough tang that offsets the molasses; a very slow chilled rise ensures an even and small crumb. So we always prep tomorrow's dough today. Herman has the same devotion to his meal schedule that Bubbles does.

"Sounds good."

"And, Herman? If you want a little lie-down, feel free. I can always ring the bell if we get a rush." Herman has, essentially, a Batphone: what looks like a little doorbell behind the counter that rings upstairs in his apartment.

"Well, maybe for just a few moments." Which means I won't see him till about three.

"I'm not expecting to be busy." I gesture out at the rain sheeting down the windows.

"April showers, my dear; we'll be grateful in May." He

tweaks my cheek between two knuckles and heads to the secret
door behind the counter and up to his apartment.

I shake my head and stretch my shoulders before walking
back to the kitchen. The bells on the front door will warn me if
anyone comes in, unlikely as that seems in this downpour. In
the walk-in, I grab the bowl that has the dough from yesterday's
bread that we kept for making the starter. It is fluffy and smells
the slightest bit tangy. I put the water in the big Hobart mixer
and mix in the molasses. I add the rye and wheat flours, some
salt, some pinches of fresh yeast, and the dough starter, which I
pull into shaggy golf-ball-sized portions before throwing it in. I
mix the dough till it just comes together, and then throw a large
linen towel over the bowl and let it rest. When I come back in
about a half hour, I'll separate it into two batches—one will get
caraway mixed in; the other will stay seedless—and give it a
good knead and then let it proof till it doubles.

Smelling the dough gives me an idea, and I head back out to
the front and grab the little notebook I keep under the counter. I
love the caraway seeds in the classic rye bread, but I wonder if
the rich dough might not also hold up to other flavors. I jot down
some notes. Aniseed. Fennel seed. Orange zest. Golden raisins.
Coarse salt? Maybe if Herman doesn't come down when I am
working on the dough, I can use a small batch for a little experiment. I'm thinking rolls, not loaves. The kind of rolls you want
to smear with cold sweet butter at dinner, or split and toast and
spread with cream cheese for breakfast. Savory and sweet. Maybe
semolina on the bottom instead of the coarser cornmeal we use
for the regular rye loaves.

I'm sketching out a look for potential rolls in my notebook
when the bells on the door peal, and with a gust of wind, a little
girl gets blown into the bakery, struggling with an umbrella
twice her size. She gets the thing closed and pulls the hood off

her head, revealing that she is, in fact, a woman, if a tiny one, with long, dark, straight hair sticking to her wet cheeks.

"Hi," she says breathlessly.

"Hi. You must really have a sweet tooth to be out in this mess. What can I get you?"

"I need to talk to someone about a wedding cake."

Oh boy. In the five weeks I've been working here, this is the first special-occasion cake that someone has been interested in. Which has been fine by me, because when Herman took me through the ancient order forms, I again questioned how on earth he stays in business. Whether you're a bride or a birthday boy, your options are much the same. Cake comes in chocolate, yellow, or white. Frosting comes in chocolate or vanilla buttercream, or you can opt for whipped cream. Fillings are either chocolate or vanilla custard, fresh bananas, or strawberries or raspberries in season. For birthday cakes, you can have either flowers or balloons in your choice of colors. For wedding cakes, you can add either fondant or marzipan covering, or either smooth or basket-weave buttercream, in white or ivory, with either pearl-like dots or ribbony swags made of frosting, and fondant faux flowers are extra. Tiers are either on columns or resting right on top of each other. Full stop. No bells or whistles, no cake tastings. If you want to decorate with real ribbons or fresh flowers or anything else, you are welcome to DIY that crap once the cake is delivered. Hence the entire lack of special-occasion cake business, which was once probably at least half the profits of this place.

"I can help you if you like, but first, you're shivering; can I get you some tea?"

"Actually, that would be great."

"Have a seat, and I'll bring some." While we don't sell tea or coffee here, which is good with the new coffeehouse recently opened down the block, Herman and I do make a pot of coffee (for him) and tea (for me) every morning that we keep in thermal pitchers for ourselves. I pour out two cups of tea and walk them around the counter. "Sugar?"

"Black is fine." The woman takes the mug gratefully and wraps her delicate hands around it, breathing in the steam. I grab an order form and a pen, and join her at one of the café tables.

"I'm Amelia."

"Hi, Amelia, I'm Sophie. Congratulations on your engagement. When is the wedding?"

"June."

"Naturally." I chuckle.

She laughs. "I know, right? But I swear, it's not that kind of wedding; I'm not that kind of bride. We actually picked the date because it is my fiancé's thirtieth birthday, so we are inviting everyone to what they think is his big birthday party, and we are going to surprise them with a wedding!"

"Wow. That is amazing. What a cool idea." Actually this sounds like a horrible idea. How do you organize a surprise wedding? And why?

"Yeah, we're not really wedding people; we prefer casual parties. But his whole family was already planning on coming for his birthday, so we figured, kill two birds!"

Killing birds? For your *wedding*? Like it's just some annoying exercise you have to get through? This woman is insane. But hey, it's her life; if she wants to spend the rest of it with fond memories of the people who blew off her wedding because they thought it was just a casual birthday party, that's her business. And if she wants a basic boring wedding cake, then I'm grateful, because after over a month of butter cookies and rugelach, I'm definitely ready to make something, *anything* a little bit challenging.

"Well, that seems smart."

"Yeah. We think it will be great fun and, actually, will save my life."

"Why is that?"

"Our parents are all sort of traditional people, you know? When we got engaged, both our moms all of a sudden went full-tilt insane and started talking about showers and bridesmaids, and *colors*. Like seriously, all that 'my colors are blush and bashful' bullshit. We finally got them to stop by telling them to agree to let us be happily engaged for six months before pressuring us about a wedding. Brian's birthday is our six-month mark, and we just thought, this way? We get to plan a great fun party and do it just the way we want with no outside input, and then we don't have to do all the crap we don't want to do. Plus, we both have pretty large circles of friends, so we are already at about a hundred and fifty people; if we got the families involved? There would be so much pressure to include, like, all the third cousins from Atlanta, and all the parental business associates, just too much."

I laugh, thinking about my own wedding planning, and the debacle that ensued, and wonder if this girl isn't onto something after all. "Too bad you don't have my parents. They have never gotten married themselves, and the idea of a wedding at all, let alone a traditional one, gives them hives."

"God, that sounds amazing; can we adopt them?"

"You're welcome to them. I could have used your parents when I was planning my wedding . . ." This slips out, and when I see Amelia sneak a peek at my bare left hand, I can feel my face color. "Runaway groom." Usually the wedding that wasn't is an off-limits topic for me, but the damn Canyon Ranch counselor told me that I will never fully move forward to the future I deserve until I am able to claim the whole event as an important part of my past.

"Ouch."

"You're telling me. Literally left at the altar. Well, left in the foyer very near the altar, but close enough."

"You are freaking *kidding* me? No way."

"Way." And then, for no reason other than this girl's wide brown eyes full of empathy, and the strangely intimate air of the bakery with the rain pelting the windows, I tell her. *Everything.* The perfect wedding, the plans, the cost, the crushing debt, how I ended up here at this run-down little bakery part-time instead of at the helm of my own fancy restaurant grinding it out for Michelin stars. I tell her about the meticulous details and the photographer, and how I went totally off the rails and lost my job and am now hiding out here. She listens rapt to my tale of woe and at one point reaches out and grabs my hand and doesn't let go. By the time I've shared every bit of my secret shame and public humiliation and personal financial devastation, we have finished the entire pitcher of tea and half of a chocolate babka.

"Damn, girl, that is just the most amazing terrible story I have ever heard. I mean, seriously, that is *epic.* When does the movie start filming? Please tell me you are going with Sandra Bullock to play you."

This makes me laugh. "Yeah, it feels about that real. But please, I'm holding out for Melissa McCarthy to play me. Sandra can play my best friend, Ruth."

"I'm coming to the premiere." She pauses and tilts her head a little bit. "Is it hard? Making wedding cakes, I mean, after all that?"

I think about this for a moment. "I dunno, yours is the first one I'm doing since then. But I don't think so. The sad thing is I still believe in marriage and I still believe in weddings. I may have really picked the wrong guy, but my wedding was perfect. It was everything I ever wanted, except for the whole not-actually-getting-married part. So no, I don't think it is going to be hard to make wedding cakes. I think it is going to serve as a constant reminder to me to be hopeful." This sounds really good, and I'm shocked to hear it come out of my mouth. Maybe someday it won't be a pile of bullshit.

"That is a very cool way to think about it. I'm really glad you are going to make my cake." She grins at me.

"Well, then we need to talk about details, because I hope that I actually get to make your cake after you hear your options . . ." I fill her in on the limitations of Langer's wedding-cake offerings and keep apologizing for not being able to give her more choices. She shakes her head at me.

"Sophie, that is exactly why I'm here. My Brian? He is a steak-and-potatoes, simple-is-better, total-nonfoodie kind of guy. I'm here because I took him to a cake tasting at a fancy place, and when we left he looked like I'd shot his dog. Every year I get his birthday cake at the grocery store, because that is what he really likes. A girlfriend of mine posted a Throwback Thursday pic on Facebook of her parents' wedding, and I took one look at the cake and thought, That is the one! I called her and she said they got it here, and so here I am."

"Well then, I'm glad we are so perfectly retro."

"I'm a little relieved myself. I mean, don't get me wrong, the tasting was awesome, and eating one of those complicated taster cakes as a dessert in a restaurant would be fantastic, but to be honest? I like the idea of a simple wedding cake. No worrying about anyone's nut allergy or trying to make sure everyone would like the flavor combination."

I've never really thought about that before, since I love to find the perfect and unexpected blend of flavors for a complex cake, but I can see her point. Comfort food is comforting for a reason, and the basic cakes that evoke your earliest happy food memories? There is certainly something to be said for bringing that pure joy into a day like your wedding. Which gives me an idea.

"If Brian could have one dessert for the rest of his life, what would it be?"

Amelia thinks about this for a minute. Then she smiles. "My little gourmand? Probably Hostess Twinkies. Maybe a strawberry shortcake like his grandmother used to make."

"And what about you?"

"I'm a chocolate girl. Chocolate on chocolate. But less of a cake person. My desert-island dessert would probably be a really great chocolate pudding. With plenty of whipped cream."

"So tell me what you think of this . . ." I begin to describe a three-tier cake. The bottom tier would be a deep, dark devil's food cake filled with thick chocolate custard. The middle tier would be a vanilla cake filled with a fluffy vanilla mousse and a layer of roasted strawberries. The top tier, designed to be removed whole and frozen for the first anniversary, would be one layer of chocolate cake and one of vanilla with a strawberry buttercream filling. The whole cake would be covered in a layer of vanilla buttercream, perfectly smoothed, and the tiers separated by a simple line of piped dots, looking like a string of pearls.

"I love it. It sounds perfect."

My heart is beating fast, as it always does when I'm getting into a groove. "I'm so glad." I make a bunch of notes on the form, keeping things to shorthand, since while I am technically working within the allowable restrictions, there are some changes I'm going to make in the execution that are not quite "Herman approved."

"The other places said we would be looking at about fifteen dollars per person, so by my math, we are somewhere in the $2,500 ballpark, is that right? I can give you a credit card or a check for the deposit, whichever."

I look down at my notes. Based on Herman's pricing structure, she is coming in just around six dollars per person. Part of me wants desperately to just say yes; she seems totally prepared to pay that much. I'm ashamed to admit that my first sick impulse is to take it and pocket the difference. Herman would never know, and sending an extra $1,500 to Visa would certainly feel good. But thankfully the larcenous thought leaves almost as soon as it comes. "Well, those other places are charging you for extra-fancy ingredients and complicated assemblages, and their very posh overhead." I gesture around the store. "We here at Langer's keep things a little more reasonable. How does $1,000 all-in sound?"

Amelia's little rosebud of a mouth makes a tiny O. "Really?"

I nod. "Yep. Tax and delivery included. You will have to provide your own toppers."

She narrows her eyes at me. "You know that I was fine with $2,500."

I shrug. "I know. But this isn't a $2,500 cake. It would be highway robbery to charge you that much for something so simple. And I know how quickly the expenses pile up on these things."

"You're going to go out of business if you turn down good money when it is offered."

"We might go out of business anyway, but it won't be saved by gouging our customers."

"You're a good person, Sophie."

I think about thirty seconds ago when I was toying with the idea of overcharging her and stealing from Herman. "I'm working on it."

"Would you mind if I asked you a couple of other questions? I mean about the wedding. I get it if you don't want to talk about it, in light of everything, but Brian keeps saying he doesn't care, it should be whatever I want, and there are so many decisions to make . . . and you seem so great at it all."

"Ask away. My brains are mush, but you are welcome to pick them. But you have to do it while I'm kneading rye bread."

Amelia follows me back into the kitchen and perches on a stool next to the kneading table, a long antique wooden table that is covered in a heavy canvas sheet. I flour the table and dump the large batch of proofed dough onto it. I separate the dough into two large mounds and one small mound. I start kneading the first big mound, my movements smooth, the dough coming together under my hands.

"Shoot," I say to Amelia.

"So, we are doing the party at our office."

"Your office?"

She laughs. "Yeah, I know, it sounds bizarre. Brian and I both work at a digital software company, and even though we aren't quite a start-up anymore, the building we bought to house the office was, let's just say, purchased with an eye on the future. It's a huge warehouse space, and the actual offices only take up half of it, so we put up temporary walls, and we leave the other half open for shenanigans. You know programmers; they go back there and skateboard or play basketball. It's just a huge open room, about six thousand square feet, and it's free, so we figured blank slate, have the party there."

I'm starting to understand why the prospect of a $2,500 cake on her own dime didn't faze this girl. "Okay."

"But I was in there yesterday and got to thinking. It's just a huge room. Twenty-foot ceilings and polished concrete floors and blank walls. What on earth do we do with it?"

I can feel that the dough has come together properly, so I quickly portion it into two-pound chunks and form them into the traditional oval shape. I grab three large sheet pans and give them a liberal covering of coarse cornmeal. After gently transferring the loaves to the pans, I slash the tops with Herman's homemade lame, a slightly curved razor blade duct-taped to an old toothbrush handle, and slide them into the proofing box for the final rise. Then I grab a large cup of caraway seeds, sprinkle them over the second large mound of dough, and begin the process again.

"What sort of vibe are you going for with the event? I mean, I know the cake will be retro because of Brian's personal taste, but is the whole party going for that feel?"

Her face lights up. "I hadn't thought of that, but some sort of theme might help narrow down decisions. I swear, if I spend one more minute on Pinterest looking at faux farm-to-table, mason-jar hipster weddings, I'm going to poke my eyes out."

"I know what you mean. Well, for what it is worth, I think embracing the old-school idea might be fun. And might make Brian feel really comfortable, especially since it's his birthday as well. Plus, it could let you literally get through the cocktails before the ceremony without letting the cat out of the bag, so to speak."

"That would be amazing."

"So here is what I'm thinking . . ." I start to let the ideas flow with the rhythmic kneading. "Think about it like those old-school family-style banquets from the seventies; maybe almost treat it like a family-reunion vibe. Right? Keep the décor simple. Find great pictures of the two of you, your whole lives, you as kids, with your families, great memories, your times together, and have them printed in black-and-white on big foamcore boards. You can stick them to the walls all the way around the room, almost like a photographic exhibit at an art gallery. Maybe some uplights on the floor to make them pop. Put up a stage for the band or DJ that is big enough to have the ceremony on; that way you don't need to do some fancy altar thing that will tip them off." I portion out the dough, which now has the caraway seeds fully incorporated, prep a new set of pans, and sprinkle more caraway seeds on top of the loaves before slashing and sliding them into the proofing box. I grab the smaller mound of dough and find some fennel seed and aniseed to sprinkle over it. I add some orange zest and a couple of handfuls of golden raisins, and begin to knead, the scent of orange and spice wafting around me.

"I love it. What about food?" Amelia asks.

"You do a simple buffet for appetizers, your basics like a cheese platter and a veggie platter, a shrimp display, maybe some chafing dishes with sweet-and-sour meatballs or chicken drumettes. Then long communal tables; let everyone find their own seat." I think about my own little unused table. "Set aside a small table for just you and Brian. Cozy, and you won't offend anyone. Simple flower arrangements, maybe gerbera daisies, in a bunch of different colors, but only one color per vase. Then after cocktails you can ask everyone to find a seat at the tables, head up for what would appear to be your welcoming toast, and boom! Ceremony! Quick and simple before they know what hit them. Then do the meal family-style; have large platters of food brought out, one set of platters for every eight seats, and let them help themselves. Bottles of water and wine already open on the tables. Keep it to foods you and Brian love, maybe whole roasted beef tenderloins that have been sliced up, and simple roasted chickens with some lemon and garlic, just portioned into pieces. A great salad. Some steamed asparagus or green beans. Something whimsical or unexpected like twice-baked potatoes or macaroni and cheese."

"I think Brian might want to marry you instead of me; you literally just named all his favorite food groups."

I divide the new dough into a dozen small balls, and two at a time, I roll them under my curved palms on the canvas, feeling them tighten into perfect spheres. "You're going to all the trouble of keeping it secret so that it can be what you want, so I say embrace it fully." I grab a small sheet pan, sprinkle a layer of semolina on the bottom, and gently arrange the rolls on top. I brush them with egg wash and toss on a little coarse pretzel salt before marking them with an X and adding the pan to the proofing box.

"What else?"

I brush the excess flour off the table and head over to the sink to wash my hands. "Do you and Brian have any traditions or habits that are personal to you?"

Amelia thinks about this. "Well, anytime I take a bath he brings me a glass of milk and a little plate of Chips Ahoy."

"Awesome! So towards the end of the evening, have your servers pass platters of warm chocolate chip cookies and little glasses of milk. Maybe add some vanilla and a little bit of sugar to the milk; with straws could be cute . . ."

"Oh my god, I love that idea!"

"Is there anything else like that you do for each other?"

"He has really sensitive skin, and in the winter his hands and lips get really rough and chapped, but most of the store-bought stuff causes him to break out, so I make these custom coconut oil balms and lotions for him and stash them all over the place. And he brings me splits of champagne anytime he knows I've had a long day."

It is clear to me that this girl has pretty deep pockets. I swallow the jealousy that is pricking my brain and keep going. "So what would you think about making a bunch of sets of your custom products to give to your guests as they leave? A little gift bag with a lip balm and some hand cream with a note encouraging hand-holding and kissing? Maybe with a little bottle of champagne with a custom label?"

Extravagant gift bags like these were absolutely a part of my madness; I'll be paying for them for the rest of my natural life, but that doesn't make them a bad idea if one can actually afford them.

Her eyes pop open. "You're a genius, you know that?"

"I do what I can."

We head back out of the kitchen to the front, and I take all her information down, run a deposit of $500 on her credit card, and then write down my email address on the back of one of Herman's business cards.

"If you need anything else, just holler. Otherwise, I'll be in touch to confirm delivery details the week before the wedding."

She grabs me in a hug, surprisingly strong for such a wee pixie of a girl. "You are the best. Are you sure I can't hire you as my wedding planner?"

I shake my head. "No can do. I'm more comfortable in the consultant arena . . . I don't actually want to do what I propose; I just want to propose it."

"Well, your consultancy makes me feel like I have a handle on this whole thing, so don't dismiss the value of offering good advice."

"I'm very glad to be of help. And, Amelia?"

"Yeah?"

"Want a cupcake for Brian?"

"What do you think?"

"Something smells different in here," Herman says, reappearing promptly at three thirty, one cheek subtly patterned in the herringbone of his couch.

"I did a little experiment," I say, handing him one of my rolls.

He pulls the roll apart, and I'm pleased to hear the crackle of the crust. He sniffs the interior and then takes a bite, chewing thoughtfully. His eyes light up.

"This is wonderful, Sophie, just wonderful! What are they?"

"Just something I was noodling with. I started with the basic rye dough and then fancied it up a little."

"Well, it is delicious. Fennel?"

"Yes. And aniseed."

"The orange is good, keeps it fresh and from going too perfumed. The raisins work well. But the salt is what makes it, truly. It wants butter or cream cheese most urgently."

I laugh, always loving his very formal turns of phrase. "Exactly what I was thinking."

"Well, my girl, perhaps we should put them on the agenda, since it is just using the basic dough, see how the people like them?"

I blush. I wasn't trying to get my invention into the case, just wanted to see if it would work, but Herman's praise feels wonderful.

"That would be great, Herman, thank you. And I have some other good news."

"Yes?"

"We got a wedding cake."

He beams and touches the tip of my nose with the tip of his finger. "You're my good luck charm, Sophie."

I almost believe him.

No Man of Her Own

(1932)

You'd be lovely to have around, just to sprinkle
the flowers with your personality.

· CAROLE LOMBARD AS CONNIE RANDALL ·

"Can I get you girls anything else?" Bubbles asks.

"No, thank you; this is perfect," says Ruth, wrapping her long, elegant hands around her cup of tea.

"You can get me the recipe for these muffins," Jean says around a mouthful of Bubbles's famous lemon-blueberry streusel muffin.

Bubbles beams and places a hand on my shoulder. "Sophie can give you that anytime you like. Now, I'm going to leave you and take the dog out for a bit, but it was lovely to see you all, and I hope you'll be back soon."

She leans down and kisses all three of us on the tops of our heads and then leaves the dining room, where we have all been visiting.

We hear her in the front room. "Snatch! Stop scratching! Oh yes, I know, my little itchy Snatch; just try and leave that alone, please. Let's go walkies."

The three of us chuckle into our tea and then hear the front door latch.

"She cracks me up," Ruth says.

"I just love her," Jean says, beginning to reach for another muffin, but Ruth gives her a withering stare, and she pulls her hand back.

Jean, like me, is a curvy woman, and while she is comfortable in her body, she has recently begun to make noises about wanting to get healthier and lose some weight. We assume this is because her crush du jour is a lithe little actress/yoga instructor who is in the show Jean is currently costuming. Ruth, having never had an issue with her weight a day in her size-six life, is a big proponent of making choices and owning them. She couldn't care less if Jean or I am a size two or a size twenty-two, as long as we aren't waffling. She is always quoting a Robin Williams line from that movie *Dead Again*: "Someone is either a smoker or a nonsmoker. There's no in-between. The trick is to find out which one you are, and be that." She takes it personally when Jean says in one breath that she wants to lose weight and then in the other asks her to pass the fries.

"How is it, really, living here? I mean, I know she's the best, and you adore her, but it's still a really big change."

I take a sip of my hot, sweet tea and pop the last piece of my muffin into my mouth. "It's mostly wonderful. I think it is a change for both of us; obviously, neither of us has lived with someone in a long time. And it's a new adventure to live with someone her age." As much as I love Bubbles, she certainly has her moments. The rigid scheduling of meals, the fact that she is just hard enough of hearing not to know how loud she is in the house at odd hours. "It's difficult to watch when she gets a little bit forgetful or doesn't have the energy she used to, because I do have to face that she is slowing down, which is sad and scary."

"Then so much the better that you have this time with her now, this quality time; what a gift for you both," Jean says.

Ruth nods. "I agree. You'll look back on this time with her

as one of the best things you ever did. What about the job? How's that been?"

"Good, mostly. The work is constant enough to keep me busy and feeling productive, and easy enough that it isn't stressful. Herman is sweet as anything, but I worry for the business. I have no idea how he is keeping afloat. Our regular customers are solid, but they're mostly ancient. He's forever sneaking freebies to people. And the new neighborhood hipsters and stroller set aren't exactly embracing him. They'll come in once, but the minute they start asking about 'organic' this and 'gluten-free' that, it's over. And god forbid someone asks for a *Frozen-* or Minecraft-themed birthday cake; just forget about it. Apparently it doesn't encourage business to tell a devoted Pinterest mommy that her precious pumpkin is not going to remember his second birthday party and balloons should be enough decoration for anyone."

"You'll never get the modern-mommy brigade, not until you start sneaking a full serving of organic, locally foraged eggplant into every gluten-free non-GMO cookie, but you'd think the hipsters would love the retro old-school vibe," Ruth says.

"You'd think," I say. "And actually, I'm sure that if we just up the quality of the ingredients a little bit, bring in the basic-level organic stuff, which isn't that much more expensive these days, up the 'artisanal' factor, and maybe add just a few more items to the roster, we could get their attention."

"You have to raise the prices," Jean says, breaking off half of a muffin and sticking her tongue out at Ruth when she looks over.

"I think so too, but Herman is sure that his regulars would balk; so many of them are on a fixed income."

"Maybe not the prices on the things that those people rely on, but the other stuff, the new stuff. There's a weird psychological thing about pricing; sometimes if things are too inexpensive, people assume they are bad. You think those four-dollar fancy doughnuts are really four times better than a one-dollar glazed right out of the fryer at some dive? Nah. But the existence of the four-dollar doughnut makes the one-dollar doughnut look suspect to a certain branch of the population," Jean says.

"She's right, you know," Ruth says. "I can't tell you how many clients I have advised to double or even triple what they charge, and watched their businesses explode. People are weird; they perceive cost as equal to quality. And whether he likes it or not, the demographic of his neighborhood has changed and isn't going to change back. The old biddies might still need their three-dollar challahs and ryes, but the new people aren't going to come for low prices; they will only come for awesome product."

"I know, and I do think there could be some manageable changes, but I don't want to rock the boat. After all, who knows how long I'm even going to be there?"

"You still looking?" Jean asks.

"Yeah. I check the boards; I have alerts out on stuff that is relevant. It's just all either really entry level, so I'm overqualified, or restaurant stuff, so I'm persona non grata."

"What about teaching? Could you go back to your pastry school and see if they need instructors?" Ruth asks.

"I'd be terrible at it. You know me." I barely had patience when Georg had people doing stages, those brief unpaid internships designed to help train chefs, which are often just annoying babysitting jobs for a bunch of kids who think they are going to be either the next Food Network star or the next Grant Achatz, and who mostly get underfoot and screw up the prep. I'm just too much of the school that if it takes longer for me to explain how to do something than it would take for me to just do it, I bail.

"Have you given up on having your own place?" Jean asks.

"I think so. At least for now. It's too big a risk, too difficult to pull together from scratch. I'd have to be the face of the business, and my face is still a little bruised from my previous fifteen minutes of infamy. I think I just need to try and find something in high-end hotel work, something that uses my skills but doesn't make me be out front. Something second-in-command. Unfortunately, at the moment, all of those jobs are well staffed, and no one is going to let me in the door at the bottom."

"That being the case, would it be the worst thing in the world to do what you can for Langer's? If you know what you want, but know that it might take a while for something like that to open up, what would be so wrong about you dragging his place into the twenty-first century? If nothing else, for your own sanity?" Ruth stands up and carries the plate of muffins into the kitchen; Jean and I follow her with our plates and teacups.

"I have to think about it. I wouldn't want to set something up over there that is too dependent on my ideas or my work. But it would be nice to bring the business back a bit, just to get him more financial stability."

"Well, I, for one, think you should turn the place around, make it hot and happening, and then take it over when the old man retires," Jean says definitively.

"A bakery? A neighborhood bakery? Not really me, you know?"

"And why not? You too fancy?" Ruth's questions drip with sarcasm. "Honey, you know I love you more than my Birkin, and you know I hate everything you've gone through. But let's be clear. Your claim that the restaurant business is dead to you is more than a little bit of bullshit. You know very well that if you went hat in hand to Georg and were humble and contrite, and *honest*, he would probably give you a decent reference, or at least would agree to not blacklist you in the community or shame you if someone called about your work. There are plenty of off-the-rails divas in your business, plenty of people who come back from all sorts of issues; you just don't want to face those people. You hate the idea of the whispering. You hate that everyone knows your secret shame. The world was shown your ass, quite literally, and I get that it was horrific and mortifying and all you want to do is hide. You know me; I'm going to support whatever you choose, so if you are choosing hiding, hide away! But don't hide *and* claim you aren't hiding. Don't hide *and* give up. Don't hide *and* stop dreaming. Your dream died? Fine. Give it a decent burial and dream a new dream. Take off the black armband and figure out the next thing. Be open to the universe plopping it in your lap. What's the worst thing that could happen? You make old Langer's place a smashing success so he has some financial juice in his dotage, and then let it launch you into your next big thing. Or you discover you love it and take it over when he's through and become the best neighborhood bakery in Chicago. Why would that be so bad, so beneath you?"

Jean slides her arm around my waist, not quite trying to protect me from Ruth's rant, even though it is coming at me with a slight edge of frustration peeking through, but in a way that indicates that while she might not have said it so pointedly, she isn't exactly in disagreement with the sentiment.

I hate that Ruth is right. I should be used to it. Ruth is always right; she has been our whole lives. It's fucking annoying.

"Can we put a pin in this conversation and just say that I heard you and I will not dismiss it out of hand?" I don't want to fight; I don't want to push back; I don't want to list all the many, many reasons why someone of my background and experience would be wasted trying to eke out a living in bread and cookies. And I really don't want to discuss the stomach-churning idea of my reentering the Chicago fine-dining scene. Of facing Georg, who was like an uncle to me, who was supposed to be the one leading me through my "I do's," and who I treated so very badly, who I disappointed so much. My behavior was poisonous, and I wouldn't begin to know where to find the words to apologize, especially if any part of that apology also had the mercenary aspect of my wanting a good job reference. Too ghastly to consider.

"I've said my piece; you do with it what you will," Ruth says, putting the tea things in the dishwasher while Jean, winking at me, sneaks a last piece of muffin behind Ruth's back. "And leave those muffins alone, Jean," Ruth says, without turning around.

Jean looks so shocked that it makes me giggle, and when Ruth finally faces us, Jean gives her some serious eyelash batting.

"Don't play winsome, woman; you know that shit stopped working on me in 1999."

I walk the two of them to the door. The hugs I get are strong and warm.

"Love you, Soph, you know that," Ruth says.

"I know. I love you back."

"Can we have a girls' night soon? Cheap and chic?" Jean asks.

"Of course. My evenings are pretty open these days."

"There's more ahead than there is behind. Don't let that math reverse on you," Ruth says ominously.

I look past her shoulder and see Bubbles slowly heading back up the block with Snatch, think about where she is in her life.

"I won't."

❧

When I get to work, Herman leaves me up front to handle the few customers while he heads back into the kitchen to continue dealing with the challahs for tomorrow. Thursdays always mean a constant round-robin of baking challahs all day. There is a local Jewish day school that gives all of its students and staff members a challah every Friday to take home for Shabbat, 260 loaves a week, and there are times I think it is that one client who really keeps the lights on here. This is in addition to the forty or so loaves we need for our regular Friday customers. Herman, despite the arthritis, is still twice as fast as I am at the braiding, so I come in at midnight on Wednesdays to make all the dough, and then start my day late on Thursdays, leaving Herman to shape and bake off the loaves. After we close at seven, Herman and I will slide each finished and cooled loaf into a plastic bag with the Langer's sticker on it, adding a twist tie at the top, and load them into the large plastic delivery trays. The school will send their van in the morning to pick them up, and they'll return the plastic trays on Monday.

We have a brief lunchtime rush from eleven till noon, and I busy myself with cheerfully attending to the needs of precisely three octogenarians requiring sweets for, respectively, a charity meeting, a mah-jongg game, and an impending visit from grandchildren. Each of them generously offers to connect me to a single Jewish son/grandson/grandnephew. They are darling, and it doesn't even bother me when they debate endlessly over the perfect combination of butter cookies, or waffle over buying the walnut rugelach, which is apparently everyone's favorite but dangerous when one has guests who have diverticulosis, whatever the hell that is. I send them happily on their way, with a promise to "think about" their potential fix-ups. Herman comes out of the back, winks at the ladies, and makes sure to hand them each a piece of mandel bread for the road, and then heads upstairs to have his lunch, leaving me in total quiet with my thoughts.

I haven't for a moment contemplated men or romance or dating since the non-wedding. In the beginning, I was just too raw and embarrassed, and then I was too focused on my other boyfriends Mr. Hendrick, Ben, Jerry, and Chester Cheetah. And ever since I moved in with Bubbles, all the romantic inclinations in my life have been satisfied by black-and-white flickery images on the television. Exactly what sort of flesh-and-blood boy is going to compete with Cary Grant and Jimmy Stewart? Not to mention the fact that trying to date as a nearly-thirty-five-year-old famously-jilted-at-the-altar woman who lives with her grandmother while working part-time in a little bakery seems pointless. Frankly, I'm not so sure that anyone who might deign to date me in my current condition is someone I would want to date, which I know is terribly morosely Woody Allen of me.

I catch my reflection in the mirrored backsplash above the counter behind me. I'm the heaviest I've ever been, officially beyond voluptuous and well into lumpy. My hair has been neither cut nor colored in about six months, so it is dull brown and frizzy, but I keep it up in a bun all the time, so I'm hard-pressed to care much. I'm living in black long-sleeved T-shirts and the two pairs of jeans I own that have Lycra in the mix, since the regular denim ones don't button anymore without cutting off my circulation. It's a good thing Cary and Jimmy can't see out of the television, or they might refuse to continue acting for me.

I'm chuckling to myself about the image of Cary Grant scolding me personally through the television set in some magical realism comedic moment, when the bells on the door peal. And in walks a man who seems to have serious purpose in his step. He's not terribly notable looks-wise, average height, average build, dark hair thinning a bit at the hairline despite the expert cut that is designed to hide it, maybe fortyish. His suit is impeccably tailored, good shoes, a long overcoat that I can tell from here is probably a cashmere blend. My time with Dexter made me a devotee of well-tailored men's clothes. Actually, if you put a fedora on this man, he could step right into an old movie. Good chin, the kind of guy you would call nice-looking but not handsome. Or rather, he might be good-looking if he weren't sort of scowling. My best guess is that he has parents in the area and is stopping by to grab something to bring on a visit that he doesn't really want to be having.

"Hello there, welcome to Langer's. How may I assist you today?" I'm determined to stay cheery. "Would you care to try a sample of one of our newest offerings?" I extend the platter of samples. "This is our new salted spice rye roll with raisins, and this is our new sour-cherry chocolate rugelach." Herman has been letting me play, and while he hasn't loved all of my new ideas (the sweet potato financiers were definitely not a hit with him), when he likes something, he insists we try adding it into the case to see how people respond. So far the rolls have done pretty well, and the chocolate cherry rugelach are now outselling both the apricot and poppy seed versions.

"Of course," he says, taking one of each sample, popping the piece of roll into his mouth, and chewing thoughtfully. "Hm," he says, then follows it up with the chunk of rugelach. "These seem a little bit nontraditional for this place."

"Well, here at Langer's we are committed to providing for your old-world needs, but we recognize that now and again it doesn't hurt to amp things up a bit."

"I see. Do I take it from your enthusiasm that these are your additions to the menu?"

I blush a bit. "They are."

He nods and reaches for another sample of the roll. "So what do you think? Add a few new things in here and there, see how they work, maybe move towards a larger overhaul of the menu? Taking the old familiar flavors and just making them sing like new? Thinking about eventual expansion?"

I can hear Jean and Ruth in my head from this morning. I was bound and determined not to even think about a bakery as my destination, but maybe I was too hasty. After all, what would be so terrible? What if, like this guy seems to be implying, I could keep what's great and nostalgic about Langer's but bring in enough modern touches to rejuvenate the business? Overhaul the special-event cakes for sure, and tweak things here and there to make it relevant, maybe even replicable? "One never knows," I say, almost flirtatiously, figuring whoever he is, he certainly doesn't need to know this isn't my dream.

"Must be hard to compete in the market with the current menu."

"We like to think of it as sticking with the classics."

"Still, I'd imagine for someone like you, who clearly has a lot to offer, it must be a challenge to work somewhere so outmoded."

This man is terribly presumptuous, and I feel the need to defend Herman and, by proxy, myself.

"Not at all. Fads come and go, but classic is classic for a reason. When you have products as proven as ours, you don't need to chase every new thing that comes down the pike."

"And yet . . ." He gestures to the tray of samples. "You certainly aren't above breaking the mold."

I shrug. "Bringing the occasional new twist to something familiar is fun for us and fun for our customers."

"I'm sure they appreciate it."

This guy is beginning to make me a little bit nervous. "Is there something I can get you?"

He shakes his head. "No, thank you . . ." He raises an eyebrow at me, letting the sentence trail upwards quizzically.

"Sophie," I say, taking the hint.

"Sophie." He nods. "No, thank you, Sophie. I think your samples are probably all I need for the moment."

How weird. I assume he must have come in for something. "Well, if you're sure."

"Oh, yes, quite sure. Thank you for your time, Sophie." He says my name like he is tasting something new and unfamiliar, and is deciding whether he loves it or hates it.

"My pleasure . . ." I imitate his eyebrow raise.

He laughs wryly. "Mark," he says.

"My pleasure, Mark. Come back again."

"I will. You can count on that." And then he's gone, leaving me feeling somewhat perplexed and weirdly exhilarated by the exchange.

And something tells me that while I'm not remotely thinking about being back on the dating market, at the very least, it might be time for a haircut.

The Shop Around the Corner

(1940)

JAMES STEWART AS ALFRED KRALIK: There might be
a lot we don't know about each other. You know,
people seldom go to the trouble of scratching
the surface of things to find the inner truth.

MARGARET SULLAVAN AS KLARA NOVAK: Well, I really
wouldn't care to scratch your surface, Mr. Kralik,
because I know exactly what I'd find. Instead of a
heart, a handbag. Instead of a soul, a suitcase.
And instead of an intellect, a cigarette lighter . . .
which doesn't work.

⁓

"Good morning, sweet girl," Bubbles says as I schlump into the
kitchen.

It was a long night; I went in late to do the week's challah dough
so that it would be ready for Herman today. Usually when I get
home after that, I just go right to bed, but last night I returned to
an email reply from a query I had sent to the Four Seasons, where,
I'd heard, there might have been an opening. The terse "Thank
you for your interest, but there is no position available at the
moment; we'll keep your résumé on file . . ." form letter was disappointing and annoying, and I tossed and turned for hours, and fell
into fitful sleep. I am not exactly feeling rested. Bubbles's serenad-
ing Snatch with Sinatra from the shower at six did not help, despite
her adjusted lyrics: "My kind of dog, Snatch is my kind of dog . . ."

"Coffee," I croak.

"Coming right up. And eggs?"

"Yes, please."

I grab the *Chicago Tribune* that Bubbles has left on the counter, minus the sports section and the crossword puzzle, her two favorite things. I grab the dining section and shake it open. And there, big as life above the fold, is the smiling visage of the Cake Goddess. The relentlessly perky MarySue Adams, darling of the food networks, is grinning her veneered grin, hair shellacked into place, wide blue eyes sparkling with a combination of smugness and condescension and faux hominess. She's everything I loathe about the celebrity-chef movement. She started with a little cake-baking business in Atlanta, a way to earn some money after an acrimonious divorce while raising three little girls on her own. Back then she was sweet and real and plump like a milkmaid, wide-eyed with charming little crooked eye-teeth and a thick accent. I met her once after a panel about women in the industry at the Music City Food and Wine Festival in Nashville. I was on the panel; she was in the audience, having been brought to the festival by a well-known country music star who had loved her cupcakes in Atlanta and flown her up to bake desserts for the party she was hosting for the festival. Back then MarySue was effusive and energetic and authentic. We ended up back at the hotel having drinks and snacks, and it was a memorable evening with a fun gal.

But that was ages ago.

She met the Food Network people at that same festival; they signed her and proceeded to completely make her over. Today she is a trim size four, with cheekbones where cheeks used to be; a slight hint of a southern lilt has replaced her full-blown drawl. The teeth are now a scary row of perfectly even and blindingly white fake choppers. Once a week she is the Cake Goddess on national television, making "simple, straightforward home-cooked desserts that the busiest mom can manage in a jiff!" and she's opening stores all over creation. She publishes a bestselling cookbook once a year like clockwork and does a regular weekly cooking segment on *Today*, as well as a column in *Marie Claire* magazine. Last year she went public with her longtime boyfriend, Chicago venture capital billionaire Charles Monroe, once his endless divorce was finalized.

According to the article, Cake Goddess, fresh off its successful recent IPO, is apparently expanding its monolithic cake empire into Chicago. Twelve flavors of cupcakes, with eight different frosting options. Five types of chocolate chip cookies alone, and eight types of brownies. A dozen different breads daily, and nearly two dozen on weekends. And a full range of organic/vegan/gluten-free choices. And they specialize in over-the-top wedding cakes, the cornerstone of their empire. MarySue is so excited to finally be in Chicago after successful endeavors all over the South and Northeast, and on the West Coast. Chicago will be her flagship midwestern store, and she is going to make it the biggest and best. She plans to set up her testing kitchen here, and the store will serve as the place where she'll first roll out new offerings, including event spaces for parties and a small café for lunch and high tea.

She will be keeping her sprawling Atlanta mansion, a pink-stuccoed nightmare that looks like Dixie Barbie's Nouveau Riche Dream House, but has bought a multimillion-dollar Lake Shore Drive penthouse condo, which I recognize immediately from Anneke's portfolio. She showed me the before and after pictures when we were working on the restaurant, and the before had the most amazing and ridiculous kitchen covered entirely in blue-and-white floral delft-patterned wallpaper with matching countertops and ceiling and cabinet pulls. We had laughed about the matchy-matchy and the ancient appliances and the general insanity of the space, and when she said she promised me that the restaurant would not look like that, I knew that Anneke, beaming at me over the swell of her enormous belly, was the perfect person to design my dream restaurant. It sort of hurts my heart to know that MarySue Adams gets to reap the benefits of Anneke's gifts in her home and that Dexter and Cookie get to reap the benefits in their restaurant, and that I will now never again be able to afford to work with her.

I keep hate-reading the article, learning about how much MarySue has fallen in love with Chicago, that she has some fun new treats that will be Chicago themed, and that she is delighted to announce that she will be breaking ground soon in one of Chicago's most historic and storied old neighborhoods.

Less than four blocks from Langer's.

My eyes fly open, my stomach turns itself into a pretzel, and I'm suddenly powerfully awake.

"Shit," I say as Bubbles comes over and slides a plate of scrambled eggs and toast in front of me and puts down a large mug of steaming coffee, light and sweet.

"What is it?"

"A nightmare." I show her the front page of the section.

"Oy, that woman. She gives me the creepy-crawlies. I always feel like she is peering into my soul through the television. Her teeth look like she wants to eat me. And I don't think anything I've seen her cook has ever appeared appetizing."

"She's bringing her bakery here."

"To Chicago?"

"To the old Woolworth's space on Milwaukee."

"Over *there*?" Bubbles says, gesturing to the backyard and beyond, where the long-empty building has been awaiting development, less than a half mile from where we sit.

"Yeah."

The realization of what that will mean flashes across her face, and she flops into the chair opposite me, hand over her mouth. "Poor Herman."

"Exactly."

I hand her the article and eat my eggs and toast, which are at once delicious and suddenly leaden. By the time I'm finished with my breakfast, she is finished with the article.

"Vey iz mir."

"Exactly. I think I'd better go in early today. I don't know if he's heard yet, but if he hasn't, it should probably come from me."

"Good girl."

I drop my dish in the dishwasher and head upstairs to get dressed. As I pull on my work clothes, I think about poor Herman and what this will mean, and then about myself. Last night's email means I'm no closer to the type of employment that I really need, and while Langer's isn't my dream job, it is a job, and a pleasant one at that. What if Herman just throws his hands up and closes quickly? I'll be totally back to square one. I shake this off, knowing that Herman's best bet is probably to just try and sell his place as fast as he can before Cake Goddess opens so that he doesn't face the humiliation of being put out of business. I would hate to see him suffer that, especially after so many years.

I grab my bag and zip down the stairs, yelling my good-bye to Bubbles, and head for the bakery hoping upon hope that Herman already knows and I'm just there for comfort, and that I don't have to be the one to tell the sweetest old man in the world that his business has one year left at best and whatever nest egg he was aiming to get out of it has likely fallen right into the toilet.

❧

When I push open the door at Langer's, slowly to prevent the bells from ringing out, the first thing I hear is Herman on the phone.

"I can't worry about some other bakery." Herman's voice, coming out of the kitchen, sounds weary.

There is a pause.

"They do what they do; I do what I do. It's not the same."

Another pause.

"They may in fact do it bigger. But not better."

When I walk into the kitchen, Herman catches my eye and winks at me, gesturing to the pitcher of coffee, and I go to pour myself a cup.

"You may think that better doesn't matter today, but I disagree. Bigger and cheaper and with more variety, with their big-time celebrity-chef owner. That doesn't mean anything to people who respect places like this."

Herman rolls his eyes and holds the phone away from his ear, the ancient receiver emitting the noise of a thousand angry bees.

"Please, Junior, I understand that you want to help, but I know what I know. This is my home; this is my job; this is where I belong and what I belong doing. If the new place makes things slower, so be it. But I'm not a coward. I don't run away. I stay. The business stays. That is the end of the discussion."

I hear a noise that sounds very much like "*aaarrrghhhhhh*" through the phone and then, unmistakably, a dial tone. Herman puts on a brave smile.

"Sweet Sophie. You are early! But it is good, because there are still many challahs to get ready. Can you continue for me? I need to go upstairs for something. I will return quick as a rabbit."

"Of course, Herman. Take your time; I'll get the challahs done."

He pinches my cheek on his way to the door and disappears upstairs. That must have been the son. Herman has shared very little about his son. All I know is that he is some sort of big-time businessman who splits his time fairly evenly between Chicago and the West Coast. The two of them seem to have a strained, respectful relationship. I know that they spend key holidays together and that the son does try and stop in to see Herman when he is in town and has time, but apparently those visits have been fewer and fewer ever since his mother died. I know that Herman is proud of his son but doesn't really understand him, and on the rare occasion he mentions him, I make sure not to pry or ask for more info. And it always makes me grateful that my folks, who also don't necessarily understand me, don't let it distance us from each other.

Herman returns, looking like nothing in the world is wrong.

"Sophie, you are very early."

"I saw the paper, thought I should come in."

He pats my hand. "Very sweet of you, my dear, but nothing to panic about. I'm very delighted to see that our neighborhood is attracting new and exciting businesses."

"But, Herman . . ."

He shakes his head. "There is a big building that needs to be torn down, rebuilt from the ground up. Who knows what happens between now and then? For all we know, having the new business nearby brings many more people to the neighborhood, people who love baked goods. I've seen photos of this Baking Queen woman. This is not a Jewish face. I'm sure she makes an excellent cookie, but I would bet she wouldn't know a babka from a bobcat, *nu?*"

Herman puts on his thickest shtetl accent and mugs for me, making me giggle despite myself.

"There's my girl. Bad enough I've got my son phoning in from California all gloomy and doomy. You and I know better. Don't we both still love to get that perfect French baguette at La Boulangerie? Those amazing English muffins at Summer House? The carrot cake muffins at Blue Door Farm Stand?" Herman rattles off some of the outstanding work of other local Chicago establishments.

"Of course we do."

"Of course we do. Because no one place can be all things to all people. We do what we do. She will do what she does. There is room for everyone. The tide raises all boats."

It does indeed. Even the *Titanic*.

"Okay, Herman, I'm here for you. So, since I'm here, shall we bake some challah?"

"Yes, we shall. You think that woman knows from *challah*?" He chuckles at the very idea, and his confidence puts me at ease. He's right, of course; what we do and what she does are so different. Why would her store affect ours negatively? Why can't the burgeoning community sustain both places? I think about other clusters of businesses: that stretch on Western Avenue with all the Thai restaurants; Armitage Ave. with a Kiehl's, L'Occitane, and Lush in a two-block stretch, all hocking their lotions and potions. Why can't there be two very different bakeries near each other. Four blocks might as well be four miles; you can't even see her place from our place.

You can't even see her place from our place.

Which also means that if you swing by her place and see lines or crowds or no parking, you have to know we are here for us to get overflow business. And as far as I can tell, only a few dozen people know we're here. My heart sinks anew. If we are going to stay, we have to figure out some way to at least get our name out there. I stop myself. Herman's name. Get Herman's name out there. After all, he's right about the build; it could take a year, depending on what she is planning. Do I really think I will still be here in a year?

Herman and I bake and bag the challahs, working in companionable silence, occasionally popping out to the front to deal with a customer. Whatever his bravado was with his son, with me Herman is still fairly quiet for most of the day, and when the skies darken around four p.m., he sends me home ahead of the storm, telling me that things will be very quiet in the rain and that I came in early and should get back so I don't have to run home in the wet. And I have to say, I'm grateful for the release.

When I come through the door, Snatch greets me with happy

barking, resplendent in a new sweater I haven't seen before, an ivory fisherman's number with traditional cabling and design. He looks like a little roly-poly longshoreman in need of a black watch cap.

"Hello, sweet boy. Is this a new sweater? You are very handsome."

He yips in reply, and Bubbles appears in the hall, drying her hands on a dish towel.

"Hello, schnookie. How is Herman?"

I head over and kiss her cheek. "He is doing great actually, not worried at all. Says that what MarySue does and what we do are so different we shouldn't even think twice."

Bubbles nods. "And what do you think?"

"I think that I hope he's right."

"But?"

"But he might not be. Right now we are the only game in town, so to speak. She'll be bigger and brighter and newer and more up-to-date. I don't think we'll lose our devotees, but I can't imagine how the doors are staying open now, let alone if we lose the people who use us more as 'the only local option' as opposed to 'our favorite place.'"

She nods thoughtfully. "Well, it is Herman's place, so all you can do is what he needs."

"True enough. I see your compatriot here has a rugged new look."

We peer down at Snatch, who gives a little spin as if he is auditioning for *America's Next Top Model*.

"He had one like it before, but there was an unfortunate dog park incident."

"I'm not even going to ask."

"Probably best."

I give the dog a head scratch and go upstairs to get my computer, the pug staying close at my heels. Herman might be feeling confident, but I still think my best play is to take advantage of my early dismissal to get out another round of job queries. I grab my laptop and get onto my bed. Snatch snuffles and snorts, doing his level best to join me, but the bed is tall and his vertical leap is roughly that of a small newt's. In Bubbles's room he has an elegant little staircase.

"Hey, fat boy. You wanna come up?"

He snorts in agreement. I lean over and grab the sweater, using it as a sling to haul him up onto the bed. "Damn, dog, you are leaden."

Snatch sniffs around on the bed, finally plopping himself down next to me, resting his head on my knee, his warm weight a comfort.

"Okay, buddy. What do you think? The Ritz-Carlton or the Peninsula?"

He raises his smooshed little face and lets his tongue loll out the side.

"Yeah, okay. Both it is." He puts his head back down on my knee, drooling slightly, and I reach out into the ether hoping upon hope that someone somewhere will want me before Mary-Sue Adams makes me even more irrelevant than I already am.

She Wouldn't Say Yes

(1945)

Ethics shouldn't even have to be considered
when a man's sanity is at stake.
· ROSALIND RUSSELL AS DR. SUSAN LANE ·

"Hello?" I don't recognize the number on my phone, but I answer anyway, hoping it is one of the hotels I sent my résumé to, calling with an interview for me.

"Hey, Sophie? It's Amelia. The wedding cake for June sixth?"

Damn. I hope she isn't cancelling. "Hi, Amelia. Everything okay?"

"Yes . . . well, yes and no. I was wondering if I might take you to lunch? Pick your brain some more on the wedding stuff?"

On the one hand, this is the last thing I want to do. It was one thing to hang with her that day at the bakery, but I definitely meant it when I said I was not up for being her wedding planner. On the other hand, since I left the restaurant having pissed everyone off, Ruth and Jean are about my only friends, and with both of them so busy with their own lives, Bubbles and Snatch are my main companions. Lovely, both; but not exactly a full social roster. Amelia was sweet and smart and funny, so it would probably not be a terrible thing to have lunch with her, just for the change of pace.

"Sure, when were you thinking?"

"Um, what does your week look like? Would noon tomorrow work?"

Tomorrow is Wednesday, which I have free until I have to go in at midnight to do the challah dough. "That would be fine."

"You like Mexican?"

"Love it."

"Nuevo Leon?"

"Perfect. See you there." At least the food will be great. I slip my phone back into my pocket and head out front, where Herman is sitting with Bubbles, sneaking bits of butter cookie under the table to Snatch.

"Well, this is a nice surprise," I say, walking around the counter to give her a kiss. She sips her tea and nibbles on an almond horn.

"This is very delicious." She waves the crescent cookie at me. It's one of my new items, a chewy marzipan-like cookie rolled in toasted sliced almonds, with one end dipped in dark chocolate.

"Your Sophie is a wonder, Betty, a true wonder." Herman winks at me. "Her talent is a bit wasted here with me."

"Don't be silly, Herman," Bubbles says, patting his hand. "This is a wonderful thing for Sophie; it's important to know where she came from. After all, yours were among the first cookies she ever tasted. Where else should she be but where her love of baking began!"

"Alright, now, do either of you need anything else up here? Otherwise I'm going to take my prodigious talent into the back and get a cupcake party happening."

"We're fine, dear. I was just taking Snatch on his walk and thought we'd stop in to say hello."

"Sounds good. You two have a nice visit. Herman, call out if you need me up here."

"Will do. And if you are thinking of doing something new

with those cupcakes . . ." He pauses and my stomach drops as I contemplate the prep I've laid out in the back, including ingredients for a banana cupcake with peanut butter frosting in addition to our usual vanilla and chocolate. "You just go right on ahead." He winks at me again, and I make my way to the back.

I look over the basic cupcake recipes, which, frankly, might as well use a boxed mix for all the oomph they have. To Herman's credit, they are always a great texture and have a certain bland nostalgia, but the flavors don't pop; there's not much *there* there. I've been keeping notes, and now that I have his blessing, I'm going to make a couple of changes to the usual suspects, in addition to trying the new one. Starting with the chocolate version, I swap out some of the cocoa powder with melted bittersweet chocolate and add some sour cream for balance and moistness, as well as some instant espresso powder, my secret ingredient for anything chocolate, which doesn't so much make something taste like coffee, but rather just makes chocolate taste more chocolaty. While the chocolate cupcakes are baking, I turn my attention to the vanilla recipe, adding some vanilla bean paste to amp up the vanilla flavor and show off those awesome little black-speck vanilla seeds, and mixing some buttermilk into the batter to prevent it from being overly sweet and unbalanced. The banana version uses very ripe bananas that I've been stashing in the freezer, as well as a single slice of fresh banana that has been coated in caramel and is pushed halfway into each cup of batter for a surprise in the middle of the cupcakes.

Herman's frostings are close to the frostings of my youth, simple faux buttercreams made with softened butter and confectioners' sugar. Nothing fancy. In my newer versions, the chocolate gets melted chocolate and chocolate milk mixed in, the vanilla gets more vanilla bean paste and a tiny hit of lemon zest, and the peanut butter gets a blend of butter and cream cheese for some tang.

"It smells good in here," Herman says, pushing through the door. He walks over and peers into my bowls. He grabs three of the small teaspoons we keep in a jar on the worktable for tasting, and one by one he tries the frostings.

"These are good, Sophie. Better than mine." His voice is a little sad, and I worry that I've gone too far, pushed too hard.

"Not really better, Herman, just more of what people expect. Flavors are much more intense for people these days, so some of the old recipes don't stand up the way they used to. Think about what people are eating now, all kinds of hot sauces and spicy foods. Intensely spiced global cuisines. Bitter kale instead of buttery spinach, funky goat cheese instead of mild cheddar."

He tilts his head at me, pondering. "So what you are saying is that because people are much more exposed to these things, the original recipes taste different to them?"

"Exactly! Sriracha is as common as ketchup in most houses these days, so people's palates are used to more oomph in their flavors. Think about how it all used to be basic caramel, and now salted caramel is everywhere! When I was a kid it was all about milk chocolate, and now the darker and more intense the better. I just took your recipes, which work so well, and brought in the little extras that make them compatible with the way people eat today."

"Do you think it will help?"

"Help?"

"With the business. To bring in more business?" I see the look in his eyes and realize he isn't as confident as he might want me to believe. Maybe it is beginning to sink in that his days here may, in fact, be numbered.

"I think it won't hurt."

He nods. "They are very good. You'll show me how?" he asks, sounding a little defeated, but resigned.

"Of course."

He pulls over a stool and sits while I take him through my changes to his recipes, and when the cupcakes are cooled, he and I frost them together, giving each pillowy cake a generous swirl of frosting on the top. Despite the arthritis in his hands, his touch with the little offset spatula is graceful and deft, and his frosting ends in perfect little curls every time. We talk about some of the other bakery offerings that might be up for a revisit, and when we put the finished cupcakes in the case, he smiles at me.

"I'm going to get one of those chalkboard things for the front. So we can tell the world about our new cupcakes."

"I think that would be good."

"What else would you do, Sophie, if the place were yours?"

This makes me stop cold, because whatever Jean and Ruth may think, I am definitely not here permanently, and I don't want Herman to view me as his succession plan. But his face is so open, and I can see that the idea of bringing the business back a bit is exciting to him, so I have to tread lightly. "Well, the most important thing about this place is that it is *yours*. Your energy, your family recipes, even if we are changing them a little bit. *You* are what makes the place special, Herman, always will be. Having said that, if you really want to try and get more business, you ought to think about the new people in the neighborhood and what they want, and try to give them enough of it to bring them in."

"Oy, not all that vegan, gluten-free nonsense."

I laugh. "Herman, I don't think you need to be a vegan, gluten-free bakery. But I do think that perhaps switching out at least your basic ingredients for organic versions would appeal to them. Having special products that are only available on the weekends, when it makes sense to have more items stocked for people who might wander in. Looking into doing some seasonal items, maybe in conjunction with a few of the local farms. Creating the kind of items that make people wait all year for the brief time you bake that special summer berry tart or fall pumpkin bread."

He rubs his chin. "I will think about it. It might be worth trying."

I consider the specialty-cakes issue and decide that is a conversation for another time, and only if he brings it up. As I'm discovering by living with Bubbles, there is only so much change one can ask a senior citizen to absorb at one time.

"Sounds good."

He checks his watch. "I'm going upstairs for a bit, Sophie. My son Herman Jr. is coming over. If he comes in down here looking for me instead of going right up to the apartment, you can send him up the back way."

"Will do." I wonder again about the son. Bubbles, who is a fount of all gossip, filled me in a little bit. Apparently there had been a second son who was killed in a car crash when he was in college. There is some fuzzy stuff about one of the boys maybe taking over the bakery, so I assume it must have been the one who died. Poor Herman. With his wife gone and one son lost, it would be so nice for him to have at least one family member he could connect with. And again I remind myself not to get too close, to make him too dependent. I would like to believe that it is about protecting him, for when I find my real job, but deep down, where I don't like to look, I know it is more than a little bit about protecting myself.

Herman heads up the secret stairs, and I zip into the back to clean the table with a mild bleach solution, wash all the bowls and beaters, and return the kitchen to pristine condition, ready for the next round of dirtying.

I'm wiping down the tables in front when the bells on the door peal.

"Hello, Sophie."

I turn around to see Mark in the Suit. A different suit today, though no less beautiful, with a lighter trench coat in honor of the sun. It's still brisk outside, but there is a hint of spring in the air.

"Hello, Mark. Welcome back. What can I get you today?"

"Anything new I should be tasting?"

"As a matter of fact, there is. How do you feel about cupcakes?"

"Generally I have no feeling about cupcakes other than the fact that they are food for children and giggly young women, and that if the craze for them ended tomorrow, the world would not suffer overmuch."

Hmm. Mark in the Suit is sort of a grumpy goose today. "Well, I can't speak to other cupcakes, but I assure you that ours are very much appropriate for grown-ups, and while we have no intention of launching yet another cupcake empire, we do want to be sure that when our customer has a hankering for a bit of cake, that desire can be fulfilled."

This comes out a little breathier than I intended, which makes it sound like there are double entendres embedded in my cupcake talk.

"Don't you just have chocolate and vanilla?"

"We do, newly revamped. And banana with peanut butter frosting."

"Well, I suppose I'll have to taste them all."

I remove one of each cupcake from the case and pull the tasting-sample platter out from underneath the counter. I cut each cupcake into six pieces, arrange them on the platter, and then place it on the counter where Mark can reach it. He tastes the vanilla first, then chocolate, then banana. After each piece, he nods.

"As cupcakes go, these are clearly superior. I doubt it will make me a cupcake fan, but . . ."

"You wouldn't kick them out of bed for dropping crumbs." Oh good lord, Sophie, why on earth would you say *that* of all things? I clearly have lost all ability to converse with a man.

Luckily, Mark laughs. "No, I suppose I wouldn't. Why don't you give me a dozen, four of each. The girls in my office will love them."

"Wonderful!"

I put the cupcakes in a box, with a special cupcake insert to keep them from falling over, and seal it with a Langer's sticker. I ring him up, deciding on the fly to up the cupcake price from two to three dollars each, take the cash he offers, and give him change and his receipt.

"Is the owner in back?" Mark asks. "Or do you have him tied up and gagged somewhere while you make all of these fancy new changes?"

While I love a good *9 to 5* reference, I resent the implication that somehow I'm going all rogue or something up in here. "For your information, the owner is in a meeting at the moment, but he and I are making these changes together. He's very progressive-minded, and there is more to come."

"Really?"

"Of course. You'll have to come back and see what we have up our sleeves."

"I see. So all of this is his idea? The new products, the changes to the old recipes? He woke up one day after sixty years in business and thought it was time to shake things up?"

I'm starting to get annoyed at this Mark fellow. Which, frankly, feels much more manageable than the minor attraction that had been brewing. "Mr. Langer recognizes that the neighborhood has changed significantly in recent years and that he should serve the changing needs of his community. He is forward-thinking enough to know that by making a few simple changes in what he offers, he lets his customers know that he is considering what they want and is attempting to provide it with the same level of quality and dependability that have allowed him to be here for sixty years."

"Or he's grasping at straws to try and stay afloat in a market that has blown right by him and made him nearly obsolete."

Now he is just pissing me off. "Any place that doesn't change to reflect change around them is simply doomed. That isn't grasping at anything; that is just smart business."

"Well, Sophie, as good as they are, your cupcakes aren't likely to save a place like this."

I narrow my eyes at him. "Langer's has no need of saving, not by me, or anyone. Was there something else I could get for you?" I thrust the bag containing the box of cupcakes at him. He smirks at me and takes his purchase.

"Not at all, Sophie. Thank you for the cupcakes. And the business lesson."

He turns and walks back out the way he came, and as much as we could use the kind of business that buys a dozen up-charged cupcakes on a whim for the "girls in his office," I won't exactly be terribly disappointed if he takes his superior, smirky, snarky business elsewhere.

⚬⚬⚬⚬⚬

I walk into Nuevo Leon promptly at noon and pass the large group of Mexican families and Chicago's finest waiting for tables. Amelia had texted that she was already seated in the back room. The place is packed as always, and heady scents of spices and grilled meats fill the air. Amelia waves me over, and I join her at the table. She is noshing on the bowl of house-made pickled vegetables they always put on the table, and in less than thirty seconds, we are given menus, a basket of still-warm tortilla chips with salsa, and small cups of chicken soup. They always provide a little amuse-bouche of some sort of soup when you arrive, and I'm always grateful, since the minute I walk in here I get ravenously hungry.

"Thanks so much for meeting me here. This isn't exactly

Brian's favorite spot, so I'm always looking for lunch companions who are a little adventurous."

"I've always loved this place; you don't ever have to ask me twice."

We glance at the menu, decide to split a queso fundido with chorizo and poblanos, and then we both order the skirt steak special. The melted-cheese dish arrives quickly, lava hot and packed with spicy sausage and roasted chiles. We dig in, rolling the cheese mixture in hot fresh tortillas.

"Heaven." Amelia rolls her eyes in pleasure.

"Amazing," I agree, letting the flavors wash over me.

"So, I suppose you're wondering why I summoned you here."

I take another bite. "Nah, I couldn't care less. I'm just happy to be eating this."

She laughs. "Well, there's that. But I'm coming up on some unexpected snags, and since you had such amazing advice for me before, I thought that if I bribed you with lunch, you might let me pick your brain again."

"I don't mind singing for my supper. Lay it on me."

Turns out that keeping the wedding part secret and just promoting the event as a big thirtieth-birthday bash means that a few of their friends and family are creating some unexpected complications. For starters, at least three of the out-of-town guests have asked if they can stay with Amelia and Brian. They have all been temporarily put off by being told that someone else requested housing first and that there's only one guest bedroom. But all have offered to do couches or blow-up mattresses on the floor, so now Amelia and Brian are worried that these people might not be able to afford the hotel where they got a block of rooms, and won't come if free housing isn't available. Under normal circumstances, they wouldn't mind turning their town house into a crash pad, but it isn't exactly ideal for a wedding weekend. And since the party is on a Saturday night, their friends are also trying to make plans to get together Saturday during the day, and she isn't sure of the best way to get out of it.

I scrape the last bit of cheese out of the cast-iron skillet, and a busboy whisks it away like magic. "What was your plan for Saturday?"

"I figured we'd spend the morning and early afternoon getting the place set up and then scamper home to get ready."

I shake my head at her just as our skirt steaks arrive. "No. No can do. You'll make yourself crazy."

She cuts a piece of steak, seared crisply on the outside and pink and juicy on the inside, and pops it in her mouth. "Whaddoido?"

"For starters, for Saturday you need a wedding coordinator. Not a planner; they'll charge you an arm and a leg, and you've already done most of the work. You need someone to be there the day of to get everything set up, to deal with the different vendors, to manage the timing and execution of the event. And no, before you ask, I am not volunteering. But I have someone for you."

I take out my phone and scroll through my contacts. I send her Bernie's contact card. Bernie coordinated tons of events at the restaurant, and while we were never close friends, he did reach out after I got fired to say that he hoped I was doing alright. I'm reasonably sure he will welcome the referral. "Okay. I just sent you Bernie Tarkington. He's a dream. He will handle the day so that you can just show up and get married and enjoy your party. He's English and charming, and he will whip your whole party into shape and take care of anything that comes up without breaking a sweat and without bothering you. That way, you could make brunch or lunch plans with pals without worrying."

I eat a slice of my steak, wishing that I could figure out their secret marinade.

"Okay, that will help a lot, but what on earth do I do about houseguests?"

"Give them your house."

"What?"

"Get a fabulous hotel suite for the whole weekend, and give your friends your house. Check into the hotel Friday morning with everything you need for your whole weekend of festivities, and have a cleaning service come that day to clean your place and put new sheets on all the beds, et cetera. Get a blow-up mattress if you think you'll need one. And then just let them use your house like a hotel for the weekend. Don't leave the hotel till Monday, and have the cleaning service come back to set your place to rights before you return. Tell your guests you are surprising Brian with a fabulous hotel weekend, so they can't say anything to him about staying at your town house. Better yet, tell them you have booked a couples massage and some other stuff for the two of you Saturday during the day, to keep Brian out of the way and prevent him from suspecting too much about the party, so they also have to be prepared to fend for themselves until the evening."

Amelia's jaw flops open. "I never would have thought of that."

I shrug. "It's cheaper than springing for their hotel rooms, allows you to be generous with your hospitality, and also will help make your wedding weekend a little more special. Get a great suite, big enough to have the hair and makeup people come get you ready in one room while Brian is getting ready in the other, and then it is your oasis all weekend."

"Seriously, Sophie, you are amazing. And it's worth so much more than lunch; you have to let me pay you something."

I shake my head. "I'm happy to help, but you have to stop offering me money."

"Can I ask you something? No pressure?"

I shrug.

"I know that you have all that debt from your wedding. Why won't you take some extra cash?"

"It's going to sound weird and a little bit lame."

"Try me."

"I don't have many friends left. I mean from my life before. The restaurant business is all-consuming; it is hard to make close friends outside the industry, especially because your life is so weird—strange hours, working nights and weekends. It's just easier to have your social life connected to your working life. And so when I was screwing myself out of a job, I was also pretty much screwing myself out of my circle of friends. I have my two best girlfriends, thank god. I have a few pals from culinary school, but they don't live here, so I don't see them much. Any friends I thought I had through Dexter are . . . well, you can imagine. I have to get to a place where I can meet new people, nice people. Normal people. And maybe make some new friends. I know that probably sounds creepy, like 'Please be my friend, I'm so desperate,' and that isn't it exactly. But I feel like I have to relate to people as people, and if I let you give me money for offering friendly advice, then it makes this"—I gesture between us—"commerce and not company. And as much as I need money, I sort of feel like I need company more."

I know I'm blushing, so I stare at my plate, pushing the rice around.

"I'd love for us to be friends. So I'm going to stop offering you money."

I look up and she is grinning widely at me.

"I work in *tech*. I'm surrounded at all times by *boys*. Have been since college. There is one other woman in our office, and she's the chief operating officer, and she's in her sixties with grandkids. I could totally use some girlfriends, seriously."

"I wouldn't have thought that."

"Yeah, it's still a guys' club. I love them, but they won't go shoe shopping with me."

"I will totally go shoe shopping with you."

"Deal."

"And I'll still talk about your wedding, really, anytime. Just don't try to pay me."

"Done. On the flip side, while they won't go shoe shopping, a lot of the guys I work with are really terrific people, so if you ever want a fix-up, we can do a double-date introduction sometime."

"Yeah, I think my guydar is broken." I tell her about Mark and how quickly that went from intriguing and flirty to completely insufferable and annoying.

"He sounds like a tool."

"Yeah. And, which is worse, now I'm starting to wonder if he isn't doing some sort of recon."

"Like a spy?"

"Well, think about it. Why does he care so much about what changes we are making in the bakery? What could be his motivation for prying and pushing? The first time he came in, he didn't even buy anything, and then this time he bought but proceeded to interrogate me." I tell Amelia about MarySue's plans to open a bakery four blocks from Langer's. "What if he works for Cake Goddess and just keeps coming in to see what we are up to?"

"Can't worry about that."

"Of course I can worry about it; this awesome new bakery so nearby could well put us under."

"Not if you are awesomer."

"I dunno, shiny and new . . ."

"There are new tech start-ups every day. Every time one gets announced, someone in the office goes all wiggy. We keep saying, 'You can't be overly concerned about what other people are doing in your industry; you can't be reactionary to everything that is new; you have to do what you do best and let the rest of it shake out as it will.'"

"I suppose. At least I got Herman to agree to think about making some changes. If Cake Goddess is coming in, we're going to have to be at the top of our game."

"Keep that as your focus, being your best; the rest will make you crazy."

We finish our lunch and make a date for next week to shop for her wedding shoes, and I head home sated and surprisingly happy, with a package of still-warm fresh corn tortillas and a new friend.

Wedding Present
(1936)

"Who's a good boy!" I hear Bubbles coo from downstairs as I head down the hall to the shower. A peek over the railing shows her giving the dog a good belly rub at the foot of the stairs. Regardless of my distaste for being awake at the appalling hour of seven on my day off, it's hard to stay too annoyed. Bubbles catches me peeping at her, and her round face breaks into a wide smile.

"Good morning, sweet girl. You're up and about early today!"

"Beautiful day like this, how could I stay in bed?" Especially when Bubbles was up at five clomping down the hall, singing Patsy Cline, and letting the teakettle whistle for a full four minutes.

"Wonderful! Can I make you some breakfast?"

There is the occasional benefit. "Absolutely. I'll be down in ten."

Considering the length of Bubbles's morning ablutions, I'm astounded that there is enough hot water left for me to get in a three-minute shower. I wet my hair, retrieving an earplug from the nest of tangles under my right ear, but decide against a full wash. A second earplug is discovered tucked neatly under my left boob. Just as I get the soap off my body, the water threatens to turn, so I give up, bending down to clear the hair out of the drain and finding a third earplug in the drain catch; god knows where it was hiding. I towel off quickly, put my hair in a loose bun, and head back to my room to get dressed.

"Perfect timing," Bubbles says as I wander into the kitchen, where a steaming cup of tea is already waiting. I sip it slowly, and she hands me a plate.

I laugh. "Eggs in a basket?" There on my plate are two slices of toast, each with a fried egg cooked in the middle; the two circular pieces she cut out of the centers of the bread are toasted and buttered on the side with a pair of plump sausages.

"It was always your favorite." She winks.

I use one of the toast rounds to break the yolk of an egg, which flows out perfectly liquid, and take a bite. "It was indeed, and for good reason." I haven't had an egg in a basket in probably twenty-five years, but it is still freaking delicious.

"So, what is your plan for today?"

"I'm meeting my mom and dad for lunch at the house and thought maybe I'd swing by and pick up something fun for dinner for us. Maybe we could do a double feature tonight? A little Hepburn and Tracy perhaps? I've been in the mood for an *Adam's Rib/Pat and Mike* night." Anytime I need a little confidence booster, Kate Hepburn always does the trick for me; she is so sure of herself.

Bubbles's face falls a little bit. "So sorry, sweetheart, I have plans for dinner and the opera this evening."

One thing about Bubbles: She might be an old broad, but she's no homebody. I can barely keep track of her theater subscriptions, her mah-jongg and bridge games, her charity meetings and book club. She keeps herself very busy, filling her days with other little old ladies when I'm at the bakery, and two or three

nights a week with evening plans. I can never remember if she's
meeting Mrs. Spiegel with the sciatica or Mrs. Goodman with
the cataracts or Mr. and Mrs. Barkley from the bridge club. She's
lucky to have a reasonably broad social circle that's still ambula-
tory, and I've stopped asking who she is seeing so that I don't end
up on the receiving end of way too much medical information or,
god forbid, a potential fix-up. I'm mostly cashed when I get home
from work, so if she isn't there, I'll take the dog for a walk, eat
something, watch an old movie.

I find I can't watch regular TV these days. It's all too "reality"
or depressing, or shocking and provocative, and all I can manage
is funny fluffy movies full of beautiful women and handsome
men falling in love and quipping brilliantly and wearing stunning clothes and endlessly sipping champagne and stirring martinis. I wish I could blink my eyes and have some magical realism
moment like in that *Pleasantville* movie, and just lose myself in a
world long gone. But I have to admit, it's more fun to watch with
Bubbles. She remembers those years, accentuates the movie-
watching experience by sharing personal anecdotes from her
own childhood and stories of her parents. Sometimes a movie will
spark a particular memory, so she will pull out her photo albums,
and we will curl up together and talk about old relatives. She has
the best stories.

"Well, that sounds like fun."

She smacks my arm playfully. "Little fibber. You hate the
opera."

This is true. As much as I have a soft spot for musicals, especially old movie musicals, opera is beyond me. Too screechy, too
melodramatic, too not-in-English.

"Well, I don't want to *go*, but *you* think it's fun, so it sounds
like fun for *you*. What's playing?"

"*Tosca.*"

I make some exaggerated gagging noises while rolling my

eyes. She laughs and smacks me again. I wink at her and pick up a sausage with my fingers and bite it in half dramatically. She makes a face that says she disapproves, but her eyes twinkle at me, so I know she doesn't really.

"What time are you meeting your folks?"

"Noon. Although considering them both, I'm shocked I haven't heard from them cancelling."

"Well, you haven't seen them since we went to Chinatown, and that was, what, three weeks ago?"

"'Bout that. I just think it's weird they wanted to meet for lunch, and at the house."

"Maybe it's a good sign, a sign they are thinking about taking more time for themselves. Not working such crazy hours."

I give her a classic single raised eyebrow, a gesture I learned from her.

"Okay, maybe not." She waves me off.

I grab my plate and teacup and load them into the dishwasher.

"*Snatch!* Time for walkies," she yells out into the hallway as she leaves the kitchen. I can hear her put the dog's leash on. "We'll be back in a bit," she calls back to me before heading out the front door.

I go upstairs to check my email, and see I have a note from Amelia.

A few quick questions, since we are getting so close . . .

Since no one knows it is a wedding, no one will be prepared for toasts. Which is fine by us, we aren't interested in toasting, but how do we handle people who want to make a toast in the moment?

The invite specifically says "No gifts please," but Brian thinks that people are going to want to send us stuff anyway after they find out it is our wedding, even though we don't want anything. How do we handle that?

We sent his cousin from Indiana an invite that was specifically "Mr. and Mrs." But they RSVP'd with their three kids. This is not a kid-friendly event. What do we do about that?

Thank you thank you thank you. And I've been doing what you said and walking around at home in the shoes we bought with a pair of socks on, and you're right, they are totally getting more comfortable. Let me know if you are up for dinner or drinks or something one of these nights!

A

I think about this for a minute and then reply.

A—

I think after the ceremony, when everyone is seated for dinner, you and Brian welcome them and thank them for going along with the surprise. Let them know that anyone who wants to share a special message with you can tell the videographer, and he will help them tape a "toast." That should take care of your friends. If parents want to toast, let them. They may be longwinded or bumbling, but they're your parents, and they are already going to feel like they missed out a little bit, so if they want to toast, suck it up. But be sure the DJ knows not to give the mike to anyone not pre-approved by you.

In your little gift bags at the end of the night, put a small card that says "Your presence was our present, but if you feel you must honor our nuptials in a tangible way, we would love for you to make a donation to one of the following charities in our name." And then list two or three places that mean something to you where they can go and donate. I can't guarantee you won't still find some Crate and Barrel boxes on your doorstep in the coming months, but it should keep it to a minimum.

Book a babysitter for the cousin's kids for the evening, and send them a note saying you are so glad they are able to use the occasion of the party to have a family getaway weekend, but that the event is adults only, so you have made arrangements for appropriate childcare for them so that they can have a date night!

Glad the shoes are loosening up, they are gorgeous!

I pause for a moment and then type:

I know it's last minute, but I happen to be free tonight if you want to hang out.

S

What the hell? Bubbles is going to be out. I'm trying to be open to new people. Amelia has been fun to get to know, and I really like her. She replies almost immediately.

Tonight is perfect, actually! Brian is working on a new piece of programming for a client that is due in a couple of days, and there is a glitch he can't seem to fix, so he's already warned me that he is probably pulling an all-nighter at the office with his team. What did you have in mind?

A

- - - - - - - - - - - - - -

How do you feel about classic movies?

S

Not familiar with many, but if you mean like John Hughes stuff, I love those!

A

Sigh. Bless her heart. I believe an education is in order.

I mean a little more classic than that. Why don't you come to the house around 6:30? I'll make something simple for dinner and I can introduce you to something fun.

S

I pull my car in front of the ramshackle house on Mohawk where I grew up. I have mixed feelings about the old girl. On the one hand, the redbrick house has the kind of history I love. It was built right after the Great Chicago Fire, about 1872 or so, on an extra-wide double lot, set back a bit from the street, and has some wonderful details about it. The transom over the wide double door displays the house's number in original stained glass. The staircase is also original, with its carved balustrade and turned spindles. And the living room fireplace is surrounded by limestone and a mahogany mantel. On the other hand, it's also always been a mess. It still has the original steam radiator system for heating, with an ancient boiler taking up half the basement. No central air-conditioning, so early summer requires the installation of window units throughout the house, which can only be run in strange sequences, as the electrical system hasn't been upgraded since the 1970s. If you turn on more than two at a time, you blow fuses. The beautiful stairs are also a death trap, with skinny winders instead of landings, and the balustrade is somewhat wobbly. And the fireplace, while decorative, can't be used because the lining of the chimney is in complete disrepair, not to mention coated in so many years of built-up creosote that the chimney sweep they tried to hire turned down the job and told them if they ever lit a fire, the whole chimney could catch and make the house a Roman candle.

The hardwood floors squeak and give splinters, none of the bedrooms have closets, and the bathrooms are tiny. The pantry in the kitchen has walls coated in stucco so pronounced and spiky that every trip to fetch ingredients for dinner is an opportunity for shredded skin and blood loss. I still love the old apple tree in the backyard, but the screened-in porch it shades is rotting away, and the garage is so rickety that my folks haven't parked in it for the better part of the last two decades.

Mom and Dad bought it for only $30,000 in 1975, back when it needed a new roof and all new electrical and plumbing, and some serious tuck-pointing and foundation fixes. To their credit, they enlisted all of their hippie-dippie pals, housing up to a dozen of them at a time and feeding them brown rice and black beans and cheap beer and pot brownies in exchange for labor, both un- and semiskilled. Over the course of six years, while my dad passed the bar and joined the overworked and underpaid team at the public defenders' office, my mom oversaw a constantly changing set of houseguests and squatters, learning from books how to DIY every possible aspect of renovating an old house. Two years in, they bought the vacant lot and a half adjacent to the house from a cash-strapped neighbor for another twenty grand, fenced it in, and my mom planted her urban garden, all sorts of vegetables and herbs— culinary, medicinal, and probably illegal as well—and set up a beehive. By the time the house was fully watertight and structurally sound, she was pregnant with me. Slowly they managed to move their motley crew along, and apparently, for the first six months of my life, it was just the three of us. But that didn't last. Some complications when I was born meant that my mom had to have a hysterectomy, so I was destined to be the only one of my kind.

Eager to give me a sibling experience, my folks embarked on hosting a steady stream of foreign exchange students. My childhood was a cacophony of languages and accents, young men and women of all nationalities coming and going, alternately doting on me or resenting my presence. In my memory, the dining room table was never *not* covered by textbooks and school projects. But I also remember celebrating every conceivable holiday from every religion and nation, and I recall a constant influx of exciting new foods and flavors, each "brother" and "sister" bringing in the spices and tastes of his or her homeland. As soon as I was old enough to hold a spoon, I was the official kitchen helper, and under the watchful eye of my mom's charges, while she was upstairs studying or working on her doctoral thesis, I learned about the food of the world.

"Hi, Mom," I say when she opens the door.

She pulls me into a deep hug, kissing the side of my neck with loud smacking noises. "Hello, honey. Come on in."

The house smells, as it always does, of a combination of old books, exotic cooking, beeswax candles, and the essential oils my mom uses instead of perfume.

"There she is! Princess Summer Sunshine!" My dad comes down the stairs and grabs me in a bear hug, then leads me, in his lumbering way, in a dance around the living room.

We half waltz, half polka through the living and dining rooms and into the kitchen. Where I stop.

"It's really, um . . ."

"Clean!" my mom says, smiling.

"Yeah. Clean," I say, gobsmacked. For my whole life, between my parents' crazy work schedules and the endless stream of students from far-flung places, the kitchen was occasionally tidy, rarely organized, and never truly deep-down *clean*. My parents laugh at my shock, and it occurs to me that they seem to be in particularly good moods. Even their physical affection, which on any normal day is just shy of pornographic, seems somehow full of love instead of lust; there's an electricity between them that seems palpable and full of joy. I squint at them. Something is up.

"Let's sit," my mom says, gesturing to the worn white laminate table that is in the dining section of the kitchen in a large, curved bay window. The oval table, shiny white when they got it, is now matte with years of use and abuse, the edges chipped, chunks of laminate veneer missing. I used to love hiding in the half-moon nooks in the base when I was small. The table is set with Mexican woven place mats that look like little serapes, and the plates my dad made when he took a pottery class over at Lillstreet Art Center. In the center of the table is a classic deli platter of lox and tuna salad with all the fixings, bagels, and cream cheeses. And on a trivet, a noodle kugel, a casserole of egg noodles suspended in a light sweet custard, with a crunchy topping of crushed cornflakes mixed with cinnamon and brown sugar. It was always my favorite thing my mom ever made.

"All your favorites." My mom beams at me.

"And mine too. Let's eat!" my dad says, swatting my mom on her ample tush.

We make our plates; I grab a plain bagel and top one half with tuna salad and dill pickle, and the other with chive cream cheese and cucumber. I also help myself to a large corner chunk of kugel, for maximum crispy edges, and some coleslaw. Clearly someone went all the way out to Kaufman's on Dempster in Skokie; I can tell by the bagels. A slight crunch on the outside gives way to perfect dense chewiness.

"Okay," I say, after a large mouthful of kugel. "What's up? What's wrong? Is someone sick or something?"

My dad laughs, and my mom looks startled.

"Why would you think something is *wrong*?" my mom asks.

"Because *both* of you have clearly taken today off from work, which is unheard of, and the house looks really good, and you've brought in my favorite brunch stuff and made a homemade kugel, which you never do except for the holidays, so clearly something is going on, and this feels a lot like softening a blow. So I'm just asking what the blow is."

She shakes her head at me and takes a bite of tuna fish salad.

"Not a blow, honey; just a change," my dad says. My mom reaches over and squeezes his hand. I brace myself.

If my dad wants to be a woman, then he should be who he is, and I will support the crap out of him, and call him Roberta or something. Some things would make sense—the devotion to his ponytail, that year they came back from Scotland with a kilt that he wore endlessly on the weekends.

"A really positive change," my mom says. She is clearly also being great about this, which doesn't surprise me. If ever there was a woman to stay with her partner post-transition, it is my mom. And it won't be so bad; after all, my best friends are both lesbians. If my parents become lesbians, so what? As long as everyone is happy and healthy, love is love.

"Well, whatever it is, I support you both unconditionally." I try to fill my voice with love and calm.

"We appreciate that so much, sweetheart, because it will be a huge shift for us all," my dad says, his voice full of kindness, as I scan his face for signs of hormone treatments having softened his features. Looks pretty much the same to me.

"We're selling the house," my mom says.

Wait, what? "You're selling the house? That's it?"

"What else would you prefer?" my dad asks. I decide this is not the time to tell him I was picturing him in a tasteful wrap dress.

"I'm just surprised; you guys love this house. Why are you selling?"

"We'll always love the house, honey, but it is a lot of house for the two of us," my mom says. I can see that; it is three stories, over 4,500 square feet, full of bedrooms that have been mostly empty since they stopped taking exchange students about six years ago after one of them was discovered to be running a streaming-video porn site from her bedroom.

"And we always thought that our retirement project would be to do a systems overhaul, but at this point we'd have to move out for the better part of a year to do it, and there is something about heading back into construction mode that is just beyond our ability at this stage of our lives," my dad says.

"So when we were approached by a developer," my mom says, "we had to really listen to his proposal."

Which apparently was beyond substantial. Between the house itself and the fact that it sits on a lot that is effectively more than three and a half lots wide and in the heart of Lincoln Park, the developer offered my folks $5 million. Cash. No contingencies, as is, covering all closing costs, with a flexible closing date that gives them up to eight months to find a new place and move.

I almost choke on my tuna salad.

"Seriously?"

My dad nods. "Seriously."

"My god, that is amazing." I knew the place would be worth a ton, particularly because of the land, but I had no idea it'd sell for that much, especially since the market isn't fully recovered yet. But apparently, in Lincoln Park, what they are sitting on is a gold mine of insane proportions.

"It's enough that we can buy something scaled properly for the two of us, easier to manage and maintain, and it'll go a long way towards bolstering our retirement savings, giving us some extra to travel with, maybe even think about a little place out west to spend the winters when we are ready," my mom says, and

I can see that they are both really excited about the prospect of moving on.

"Well, then congratulations are in order!" I wish that I were fully openheartedly happy for them. It is an amazing financial opportunity and will change their lives and future for the better. I know that over the years, they have often reduced the amount they put away for retirement to support a cause they believed in, or dipped into savings to be able to pay bills while providing services for free to those who needed them. But taking the money and running seems so antithetical to who they are and how they have always behaved that I can't really wrap my head around it. Additionally, knowing that my finances are such a mess, and that my own foray into real estate left me no better off than if I had never owned my own place, adds a layer of bitterness. Especially since I would never ask them to share their windfall with me. If they knew how in debt I was, let alone the reason? Their disappointment would be oppressive and debilitating. They may not have always approved of the focus of my career path, but they have always been supportive of me and proud of me. If they knew about my abusive co-dependent relationship with Visa and MasterCard? I'd never get over the shame. In one moment it occurs to me that it is sort of horrid that I was fully prepared to embrace my dad's wanting to be a woman, but am struggling with the idea of my parents' wanting to have money for their third act.

My dad jumps up, runs to the fridge, and grabs a bottle of champagne. I get a peek at the label. Krug. Apparently, for all their simple, frugal tastes, you throw a bunch of money at them, and they go all Robin Leach in a hot minute.

"To a new adventure," my dad says.

"To the end of an era," my mom says.

"To the two of you," I say. Whatever my own bullshit is, I love them both and I am very happy for what this change will mean for them. And if the new reality means I occasionally get to sip Krug on their dime, how bad could it be?

⁓

Bubbles looks wonderful in a simple navy blue dress, the top showing off her still-lovely collarbone, which is accented with a necklace of sparkly green peridots. The diamond drop earrings my grandfather bought her when my dad was born add a touch of glamour. In the last few years she has given up her trademark stilettos for more manageable kitten heels, but she's lost none of her sass; tonight's shoes have a super-pointy toe and are in a jaunty leopard-print patent. Her silver hair is up in a chignon, courtesy of an afternoon salon appointment. She takes from the closet her prized possession, an embroidered moss-green velvet cocoon coat that had been her mother's, from the 1920s or so, with ermine cuffs and collar. It is the perfect thing for a chilly spring evening, and she looks simply gorgeous and elegant, and could have stepped right out of one of our movies.

"You are a vision." I come over to kiss her soft cheek. "If Nick Charles is at the opera tonight, then Nora has some serious competition."

"Pish," she says, blushing prettily. "I'm just an old lady all tarted up."

"Well, don't let Mrs. Barkley see her husband flirting with you; people will talk."

"The Barkleys hate opera as much as you do, darling."

"I can never keep track."

"Nor should you. Us ancients are terribly boring. Something smells good in here. Spicy."

"Lamb shawarma." I figured that Amelia would appreciate something of a Middle Eastern/Mediterranean feast filled with things Brian would hate.

"Yum. I almost hate to leave."

"I made plenty for leftovers; we can have it for lunch tomorrow."

"Not if you burn it," she says, sniffing the air, and I run for the kitchen, shouting at her to have a lovely evening, and grab the pot of freekeh that is boiling over on the stove. I turn down the flame and return the pot to the burner. After my lunch shock with Mom and Dad, who asked that I not share their news with Bubbles just yet, I headed for the stores up on Devon and loaded up on goodies for this evening. As soon as I got home, I took a hot bath, followed by a nap. I let the news of the day wash over me and made a conscious decision to just be happy for my folks. Or at least to pretend that I'm happy for them until I'm actually happy for them.

The doorbell rings promptly at six thirty. Amelia, as per my instructions, has arrived in comfy couch clothes, and is carrying a six-pack of beer. I've got the dinner laid out buffet-style on the coffee table in the den, and *Auntie Mame* queued up on the DVD player. I figured I'd better start her off with something fun and fluffy and in color, and see how she takes to it, before springing black-and-white on her. We load up our plates, making sandwiches with the tender, well-spiced pink lamb drizzled with both creamy, nutty tahini sauce and a spicy green sauce, with feta, fresh tomatoes, and parsley on top. On the side are scoops of the freekeh and lentil pilaf, and cucumber yogurt salad and olives.

"I'm madly in love with you, you know?" Amelia sneaks Snatch his umpteenth piece of lamb and makes smooching noises at him.

"You can have him for a very low price."

"Don't I wish! Brian is allergic. Or I would take you home. Yes, I would! And maybe change your name a little bit." She grins at me.

"I know. Isn't it awful?"

"It's kind of hilarious." Amelia leans back on the couch, and

Snatch launches himself into the air, landing on her tiny lap with a mighty oomph.

"*Snatch!*"

But Amelia is unfazed, holding his head in her hands and snorting at him in a perfect imitation of his piggy little language, and receiving his slurpy kisses without revealing a hint of being grossed out.

"I could leave the two of you alone for a bit if you like?"

She swats at me and then holds her face next to his face. "Don't be jealous of our love."

I see Snatch do a very particular sort of wiggle. Good lord. "I'm not going to be jealous of anything. Especially in three . . . two . . . one . . ."

"*Holy crap!*" Amelia says, clapping her hand over her nose and mouth as a funky meaty stench rises around us.

"Yeah. Lamb makes him farty, by the way. Still want to take him home?"

Amelia makes an exaggerated gagging noise and pushes the dog back off the couch.

By the time Auntie Mame outruns the fox at the hunt, we are stuffed to the gills. Amelia laughs throughout the movie, exclaiming at the transformations of Mame's Beekman Place apartment, and the fabulous costumes. After the movie is over, Amelia helps me get all the leftovers into containers in the fridge, and we head to the Nook with mugs of tea and our desserts.

"I have a present for you, and I don't want you to be mad," Amelia says, crunching into a pastry and dropping honey-sweetened crumbs and bits of pistachio down the front of her U of C sweatshirt.

"As long as it isn't a check, I'm not mad," I say. "I generally love presents."

She runs to the front room and grabs her tiny laptop out of her bag, then asks for the Wi-Fi password. "HildyJohnson1940,"

I tell her. She types rapidly and then hands me the computer. There is a website up on her screen.

Welcome to WeddingGirl.com! All of your nuptial questions answered and problems solved.

I scroll through the website, which is cute, full of images of details from weddings, samples of questions from brides and grooms, and a large button that says Ask Wedding Girl. When I click the button, there is a form to fill out, with a drop-down list of possible topics for questions, like Food, Etiquette, Décor, Handling Family, and Disasters. And at the bottom, a clear message:

Free advice is worth what you pay for it. All initial questions for Wedding Girl are $4.99, with up to three follow-up questions at $1.99 each.

"It's a cute site, good idea. One of yours?"

"It's yours." Amelia smiles at me.

"Mine?" I'm not getting it.

"If you say so, it's ready to launch; all I have to do is push a button. I made it for you. You won't take money from a friend, but I thought maybe you would take it from strangers. Your advice is so great, and your ideas are so cool. I know you don't want a wedding-planning business, but I thought, for some extra income, why not just an email consulting business? I've set it up for Pay-Pal, so they can pay however they want, and the money goes straight into an account for you—some easy income to help pay down your debt. And you can do the whole thing anonymously!"

"Wait, I don't get it. *I'm* Wedding Girl?"

"Exactly. I set up the code so you should come up fairly high on Google searches, and I hacked your Pinterest wedding boards, copied them completely, and used your pins to populate a Wedding Girl Pinterest. And I've got both a Facebook page and a Twitter account all set up for you as well. You can promote as much or as little as you want, but I think you could get enough questions a month to start making a dent in your credit card balances."

"I don't know what to say." I really don't. The site is adorable, and the idea is genius, but the thought of promoting myself as a wedding guru? That seems farcical.

"I know what you are thinking, but it isn't a relationship counseling site; it is a wedding site. Questions just like all the ones I've been asking you that you've been answering so perfectly. And there is a button on your end for if you ever just don't want to answer something; you can decline the question, and it sends an email saying that they have 'stumped the Wedding Girl,' that the team doesn't have an answer and their payment was not charged."

"And you really think I could make money this way? Enough to matter?"

"I know you can. I've got some ways to drive traffic that are built into the launch, and I think once you answer a few questions, you are going to get some great social media traction. And again, it says on the site that Wedding Girl can decline to answer any question due to time constraints or content incompatibility, and that no unanswered question will be charged. So if the traffic gets to be more than you want to handle, you can just decline a bunch of stuff."

"And what if they don't like my answers?"

"No money-back guarantees; if they don't like the answer, too bad."

I have to admit, the thought of some extra income, income that I can earn in my ample spare time, in my sweatpants? That is appealing. "What do I have to do?"

"Just say yes!"

"Okay, yes. But you have to show me how it works."

"Yay! Okay, couldn't be simpler. Watch." Amelia hits some buttons and then asks me to go grab my laptop. By the time I get back downstairs and log in to my email, there is a message from WeddingGirl.com. I open it and read a question: Dear Wedding Girl, are you ready to be Dear Abby to the engaged people of the world? Below are two buttons: Accept and Decline. I press Accept, and a box pops up with a form for me to answer the email. I type, Ready as I'll ever be, and hit Send. I hear a ping on Amelia's computer and realize that she sent me the email through the site and I answered.

"That's really it?"

"That's it. At the moment it is set up to forward to your personal account, but I think we should set up a separate Gmail account for it to forward to. But that is how it works: It sends you an email with the content of the question, and you hit 'accept' to answer and get your money, or 'decline' to send the auto-decline response and no payment is processed. When they get your email response, it looks like this." She shows me her computer, and the email has the Wedding Girl logo, my brief response, and buttons on the bottom: Follow-Up Question on This Topic $1.99, New Question $3.99, and Feedback Reply FREE. "So if you answered the original question but it brings something else up on that same topic, they can follow up with you for a smaller charge; or they can ask something on a new topic for a discounted price; or they can send you a little thank-you for no charge."

"Or a complaint about how I ruined their big day."

Amelia shakes her head. "Pessimist. I cannot imagine you could ruin someone's big day."

Except my own, I think. "Wow. This is crazy."

"Not crazy. Just trying to parlay your skills into some cash flow."

It takes Amelia about an hour to walk me through my new Facebook and Twitter and Pinterest accounts, all of which seem to have about a thousand followers each. "I just followed a bunch of folks in the industry so that we could build you up some people; in this business, everyone has a follow-back policy, so it didn't take much time to get you some decent numbers. If you start using the accounts, you'll find those numbers will go up even more."

"I don't know what to say."

"Look, if it doesn't work, or you hate it, no harm, no foul. I never get to work on fun stuff like this, and it was totally easy to do. But if it works, you can take me to dinner."

"Deal." I'm a little overwhelmed. No one has ever done something like this for me before, been so kind and selfless, and even though she is downplaying how much work it was, I know it must have been complicated and time-consuming. And while a few weeks ago my every impulse would have been a "thanks but no thanks," I immediately recognize that I cannot sanely turn down any opportunity for extra income, not with Cake Goddess breathing down our necks.

Amelia gives me a hug, picks up Snatch, and dances him around the kitchen while I clean up the teacups and give her the rest of the baklava to take home. I say that I want to make plans for a girls' night for her to meet Ruth and Jean, and she seems genuinely excited. When she leaves, I take Snatch for a walk, the lumpy pug snuffling in the moist patches of grass around every tree. Now that we have had a full melt of all of winter's ice and snowpack, things are a little boggy.

I check my watch after we get home, but Bubbles isn't back yet. It's after eleven, but I know opera can go forever, so it doesn't really worry me. I give the dog a treat, which he snarfs down quickly, pour myself a small glass of the sherry Bubbles keeps in a crystal decanter in the bar, and head up to my room. I plug my laptop back in on my desk and open it up. I log in to my email account, and there it is: Email from WeddingGirl.com.

I open it, and there is a question.

Dear Wedding Girl—

My future in-laws are insisting that it is socially essential for them to invite a bunch of their longtime business colleagues to our wedding, but my parents are paying for the wedding, and my in-laws have not offered to cover the cost of this potential significant increase in the guest list. I just want to tell them no, since we don't really know any of these people and my parents aren't inviting business associates, but my fiancé thinks that is petty of me. If we do decide to include them, is it appropriate to make that inclusion contingent upon their financial participation?

Respectfully,
Put-Upon Bride

I look at the bottom of the email, take a sip of my sherry, and hit Accept.

Adam's Rib

(1949)

And after you shot your husband . . . how did you feel?

• KATHARINE HEPBURN AS AMANDA BONNER •

"Thank you! Come again!" I say to the noisy gaggle, and they all wave and laugh their way out the door. Herman and I look at each other and burst into laughter.

"There were so many!" he says.

"And they were so hungry," I say.

"We're going to have to refill out here." He gestures at the case, which, for the first time since I started working here, is pretty well decimated. About a half hour ago, we got slammed with nearly twenty women from the twenty-five-year reunion class from the neighborhood high school. Apparently, in a fit of nostalgia, the entire class-of-1990 cheerleading squad had toked up behind the school, the former head cheerleader being in possession of some serious medicinal-grade weed for her osteoarthritis. They all got smacked with a killer case of the munchies, and one of them remembered Langer's was nearby. Between the sweets they shoveled in as fast as we could hand them over and the boxes they had us pack up to take back to the reunion, about all we have left in here is a few sad little butter cookies, some poppy seed rugelach, and roughly a quarter of our stock of breads.

"It's a good problem to have." Even better, a good portion of the women who were here are still local, so I'm hopeful that maybe we will have some new fans and regular customers.

"Yes, it is." Herman has been in a very chipper mood of late. I'd love to think that it is because business has been on an uptick—not over-the-top bonkers, but a steady increase, steady enough that it's noticeable. But maybe it's just that spring has fully sprung. The rains and winds of April gave way to the soft breezes of May, and now that we are knocking on the door of June, Chicago is in full rapturous bloom. The flowers are all up; the trees are lush and green. It is the magical few weeks before the oppressive heat and humidity of summer drop on our heads like a ton of bricks. The neighborhood has been out and about in force, and while we still aren't getting much of the mommy crowd, at least the hipsters and young couples have started stopping in for bread and nibbles now that we have a sign up front proudly announcing our use of organic products and our daily specials. Weekday business is still relatively quiet during the day, but we do get more end-of-day walk-ins, mainly people coming home and getting off the train at the stop up the block, and weekends are officially hopping.

"Let's get this place restocked before the after-work crowd pops in."

"I'll restock. You need to work on that cake." I've just started on Amelia's wedding cake. It's been so long since I've done one I'm giving myself a full week, just in case something goes awry. It should only take me three days, so I've got plenty of time to make one completely wrong and still be able to do it all over.

"Okay. But if it gets busy out here again, call me."

He winks, takes the cupcake tray out of the case—its contents now reduced to crumbs and a couple of smears of frosting—and heads back to fill it up again. I follow him with the empty cookie tray, leaving it for him in the rack, and begin making the batter for the bottom tier of the cake.

My biggest fear with this cake is getting these large circles out of the pans in one piece without chunks of moist cake sticking to the bottoms. I fill the pans with batter, slide them both into the oven, and clean up the worktable and the mixer bowl. I love getting into the groove in the kitchen. It keeps my head clear. I know a lot of chefs who say that while they are working, they think about all sorts of things, getting ideas for new recipes or working out personal relationship issues. One of my classmates from pastry school said that when she cooked alone, she had conversations with herself, arguing out loud with people she was mad at and speaking both sides of the exchange. I've never been like that. My brain tends not to wander too far. I think about the steps of the recipe; I go over the details; I focus on technique.

When I'm cooking, there is nothing else. Which is probably why I could never date another chef. Dexter wasn't a cook; he was a gourmand. And when it came to the kitchen, that was my domain. Just how I liked it. It isn't that I'm not a team player; from a professional standpoint, I may not have been warm and fuzzy, but until those last few months, I was good with the other people in the kitchen at S&S. And I genuinely like working with Herman; since the work itself is fairly easy and repetitive, his chattiness is fine and doesn't distract me from getting things done. But personally? I've never understood all those movies that show the couple cozily cooking together, chopping at side-by-side cutting boards, feeding each other tastes of things, offering sauces on spoons or frosting on the tip of a manicured finger; it always looked fake to me.

The door cracks open and Herman pokes his head in and says that Mrs. Freidman called to see if we had any of the strawberry cream puffs left; her family is coming for dinner, and she doesn't have time to make dessert. They were our special of the day yesterday, and we still have about a dozen of the shells baked off already, and the pastry cream and strawberries are in tubs in the walk-in. But the whipped cream is gone. I could have sworn there was some left last night when I went home, but I must be wrong.

"How many does she want?"

"Can we make her eight?"

"Yep. We only have a dozen of the puffs left. Should I make the other four and hope that one of the walk-ins tonight grabs them?"

"Might as well, unless you want to take them home."

"Herman, if I keep taking things home, neither Bubbles nor I will be able to fit in our pants."

"Bubbles fills her pants just fine," he says with a wink, in a shockingly knowing tone that is probably making my grandmother wonder why she is blushing right now for no reason.

"Wicked man. Go watch your store."

He disappears, and I grab the pastry cream and strawberries out of the walk-in and put them on the table. The amount of cream we need for a dozen puffs is fairly minimal, just three cups, so there is no point in dirtying a mixer. I grab a large bowl and the immersion blender with the whisk attachment. Back in the day, I might have done it by hand, just to show off, but these days my attitude is that technology is my friend, especially since there is no one here to impress. I dump the cream into the bowl and turn the blender on. I hold the bowl tight to my waist as I move the blur of a spinning whisk around in the cream in a wide figure eight. Watching the white liquid start to swell the smallest bit as it begins to absorb air, I get a little mesmerized. I start thinking about the email I got last night from WeddingGirl.com. It had been a few days since I had gotten anything from the site, so I thought perhaps the first couple of weeks of one or two emails a day had been some sort of fluke, and that business was just going to trickle away until it stopped. The questions I'd gotten so far had all been pretty mundane and easy to answer: suggestions for favors, or how to handle dietary restrictions, or how to tame a maid of honor whose nickname is Tequila Tina. I've officially earned enough to have one dinner out. Provided I don't drink. To be honest, I'd almost forgotten the site even existed until I saw the email last night.

Dear Wedding Girl—

I'm not sure if I should be getting married. I love my fiancé and he makes me happy, and I believe we would have a great life together. I don't want someone else or anything like that. And his family is lovely to me, everyone gets along well. But there is just something nagging in my gut that makes me want to run away, and I don't know if it is just cold feet and nerves, or if my subconscious is trying to tell me that I'm not ready or don't want this.

How do I know if I should go through with it?

Bride in Crisis

I almost declined to answer when I first saw it. On the one hand, I'm a big believer in going with your gut, and if your gut says don't do it, don't do it. But then I thought about a loving fiancé, a beautifully planned event, and the devastation that comes when someone runs, and I shut the computer down and went to bed. What can I tell her? She has a fifty-fifty shot either way. Half of marriages end in divorce however they begin. So barring a real "reason" beyond some butterflies, should she, in what is from her own account a happy and loving situation, go for it and hope they are in the lucky half that makes it? And if I suggest that and in a year it all falls apart, will she blame me? Would I blame me? I never thought about Dexter's end of things, assuming as everyone did that he made a cold and calculated financial-and business-driven decision and not an emotional one. But what if that wasn't the case? What if he didn't want Cookie for her money but just wanted her more than he wanted me?

I'm wondering this very thing when my grasp on the bowl loosens a bit. The bowl starts to spin on the metal tabletop, and the cord of the immersion blender gets caught between the side of the bowl and the spinning whisk. The bowl slips completely out of my hand, doing a wild spin and sending a wave of barely soft-peak whipped cream all over me, the work surface, and everything in a six-foot radius. I drop the immersion blender in my shock, and the whisk continues to spin, sending thwacks of cream shooting out as it skitters along the table, knocking things over and creating a sound like machine gun fire, until I grab the cord and yank it out of the socket to make it stop. This is why I don't let my mind wander when I cook. Because I'm a total klutz by nature, and the only way to tamp that down is to stay super focused.

The door flies open, and Herman comes running in.

"Are you okay?" he says, looking stricken.

"Yeah, just a small whipped cream incident." I look down. I've got a swath of cream straight across my boobs, and I can feel it all over my face, in my hair.

Then I look over Herman's shoulder and through the open door, and see Mark in the Suit. Great.

Herman starts to laugh and walks over to me. He gently takes the immersion blender cord out of my hand and offers me a side towel.

"Sophie, my girl, I want you to meet my son Herman Jr."

"Sounds good. Is he out front? Can I clean up first? Want to make a good impression."

Herman looks at me quizzically, and then Mark in the Suit heads into the back room and waves at me. "Hi there," he says, smirking.

"But you're Mark," I sputter.

"Mark is his middle name, and he prefers it, but his mother and I named him Herman Jr., and so he will always be to me," Herman says with an edge in his voice. Mark winks at me. I don't know how to take this. I certainly get the whole "use the name you want and not the one you were given" thing, which weirdly endears him to me a bit. But then I remember he has been in twice and neglected to mention his connection to the place, which makes me feel retroactively idiotic.

"Well, Herman Jr., nice to meet you." I hold out my hand, which he looks at. When he raises an eyebrow, I glance at my hand; there is a glob of whipped cream on it. I wipe it off on the towel and let it drop to my side.

The bells on the door up front peal, and Herman heads back up front to manage the customer, leaving Mark behind. I start to clean up.

"Nice to see you again, Sophie."

"Why didn't you say you were Herman's son?"

"You didn't ask, and it didn't seem relevant."

What a pompous ass. "It didn't seem relevant that you were in the store and you are my boss's son, that maybe I should know that?"

"Would you have done anything different?"

"I dunno. Maybe." Flirt less, probably.

"Exactly. My dad ran this place on his own since Jose left over ten years ago. Never replaced him, never hired someone else to help. Suddenly there is some random girl working here, making new things, changing recipes. I wanted to get a sense of you, and if you knew I was his son, you wouldn't just be yourself; you would have been trying to make some sort of impression."

Suddenly a clump of whipped cream falls from the ceiling and onto his shoulder. It totally looks like he got nailed by a pigeon. He doesn't seem to notice, and considering his accusatory tone, I'm inclined to just let it sit there.

"So, what, you think I've got some nefarious plan where your dad is concerned?"

"Do you?"

"That's a shitty thing to ask."

"Trust me, it's a shitty thing to wonder."

I can feel my face burn. "What on earth could I possibly be plotting here? I mean, your dad is adorable, but if I were an Anna Nicole type, he isn't exactly rolling in it."

Mark laughs. "No, I'm certain you aren't trying to marry him for his money. Nor, before you mention it, do I think you are trying to become 'like a daughter' to him so that he writes you into the will and denies me my birthright."

If his air quotes around "like a daughter" didn't infuriate me enough, his sarcastic tone on the word "birthright," accompanied with a dismissive wave around the kitchen, implying that inheriting the bakery would be like getting some horrible ugly piece of battered old furniture you never liked, makes my eyelid begin to twitch with rage.

"I see, so we've established that I am neither trying to get in your dad's pants nor oust you as favorite child. So tell me, *Junior*," I say with deep emphasis, "exactly what about me worries you so damn much?"

He peers down his nose at me and lowers his voice. "You're making it better."

I throw my hands in the air. "God forbid! I am so sorry. Shall I make it crappier?"

He sighs. "Look, Sophie, I'm sure you're a very nice girl with perfectly good intentions. And my dad says he's known your people forever, so I believe you genuinely think you are doing a good thing for a family friend. But here is the reality. I had almost convinced my dad to sell this place, the whole building, to move into a really spectacular retirement community, where he could rest and relax and make friends and enjoy the time he has left. But now the business is picking up, and you are revitalizing things, and new customers are coming in, and it is getting him excited."

"And this is bad because?"

"Because he is eighty-three years old and has a heart condition, and because *you will leave*. Cake Goddess is coming in *six months*; they announced it in the trades this week. Once she is spitting distance? This place already is barely worth the price of the bricks it's made of." Now he seems to be getting mad.

"This isn't my fault."

"It's not *not* your fault."

"That's unfair."

"You're not kidding!"

"How on earth could I possibly know that the goddamned Cake Goddess was going to plunk herself down around the corner?"

"How on earth could you possibly *not* know that my dad's business is a dinosaur in a changing hipster neighborhood? How could you not know that how this place runs and what it sells is none of your business, and certainly not your place to change!"

"All I did was try to help your dad make more money!"

"Did you? Or did you try and change things to your own taste and sensibility?"

This makes my blood begin to boil. The unmitigated *gall* of this pompous, self-important poopweasel. "Look, *Junior*, I didn't come in here begging for a job; I came in for rye bread. And your dad put on a full-court press to get me to accept his offer. I told him not to take the sign down!" I gesture towards the front, where the faded, dusty "Part-Time Baker Wanted" sign still sits on a shelf. "I told him that I would be temporary and part-time till either he or I found something permanent. So don't get all up in my grill about what a terrible person I am and how I screwed everything up around here. You might want your dad to sell and move and go live in some retirement community for your own convenience, but I'm pretty sure he is a grown-ass man and can make his own decisions about his life and livelihood. And while he might be slowing down a bit, his mind is sharp as a tack from what I've seen, so if that mind has weighed his options and wants to stay here? Then I do consider it both my business and my *job* to help him make it as lucrative as I possibly can."

"Thank you, darling girl." I hadn't heard Herman come back into the room, so intent was I on putting Mark in his place.

"I'm sorry, Herman. I . . ."

"Shush. Don't ever be sorry for speaking your mind or defending someone you think needs it. I am deeply grateful for both the sentiment and that you have the courage to express it." He takes my hand and kisses it before patting it solidly with his own; when he gives it a tight squeeze, he doesn't let go. "Junior? I love you, my son. I know your heart is in the right place, and you want what you believe is best for me, and so I am willing to listen to whatever crap you care to sling in my direction. But you may not harass my partner here. Ever. Clear?" His voice is low and steady, and sends a very distinct message.

"I give up." Mark throws his hands in the air. "And, Sophie?"

"Yeah?"

"Something's burning . . ."

I run to the oven and retrieve the two enormous pans of charred cake, tears prickling at my eyes at the stupidity of not setting a damned timer, as Herman escorts Mark back out to the front.

⟋⟍⟍⟋

"So, now that we have announced our crazy idea to Mark, what next?" Herman says, bringing me a steaming mug of tea.

"I dunno, Herman. I don't like the tone he used or the way he said what he said, but Mar . . . Herman Jr. isn't exactly wrong. He said the Cake Goddess has only six months before she opens her doors over there." I wave in the direction of the future site of our downfall.

"Six months."

"If we're lucky."

"Six months to become indispensable. Will you give me six months? If I shift you up to full time, can you promise me that you'll stay the full six months to see what we can do together, to see if we can save ourselves? I know it is a lot, I know this isn't where you want to end up, but I can't move forward without you." His blue eyes are extra-shiny, not quite welling up with tears but full of both determination and worry.

I look him right in the eye and, with my whole heart, say, "You got me."

He smiles and nods. "We are going to need a plan."

"Yeah."

"And some new offerings."

"That too."

"I'm too old. I don't know what to do or how to do it. When all the cakes changed and everyone stopped coming, I just didn't know how to shift gears, how to bounce back. But you will know. Do you think you can do it? Do you think you can come up with a plan?"

"I can certainly try."

"Okay. Do this. Redo your burnt cakes. And then go home. And take tomorrow off. I can handle the challahs. Come back

Saturday, and after we close, we'll have dinner upstairs, talk about the plan. And bring your grandmother. She's a very smart lady; I will want to hear her thoughts about the plan as it relates to the old neighborhood regulars. Whatever we do, I don't want to leave them out in the cold."

"Okay. On one condition."

"What's that?"

"You let us bring the dinner."

Herman laughs. "Deal."

"You do know he's right, don't you?" Ruth says, smacking Jean's hand when she tries to steal one of her fries. Jean pulls her hand back and returns to moving her spinach salad around on her plate, looking wistfully at Ruth's burger and my grilled cheese. We were having wine at Jean's and got hungry, so we walked up the block to Four Moon Tavern for some pub grub.

I narrow my eyes at Ruth, pick the largest onion ring off my plate, and hand it to Jean.

"Right in what way exactly?" I haven't been able to stop thinking about Mark/Herman Jr. All I ever thought about while working at Langer's was making some money, feeling productive and useful, and waiting for the dust to clear so that I could get a decent job and move on with my life. But the fact that I even think about looking for a "decent job" does sort of weirdly imply that I think my current job isn't decent. I don't like that Mark was so certain my departure is inevitable, despite the open-ended nature of my agreement with Herman. I hate to think of anything that would be bad for Herman. I certainly didn't know about any heart condition, and that really worries me. Which doesn't mean I'm not fully prepared to be irrationally defensive about the whole thing. Especially because I'm so in my head about it that I've now remade the devil's food cake layers twice more, having forgotten the cornstarch in the second batch, so it sank in the middle. And while the vanilla layers came out perfectly the first time, so far the buttercream has broken on me twice, because the spinning mixer blade gets me all hypnotized and thinking about Herman and Mark, and I lose concentration. I'm committed to going back to the bakery tonight after dinner to get a batch done right, so that I can assemble and crumb-coat the tiers and get started tomorrow on decoration.

"In the way of not being wrong. Don't play dumb-ass; I hate that shit," Ruth says.

"Don't be mean, Ruthie," Jean says. "It's a difficult situation."

"No, it isn't. It is a simple situation. Our darling girl over here has to decide what it is she truly wants. If she wants to turn Langer's into an amazing retro destination neighborhood bakery, as they seem to be planning, then she should embrace that and own her part in it. Or she should decide definitively that Langer's is just a placeholder for her, in which case, Marky Mark is absolutely right: She needs to stop meddling, put her head down and be a good little employee, and handle her eventual exit with grace and integrity. And, Jean, for the love of god, either eat the damn salad and ask the girl out, or order the sloppy joes you actually want and find someone less scrawny to obsess over." Jean is still pining for Yoga Actress, who has landed solidly somewhere in the "affectionate friend" zone, but trying to maintain the healthier lifestyle she adopted as part of her wooing process has made Jean so morose that she has lost her oomph for taking things to the next level.

"It isn't as easy as all that, Ruth. You might be interested to know that Jean and I don't necessarily live in your black-and-white world of numbers that add up or don't. You might give us both a little bit of support for the stuff that falls into the gray areas."

"Thank you," Jean says, reaching over to my plate and taking another onion ring.

"Don't push it, lady; order some of your own if you want more," I say, winking at her. "Look, Ruth, I get where you are coming from; I get where Mark is coming from. I'm just saying that I don't know whether I'm actually ready to be sure about the situation yet, and I don't want to make a mistake, for me or for Herman. But I do know that in the short term, I'm not going to feel bad about making him more money. Because until I hear from Herman that his goal is to sell and leave, and that it isn't just what Mark wants, then I don't see harm in his business improving. How do I know what Mark's motivations are? Maybe he just wants his dad in a facility so that he doesn't have the inconvenience of having to check in all the time, or schlepping to the old neighborhood to visit."

"Which is both possible and none of your business," Ruth says, taking a small handful of her fries and putting them on Jean's plate by way of peace offering.

"It's—"

"None. Of. Your. Business." Ruth shakes her head at me. "He is a nice old man who is not related to you by blood or choice; he is your boss, and not your responsibility, and his relationship with his son or his son's motivations are not your concern. If no one is doing anything that should be reported to the police, keep your pert little nose out of it, Soph, seriously. Figure your own shit out and act accordingly."

"While I may disagree with the tone, I do agree with that part of the message. He's a dear old thing, but Ruthie is right; you have to keep things separate. Decide what you want and need, but don't try to meddle, especially between a parent and a child; it is too complicated." Jean's dad died when she was little, and her mom has Alzheimer's and is in assisted living near Jean's sister in the burbs.

This is the moment I decide that I am never going to tell them about WeddingGirl.com. If they think that adding some stuff to the menu at the bakery is meddling, god knows how they would react to my giving advice to strangers on the Internet, and for money no less.

"Fine," I say. "I get it; duly noted. I will keep you posted." I wave the waiter over. "We are going to need a basket of chicken tenders with both ranch and BBQ sauce, and a basket of the sweet potato fries." I stick my tongue out at Ruth and smile at Jean. What's the old saying? "Never trust a skinny chef"? I'm embracing all of my trustworthiness.

Ruth shakes her head. "And another round of drinks. Go big or go home, ladies."

"And you can take this," Jean says with a grin, handing him her half-finished salad with a flourish. And he leaves the three of us laughing.

Love Crazy

(1941)

WILLIAM POWELL AS STEVE IRELAND: She's married now—got a husband.

MYRNA LOY AS SUSAN IRELAND: Yeah? Whose husband has she got?

⁂

I reach up and remove my earplugs. The low thumping that woke me is now clarified as a consistent banging, which only means one thing. Bubbles is down there whaling away on chicken breasts with a cast-iron skillet. My parents are coming for dinner, and she has gotten it into her head to make chicken Kiev, which was my dad's favorite growing up. So much for sleeping in on my day off. I'm supposed to meet the girls for lunch today but had really hoped to just stay in bed until I need to get dressed. Bubbles got home late last night from a play at Writers Theatre; we made some honey-ginger tea, retreated to the den, and discovered that *Gone with the Wind* was just starting on TCM, and that settled things. Bubbles, trooper that she is, made it almost to intermission before dropping off, and when the music woke her, she headed off to bed with Snatch clicking sleepily at her heels. But I couldn't follow suit, so I was up till three finishing the movie. I was amped up anyway. Amelia had emailed me to tell me that not only had the cake looked spectacular, but it had been the most

delicious wedding cake anyone had ever had. The surprise apparently went off without a hitch, thanks to my other advice. Ever
since they got back from their five-day mini-moon in Austin, they
have been inundated with people telling them that it was the best
wedding they had ever been to. And all the parents loved the
whole thing and weren't mad in the least. More importantly,
everyone raved about the cake. I didn't tell her it took me three
full tries on almost every aspect to get it right; all I cared about
was that it was what they wanted and it made everyone happy.
Amelia and I have plans for a girls' night next week to introduce
her to Ruth and Jean, and I'm strangely excited that she seems to
be becoming an actual friend.

Bubbles is still thwacking away down there, so I get up and
stretch a bit. I check my phone. It is nine thirty, so at least I'm
up at something of a rational hour, despite my long night. I
might as well get dressed and go help her. The phone also tells
me I have an email from the website, so I log in to my laptop.

Wedding Girl—

Not sure if you can help. My boss is having something of a best
man problem, and has asked for my help, but I don't have the
foggiest idea how to deal with it. A girl in my book club mentioned your service, so I thought I would reach out on his
behalf. I don't know if you handle this sort of thing, but if you
do, I would like to suggest to him that he get in touch with you
for assistance? I think he needs to plan a bachelor party and
isn't feeling terribly confident about how to go about it. If you
think you can help, let me know and I will have him reach out.

Thanks much.

Why not?

I'd be happy to hear from him, and hopefully help him out. Feel free to send him to the site and have him get in touch. And be sure to charge the fee for this first email to him!

Best,

Wedding Girl

I head off to the shower, retrieving only two lost earplugs, which means that for the few hours I was asleep, I was really dead. I get my hair up into its traditional messy bun, remember to slap on some moisturizer, and pull on a pair of leggings and a T-shirt from the Police reunion tour. I'm just getting ready to head downstairs to help Bubbles when I spot a new email on my still-open laptop.

Wedding Girl—

Well there is a first time for everything, if you had told me this morning I would be writing into a website like yours I would have bet against it. But I have something of a social conundrum, and really have neither time nor inclination to put too much effort into figuring it out on my own. My assistant assures me that you may be of help, so I am contacting you. A friend from high school recently became engaged. He has asked me to be his Best Man, and I have, of course, accepted, but now I have a bachelor party to plan, and as it turns out, the bride-to-be has five brothers of the overgrown frat boy variety. My pal and I, and our circle of friends, think the best kind of bachelor party involves steaks, martinis, good cigars, maybe some old single malt at the end of the night. They believe in more of a porno keg party with strippers/hookers. I've prepared myself to pay for the entire event so that I don't have to worry about making choices for the evening that are financially based, since her brothers can't afford the places I would like to go, but I'm also worried about setting up an evening where there are two groups of people having separate experiences. I'm not sure how to handle the whole thing. If I plan the party I want and that I think my friend would want, it is likely to alienate his new brothers-in-law. If I give in to what they want, it will probably devolve into some debauched drunken event that will make our side of the group very uncomfortable. Not at all sure how to handle creating an event that will bring the two groups together.

Thoughts?

Best Man

It is my first email from a guy, albeit obviously a very reluctant one, which seems weirdly significant. The past week I've been getting one or two a day, so still not enough to have me rolling in dough, but steady enough that I'm hoping it might at least support the little social life I currently have. Every bit helps. I accept the question and type a quick reply.

Dear Best Man—

I'm happy to try and help. Where is this event taking place?

Wedding Girl

I scan through the rest of my emails, mostly junk. I get endless spam, the majority a result of all the research I did for my wedding. Every wedding-related solicitation you can imagine. I used to diligently unsubscribe, but now with WeddingGirl.com, I just file them away in case I need them for inspiration. While I work on this, I get another email.

Wedding Girl—

The event is in Chicago.

Best Man

Easy.

Dear Best Man—

Perfect, I'm a Chicago girl myself, so this should be a slam dunk. I feel like the key to bringing together two groups is to avoid all the situations that would appear antagonistic to either side, and look to find something that everyone would have in common. If you are steak and martinis and cigars, and they are beer and wings and boobs, then I would just avoid all of those entirely.

Since you clearly are in a position to be generous, have you thought about something that is more of an event instead of just a meal? Schedule the party on a night when there is a Cubs game at Wrigley and get a private suite. They have a pretty good catering program there, and even fancy guys appreciate the nostalgia lowbrow grub at a game, so you can have a combination of hot dogs and burgers, but also some nicer foods, and you can order the high-end booze package so that the beer is better quality and there are cocktails for those who want them. They also do special upgraded packages that can include tours or access to batting practice.

If that is beyond what you were thinking, budget wise, let me know and I will see what else I can come up with.

Wedding Girl

I head downstairs to see Bubbles at the kitchen counter, cast-iron skillet over her head.

"Good morning, *shayna punim*! Did I wake you with the banging?"

"You know you did. But it's fine. I should have been up anyway." I kiss her cheek before she brings the skillet down with a definitive whap on the chicken breast.

"You finished the movie, didn't you?" *Smack.*

"You know I did."

"That Scarlett, you have to love her despite herself." *Smack.*

"That you do. How can I help?"

"Did you want to make the butter filling for me? Butter is already soft." *Smack.*

"Of course. Chives and shallots?"

"Perfect." *Smack.*

"How about a little bit of lemon zest just to perk it up?"

"Ooooh, that sounds delicious." *Smack.* She takes the now enormous and thin chicken breast and puts it on the stack with the rest. "Breakfast?"

I check my watch; it is ten thirty. "Maybe just some toast. I'm meeting the girls for lunch in two hours."

"Of course. Can I offer you a slice of this amazing caramelized white chocolate apricot brioche made by my favorite granddaughter?"

"You may indeed."

When you slice the rich, buttery bread topped with crunchy bits of pearl sugar, you get a swirl of white chocolate, which now also has hints of caramel flavor from having been roasted, and chunks of apricot. It is a good one. Herman loved it and immediately said we would have it in the rotation all summer and to order more apricots.

Bubbles hands me two thick pieces of my bread, lightly toasted and lavished with butter. It is delicious, if I do say so myself.

"So, where are you girls headed today?" Bubbles pours us

both tea from the battered and chipped china pot that had been her mother's.

"Kiki's Bistro."

"Ooh la la! I do love their liver and onions."

Gack. "I know you do, Bubbles, but that is seriously gross."

"For a fancy chef person, you certainly do have pedestrian tastes. Liver is delicious, and good for you."

"I'm a muscle-only girl. If the meat had a larger purpose, I'm out." Seriously, that whole "rooter to tooter" thing just squicks me out.

Bubbles sighs dramatically. "Poor girl. The wonders you are missing."

I'm perfectly fine with my inability to choke down offal. I don't mind an off-cut like oxtail or even a crispy duck tongue garnishing a salad, but the whole innards thing? Ugh. "Well, I just prefer that *my* sweetbreads are *literally* sweet breads. Can't fault a girl for that."

"I suppose. Do you still have time to help Kiev with me before you go?"

I check my watch. "Yep. Let's do it."

It takes us barely twenty minutes to have eight fat Kievs all lined up. Bubbles drizzles some melted butter over the tops and then puts them in the fridge, ready to bake later.

We wash up, and I give her a kiss on top of her head before going back upstairs to make myself presentable for lunch. She is shrinking at a rapid rate. She wasn't a tall woman to begin with, but I never used to look down at her. This tugs at my gut a bit.

When I get to my room, I see that I have another email.

Wedding Girl—

My assistant mentioned that you were from Chicago. I believe you may, in fact, be a genius, and I apologize if my original email was dismissive of your services. This idea is terrific and I've already booked the suite. Thank you for the suggestion. We may not have much in common, but luckily we are all Northsiders, so the Cubbies trump everything. I'm wondering if you had any ideas of a place to go after? My best guess is that the group will want to head somewhere post-game, and the idea of ending up at the Cubby Bear with drunken sorority girls makes my skin crawl. And if possible I'd like to avoid the kind of bar where people will start ordering rounds of shots and suggesting ending the night at VIP's Gentleman's Club. I can have transportation organized, so that isn't an issue.

Really appreciate your help.

Best Man

I notice that he has sent this not in reply to my original note but as a new question, which means he is paying full freight on it, despite it technically being a follow-up. For some reason this seriously endears him to me. I do like making ten dollars before I digest my breakfast.

Best Man—

Hmmm. Afterparty is a little bit trickier. What if you planned something out of the box instead of just going to a bar? Something active. My best recommendation would be WhirlyBall. The Chicago location also offers lasertag for those who aren't on the WhirlyBall court, they have food and drink packages, so you can make sure that those who are continuing to party are also continuing to eat so that they don't get overly hammered. Again, play into the guys being guys thing, competitive spirit, keep their minds off the fact that there are no G-strings to pop dollar bills into, and just distract them with clean fun. WhirlyBall is open till midnight, so it makes for a plenty late enough night. If that doesn't appeal, my second guess would be to reserve some lanes at the Diversey Rock 'n' Bowl, pre-order pizzas and buckets of beer. Whichever you pick, when you are done, just to completely avoid the issue, have your transportation take you from there to Five Faces Ice Cream Shop for a late night sundae. By the time they have all sobered up a little with sweets, after a night of being a kid again, hopefully naked ladies will be the last thing on their minds, and they'll be ready to go home.

Wedding Girl

- - - - - - - - - - - - - -

Wedding Girl—

Again, cannot thank you enough, I think I will go for the WhirlyBall option, and had no idea that there was still a late night ice cream joint in Chicago, ever since Zephyr closed I've been bereft.

Best Man

Oh. My heart. Zephyr was a magic place for me. Bubbles first took me there on one of our sleepover nights, when she decided we needed French fries and ice cream for dinner. It was a wonderful art deco place, with deep booths upholstered in cobalt blue and sparkly silver vinyl. The sundaes were enormous, and everything was made in-house, from the ice cream to the hot fudge and caramel sauces to the real whipped cream, served unsweetened in a heavy glop with serious substance instead of sprayed from a can and so full of air it melted away into nothing with your first spoonful. Zephyr was a traditional hangout for me and Ruth in high school, especially because we both had serious crushes on their particularly gorgeous waitstaff: for Ruth, a blond stunner named Josie; for me, an actor/waiter named Patrick. Neither of them ever called despite our leaving our numbers written on the checks, with tips a little ostentatious for teenagers.

Best Man—

Sigh, Zephyr was one of our favorite hangouts in high school. My friend Mikey could take down one of their 64 oz shakes in under 15 minutes. I still dream of their Yellow Brick Road sundae. The parking lot was the scene of one of my most embarrassing car-related debacles.

Wedding Girl

I send this and then wonder why I did. Seems terribly unprofessional of me, but his tone threw me a bit. Oh well. Too late now. I pull on my one pair of "going out" jeans, thanking god as I always do for NYDJ and their magical stretchy denim that allows me to go out in public looking like a civilized human and not ten pounds of sausage stuffed in a five-pound casing. An oversized ultrathin sweater, two reluctant swipes of mascara just so Ruth doesn't give me shit, and some clear lip gloss. I shake out my hair to see if I can get away with wearing it down, and determine immediately that I cannot, and it goes back up into a somewhat less messy bun. A pair of small diamond hoop earrings and my granddad's ancient Rolex with the worn brown leather strap that Bubbles gave me as my culinary school graduation gift. I try to put on a cuff bracelet, but at my new, exciting "the hell with it all" weight, it is tight and uncomfortable, so I swap it out for a simple leather strap that has adjustable snaps. I'm perfectly acceptable in my current state and actually looking forward to a nice lunch. I'm just about to head downstairs when my computer pings.

WG—

I was a War of the Worlds guy myself. And how on earth did someone drink that whole milkshake and not throw up???? We used to order one for a table of 6!

I'm afraid you can't just leave a car-related debacle reference out there and not clarify the specifics.

Best Man

I check my watch. I have a few minutes. It seems strange to be sharing a story like this with someone who emailed me for advice, but I opened the door, and he seems to want to know. And maybe he will recommend me to other guys for advice, which wouldn't be the worst thing in the world. Plus every reply he has sent has cost him money, on top of the two initial full-price emails.

Best Man (can't shorten that to BM, it sounds scatological)—

The week after I got my driver's license my dad got paid for a legal case with a 1985 Cadillac Sedan de Ville. Don't ask. At any rate, the thing was massive, which was great because I could fit like eleven friends into it. A bunch of us piled in and headed for Zephyr. Their parking lot across the street was perpendicular parking, not diagonal, and there was a spot available next to a Chevy Nova. In pulling into the space with the damned land yacht, I somehow managed to swing the thing around so that my driver's side mirror was behind the side mirror of the Nova, and the rear bumpers were practically touching. So I couldn't even try to pull straight back, because I would have taken off one or both side mirrors, and if I tried to turn it out at all, I would have taken off the bumper on the Nova for sure. We had to go inside and get all of the busboys and waiters to come out and physically PICK UP the Nova and move it over so that neither car got damaged.

I should probably admit to the fact that in that week alone, I had locked the keys in the car at the DMV after getting my license, AND sideswiped a car changing lanes on Ridge Road. Luckily my driving and parking skills are much improved.

WG

I hit Send before even thinking about the fact that I am one hair shy of flirting with some random guy whose name I don't know who paid me for advice on the Internet. Whatever. Considering my current state of affairs, this is about as close to meeting a new guy as is likely to be possible.

"You know if you don't stop that, you will be a bald Snatch!" I hear Bubbles as I come down the stairs, and find her trying to get the dog to stop licking his leg. He occasionally gets anxiety and chews off the fur on his feet and legs in patches. I give her a kiss and tell her I should be home by two thirty or three, and ask if she needs me to pick up anything.

"Can you just pop into the bakery and grab some yummies for dessert?"

Good lord. "Bubbles, I'm a pastry chef. Just tell me what you want for dessert and I'll do it!"

"I don't want you to make a fuss."

"It's my pleasure. Any requests?"

She gets a wicked gleam in her eye. "Well, you know how your father loves chocolate pudding."

I laugh. "And I wonder where he gets that?" Chocolate pudding is Bubbles's favorite dessert as well. "Chocolate pudding it is."

Ruth is waiting alone, staring at her iPhone, when I get to Kiki's. I was delighted that she wanted to come here; it is wonderful classic French bistro food, and very old-school. Which means that it is blissfully separate from the Chicago fine-dining "scene," so no one will know who I am. I suppose it is somewhat lucky that I can't currently afford to go to any of my old favorite haunts.

I move in to give her a hug, but she holds up her finger at me to indicate that whatever she is typing furiously needs to take precedence. I wait, tapping my foot and feigning irritation and impatience until she finishes.

"Sorry, darls, you'd think the financial world would survive without me for two hours."

"Well, you are teddibly teddibly impawtant." I fake a bad snooty British accent.

"True," she says so seriously that it gives me pause, and then we both crack up.

"*Stop!* No hilarity without me!" Jean says, flying into the foyer in a swirl of scarves, her long hair streaming behind her. She envelops us both in one big hug.

"Good lord woman, is Stevie Nicks your stylist? Who dressed you?" Ruth says, looking Jean up and down. "For someone who designs clothes for a living, you look like an escapee from Coachella."

Jean blushes a bit. "I design *costumes*, not clothes, and Hanna likes it."

We follow the impeccably French hostess to our table and order a bottle of sparkling water.

"Holy crap, you sealed the deal," Ruth says with a snort. "I would recognize this particular glow from a mile away!"

Jean blushes harder. "It's been a very nice few days."

"Have you been out of bed *at all*?" Ruth asks.

"Well, I'm *here*," she says with a grin.

"Oy," I say. "Should I start planning the wedding cake?"

"I am *not* one of those cliché les-beans, I would have you know; I don't believe in shacking up ten minutes into a new relationship."

"True enough. She made me wait till our sixth date." Ruth smirks wickedly.

"And look where *that* got me!"

"Alright, ladies, behave. I want to hear Jean's magical love story."

"It was less magical and more organic," Jean says. "The lead got a wicked case of midnight food poisoning, so we got called in at the crack of dawn to get Hanna geared up for her understudy role; she was nervous, excited, freaking out, and asked if I would be there for the show. She said if she knew I was out there in the dark, it would calm her. I promised I would and said we could go out to celebrate after. And she leaned over and kissed me and asked if we could stay in and celebrate instead!"

"Svengali. How old is this child?" Ruth asks.

"She is twenty-nine."

"Well, not as bad as it could be, I suppose. Have you actually had any conversation yet, or is it all just grunting?"

"Seriously, Ruth, be nice. I think it's great," I say, since Jean, unlike Ruth, is a relationship girl, and I know it's been a long time since she has had anyone in her life or her bed.

"We talk about everything. She's very lovely, smart. And what's more? She said she was worried that I was losing weight and asked if everything was okay. Apparently she likes me curvy." Jean smiles ear to ear.

"So we get to actually eat lunch?" I ask.

"Absolutely. I'm starving!" Jean says, and we settle in to look at the menus. Not that we really need to look; we all usually get the same thing.

After escargots swimming in garlic butter, steak with the crispiest, thinnest fries imaginable, and simple salads of butter lettuce in a peppery Dijon vinaigrette, we share a cheese course, followed by a trio of desserts: lemon tart for me, blueberry bread pudding for Jean, and a poached pear for Ruth. Jean eats like she hasn't had a decent meal in ages, which I suppose she hasn't.

I fill them in on Amelia's wedding cake and the responses, Ruth tells us about the partner at her bank who is about one side-of-the-mouth sexual comment away from a lawsuit, and Jean waxes poetic about Hanna and the first flush of a new relationship. It's sweet. Ruth never really talks about her romantic life. Jean once told me that Ruth is something of a loner lesbian, preferring uncomplicated hookups to actual dating. She says that one of these days Ruth is going to fall, and fall hard, and it will be all nesting and house buying and hers-and-hers engagement rings, but she doubts it will happen before Ruth makes full partner.

"So, I can't stand little Miss Glitter Face over here; she's too lost in love. What's going on for you? Any more news from Herman Jr.?" Ruth asks.

"Nope, it's been quiet. Keeping my head down, doing the work."

Ruth shrugs and snags the bill. "This one is mine, ladies," she says in a tone that indicates we shouldn't pretend to argue with her. Ever since she accidentally slipped a couple of years ago and told us what she makes, Jean and I have never pushed back when she reaches for a check. We always offer, we always expect to cover our share, and Ruth is good about not picking up every tab, but when she does, we just thank her and move on.

"Can I bring Hanna to girls' night next week?" Jean says as we are walking to the door.

"No," Ruth says. "This one is for you and me to meet Amelia. If you are all wrapped up in your girlfriend, you don't focus. You can bring her to the one after that."

"Fine. I'll talk to you all later." Jean heads up the block to her battered Volvo station wagon.

"You good? Really?" Ruth asks me, looking deep into my eyes.

"I'm as good as I can be for now."

"I'll take it. Call me tomorrow?"

"Done."

She kisses my forehead in a rare moment of physical affection and then jumps into her UberBlack car to head back to work.

⁓

When I get home there is a note from Bubbles that my parents had to cancel. One of Dad's clients got arrested late in the day, and there is some family that the Department of Children and Family Services found in total crisis. Consequently, Bubbles decided to head out to an afternoon movie followed by dinner, and hopes I have a lovely evening.

Feeling half relieved and half disappointed, I change my clothes and go to the kitchen to make the chocolate pudding anyway. It will be delicious tomorrow and will keep me feeling somewhat productive. When I get it into a bowl and into the fridge, I call Snatch over.

"Who wants to go for a walk?" It's hard to believe that I'm hungry again after my enormous lunch, but I am. And there is a great little hot dog stand nearby.

I snap on Snatch's collar, and we get a good half hour in before I feel that I've earned my dinner. I know just what I want. A junk food mini-binge. We stop at the hot dog stand, and I order two jumbo char dogs. Once they are wrapped up for me, we head over to the little convenience shop around the corner, where I buy a huge bag of crunchy Cheetos and a pound of mini Swedish Fish. I'm a sucker for anything gummi, and if I'm going to keep my face out of the pudding, I'm going to need some treats.

Back at the house, I grab some paper towels and a ginger ale from the fridge, take my sacks of indulgences upstairs to my lair, with Snatch on my heels, huffing up the stairs, and get set up on my bed. I bring over my laptop, open my email, and there it is, Best Man's reply. I scroll through it with one hand while I stuff hot dog into my face with the other.

WG—

Wow. That is pretty impressive on all fronts. If it makes you feel better, I had my first fender bender while driving on my learner's permit. And the car I ran into was a police cruiser. Not kidding. I was also in a big pile up on the Edens in high school, but that one wasn't my fault, I was like car number 11 out of 15 on a snowy day. Scary, but at least no one was really hurt. I too am a much better driver than I was back in the day. So other than great advice for wedding people and much improved driving skills, what else do you do well?

B (I agree, BM is terrible)

I chew thoughtfully on the last bite of hot dog. The question at the end encourages further conversation, and while he seems smart and funny, I'm not really sure if I should be continuing the more personal connection with this stranger. I slowly eat the second hot dog, breaking off a piece for Snatch, who wolfs it down noisily. I open the bag of Cheetos and eat a fistful. But what could be so bad about a little innocent connection? After all, he doesn't know who I am either.

B—

Actually? That does make me feel better. Thank you.

Not really sure what you mean about things I do well, but if I had to list a few, I'm pretty good at being generally klutzy, eating hot dogs, watching old black and white movies, napping, and I make a killer pie crust.

WG

I suddenly feel like my bladder is going to explode. I get off the bed and head for the bathroom, where I pee for what feels like an eternity. It is shocking. I wash my hands and find that the mascara I so deftly applied earlier today is halfway down my face. I pull a makeup-remover sheet out of the drawer and get the raccoon look off, and then follow it with a really hot washcloth and some night cream. Heading back to the bedroom, I'm confronted with an odd sight. Snatch is standing in the doorway, and his entire head is orange.

"What the . . . ?"

I lean down, the dog gives a massive sneeze, and his whole head explodes in an orange poof. *"Damn dog."* I can see the empty bag of Cheetos on the floor behind him. He goes running out of the room, and I chase him all over the house as he leaves little orange smears on the rugs and doorjambs. Luckily for me, the fat little beast isn't terribly fast, so I catch him and throw him out into the backyard. If he's going to be any kind of sick, he can do it out there. I go back inside, grab a damp rag from the kitchen, and retrace our steps, getting orange dust off all the Cheetos-dirtied surfaces I can spot. I wish I could say that I'm more pissed off at the mess I have to clean up than at the fact that he ate all my Cheetos, but that would be a lie.

I head back upstairs to wallow in Swedish Fish, and find that my email has pinged again.

WG—

That is quite the list of skills. What is your secret?

B

B—

Most of them come naturally, but the secret to the piecrust is lard and vodka.

WG

- - - - - - - - - - - - - -

WG—

Lard I get, does the vodka make you loose so you don't over-work your dough?

B

- - - - - - - - - - - - - -

B—

The vodka replaces some of the water because when the alcohol evaporates it makes the crust flaky. But I suppose I could try putting some in me as well as the dough.

WG

- - - - - - - - - - - - - -

WG—

Pie and martinis sound good.

B

- - - - - - - - - - - - - -

B—

Martinis are made with gin, silly boy. I know because I'm pretty good at those too. Altho, looking back at this thread, I may be sounding a little bit lushy which I am not.

WG

WG—

Not sounding lushy at all. Must be all those black and white movies, aren't they full of martinis? I have to confess, I am something of a Technicolor guy myself.

B

- - - - - - - - - - - - - -

B—

That breaks my heart. Black and white is where it's at.

WG

- - - - - - - - - - - - - -

WG—

Well, maybe I've just seen the wrong ones. You'll have to give me some suggestions.

B

I stuff a handful of fish into my mouth and chew, wondering if there is any way to mimic the flavor of a Swedish Fish. I can't break down the elements to save my life. But they are delicious.

B—

I'd start with The Thin Man, His Girl Friday, Out of the Past, and The Women and let me know how you fare.

WG

- - - - - - - - - - - - - -

WG—

I will. Stay tuned. And have a good night.

B

I look at the screen and am suddenly both sad that he is clearly cutting things off for the night and relieved it didn't devolve into a suggestion of a hookup or anything remotely unchaste. I've heard all sorts of nightmare stories from the people at S&S about what seemed to be an easy connection from online that all of a sudden went sexual at a staggering pace. One of the waitresses said that she was connecting with someone off an alumni page from her college and it went from "Remember the cheeseburgers at Bruno's?" to "Here is a picture of my erect penis" in fewer than three emails. No thank you.

But then, there is that tiny little part of me that wonders, what happens if he does actually watch the movies? And likes them? What comes next?

I look down at the half-empty bag of fish. What comes next for sure is that I'm going to finish these fish downstairs in front of the TV. If Snatch is done polluting the backyard with his post-Cheetos-debacle effects, I'll let him come snuggle with me so that he knows he is forgiven.

Third Finger, Left Hand
(1940)

By the time I get home from the bakery, I fall like a lump on the bed. I'm exhausted; my lower back is in spasm; my feet are throbbing. Ever since Herman and I officially started our charm offensive, I've been reminded that one should be careful what they wish for. Between learning the ins and outs of social media business marketing on the fly, testing new recipes, freshening up the space in the evenings after closing, and gearing up for the official "relaunch" two weekends from now, I'm cashed mentally and physically.

The plan is somewhat simple on its surface. We are rebranding ourselves as a retro neighborhood bakery, with a fresh coat of paint and new offerings that will take you back to your childhood. I've been developing killer updated versions of things like Black Forest cake, now with bittersweet devil's food cake, a dried-cherry conserve, and whipped vanilla crème fraîche. I've perfected a new carrot cake, adding candied chunks of parsnips and rum-soaked golden raisins to the cake and mascarpone to the frosting. And my cheeky take on homemade Pop-Tarts will be available in three flavors—blueberry, strawberry, and peanut butter and jelly—and I've even ordered fun little silver Mylar bags to pack them in. The hope is that by tapping into everyone's nostalgia buttons, we will be able to offer things with a personal touch that Cake Goddess can't match.

My pitch to Herman was that we couldn't beat her at her own game, but she can't beat us at ours either. So instead of trying to do what she does, we just have to do what we do at a higher level. We won't offer as many items; rather we'll have a standard set of things that can be counted on year-round, with one specialty item that is seasonal or new available every day, and several new items on weekends. I've got a Facebook page and a Twitter account and an Instagram up and running, and have been up till all hours friending and following and liking and commenting on any other site I can find, encouraging people to follow us back. Amelia is working on a basic website for us, which should go live in time for the relaunch. Slowly but surely, I'm building a presence for us, but it always freaks me out when a note pops up that some chef I know in town is now "following." I have to remind myself that I've diligently kept my name out of everything. I told Herman that he had to be the face of the business, and even though he insists that I'm his partner in this and says he wants me to get credit, I've convinced him that for the premise to work, it has to be his smile that people associate with the bakery.

Every day we'll post a series of three clues on our various outlets hinting at what the special item of the day is; first person to guess will win a freebie. And while we have upped the flavor game on the event cakes, we aren't going to try and mimic the level of over-the-top customization Cake Goddess does. Instead we now have a solid set of old-school decoration options for kids' birthday cakes: basic trains, teddy bears, princesses, and other simple themes, none of which use famous or registered characters.

Bubbles is chipping in, making the rounds of the little old ladies in the neighborhood, ensuring that they don't feel pushed out. The feedback is that they're happy so long as we still have rye bread and at least a couple of flavors of rugelach, and challah on Fridays; they are surprisingly unsentimental about a lot of the other things we thought we would have to keep stocked every day. Any nonseasonal item we have ever carried will be available by special order with twenty-four hours' notice, so if they know the kids are coming to visit, they can preorder the old favorites. Other than that, Bubbles says they are all very excited for the changes, can't wait to taste the new items, and most of them have invited their kids and grandkids to come to the party.

We're planning a two-day summer open house to coincide with the annual neighborhood street fair. We'll have giveaways and balloons for the kids, and specialty home-baked dog biscuits for the endless French bulldogs and Boston terriers that have invaded along with the hipsters. I've put out calls to every party planner and event manager in the city, from the big hotels to the small restaurants to the independent organizers, always announcing myself simply as Herman Langer's assistant. No one yet has asked for my name, and so far no one has recognized my voice, despite the fact that several of the folks I've contacted are people I worked closely with dozens of times over my tenure at S&S. I've offered special discounts on orders for things like party favors, and a "frequent fliers" program for specialty-event cakes—send ten clients and you get a free cake for either your own personal use or a charitable event of your choosing. So far the response has been great, and one of my favorite event-planning companies, SineQuaNon, has already booked us for wedding favors for two upcoming parties: One couple will be handing out huge black-and-white cookies as their guests depart, and another will be giving out mini loaves of banana bread with chocolate chips.

I can feel my eyes begin to close, so I drag my ass off the bed and towards the bathroom. I run the water in the shower as hot as I can stand it, strip off my batter-spattered T-shirt and jeans, and get in, letting the stinging needles of water work on my back. I can feel my shoulder blades begin to unclench a little bit, and I let the water soak my hair. I grab a fistful of shampoo, begin to lather my mane, and discover an earplug buried deep inside my curls. I wonder exactly how long it's been in there, since I haven't washed my hair in about three days. By the time I finish, I'm feeling somewhat more energized, and dress quickly so that I can get downstairs to help Bubbles. I'm slipping on my shoes when I spot my laptop.

I have fifty-seven new messages.

Fifty-seven.

That seems odd. I open my inbox and begin to scroll through. One is from Ruth, confirming our girls' date with Jean and Hanna for Thursday night. It is our official version of "meet the parents" for the new couple, and Ruth has been practicing squelching her impulses to be dismissive. One is from Jean, asking me to jump in if Ruth gets too "Ruth-y" at our girls' dinner.

Fifty-five of them are from WeddingGirl.com. Must be a glitch in the system; so far the most I've gotten in a given week is eleven, so fifty-five of them in one day probably means that they are fifty-five copies of the same email. I just hope it didn't also charge the person fifty-five times for one question.

I start to scroll through.

They are not the same. They are all from different people. And the first few I scan all start the same way: "I saw your ad on YourPerfectWedding.com."

I type the address into my browser. The top banner indicates that it is the number one wedding website, recommended by Oprah and Martha Stewart, and has been featured on *Today*,

Good Morning America, and *CBS News Sunday Morning*. And in the top right corner, there is an ad.

The image is a picture of Amelia's wedding cake.

I pick up my phone.

"Hey there!" Her bright voice makes me smile.

"Hi. Um, did you place an ad for me on some wedding website?"

She laughs. "Yep. Are you seeing some traffic?"

"I have fifty-five emails."

"That's fantastic! They hired me to do a website revamp, and I always put in my contract that I get one of the top ad spaces to plug in an ad for one of my other clients. It's a quid pro quo thing; they know if I put another client's ad on their site, they will get one on another site, so they don't mind losing the ad revenue. Figured you were the most relevant choice!"

"You are amazing. But you could have warned me. How on earth am I going to manage this many emails?" I look down at my laptop. "Two more have come in just while I've been talking to you!"

"Deep breath. Don't forget; you can decline anything you don't want to answer. And I bet a lot of them will be redundant questions. Just copy your answers to basic questions and save them in a Word doc; you'll build up a bunch of standard answers that you can cut and paste to streamline things."

"Wouldn't people find out I'm just using a bunch of standard answers and not giving them ideas that are original?"

"This is the Pinterest generation. Find something you like

online that someone paid a professional wedding planner thousands of dollars to come up with, and steal it wholesale. 'Original' essentially means mimicking what someone else has already done. Have you seen the movies lately? Remake city. No one cares. Besides, for only $4.99, they can't expect every answer to be handcrafted for them."

"Okay. That sounds sort of manageable. If I weren't ass-deep in the bakery relaunch."

"Sleep is for the dead, kiddo. Besides, that is nearly three hundred smackers sitting in your inbox in one day. That is a potential extra twenty-one hundred a week for the debt collectors. And so much easier than stripping. No glitter in your nooks and crannies."

"Thanks for that visual."

"Relax. I changed your site so that it says emails will be addressed in the order received, and may take up to ten business days for a response. I also added an 'emergency' feature so that if they want an answer within twenty-four hours, the price is $9.99. Emergency emails will show up in your inbox with a red exclamation point in the subject line."

I can hear Bubbles start to set the table.

"Okay, I have to go; my parents are coming for dinner, and if I don't get downstairs, my grandmother is going to have a fit. Thank you, I think." I look down. Another email has arrived.

"Have fun!" she says. "And thanks for introducing me to Ruth and Jean last week; it was totally fun. I'm going to plan another one soon for all of us! Talk later."

I think about Wedding Girl. So far the answers seem to take about three to five minutes max to come up with. That means I should be able to write about twelve to twenty of them an hour. So my inbox is about four hours' worth of work. That's seventy-five dollars an hour. More than I've ever made for anything in my life. And suddenly, I'm not so tired after all. If I can fit in solid hours on my days off and in the evenings, I could make some serious money. Enough to really make a dent in the credit cards for the first time since the non-wedding. Enough that if things go south fast post–Cake Goddess's arrival and I haven't found something else, I could keep up with my minimum payments.

There is a little spring in my step as I head downstairs.

"Mom, that was truly perfect. Thank you," my mom says, bringing plates into the kitchen after dinner. I'm manning the sink while Bubbles packs up leftovers into plastic deli containers— one set for us, one for my parents to take home.

"Indeed it was," my dad says morosely as he brings in the salmon platter and hands it off to Bubbles. He's pouting. Dinner, while delicious, was also light and healthy. Poached salmon, steamed green beans and new potatoes, salad. My mom, ever concerned about his health and cholesterol, has been making him eat "clean" at home, so he really relies on Bubbles and me to provide the stuff he loves. But it was too hot for the heavy, fatty dishes he tends to crave. He's going to have to get over it.

"My pleasure. Now both of you scoot; not enough room in here. We'll meet you in the living room for dessert in six minutes." She waves her hands at them, and they wink at me and follow instructions. One thing about Bubbles: She knows timing. Precisely six minutes later, with the first load of dishes running in her ancient dishwasher, we head for the living room, Bubbles carrying the bowl of sweetened sour cream, and me carrying a deeply purple red and glistening summer pudding that thankfully departed its mold with a squelching sound and no drama. Just macerated berries and buttered bread, it is sort of a magical dessert.

I cut thick wedges for everyone, Bubbles generously dollops

cream on them, and the four of us tuck into the moist, delicious pudding, which tastes like pure summer.

"You've outdone yourself, Sophie," my dad mumbles around a mouthful, getting a little of his sparkle back.

"So good, honey; really delicious." My mom licks cream off the back of her fork with nearly lascivious delight.

"So," my dad says, handing his plate to Bubbles for a second slice, "we have some news." He grins over at my mother, who I swear actually blushes.

"Did you sell the house?" Bubbles asks, since my folks had filled her in on the possibility last week. She hands him another slice, this one even larger than his first, making my mother sigh audibly to announce her displeasure as she waves Bubbles off virtuously, patting her stomach in the universal "I'm just too full for seconds" signal. I've decided to just embrace the current acreage of my person and not feel bad about the weight gain. I went to Nordstrom Rack and bought some new clothes that fit me properly, and told the universe that if a size eighteen/twenty is the new me, so be it. There is not a thing wrong with me, and while I can absolutely be embarrassed about the way I lost my job, or the stupid wedding debt, or even that I lost my home and have to live with my grandmother, I refuse to be one of those girls who is shamed by the size of her ass. Whatever. Life is too short, and cake is delicious, and there is nothing wrong with taking up some space in the world. I hand my plate to Bubbles, who winks at me and slices us each a lovely second helping.

"Yes, we did. A very nice man named Andy who owns a development company called Middlefork."

"Wonderful! How much did you get?" Bubbles asks pointedly.

"Bubbles!" I say, a little taken aback, but also curious how the numbers finally shook out.

My dad snorts as he laughs. "He upped it to five and a quarter million when we didn't respond right away, Mom; ultimately seemed like a good offer."

Bubbles nods in agreement, and I try not to choke on my cake as the reality of the figure swirls in my head, still shocking even though I knew it was coming. I mean, don't get me wrong; from what I hear from Ruth, the land alone is worth every bit of that amount, as outlandish as it seems. In Chicago, Lincoln Park is second only to the Gold Coast in pricing. The kind of homes that can be built on a three-and-a-half-lot parcel could go for as much as $4.5 to $6 million each, depending on square footage and amenities. And a huge single-family home on land that big recently sold for $14.5 million, so there is plenty of money to be made on the flip side.

"And we've found a new place," my mom says.

"It's a wonderful loft-type condo in Ukrainian Village," my dad chimes in. "Two bedrooms, two and a half baths, and it's on the top floor, so the roof is also ours. It's all kitted out as a roof-deck, and we'll get plenty of planter boxes up there for your mom to be able to maintain a little garden."

"That sounds amazing. When do you move?"

"We close both places middle of next month, but we will rent our house back from him for a few months, so we can do some small renovations in the new place. The kitchen needs some new appliances, and we'll want to build out the roof, get it all repainted. We'll move out of our place sometime after the end of the summer."

"Mazel tov, my darlings. That is just wonderful," Bubbles says.

"There's more," my dad says, his eyes twinkling, and he looks at me with a face filled with love and excitement. And my heart stops. Maybe they are going to give me some of their windfall after all! It's so much money, and their new place can't be costing them that much. Maybe they are going to give me a big chunk of money, and I can pay off my debt totally. They will never have to know, and I won't have to spend the next year answering endless questions about weddings to get the debacle completely behind me, so I can figure out what I'm supposed to be doing with my life.

"We're getting *married*!" my mom says, giggling like a schoolgirl, and the needle scratches straight across the record of delirious blissful salvation that is playing in my head.

"What?" I squeak, the air leaving my lungs in a terribly rapid manner.

"She's going to make an honest man of me," my dad says.

"Well, it's about fucking time," Bubbles says.

"Mom!" my dad says as we all begin to laugh.

"Well, it is!" Bubbles says, completely calmly. "Congratulations, my children. I'm very glad you're taking this step before I'm dead. I'll get more champagne." And with that, she stands, kisses my dad on his cheek, and takes my mom's face in her hands. "Beautiful bride." She grins and heads to the kitchen.

"Are you okay, Sunshine?" my dad asks.

"Of course I am. I'm delighted for you, just surprised."

"It's not too soon?" my mom asks, a little trepidatiously.

I laugh. "You've been together forty-three years. I don't think you're exactly rushing into things."

My mom laughs a little. "Not for us, pumpkin, for you. Because of the—"

I hold my hand up. "I couldn't be more thrilled for you both. What a wonderful, exciting new chapter. New house, new vows—it's all wonderful, and I don't want you to even think twice about it."

I get up and go over to hug them both, wishing my heart were actually feeling what my mouth just uttered.

"Would you be okay helping me plan the wedding?" my mom asks with a bit of caution in her voice still.

"I'd be honored." I actually can't think of anything I'd rather do less, but I consider the full inbox upstairs, all those wedding questions, the strangers I'm going to help for money, and I know that not to jump into this with my folks with an open heart would be the most petty, mean thing any loving daughter could do. So I'm going to swallow the icky feelings and disappointment, put on my big-girl pants, and help my mom plan the wedding of her dreams. And just hope that it isn't some hippie-dippie barefoot thing with crocheted dresses and a Grateful Dead cover band.

Behind me I hear a loud pop as Bubbles opens the bubbly, and our little family raises our glasses to the future.

Man-Proof
(1938)

"What are we going to do?" Ruth asks. She is driving me home after our dinner with Jean and Hanna. Which was just shy of intolerable.

"We can't do anything; it isn't our business."

"The hell it isn't! That little twinklepants is clearly gearing up to take Jean for quite a ride."

I'm hard-pressed to disagree. Hanna was beyond annoying. We knew she was young, but on top of that, she is also young for her age, putting on all sorts of baby talk voices, pouting when the waiter told her they were out of the lemon tart. Pretty, of course; amazing body, to be sure; but her personality was ridiculously grating. She never stopped talking, mostly about herself, and divulged mortifying graphic details about her sex life with Jean. She insisted on ordering the wine, claiming extensive knowledge, and chose a very expensive bottle. She ordered several appetizers for the table, none of which any of us particularly wanted, and ate one tiny bite of each before saying pointedly to Jean that she can eat anything she wants, just in moderation. And when the hugely inflated check came, she slid it over to Jean, said that "they" insisted on treating, in a manner that made it clear she wasn't even considering reaching for her own wallet, and excused herself to the powder room.

Jean had blithely opened her own purse and put down her credit card. When we tried to add ours, she said, no, of course not, it was their treat, seeming to ignore the fact that it was actually just her treat.

"We can't do anything; she's in love."

"Yeah, look how well it worked out when we kept our mouths shut with you," Ruth spits out.

My heart sinks. "You never liked Dexter?"

She reaches a hand over to squeeze mine quickly before returning it to the wheel of her BMW. "Not for a hot minute. He was too slick, too many excuses, too many promises that never materialized. We wanted him to be what you wanted him to be, but we had reservations, and obviously for a good reason. Don't you wish we had said something? Intervened?"

I think about this. About what my life might have been if they had warned me off, if I hadn't stayed with him. I'd probably still be at S&S, being groomed to take over when Georg retired. Still keeping the long hours, still hanging out mostly with work people, still seeing my family only now and again, neglecting them all, especially Bubbles. My life now? There is plenty I hate. The massive public humiliation that will never be erased, that will follow me for as long as someone has access to Google. Having lost the condo and the promise of future equity, carrying a debt that never diminishes, living full-time with an octogenarian who is excellent company most of the time but still has all of the attendant quirks of the elderly.

But my heart pauses a little bit.

I might be broke and embarrassed, but there is good in my life too. Living with Bubbles, at this stage of her life. Whatever little annoyances there are, they are outweighed by the joys. The midnight Manhattans, cooking together, knowing that I'm keeping her in her home that she loves, our movie nights. I'll always have these special memories. My work at Langer's, which every day gets more and more fulfilling. Making a great three-dollar challah that graces Shabbat tables on Friday nights and reappears in the French toast on Saturday mornings for neighborhood families seems somehow more rewarding than perfecting some elegant dessert with twenty elements that's assembled with tweezers and purchased for twenty dollars by people who are more concerned about how the picture of it looks on Instagram than what pleasure it might bring them.

"I'm glad you didn't say anything."

"Really?" Her voice drips with sarcasm.

"Really," I say, resigned. "Good or bad, and lord knows it ended badly, where I am now isn't where I would have wound up if you guys had convinced me he was bad news, and for whatever reason, I do think I'm supposed to be where I am. Doing what I'm doing. Dexter was my mistake to make, my lesson to learn. And Hanna is Jean's."

Ruth makes a harrumphing sound. "Fine. I won't say anything. But if she starts making noises about moving in with or marrying that picketytwick, I'm putting my foot down."

"Fine."

"I'm glad you're feeling like you are where you are supposed to be. I wish it had happened differently, but I'm happy for you. You seem better."

"I'm getting there."

She pulls up in front of the house, leans over, and gives me a kiss good night, and as soon as I'm out of the car, she speeds off down the street. My best guess is that she is headed straight to one of the high-end hotel bars downtown. Ruth loves a hotel bar. The bartenders are skilled, there isn't a loud scene, and she has a second sense for finding the visiting executive lesbians for a brief fling. She always says the out-of-town lesbian is the best, because no one has any unrealistic expectations.

I head in and find Bubbles and Snatch cuddled up on the couch watching the news.

"How was dinner?" she asks, patting the couch next to her as I kick off my shoes, and muting the TV.

"Interesting," I say, plopping down next to her. Snatch gets up and shifts, putting his butt against Bubbles and dropping his head into my lap with a snort. I scratch behind his ears and give her the lowdown.

"Poor Jean. But you're right; you can't say anything. If she asks, if she solicits your opinion in a way that you believe is genuine and not just looking for pat affirmations, be kind but truthful. Start with the girl's positive qualities, the things you see that make you understand Jean's attraction, but then gently share your concerns. But don't volunteer. That would be friendship suicide."

"Yeah, that is pretty much where Ruthie and I left it."

"And what about you?"

"What about me?"

She tilts her head at me and raises one elegant silvery eyebrow. "Don't play possum with me, schnookie. I hear you up all night clickety-clacking on that laptop of yours. I assume you are doing the online dating? So, how is it going?"

I laugh. "I'm not doing the online dating." But I'm not ready to confess to WeddingGirl.com, since I would also have to confess to the wedding debt, and she won't believe I'm just noodling around on the Internet. Then I think about Best Man. "But I do have sort of a pen pal."

I hadn't heard from him since our round of almost-flirty

emails except for one brief note to thank me for the movie recommendations. I replied that I was glad he had enjoyed them and recommended a couple more.

I'd actually pretty much forgotten he existed. But then out of the blue I got this last night:

WG—

Mr. Blandings is indeed a very charming movie, and despite being a bit of predictable hooey, thoroughly enjoyable. I'm coming to the conclusion that I would watch Myrna Loy read out of a phonebook for two hours and find it delightful, and presume you feel the same about Cary Grant. It was the perfect thing for a quiet night in, so I thank you yet again.

B

PS My friends call me Jake.

I confess Jake's existence to Bubbles, who listens thoughtfully, then passes firm judgment.

"You will meet him," she says.

"Maybe . . . I just . . ."

"You will meet him," she says again. "You will meet him, somewhere public, somewhere safe. And in person, you will give him your real name, your real details. You will tell him enough about your past that when he gets home to Snoogle you and sees the full picture, he'll be sympathetic instead of judgmental."

I laugh. "Google, Bubbles. It's Google."

"Google, Snoogle, Schmoogle. You knew what I meant. Maybe he'll be a new friend. Maybe a new love. Maybe he'll be an asshole, and you'll never see him again. But you'll meet him and find out."

"Bubbles, you've become quite the vulgarian in your old age."

"Pish. I always said that when I got into my eighties, I'd take up swearing. And possibly smoking. But when I saw the price of cigarettes these days, I figured I'd just do the swearing."

I shake my head. "So I have to meet him."

"You do."

"He hasn't said he wants to meet me."

"He hasn't stopped writing to you either. Or watching the movies you are telling him to watch. Boys can be slow on the uptake. But this is a good test. For you. For your life. My Sophie was always a 'take the bull by the horns girl.'" She looks at me with love but also with honest concern. "I miss that girl a bit."

"She's a little out of practice."

"Well, there is only one way to fix that."

Jake—

So glad you liked Mr. Blandings, it is one of my personal favorites. And yes, Cary Grant could read out of a phone book to me for two hours and I would find it charming.

WG

PS My friends call me Sophie.

I think about this for a moment. And then delete "Sophie." And type in "Sunny." In the brief time I was Sunshine, Sunny was the nickname my playmates called me. I can't type "Sunshine." I just can't. But Sunny isn't exactly a lie and still makes me feel somewhat protected.

I hit Send and get out of my clothes and into my pajamas. I wash my face and brush my teeth, and hunker down into bed with my laptop to knock out some emails. They've been coming at a steady clip, and I've found that my response time is getting faster, especially with my ever-growing set of cut-and-paste answers. If I do an hour or two every night before bed, then I'm able to catch up on my days off, and so far, I'm keeping on top of things. It's a lot, and somewhat mind-numbing, but by the end of this week I will be able to mail a bonus check of $2,000 to Visa, which is the first money I've sent that isn't just paying interest, and it feels good to know that every email I answer takes a little tick off the principal.

I'm five responses in when I see that Jake has replied.

Sunny—

If you are at the "reading the phone book" stage, then you really need to get out more!

Jake

I take a deep breath. This appears to be an opening. And I think about Bubbles being disappointed that my gumption has been in short supply of late. What the hell.

Jake—

Yes, that is probably true. I recently found out that there is a new old school Hungarian café in town, and they are doing a special Tokay tasting event next Thursday night that I thought I might attend. The wines are rare and interesting, and the pastry menu looks amazing. Café Nizza on Lincoln Ave. If you are around and free you might want to check it out.

Sunny

I'd seen a brief piece on the tasting in a Tasting Table news-letter and had been thinking of inviting the girls. But after the dinner with Jean and Hanna, I had changed my mind. I used to go to stuff like that by myself all the time, so I'd figured maybe I would go check it out alone or see if Bubbles wanted to come, but suddenly it seemed like a perfect opening to offer to Jake.

Sunny—

Just Googled, place looks fantastic. Not 100% sure of my Thursday schedule quite yet, at the moment it is open. If it stays that way, maybe I'll see you there.

Jake

- - - - - - - - - - - - - -

Jake—

I'll be the girl with the red carnation reading Jane Austen ;)

S

- - - - - - - - - - - - - -

S—

I'll be the guy with the bad comb-over and enormous gut. (Just kidding!)

J

This makes me laugh, and I get back to answering emails. I feel good. It isn't a date, not a real thing; he might not end up being available that night. But if he is, it seems a safe and casual way to connect in person. Just to see. And if nothing else, making the offer feels like the kind of thing the pre-Dexterbacle me would do.

It's a big night and I'm feeling very productive, having told three people to do various edible take-home gifts; two to skip expensive flowers in favor of potted succulents or flowers; three to not do an expensive open bar but instead to have wine, beer, sparkling water, and one signature cocktail; and six to suck it up and invite their future mothers-in-law to the bachelorette party. I've suggested to one woman that she ask her fiancé if perhaps they could take the lovely stones out of his mother's ghastly engagement ring setting and reset them in something more her taste. I've gently told one bridezilla that she cannot ask her bridesmaids to lose weight, one that she can't make hers change their haircuts, and a third that she can't ask them to sign a contract promising not to sleep with any of the groomsmen. I've offered one mother of the bride with a nervous stomach some wisdom about the effective use of pre-wedding Imodium.

I'm just gearing up to log off when my email pings.

Peanut—

Just got done with a long brief and realized I wanted to ask you something the other night, but couldn't get you alone.

I'm thinking if your mom and I are going to do this thing, she deserves something shiny to make it officially official. Would you be available next week sometime to go ring shopping with me? You know I'm useless with this kind of stuff, and if you wait forty-some years to propose, the ring better be the right one.

Love, Dad

- - - - - - - - - - - - - - -

Dad—

I'd be honored to come shopping with you. I'm free Thursday during the day, why don't I make us an appointment with Ruth's client, the diamond broker? That way you can actually design the perfect ring, and we'll get a good deal. Would 11 work for you?

Sophie

Soph—

11 would be perfect, and then maybe I can take you to lunch?

Dad

- - - - - - - - - - - - - -

Dad—

Only if we can go to Eleven City Diner.

XO

- - - - - - - - - - - - - -

Soph—

NOW you're talking! Go to bed, it's very late.

Dad

Good. Now I can make sure of three important things. One, I will not someday inherit some horrible clunker of a ring. Two, I will have some distraction on Thursday to prevent me from being too nervous about my maybe-date with Jake. And three, I can eat a club sandwich the size of Wyoming with a chocolate phosphate, and really, that is always a good thing. Thinking about a chocolate phosphate suddenly makes my willingness to go to bed less interesting than a snack. I put on my robe and pad downstairs.

"What are you doing up?" I say when I discover Bubbles in the kitchen, cutting thick slices of the new challah test I brought home yesterday. The rich eggy dough is rolled with cinnamon, dried golden mulberries, and toasted pumpkin seeds.

"Sometimes the salad that seemed like a good idea for dinner disappears when you've peed five or six times."

Bubbles believes in certain food truths. You will be hungry an hour after you eat Chinese food, there is always room in the dessert compartment, and any and all salad consumed, no matter how large or full of goodies like cheese or chunks of ham or chicken, is completely eliminated through urination. And since, as she loves to say, she has the bladder of an incontinent flea, salad disappears quite quickly around these parts.

"I see. So what are you bolstering it with?"

"Well, I was going to just make some toast with your wonderful new bread, but now that you're up . . ."

"French toast with ice cream?" One of our traditional favorite late-night snacks. Sort of a faux bread pudding.

"It seems appropriate?"

I start getting out the ingredients. "I told Jake I would meet him next week."

"Good. It's the right thing to do."

"We'll see. I'm a little nervous."

"That's natural. But it's good for you. To get out. Meet new people. I'll buy you an outfit."

"Bubbles . . ." I love her impulse but hate to think of her spending money on me.

"Bubbles nothing. I can buy my only grandchild a new outfit if I want. You could use something that makes you feel good, strong. We'll go this weekend." She has her no-nonsense tone on, so I know arguing is no use.

"Thank you; that will be fun. A big shopping week for me. I'm going with Dad to help him find an engagement ring."

"Oy, thank goodness. Don't let him get some mood ring, or some horrible colored stone or weird shape. Your mother needs a proper white diamond, in a proper platinum setting. You promise me."

"I promise." I slip the bread, which has fully absorbed the egg and cream mixture, into the bubbling butter as Bubbles gets two shallow bowls out of the cupboard. After a moment I check the toast, now deeply golden and crispy on the bottom, and flip each piece, hearing the satisfying sizzle. I slide another knob of butter into the pan.

"Good. Settled."

I check the toast again and give it a poke with my finger. It is browned and crunchy on the outside and custardy within. I slide two slices into each bowl and drizzle the now-nutty browned butter over each one, then add a sprinkling of coarse sea salt. Bubbles tops them with a generous scoop of vanilla ice cream. We take our bowls and go sit in the Nook.

A grumbling snorting noise announces the arrival of Snatch, lured down from his bed upstairs by the scent of cooking, despite his girth making stairs a major annoyance for him. Bubbles puts her bowl, with one last small piece of French toast and a few spoonfuls of melted goodness, under the table for the dog, who snarfs it up greedily with exuberant grunts. The dog's smooshed face is covered in butter and melted ice cream, and I resist the urge to chuckle as he works his paws over the parts of his mug that he can't reach with his tongue.

Bubbles yawns as she retrieves the bowl from the floor; she places a hand in the small of her back as she straightens with a wince. I see the soft, thin, wrinkled skin of her face, without her usual carefully applied concealer masking the darker skin under her eyes. I hate these moments when her age announces itself so clearly; her personality is so full of life and fire that I am able to forget for long stretches that she is an old person.

"Let me get that. It's two in the morning. If you don't go to bed soon, how on earth will you have the energy to rattle around in the bathroom at four thirty?"

She smacks me on my tush as I clear the bowls. "Smart-ass."

"Better than being a dumb-ass." My standard response.

"True enough. Then I won't argue. I love you, sweetheart; thank you for snacking with me."

"It's always a pleasure." I lean over and kiss her, and take the pinch on my cheek. She shuffles off, the dog waddling at her heels, and I load the detritus of our little feast into the dishwasher, saying a prayer that I have many more years of these special times to enjoy with her.

And wondering exactly what kind of outfit I should buy to wear to meet Jake.

Kiss and Make-Up

(1934)

Every woman wants love. To deprive a woman of
love is to deprive her of life itself.
• CARY GRANT AS DR. MAURICE LAMAR •

"Sophie? What are you doing here on your day off?" Herman
says sleepily, coming into the kitchen.

I hadn't slept much at all last night. I've got my ring shopping and lunch adventure with my dad today, followed by a long
swath of time I plan to devote to the ever-expanding inbox full
of Wedding Girl requests, followed by my could-be date with
Jake. And my head will not shut off.

Bubbles and I talked about it when we were shopping for my
new outfit over the weekend, a pair of flowy linen wide-leg
pants in a soft gray, with a simple French blue cotton top that is
a faux wrap design. The shirt shows off my small waist while
masking my belly, and keeps the girls locked and loaded, while
the pants do a great job of making my ever-burgeoning tush less
obvious. It's the kind of outfit that a normal girl would think of
as a casual toss-on for a summer evening, but for me, it feels
fancy and dressed up. Bubbles is loaning me one of her antique
Hermès floral scarves for a bit of oomph. But even with a new

outfit that makes me feel almost pretty for the first time since my non-wedding day, I'm awfully nervous.

"What's the worst that could happen?" Bubbles asked me over afternoon tea and shortbread cookies after our shopping. "He seems like a nice person to you, someone who could be a friend. It doesn't have to be romance."

"What about my past?"

"What about it? We all have a past, lovey. Yours might have a few bits and pieces that are more public than others, but that doesn't make them worse, just more available. I think you should own it, all of it. After all, the only thing the world loves more than watching someone fall is watching them rise again."

"And what if I like him?"

"Would that be so bad? I know I'm good company, but a night out here and there wouldn't exactly be the worst thing, would it?"

"Of course not. But he might not like me."

"He might not. Anyone can be an idiot. If he doesn't, he doesn't; the next one will."

This made me grin. "I love you."

She winked at me and reached for another cookie.

Her words kept me mostly calm all week as I tested new recipes and stocked the walk-in with all kinds of yummies for this weekend's big party. But last night, despite being bone-tired and staying up till nearly two answering Wedding Girl queries, I couldn't sleep. So after tossing and turning for a couple of hours, I finally gave it up, threw on my clothes, scribbled a note for Bubbles, and headed to the bakery. The soft air of the summer morning was refreshing as I walked in the pale blue pre-dawn light. I let myself into the bakery quietly and relocked the door behind me. And then I went to the kitchen.

Ever since I can remember, a kitchen, any kitchen, is my

place of calm and solace. Growing up, if I was stressed about school, I'd make batch after batch of brownies or chocolate chip cookies. In culinary school, despite cooking all day, if something was bothering me, I'd be back in the kitchen tweaking it or testing some new idea. So there I was, at four thirty in the morning, head spinning circles, stomach fluttery, looking for peace. By the time Herman appears at six thirty, I've done a double batch of my version of an upgraded pinwheel, making a homemade honey oat graham cookie base, a piped swirl of soft vanilla honey marshmallow cream, and a covering of dark chocolate mixed with tiny, crunchy Japanese rice pearls. I've made a test batch of a riff on a Nutter Butter, two thin, crisp peanut butter cookies with a layer of peanut butter cream sandwiched between them. My dad always loved Nutter Butters; he could sit in his office for hours working on briefs, eating them one after another. I figured he would be my best taster, so might as well try them and bring some with me later today. And I've just pulled a new brownie out of the oven: a deep, dark chocolate base with a praline pecan topping, sort of a marriage of brownie and that crispy top layer of a good pecan pie.

"Lots to do, Herman, still plenty of things for the weekend, and I couldn't sleep. So I figured I'd pop in and be productive."

"Coffee?"

"Please." Herman shuffles out to the front to brew us a pot, and I pull together a plate of the new offerings. Might as well do a little tasting. I make some notes on the new recipes and pack up a dozen of the peanut butter cookies in a box to bring to my dad, throwing in a few of the pinwheels and two still-warm brownies for my mother, the chocoholic.

Herman returns with two steaming mugs, both lightened with cream and sweetened with sugar. Herman still holds to the old traditions: coffee light and sweet at breakfast and morning snacks, and black and bitter from lunchtime to dinner, and only espresso with lemon twists after dinner. He pulls a stool up to the table, and as I reach for my coffee, I push the plate of samples towards him.

"Homemade pinwheels and Nutter Butters, and praline pecan brownies."

Herman slowly and thoughtfully tastes each one in turn, cleansing his palate with coffee between each mouthful. I take a pinwheel first; the thin chocolate layer crackles, the little rice pearls pop like a Nestlé Crunch bar, the marshmallow is so soft it is barely set but has enough body not to drip, and the cookie provides a nutty, crunchy base that has enough salt and savory oomph to prevent the whole thing from going too sweet. The Nutter Butters are a slam dunk: super-crispy cookie and smooth, luscious filling, with deep peanut butter flavor. The brownies are going to need a little tweaking; the flavors are good, and I like the concept, but the praline topping is staying too solid, and when you bite into it, it breaks in awkward shards, making the eating complicated. If something is meant to be eaten out of hand, I want it to eat easily and with minimal mess. If it is the kind of thing that ends up half down your bra after the first bite, then it is more annoying than wonderful, and the tastes get forgotten.

"Delicious, as usual, my dear," Herman says, picking a piece of praline out of his shirt pocket and popping it into his mouth.

"I'll work on the topping for that one, so it's less messy."

"Good idea."

"Let's save the pinwheels for this weekend, you can sell the rest of the peanut butter ones today, and we'll cut up the brownies small just for samples, and tell people we sold out but they'll be available this weekend."

"A good plan. And all wonderful. But why aren't you sleeping?" Herman looks at me over the rim of his little reading glasses.

I smile at him, touched by his grandfatherly concern. "Just excited for the weekend."

"Me too. I hope everyone comes."

"They'll come. Don't you worry." Amelia has been helping me pump up the social media stuff, and we even got a small mention in the *Reader* and the *RedEye*. The weather is supposed to be perfect, low eighties and not humid, so people will be out and about, and the neighborhood street festival is just two blocks away, so there should be good foot traffic.

"My faith is in you, so if you say they are coming, I believe. Now, I need you ready and rested for this weekend, so will you please leave all this; I will clean it up. Go home and get some sleep."

I can see in his face that it is important to him, and suddenly I do feel a little tired, so I nod and kiss his cheek, then remove my apron and place it into his outstretched hand.

I'm just pulling the door closed behind me when I turn around and find myself face-to-face with Mark in the Suit. Only he's not in a suit; he's in shorts and a sleeveless shirt, and is dripping with sweat.

"Hello, Sophie. This is a surprise."

"Mark." I suppress a yawn.

"I'd shake your hand, but I'm a little damp."

Yeah. Like the polar vortex was "a little chilly." "It's okay. What brings you here at this hour?"

"I like to mix up my runs. Can't do the same route day in and out; gets too boring. Plus I wanted to stop in and see Dad while I'm in town. Is he downstairs or up?"

"In the kitchen." I pause. Then something occurs to me. He said it was a surprise, but he knows I work here. And probably knows my day off. "Figured I wouldn't be here?"

His already-reddened face turns a single shade darker. "It is your day off, I thought."

"Wow. This is a lot of effort to avoid me."

"Not avoiding, just aware, and to be honest, I just wanted to see my dad and not get into the business thing."

"You could be supportive of him, you know? What do you have to lose? If we succeed, it will make your dad both happy and financially solvent, and if we fail, you get to be right, and nothing feels better than being right. This whole thing is a win-win for you." This comes out a little bitchier than I mean it to.

"Well, I can't argue with logic like that. Have a good day off, Sophie, and I'm sure I'll see you this weekend."

"I'm glad you'll be coming. It will mean a lot to your dad."

"Oh, and just my two cents . . . The new Twinkie? The filling needs a little more structure. Right now it feels sort of like whipped cream, and it's missing that texture of the Hostess cream filling. Maybe a spoonful or two of marshmallow cream? Add some body?"

This makes my stomach tighten. I made four different batches, trying to get the right texture by adding gelatin, whipped coconut oil, pastry cream, whipped egg whites. But he's right. A little bit of Fluff might just be the ticket. And the fact that he both noticed that the pastry wasn't quite right *and* had the potential solution off the cuff . . . that really annoys the crap out of me.

"Thanks for the advice. Always appreciate having another mouth on the team. Can't make these things perfect enough."

He smacks his stomach, which I notice looks pretty flat and tight with his wet shirt sticking to it. Not six-packy, but definitely not soft. Actually I'm now noticing that his whole body is much better than what one would have presumed was under those suits. Muscles are present but not so defined as to be ridiculous. He looks healthy and fit, not ripped, and I'm reminded of the little tingles from our first meeting. Before he turned out to be an asshole.

"Always happy to help."

"Yeah, that's you. Mr. Helpful." I turn back to the door and unlock it. "Here you go. Make some noise when you go in, so you don't scare him; he never puts his hearing aids in till he opens to the public."

Mark tips an imaginary hat and opens the door forcefully, so that the bells on the back peal loudly. And I realize that whatever Zen-like calm I had achieved, however quiet my head had been five minutes ago, it's all gone with just that brief interchange with stupid sweaty Mark and his stupid smug face. I check my watch; it's nearly seven. I'm meeting my dad at eleven. Which, if nothing else, gives me a solid three hours to do Wedding Girl emails, and that should get me close to even with the inbox. As Bubbles always says, no point heading north if the path veers west. I take a deep breath, and head for home.

⌒〰⌒

"I'm going to explode," my dad says, rubbing his stomach gleefully. He's just put down a massive sandwich piled with corned beef, pastrami, chopped liver, and Swiss cheese, with a side of crispy onion strings and a vanilla malt.

"Tilt," I say, making the time-out signal with my hands. I managed to get three-quarters of the way through a turkey club with no tomatoes and Thousand Island instead of mayo, with a pile of extra-crispy fries and a chocolate phosphate. Not to mention the bucket of pickles, and the soup, chicken with kreplach and noodles for him, sweet-and-sour cabbage for me.

"But we're still splitting a piece of cheesecake?"

"Well, of course!" It's been a lovely visit. My dad was bewildered at the diamond dealer, but he was quickly put at ease. We talked about my mom's style, nontraditional; the eventual wedding ring, to be worn separately, not stacked; and the budget, which would have paid off half of my remaining debt in one whack—a thought I forced myself to forget the moment I caught myself dwelling on it. We ended up getting her a gorgeous two-carat oval with a lot of sparkle, which will be set lengthwise across the finger instead of in the traditional manner. The setting is a wide matte platinum band, and on either end of the center stone are three tiny round fire opals, glowing deep orange, which is Mom's favorite color. It is going to be glorious, unusual, but still very elegant, and I just know she will be blown away.

"Thanks for your help today, sweetheart. I really appreciate it."

"It was fun, Dad. She's going to really love it."

He smiles broadly. "I think so too. Just funky enough for your Mom, and just normal enough for you and your grandmother!"

"True enough."

A waiter whisks away our plates and agrees to wrap up my last quarter of a sandwich, and my dad orders cheesecake with two forks and a coffee. The leftover sandwich will be the perfect thing to eat before I head out to meet Jake, just a little something in my tummy so that if we decide to drink alcohol, it won't hit me on an empty stomach.

"And what about you? Bubbles says things are really getting exciting at the bakery. Your mom and I are both trying to keep Saturday afternoon a bit open, so we can swing by."

"It's a lot of work, but things are definitely picking up. One of the local food bloggers called about doing a feature, so Herman is meeting with her today to give her a tour of the kitchen and do a little interview about the relaunch. We have probably seen about a twenty percent increase in weekday business, and weekends are just hopping, so if that can continue, there's a fighting chance."

"Your words sound positive, but I know those eyes, pumpkin. What are you worried about?"

"Foodies are fickle. It's always about the next big thing, the hot new item. It's great that the business is picking up, and we don't seem to have lost any of our old regulars, but I'm not yet noticing many new regulars—just a stream of new faces, people checking us out. Plus it's beautiful weather; people are out and about. But winter? With no designated parking? People have to really be craving our products specifically to get through those slow times."

"So you're worried that this uptick is just people being curious and following the latest thing, and that they won't become a solid customer base you can count on."

"Exactly. Especially when Cake Goddess opens. Then she'll be the hot new thing in the neighborhood, with her parking lot and her massive inventory and specialty items for dietary restrictions, and I just don't know if we have enough time to get under the skin of enough people in the neighborhood to keep them once she's open."

"You're doing everything you can; that's all you can do. And you don't know what will happen once that new place opens. After all, isn't supporting local small businesses a faddish trend right now too?"

Bless his heart. "Yeah, Dad. It is. Who knows? Maybe we'll survive!"

"If you do, you do. If you don't, you'll know you gave it your all. Isn't that what counts?"

"Of course it is."

The waiter arrives with a massive slab of cheesecake and two clean forks. I thought I wouldn't have room for more than a bite, but after that first taste of dense, rich, tangy cake, I know that between us we'll clean the plate.

"Anything else going on? I know this is all a lot for you to process, us selling the house, moving, getting married."

If he only knew. All of those things are really back burner

on my list of stressors. "It's all great. I'm very happy for you on both accounts."

He nods and chews another huge bite of cheesecake thoughtfully, in a way that lets me know he isn't going to poke at me further but he doesn't fully believe me either. "Well, get ready, because now that we've finalized most of the decisions for the house, your mom is about to really get into wedding-planning mode, and I'm afraid you're going to bear the brunt."

I laugh. My mom was always something of a terror when it came to event planning. It just was never in her natural wheelhouse, and anytime they decided to have a party, whether it was a Cinco de Mayo celebration or New Year's Eve, or even the one year they hosted a party for the Super Bowl, it always turned my mother into a crazy person. Or a "dirling whervish," as I mispronounced it as a kid. "You tell her to bring it on. I'm ready when she is."

"Careful what you wish for. Last night I found her making lists and muttering to herself at two in the morning about canapés."

"Oh no. It's going to be like Obama election night all over again," I say.

"Probably worse," my dad admits. In 2008, my mom planned a big election-night party, figuring their friends would want to be together to either celebrate or commiserate. For a month she obsessed over the food, waffling between getting it catered or making it herself and unfortunately deciding on making it all herself. Then the menu choices became the thing waking her in the night. When my dad said it didn't matter what she served, she literally yelled at him that she was not going to *jinx the election* by choosing food that was either too celebratory or too comforting, somehow having decided that if they either bought champagne or made mac and cheese, they could alter the course of history. When the day rolled around, the crowd got a strange combination of canapés and crudités, hot dogs, roasted chicken, spaghetti and meatballs, brisket, and beer, and my mother spent most of the party hiding in her room with a tension headache.

"We'll have to keep her in check. And frankly, we'd better get a move on if we're looking at sometime soon after Labor Day. That's only a couple of months off!" I say.

"Well, we're thinking of moving it back a bit, maybe mid to late October. The new place is going to be done right before Labor Day, and your mom thinks it will be easiest to move first, so that the wedding is its own thing."

"Seems smart. You don't want to be pulled in two different directions. Better to focus on one thing at a time. Plus you'll get a better deal on wedding stuff not connected to a holiday weekend."

"Aren't you full of excellent advice!"

If he only knew. "That's me, your source for all things wedding." Truer words were never spoken.

"How lucky for us. We also wanted you to know that even though my dad left her well provided for, we have put some extra money in Bubbles's trust, and plan to do so every year, so her monthly income should get a nice increase. And we've created a new trust that will cover anything hers doesn't in the eventuality of her needing to either move to assisted living or hire some in-home help."

"That is so great, Dad. I know she will really appreciate it."

He laughs. "You know no such thing. The only way we got her to agree was by telling her that it was to our advantage tax-wise and that she was doing us a huge favor by accepting the money and the annual gifts. We didn't even tell her about the second trust. I manage her stuff, so she doesn't need to know."

"Papa Sol would be very proud."

"Thank you. I think he would." He pauses. "Your mother and I also wanted to do something for you."

"Please tell me I'm not getting a baby brother; it would just be too much." My heart stops. This is it.

He laughs again. "I think we are safely beyond that possibility. No, we know that you are staying with Bubbles to help her out, and also to save up some money. But when it is time for you to move on, whenever you decide that is, we wanted you to know that we have also set aside some money in a trust for you so that we can help you buy a new place. It isn't enough probably to buy something outright, but it is enough that you will have a really good down payment."

My eyes prick with tears. "Oh, Daddy."

"Now, now, none of that; this is happy! Bubbles is doing great, but eventually either she will need more help than you can provide, or you will find a different job that will make it less convenient to live there, and we want to help you get that new start whenever you are ready for it."

"That means the world to me. Thank you so much."

"In the meantime, it doesn't hurt to have a little extra *pushke*," he says, using the Yiddish word, which we always use to describe a little mad money you have stashed around. He slides over an envelope. Inside is a check for $2,500. "Just between you and me." He winks. I notice the check is from his personal account, not the joint one he shares with my mom.

"I won't tell." I think about the fat check I am about to send to Visa, and the fact that even though I didn't make any money on the sale of my condo, I will someday be able to afford a real place of my own again, and I suddenly feel ready to take on the world.

He raises an eyebrow at me as we both glance down at the last bite of cheesecake. I narrow my eyes at him, fork at the ready, and we both pounce at once.

I'm going to call that last sweet, delicious bite a solid victory, although considering his generosity and the current tightness of my waistband, good sense might have recommended I let him win.

"You look wonderful, schnookie," Bubbles says when I come downstairs. "A vision!"

After I got home I had a big thank-you call to my mom, carefully leaving out any mention of dad's extra bonus. She was glad that I was excited and reminded me that I should only take into account my own needs, and not worry about Bubbles, when considering moving to my own place. I assured her that where I am is very much the best place for me to be right now, and if that changed, I would be sure to let her know. Then I took an epic nap, sleeping the sleep of the dead for nearly three and a half hours. The side of my face still bears a faint shadow image of the pillowcase; apparently my skin doesn't bounce back the way it once did. I'm hoping the lighting at Café Nizza isn't too bright.

"I'm glad I pass muster."

"Oy. Stop licking that, Snatch. That is very rude," she scolds the dog, who is having a spectacular buttmunch at our feet. "I have something for you." She walks over to the side table in the hallway. When she turns around, she is holding a leather-bound copy of *Sense and Sensibility* and a red carnation.

"Oh, Bubbles, you are so funny. I was joking about the book and the flower. I don't think he would expect it."

"I know, but I think it's good luck. Plus it looks much better to be sitting alone reading a lovely book than scrolling through your iPhone."

I think about this for a moment and realize she's right.

"Thanks. I really appreciate it. What are you up to tonight? Hot date?"

She blushes prettily. "Just a quiet dinner out with a friend, and maybe the free concert in the park; it's such a nice night."

"Well, that sounds lovely. Enjoy it." I kiss her cheek, take a deep breath, and head for the car. I'm lucky and find a legal parking space just up the street from the café, a magical freebie spot that is blocked for loading during the day, so it can't be part of the egregiously expensive metered system we have here in Chicago.

Café Nizza is charming, and fortunately not crowded. I get a small two-top in the window, place my red carnation in full view on the table, and order a tea from the waitress. She tells me about the Tokay tasting, a six-dollar flight of three wines, or ten dollars for six, and hands me the menu of daily specials. I check my phone; I'm fifteen minutes early. I emailed Jake a couple of days ago just to say that I would be at the café around seven. He replied that he still didn't have his schedule for the day, but thanked me again for the heads-up. Even though it is possible he won't come, I figured it is always better to be the early one, the one seated and settled and calm, instead of walking through a strange place looking for an unfamiliar face.

My tea arrives, and I look over the menu while it steeps. A short list of sandwiches and salads, a daily soup special, a daily quiche special, and a long list of classical pastries, napoleons and éclairs and opera cakes. The Hungarian ownership is evident; there are Dobos tortes, several kinds of strudels, cream cake, and walnut cake. Traditional cookies and sweet breads. It all looks fantastic, and suddenly the last quarter of my sandwich, which I ate in my bathrobe while trying to apply makeup in a "natural" way that made my skin look decent and not like I'd troweled on buttercream, is gone and my stomach rumbles. And there is the description of the tasting wines, all Tokaji, from dry wines that would pair well with savory items to the very sweet dessert wines.

I add milk and sugar to my tea and take a deep draught, hoping it will stave off my hunger a bit. I check my phone again; it is 6:59. Jake could be here any second. I open my book and am immediately immersed in Jane Austen's wonderful language, and the world of the Dashwoods. It's only when I turn a page and realize I've hit chapter two that I think to check my phone again. 7:12. It isn't like we had a set meeting time; I had just said that this is when I would be here. The waitress refills my teapot with hot water. I return to my book, grateful for Bubbles's insistence, and wondering why I haven't read this one recently when I remember loving it so much in high school.

"Are you cheating on my father?" A voice comes from above my head.

"I'm not dating your father, Junior," I say to Mark, who is hovering over me. He's dressed in a pair of gray pants and a lightweight cotton shirt in a blue that seems very familiar. I look down. Same color as my new shirt. We look like the Bobbsey Twins.

"I meant hanging out at another bakery. Unless you are here on a recon mission, stealing secret recipes." He pauses. "Or you're here for an interview? You do look lovely by the way; that color suits you. Makes your eyes very blue."

"Thank you. It seems to be a very popular hue these days. You look, well, less sweaty than the last time I saw you."

"Showered and everything. So not an interview, then?"

"I'm waiting for someone, if you must know." I don't know why I even said this.

Mark looks around, as if he would recognize Jake if he spotted him. "Where is the lucky fellow?"

Crap. Now I have to salvage it. "Well, it wasn't a firm date. I just let him know about the wine tasting tonight; he said he would stop by if his schedule allowed."

Mark pulls out the seat across from me and sits down.

"What? Don't . . ."

"Relax, princess. If your prince arrives, I'll vacate. Just keeping you company. Besides, he should know better than to leave a beautiful girl waiting on him; someone else might swoop in and steal his prize."

This man is insufferable. "I'm neither a princess nor a prize, nor a girl if you want to be specific about it."

"I notice you didn't mind my calling you beautiful." The waitress comes over and asks what he would like. I begin to tell her he isn't staying, but he talks right over me. "The three-wine flight and a slice of the chestnut cream cake, please." Damn his eyes! That was the dessert I was most interested in: layers of chestnut cake with a filling of chestnut cream, apricot glaze, and dark chocolate ganache. "Well, he must be quite the catch, this paragon of manhood."

"I don't know if I would say that."

"He isn't a catch?"

I'm definitely starting to wonder. "I have no idea. We've not yet met in person."

Mark laughs. "No wonder you're all *fertutzed*. Who set you up with this charming fellow?"

I put on my most casual attitude. "We met online, the way everyone does these days."

"No shame in that. Some of my best friends have met perfectly suitable spouses that way."

"I'm not ashamed in the least."

"Good for you. After all, he might be The One. So what do you like about him? His intelligence? Wit? Washboard abs?"

I can't help but laugh. "At this stage I can neither confirm nor deny that he has much of any of the above, and I'm highly doubtful that he is The One. After all, when I mentioned that this event was happening, he never confirmed his availability, nor did he make it a firm date."

Mark's face gets a little puzzled. "Well, maybe he is nervous; those online dating sites are notorious for being a place of dishonesty. Or maybe he really thinks he might like you, and it spooks him a bit."

"Pish. If that is the case, then he's a mouse, not a man, and definitely not worthy of my time." I'm more disappointed than I should be, and being a little mean because of it. But I can't help it. If Jake really wanted to meet me, he would have figured out a way to show up here. I know I shouldn't have put so much pressure on myself, with the new outfit, the care I took with hair and makeup. Deep down I thought this was going to be a meet-cute worthy of Rosalind or Myrna, and the fact is, it's looking like it's not even going to be a meet, cute or otherwise.

"Ouch. Not playing around, is our Sophie. So then, why invite him here?"

The waitress brings over his wine and cake.

"Everyone says not to let these things go too long before meeting, makes things complicated and easily becomes a timesuck. I figured I was going to be coming here anyway, why not give him the opportunity to show up and wow me? As you can see"—I gesture around—"I'm not wowed."

Mark takes a huge bite of the cake and rolls his eyes in delight. "This is amazing; you have to try it." He pushes the plate towards me. I hesitate, but the fact is, with me, hunger wins over everything. I pick up my teaspoon and take a small bite, and am transported. The cake is nutty and moist, the cream with the barest hint of rum, the dark chocolate ganache smooth and silky with just enough bitterness, the apricot bringing that perfect amount of tart brightness, cutting through the rich flavors, and making the whole thing sing in the mouth. It is perfectly balanced and absolutely amazing, and I'm mentally making notes to see if I can replicate it.

"It's terrific, right?" Mark says, sliding the plate so that it is dead center in the table, the universal sign for sharing. I start to move it back towards him, and he stops me. "Please, you have to help me. This morning's run won't make a dent if I eat the whole thing myself. Ditto the wines."

I want so badly to be strong, to say no, but I have no pride. Not when faced with temptation like this. I take another bite. And a sip of the first wine.

"Well," Mark says, licking the back of his fork. "Looks like your fellow has definitively failed the first test. Is he off the list?"

I take a sip of the second wine. "Not off, necessarily; just no longer anywhere near the top."

"You've got hard standards." Mark sips the third wine.

"I've got standards, full stop. You know the old saying: 'It's gonna take one heck of a man to beat no man at all!'"

"Poor fellow, he has quite an uphill battle ahead of him."

I try the third wine. "If he's deserving, he'll have plenty of stamina for that climb. But enough about my no-show non-date. He's barely worth offhand mention, let alone an analysis of his viability. What brings you here solo on a night like this?"

Mark looks a little pained. "I live next door."

"Seriously?"

"Seriously. At least when I'm in town. They sent a note to all the residents of the building about the wine tasting; sounded sort of interesting. Plus I figure it's good karma. Son of a baker and all. Figured it might also be a bit of good networking; if I met anyone, I could mention the events this weekend."

"Hmm. Very Jewdhist of you. Shockingly supportive as well. So you came on a mission of goodwill, spotted me happily immersed in my book, and thought you'd love any opportunity to, what? Give me more shit for dragging your dad kicking and screaming down the path to ruin?"

"I thought I'd like an opportunity to make you an offer." His tone, which had bordered on banter, is now all business.

"It's not indecent, I hope."

"Nope, just straightforward. I've got some friends in the industry; I could get you some interviews, for serious pastry work. It wouldn't be at the level you were at before, but at least closer than where you are now."

"And this you would do to get me away from your dad."

"This I would do because as great as what you have done has been for my dad, you and I both know it is too little, too late, and in a few short months when Cake Goddess opens, she will crush the business in a very rapid fashion, and you will be out of work. So I thought I would just let you know that I can get you some interviews, and from my perspective, you might want to at least talk to some people before you are officially unemployed."

I hate how much I agree with him, but whatever willpower I don't possess with cake, I do possess with the things that actually matter.

"Thanks for the offer, but I'll be fine. I promised your dad I would be with him till the bitter end, and so I shall be. What I do after is not yours to worry about."

He shrugs. "Just an offer. An open one. You know where to find me." He takes the last bite of cake and finishes the last sip of the third wine.

"Sophie? Is that you?" I look up and there is Jason. He used to be the pastry chef at a farm-to-table place around the corner from S&S, and we'd help each other out in a pinch with ingredients now and again, have the occasional drink after work.

"Hi, Jason. How are you?" I say, wishing I could crawl into a hole. "This is Mark. Mark, Jason."

"Nice to meet you; are you responsible for this?" Mark gestures at the empty plate.

"That would be me. You like?"

"It's amazing. If the rest of the stuff in that case is half as good, you'll make a mint."

"Thanks. I appreciate that. Sophie, yours is the opinion I crave; I was so stoked to see you here. Lemme have it!"

"It's spectacular, J, truly. Congrats."

"You been out of town? No one has seen or heard from you in forever, I mean, not since . . ." And then he pauses and turns a bit red.

"Just floating."

"Floating, nothing! She's in Uptown, saving the neighborhood from pastry dullness over at Langer's Bakery!" Mark says cheerfully.

I could fucking kill him. All my efforts to be quiet and anonymous and hidden are now in vain, and it will only be a matter of time till all of the Chicago fine-dining chefs know exactly how far I've fallen.

"That's cool. Going old-school. Must be, um . . . a nice shift, for you," Jason says in a tone that makes it clear he knows I must be mortified.

I put on a brave face. "Well, you know, just consulting until I figure out my next project."

"Sure, sure," he says, and then, nothing. The moment becomes uncomfortable, and Jason finally breaks the silence. "Well, great to see you; glad you liked it. Thanks so much for coming, and I hope you'll make it a habit. I've got to get back." He gestures back to the kitchen, then shakes Mark's hand and leans down to give me a kiss on the cheek.

"Well, I don't know about you, but a bit of wine and cake always makes me hungry for dinner. Looks like your guy is officially a nonstarter. There's a great little Italian place up the block. I was going to get some linguine for takeout, but if you're up for it, I'd be happy to have you join me?"

Oh, hell no. "I think I will stay for a bit; the place is lovely and my book is a good one. I might try the other wine flight." I hope this makes me seem sophisticated and self-assured, and

not like some sad sack who is just going to sit here and drown
her sorrows in pastries and wine. I will not let him see me run
away with my tail between my legs.

   "Sounds delightful. I hope you enjoy."

   "Thanks."

   "See you Saturday, Sophie." He gets up and walks out. I wait
until I'm sure he must be well away from the café, and then
stand and gather my book. I leave the now-wilted carnation on
the table. I'm almost at the door when the hostess stops me and
hands me a bag.

   "Jason wanted me to send you off with some other things to
taste. His number is on the card; he'd love any input you might
have."

   Sigh. "Please thank him for me; tell him I'm sure it's all
perfect, but I'd never turn down an opportunity to enjoy his
work."

   "I'll let him know. Have a good night."

   I check my phone one last time in the car: no messages, no
texts, no emails. I even turn it off and reboot it. Nothing. It's
after eight, and Jake just blew me off completely with no explanation. I reach into the bag and pull out the first box on top.
Inside, an éclair, nestled in a frilled paper boat. I drive home
with one hand, eating the éclair with the other, marveling at
how pastry, which can seem on the surface so complicated and
difficult, is really easy for me, and men, who can seem so simple
and straightforward, are really so very hard.

                                   ⁓

Bubbles was blissfully still out when I got home from my non-
date. I poured myself a hefty double bourbon and retreated to
my bedroom with the rest of Jason's bounty. In the bottom of
the bag was a little note from Jason saying that it was nice to see

me and that he would love to get any relevant feedback on the things he sent me home with; he indicated that he sensed I was in self-imposed pastry chef witness protection, and said not to worry, my current location and employment would not be revealed to anyone, and if I ever wanted to get together somewhere quiet, just give him a call. Jason always was a good guy.

In gratitude for my continued privacy, and in spite of the fact that I had already consumed a small wagonload of empty calories today, I ate a piece of walnut cake, a small chocolate mousse bombe, a caramel bar, and three different cookies before effectively passing out in a sugar and alcohol coma. I woke briefly at around three in the morning to slither out of my lovely new outfit, now a mass of wrinkles, then finished my sleep of the dead. At five this morning, I got up, figured I could skip the shower since I had showered the previous evening before the festivities, and dressed for work. Today will be insane, the last day of prep before the relaunch tomorrow. I have a zillion things to do, including help Herman get the challahs out the door. I look over at my computer. I know I have to check.

And there it is. Time-stamped around ten p.m., right about the time I passed out.

Sunny—

Sorry I missed the wine tasting, I hope you had a great time! I got stuck in a crazy strategy meeting at work. My company apparently needs me to save a chunk of business in London, so what I thought was a meeting I might sneak out of early enough to meet you turned into a planning session of insane proportions. The work craziness will likely continue all weekend and through next week. I've got the bachelor party and wedding the following weekend, and the Monday after will be headed to the airport for parts both Anglo and Saxon, and won't be back for at least three months. But I was really hoping to get free to come to the event last night so that we might meet in person, and if you are feeling up to it, would love to retain my pen pal privileges while I'm across the pond, and then maybe we can set up a proper meeting when I return?

Jake

Well, I'm relieved he didn't just blow me off and seems genuinely disappointed. I'm also sort of relieved that he is heading out of the country for three months. I like the pen pal thing; it is safe and comfortable, and I don't have to worry about the whole rejection thing. In the movies, we would stay in touch and I would be witty and wise, and by the time we met, we would be inevitable.

But as we know, my life is not a movie.

And if we do continue to communicate, I'm sadly going to have to amp up my lying until I can explain myself face-to-face, which really sucks. I'm tempted to try and get myself out of the whole mess, and just tell him that I'm too busy for silly emails back and forth. I know it would save us both a lot of hassle surrounding something that isn't even a thing. Then again, deep down, I do get a little fuzzy feeling with his emails, and continuing is ultimately fairly harmless, especially if I can keep my flights of fantasy in check. So I'm going to play it cool and casual. And leave the ball solidly in his court.

Jake—

Don't think twice, you missed a lovely event, but I ran into a friend unexpectedly, and the wines and pastries were delicious, so the evening certainly was far from wasted. London sounds exciting! What a fantastic business trip. And of course, feel free to write if you like, I'd be happy to hear from you if you have time.

Do let me know how the bachelor party shakes out!

Sunny

And with that, I head to work, hoping I won't have to think about whether I've made the best or worst decision possible.

Woman of the Year

(1942)

Success is no fun unless you share it with someone.
· FAY BAINTER AS ELLEN WHITCOMB ·

"Thank you! Come again!" I say to the young man in skinny jeans and his sundress-clad girlfriend. They have just bought the last loaf of apricot white chocolate brioche, as well as two of each flavor of Pop-Tarts, and have taken a dog biscuit for their puggle, who is outside communing meaningfully with Snatch's rear end.

"We will!" she says gleefully, having tasted just about everything on the sample platter before making final decisions. "This place is awesome."

"Thanks much. Please be sure to follow us on social media; there's something new every day." Before closing their bag, I slip in a postcard, which has our links and a coupon for 10 percent off their next event cake or 15 percent off their next in-store bakery purchase.

"Cool," the guy says, and they elbow their way back outside.

Herman looks over at me, grinning, as he handles his end of the counter. He shockingly took to the new iPad register system like a champ, so we can both ring up customers at the same time, and the bakery has been packed since we opened this morning. The place gleams; we repainted a soft dove gray and had the old black-and-white linoleum floor polished. Today we have all of our café tables outside for customers, and a little buffet table with huge self-serve urns of iced tea and raspberry lemonade. We've got a line of dog bowls filled with water under the front window in the shade, and a small table with a big bowl of home-baked dog biscuits.

I turn to address the next customer and find myself face-to-face with my parents.

"Wow, quite the turnout!" my dad says, leaning his long frame over the counter for a kiss.

"So proud of you, sweetheart." My mom, not nearly tall enough to get at me physically, kisses her fingers and reaches them out to me.

"Thanks, guys; what can I get you? My treat!" I wink at them.

"I would love some of those nuttery buttery cookies you made me last time," my dad says, rubbing his tummy with glee. "They were amazing!"

"I saved some just for you; we sold out over an hour ago, and I haven't had time to go in the back and frost more." I reach behind me and grab the box where I was hoarding half a dozen for him. "Mom?"

"You know what I want."

"Chocolate babka."

Her whole face lights up. "Yes, please!"

I grab one off the shelf, wrap it up, and hand the goodies over to them. "Enjoy."

"Thank you, honey. This is just great what you are doing here. And your grandmother is having the best time!"

I look through the window to where Bubbles is holding court outside under our big oak tree, doing a cookie story time for the neighborhood kids, who are seated around her on picnic blankets, eating free organic chocolate chip cookies and listening to her read from the Mrs. Piggle-Wiggle book. I think she's already done three chapters, and they won't let her stop. Snatch is preening in a new sweater that has a huge cupcake on the back, meeting every dog in the neighborhood, and, I believe, has already eaten his weight in dog biscuits.

"She's the best."

"We're going to go outside and listen." And they slip back out the door. There are only a couple of people waiting, and I zip into the back to grab some trays to replenish, winking at Herman, who is deftly handling the next customer. I bring out a new tray of Pop-Tarts and swap it with the now-empty old one, then do the same with a tray of cookies and brownies. Herman still has everything well in hand, so I quickly frost and sandwich three dozen more of the peanut butter cookies that were such a hit earlier, and arrange them on a new tray.

"My goodness, how darling!" I hear a voice with an unmistakable drawl, and all the hair on the back of my neck stands up. I walk through the door and am confronted with the Cake Goddess herself. She is flanked by two nearly identical assistants, both petite blondes with razor-sharp blowouts and Lilly Pulitzer dresses, who are making notes in twin pink leatherbound notepads. "Hello, honeypie. I'm MarySue!" She extends a hand, not making eye contact with me at all.

I shrug, not having a hand free, and lean over to slide the tray of cookies into the case. "Hello, MarySue." She finally actually looks at me, and a flicker of recognition flies over her face. Shit.

"Sophie? Is that really you, sweetheart? My word, I barely recognized you." She says this while looking me up and down in a way that leaves no question as to her opinion of the current state and size of my personage.

"Yes, well." Not really sure what else to say.

"Is this place yours? I hadn't heard about you opening something new, you sneaky minx."

"Not mine, Herman's." Herman has walked over. "Herman Langer, proud owner of Langer's for over sixty years. This is MarySue Adams, the Cake Goddess."

Ever the charmer, Herman reaches out, takes her hand warmly, and slips her a peanut butter cookie from the tray. "Welcome to the neighborhood." She looks at the cookie as if it might bite her, and hands it wordlessly to one of her assistantbots.

"Thank you, you dear thing, how lovely." She is taking it all in, and the girls are writing feverishly. "This place reminds me of Old Mrs. Jenner's, back in my hometown."

"That's us, just the stalwart local bakery, taking you from your first cookie to your high school graduation cake to your retirement cake . . ." I say pointedly, trying to send a message of longevity and solidity. I wish my voice sounded a little bit more convincing.

"How is your construction going?" Herman asks her, and the assistant takes a tiny bite of the cookie, her wide blue eyes getting even wider as she tastes it. She breaks it in two, wolfs down the part she has already bitten, and hands the other half behind MarySue's back to the other assistant, who takes a small taste, and then, like her compatriot, nearly swallows the rest whole. Then they both start scribbling again.

"Very well, you are a dear for asking. We'll be doing the grand opening in October, on Halloween."

Ugh. Well, that gives us our timeline, a little sooner than we anticipated. "That is fast," I say.

"We've got them working round the clock over there," she says.

"I bet you do." I'm trying really hard not to imagine her on a white horse in an overseer costume on a plantation.

"Sophie, honey," she says in a loud whisper that is anything but conspiratorial. "I was so sorry about all that business with Dexter. You know I know how cruel those tabloids can be." This is true enough; she's fought her share of public embarrassment at the hands of the smear press. I wonder if we have more in common than I would like to admit. "But I'm glad to see you've landed on your, um, feet here. Good for you!" The tone is full of pity and condescension, and any potential softening of my heart towards her firms right back up. I put on a wide smile.

"I'm just so delighted to be back here, in a place that is genuine and authentic and serves the community. It's much better for my soul than the path I was on, and frankly, I'm awfully grateful to Dexter for giving me the opportunity to find that out."

Behind her, both assistants are now decimating the sample tray on Herman's side of the counter as if they have not eaten in days. Which, considering the size of them, isn't unlikely.

"I'm so glad to hear that. It is nice when things can end amicably. Have you been to Abondance yet? We were there last week, and it is just spectacular. They are really doing something special there." My stomach turns over. I knew that Dexter and Cookie were getting good press, but that is often as much about a talented PR firm as it is about what the kitchen is doing. But whatever else she may be, MarySue is a woman with a refined palate, and a lot of fine dining under her belt, and if she is raving, then it is likely great. Or she is just poking at me for the fun of making me squirm. Can't decide which is worse.

"That is wonderful for them. I wish them much success. Now, is there anything I can get for you today? We have a lot of specials for the festival, plus all of our usual offerings. Please do try a sample."

I push the tray over in hopes that if I give her something to put in her mouth, that noise will stop coming out of it. She waves me off, pushing the sample tray back with a wink.

"I would love to taste just everything! Girls, why don't you make some selections for us to take back to the office to share with the team? Put it on the card. I do have to go outside to make a call; I'll meet you in the car. Herman, lovely to meet you, and see your charming store. Sophie, good to see you, um, thriving." She looks me up and down again, clearly taking in every bit of my bulk, smiles her blinding smile, and whisks out the door.

Blonde 1 says, "Um, give us one of everything?"

Blonde 2 says, "Yeah, but maybe a couple extra of those peanut butter thingies?"

"Oh, for sure," the first blonde says, nodding. "Those are killer."

"Coming right up." I'm trying to prevent my eyelid from twitching. Usually in this business, other bakers will absolutely show up in support. So the order of "one of everything" doesn't surprise me. It's just that in this case it feels like an act of charity instead of solidarity. But I'll take every cent of her money without thinking twice. I start going through the case, grab one of each cookie, but six of the peanut butter sandwich cookies. One of each flavor of rugelach, Pop-Tart, and brownie. A pair of almond horns. A small cupcake box for one of each flavor, today a total of six: the usual chocolate and vanilla, with the new banana, plus a carrot cake version with cream cheese frosting, a strawberry cake with chocolate frosting, and, especially for the festival, a Chicago cupcake of lemon-scented white cake with white and blue vanilla icing and four raspberries making the Chicago flag across the top. I load a bag with loaves of all of our breads, savory and sweet. A bread pudding, two summer berry puddings, a chocolate babka, and a cinnamon babka. Then I ring them up, wishing I could be more gleeful at such a large total. They don't blink at the cost, hand me a Cake Goddess Amex card, and receive the bags I hand over.

"The peanut butter cookies are on the top of that first box," I say, trying to be happy they ate them and enjoyed them, and not hate the women by association.

"Awesome. Thanks." And they are gone in a swirl of pastels.

I take a deep breath, let my shoulders unclench, and turn to help the next customer, attempting to ignore the fact that MarySue Adams is now standing in front of our window, blithely signing autographs and taking pictures with adoring fans, all of our customer base basking in the glow of her veneers and spray-on tan.

❦

"You did great, schnookie, really great," Bubbles says as we walk home after dark. She stayed the whole day, reading to the kids, schmoozing the hipsters, cooing at the mommy mafia and their nut-free, gluten-free, lactose-intolerant, organic-only offspring. She sat with the old biddies drinking iced tea in the afternoon, telling stories, and enjoying the summer breezes and shortbread cookies. As the festival wound down, she wandered over to Kolmar's and picked up some of the special sausages they had made, plus homemade sauerkraut, potato salad, and cucumber salad, and brought them back for us. We split open some of our salted rye sticks and made sandwiches that the three of us snarfed up without even talking, washing it all down with some dark beer that Herman fetched from his apartment. Then she made us tea as we cleaned up and tallied the day. It had been a huge success, and I couldn't wait to check the computer to see how our social media push had gone.

"Thank you for everything, Bubbles; you were an enormous help."

"Pish. It was less than nothing, and a pleasure, every bit. But the poor dog may need a vacation." Snatch is extra slow and waddly today, having consumed a zillion treats and biscuits, and god knows how many pieces of sweets snuck to him by his adoring fans of the under-eight set. Thankfully, Bubbles was there to keep a watchful eye out to make sure none of them tried to give him any chocolate, which could poison him.

"It's his own fault for being such a glutton."

"Are you a greedy Snatch? Never satisfied? Can't ever get enough in you?" Bubbles coos at him. I have to remember to tell the girls about this one; they love her accidental porn conversations with the dog.

"Pity Herman's son couldn't come," she says. "It would have been so nice for him to see it today."

I had also been hoping to see Mark, just to witness the look on his face when he saw that the place was hopping and buzzing and everyone was raving.

"Herman said that he got called back to the West Coast unexpectedly, some work thing," I say.

"Herman mentioned it when I asked where he was. Although he thinks it was less a work thing than a relationship thing. I think he is afraid an engagement might be in the offing, and he isn't sure she is the right girl."

"Well, they're sort of like chalk and cheese, those two; would any girl Mark chose be the right girl in Herman's eyes?"

"I think he wants his son to be happy, and thinks if this girl were making him happy, he wouldn't seem so lacking in lightness. Love makes you a feather on the wind, and Herman Jr. is a little leaden."

I laugh. "He is at that." I wonder about the whole girlfriend thing. Mark has never even mentioned her existence to me, but Herman seems to believe they are really serious. Curious.

"Not our circus, not our monkeys," Bubbles says with hands raised in surrender. It's one of her favorite old proverbs, and reminds us both to keep our noses out of other people's business. If only I could. I have at least forty Wedding Girl emails waiting for me.

We get home and Bubbles immediately heads for bed, the day finally catching up with her. Snatch can't even make it up the stairs and instead snuffles over to the dog bed in the front room and collapses, snoring like a pig with a sinus infection. I pour myself a restorative bourbon with a squeeze of lemon and a splash of ginger ale, and head upstairs to see if I can knock out some of my email backlog before I pass out. Lucky for me, most of the questions are now routine, and I cut and paste, listening to some Patty Griffin on my headphones, getting into the groove. I get one email from an older bride who wants a wedding that is "all bread and no circus," so I recommend a small mid-afternoon Sunday wedding ceremony followed by cake and champagne, and then a private dinner for the immediate family only that evening at a restaurant. A May bride is worried about her December groom and how their friends will mix and mingle at the various wedding events considering the generation gap, so I suggest doing mixed table seatings based on common interests in hopes of creating easy conversation. And a bride who is about to have her own personal *Brady Bunch* moment wants to know how to use the wedding planning to bond her three boys with his three girls and begin to create a blended family. I tell her that to start, she should include his girls in all her girlie stuff, and he should do the same with her sons and the boy stuff. Then they should do some fun stuff, with the eight of them, and solicit the kids' advice on the wedding planning. Better to end up with a hodgepodge wedding that all of the kids feel they had a hand in than a perfect event where everyone's on eggshells.

I check the social media sites and see that we had an exceptionally good day, our follower and likes numbers are through the roof, and there were lovely postings on Twitter and Facebook and Instagram. Then I spot it. @CakeGoddess What a charming treasure right in my new backyard! Thanks for the delicious treats @LangersBakery! With a picture of her standing with all of her sherbet-clad minions in her office behind the detritus of their haul, reduced to crumbs and bits. She had tweeted this to her 800,000 followers, and they proceeded to follow us, tweeting how sweet she is to support other bakers. I hate that she actually helped our cause, but diligently go through and favorite and like and retweet and reply. Can't look a gift horse in the mouth, even if said mouth is full of ceramic teeth that look like Chiclets and belongs to the one person who can and probably will put us out of business.

It's just after two when I finally finish, feeling good about clearing out the inbox, when one more email arrives. It's Jake.

Sunny—

Looking forward to continuing the conversation, and grateful for your kind and forgiving nature. And of course I will report back on the bachelor party. More soon.

Jake

I smile. I go to hit Reply, but then stop myself. It's Saturday night at two a.m., and I should be either asleep or out having fun. Despite that it feels a little bit like game-playing, I don't want him to think that I'm just sitting home waiting out the summer to finally meet his fabulous personage. I'll reply tomorrow, let him sit on it a bit. I finish the last of my drink, now essentially just lightly bourbon-scented ice water with a hint of lemon, and get ready for bed.

Just as I'm about to drop off, I wonder.

Is Mark out there in California somewhere having put a ring on it?

And will I be more annoyed if I have to make his wedding cake or if I don't?

My Favorite Wife

(1940)

I bet you say that to all your wives.
· IRENE DUNNE AS ELLEN/EVE ·

"Don't you find this a little strange?" Ruth asks when she picks me up at the bakery.

We are on our way to Hanna's house in Forest Park. She has invited us to a surprise birthday party for Jean, who hates her birthday.

"Well, maybe this will flip the script on Jean's whole birthday thing. She is a little insane about not marking the occasion."

"Look, I get that for someone who is mostly all earth mother goddess, she is weird about not wanting to mark the passage of time. I don't think it's a vanity thing, but whatever, it's her bag. But they have been dating for less than two months, so throwing a surprise party? For a birthday that isn't even a special number? That is just weird."

"Maybe thirty-seven has some special astrological meaning?"

Ruth makes a harrumphing noise. "And what about the whole *kid* thing? That's not odd to you?"

Jean divulged, offhand and almost accidentally, at our drinks date with Amelia the other night that Hanna has a three-year-old daughter. From her previous marriage. To a man. "Didn't I mention it before?" she said when we all were a little shocked. She decidedly hadn't.

"Maybe Hanna just wanted to have a summer barbecue and wanted to invite people for Jean, but thought we wouldn't come unless it was a special-occasion sort of thing. It isn't like she's dumb; she has to see that it's a bit awkward with all of us."

Ruth and I have been really trying on the whole Hanna front, since Jean seems so keen on her. They are going away for a long weekend next week to the beach in Connecticut, borrowing the house of a director pal of Jean's, and Ruth agreed that only once they get back can we have any opinions on how things are going in that department as it's hard enough to get Jean to take a vacation, and really not our place to ruin it.

Ruth harrumphs again and turns off of the expressway. I'm distracted anyway. I switched my hours around this week so that I could have this rare Saturday afternoon free to participate in this party. But I hate leaving Herman on his own on a weekend day—ever since the relaunch, our Saturdays and Sundays have been busy as hell, which is great, but I worry about him handling it on his own. And which is worse, this morning I tanked a batch of this week's special Pop-Tart flavor—blueberry with lemon glaze—because all I could think about was the email I got today from the Wedding Girl site.

Dear Wedding Girl—

One of the paralegals in my office suggested that I check out your services, as I have something of a problem. I am about to make an honest woman of my partner of 43 years, the love of my life, and mother of my exceptional child. We never thought we would marry, but frankly we are at the stage of life where planning for the future is a moral imperative, and we have been advised by our estate planner that being legally married will make the eventual machinations of dealing with health issues or things that come up after death much easier on both of us, and the aforementioned offspring. Being a lawyer myself, I always knew this deep down, but the die-hard hippie in me has always balked against it.

Ever since we decided to go ahead and make things legal, my lovely compatriot has gotten, a bit, shall we say, aggressive about some things related to the gathering we're planning. I frankly had assumed we would hit the courthouse with our daughter and my mother, and then maybe have a barbecue back at the house. But apparently if you have a woman in your life, even one you know is enlightened beyond fancy parties and sparkly things, wait 43 years for a wedding? She goes a little gonzo. Last thing in the world I would have expected, but there we are. Can you give me some advice on how to gently try and rein her in a bit, get her back to rational so that I don't spend the next three months in wedding plan hell with a woman I barely recognize?

Any advice is most welcome.

Best wishes,
Robert Bernard, ESQ.

Yeah, because the only thing more awkward than being the epically-left-at-the-altar wedding advice girl is getting an email from your dad asking for advice on managing your newly shockingly bridezilla mom. Fantastic.

"Hello? We're here." Ruth pops me out of my reveries as she pulls up in front of Hanna's address. The house is a lovely little cottage style, small front yard abloom with landscaping, and has a wide driveway leading to the garage. There is a large catering truck parked in the driveway, but plenty of street parking is available, so I wonder if we are early. Ruth grabs the large beribboned bag from the backseat, our gift for Jean, a cast-iron *plancha* for her new grill. Jean costumed a show in Barcelona three years ago and got addicted to the simple grilled foods she ate at all the small restaurants near the theater. She came back and bought a grill for her back porch, and now has become one of those insane Chicagoans who is outside regardless of weather, cooking things over fire. She's been using a big cast-iron skillet in place of the traditional slab surface, but a pal of mine who works at Cafe Ba-Ba-Reeba! hooked me up with a real *plancha*, so it can be all tapas authentico all the time at Jean's from now on.

Hanna greets us with massive hugs and tells us how excited she is for us to be seeing her place at long last. The "long last" part throws me, because, *two months*, and Ruth raises an eyebrow at me. We walk inside, where there is a large open-concept great room, incorporating the kitchen, dining room, and living room. It is, to say the least, sparsely populated. She introduces us to her parents and her daughter, Pippi, a tiny thing in pigtails with a thumb in her mouth, hiding behind her mother's skirts. Which are voluminous. Hanna is dressed sort of like Donna Reed; all of the funky youthful style she's exhibited on the couple of times we've met her, the skinny jeans and ironic T-shirts with the leather moto jacket and hair in a messy bun, is gone. In its place, apparently, a rejected picnic costume from the *Mad Men* fire sale: a cotton belted shirtdress with a kicky print of twinned cherries and bluebirds, with what appears to be a freaking crinoline under the skirt.

Across the room we spot one of Jean's favorite colleagues, Gary, and his partner, Richard, both of whom Ruth and I have met at numerous opening-night parties. They wink at us, and we head to their side of the room.

"Have you taken the tour yet?" Richard asks. "It is *epic*."

"Be nice," Gary says with a smirk. "But you really should see it when you get the chance."

"Oh, I'm sure we will," Ruth says.

I walk over to kiss Jean's sister Margaret, who is looking a little gassy. Margaret is twelve years older than Jean, and lives out in the burbs. She has always been more of a mother figure for Jean, especially since their mom was diagnosed with Alzheimer's eight years ago and moved into the memory-care unit at the assisted-living place near Margaret. She is sitting on the couch with Hanna's mom, Therese, right next to her, on the receiving end of what sounds like a barrage of information about how great some person named Jeanine is. Ruth mouths "Jean" at me, to clue me in that for some reason these people are all using Jean's full given name. Margaret's husband, Glenn, is in the kitchen, where Hanna's dad is apparently grilling him about their family life and history.

"Hello, dear. So good to see you. How is your family?" Margaret is simply the kindest woman on the planet. She's been a homemaker her whole life, has three amazing grown sons who Jean spoils rotten, and recently became a grandmother for the first time, which is, according to Jean, the thing she was really born to do. She would never say a bad word about anyone, but the look in her eyes right now implies that she is having some opinions. I wink at her, and she smiles.

"They're good; thanks for asking. I know they would want me to send their love."

Margaret and my mom served on a board together many years back, so our two families got to spend a lot of time together at various events and fund-raisers.

"Please send my love back. I owe your mom a call and a lunch."

"We just love that Jeanine has such a wonderful, supportive set of family and friends around her," Therese says.

Gary is raising eyebrows at me, and Richard gestures around the room with his head. I take a closer look at our environment.

Everything that isn't nailed down has a pithy aphorism scrawled on it. You know, those "Dance like nobody's watching" Bed Bath & Beyond art pieces? They are everywhere. Pillows that have "When I count my blessings, I count you twice!" embroidered on them. Sayings are stenciled on the walls. It looks like Pinterest threw up in here. And while they aren't my personal taste, I'm not dissing these wholesale. I know many lovely people who have one of them tastefully displayed in their homes. *One.* Not *seventeen* in the great room alone. Ruth's eyebrows have knitted themselves into a knot of distaste.

"Isn't it lovely? Hanna did such a great job with this place; she designed it herself." Therese busts me checking out the décor. "You must come have the full tour!"

"Oh, yes," Richard says with profound sincerity. "You must."

Margaret makes a move to go save Glenn in the kitchen, but Hanna's mom grabs her arm and pulls her towards the stairs. "You come too, Margaret!"

"But, um, I took the tour earlier, remember?" Margaret has bad knees, bad enough that she and Glenn recently traded their three-story family home for a sprawling ranch on the same block with no basement so that she didn't have to do stairs anymore.

"Oh, I know, but don't you just want to see their reactions? Especially when we are *bonding.*"

Oy.

Margaret, unable to simply say no, sighs deeply, and we follow Therese upstairs through a series of rooms, all of them in the shabby-chic pastel mode. All the furniture is painted with that ghastly chalk paint that gives me the willies when I touch it, and more sayings have been stenciled on nearly every surface.

"Cute pup," Ruth says, looking at a photo of a yellow Labrador in the master bedroom.

"Yes, he was," Therese says, voice full of venom. "That son of a bitch took him when he left."

Margaret's eyes fly open, and it is clear that the ex-husband is none too popular with Hanna's people.

"Here is the hope room!" Therese says, back to her cheery self, as she escorts us into a fully kitted-out nursery. "Since they had so many bedrooms, when Pippi got too old for her crib, Hanna just left this all set up and moved her into her big-girl room next door. Siblings are just so wonderful. Well, you know that better than anyone; don't you, Margaret?"

Margaret has gone absolutely white.

"I could use a drink. Anyone else?" Ruth says, taking Margaret's arm and leading her down the stairs.

In the kitchen the caterer is setting up the buffet. I ask Gary, "Where are the rest of the people?"

"This is it," he says pointedly.

"Where are all of Hanna's friends?"

"Dunno."

I do a quick head count. "There's only nine of us."

"Yep."

"She hired a caterer."

"To grill the burgers and hot dogs." He nods over into the kitchen.

I look at the buffet. Sure enough, hot dog and hamburger buns, appropriate condiments, a green salad, a bowl of pasta salad, a bowl of coleslaw, and a chafing dish with corn on the cob. The caterer is indeed in the backyard grilling burgers, dogs, and chicken breasts. On the dining table is a vegetable platter, a shrimp platter, and a cheese and sausage platter. There is enough food for forty people. And if there were forty people coming, I would say, "Absolutely, hire a caterer; have at it." But for nine? When it is just casual BBQ fare and the usual suspects? Using the gas grill in the backyard? That seems excessive. We'd all have been happy to potluck if she didn't want to cook everything, and lord knows I would have been happy to man the grill myself.

I look back towards the kitchen and see that Hanna is arranging something on the counter. It turns out to be individual servings of sangria. In glass bottles. With stripy paper straws. Decorated with a garland of no fewer than three different types of ribbon, a seashell glued to the knot, and a paper tag that says "Sangria" in curly script. She is photographing them from many angles.

Richard cants his head out towards the backyard, and I look outside.

The table set in the backyard has a clear beach theme, apparently related to their upcoming Connecticut trip. And when I say "theme," I mean that the White Party is a mere dress code suggestion in comparison.

The table has striped beach umbrellas overhead, which I'm grateful to see, since today's balmy Chicagoland weather is about ninety-nine degrees. Underneath the umbrellas hang paper lanterns in the colors of the ocean. Each chair has a striped beach towel draped on it, and the place mats are brown craft paper over cardboard. The plastic flatware has been tied in a starfish shape with the same ribbon configuration as on the sangria bottles, also with a small shell glued to it. At each place is a thin piece of wood cut in the shape of an ornate square picture frame, and resting in it is a cardboard cube, the outside of which has been covered in glued-on sand. These boxes have the same ribbon and shell thing, as well as a paper tag.

Down the middle of the table are large glass containers filled with sand and seashells. Larger seashells and starfish are strewn about. There are sandpipers made of burlap, rope, and wire scampering down the center of the table. Pillar candles, with more ribbons and tags.

This tablescape makes Sandra Lee look both sane and sober.

Ruth grabs my elbow and pulls me outside, past the table, to where an easel is set up.

"Check out *this shit here*," she hisses in my ear. On the easel is a large framed print. It shows the silhouette in gray scale of two women holding hands with a little girl and walking on the beach. Over this image is printed a poem that Hanna has clearly written herself, describing Jean as being the "light in her darkness and the joy in her despair and her forever love." I think my quick intake of breath scares Ruth.

"Two months," I whisper.

"Not even," she whispers back.

Gary and Richard join us.

"Have any of you talked to Jean about her? I mean, are they both in this place, and we just didn't realize?" I ask them.

They shrug. "Not a word," Gary says.

"Not to me," Richard says. "I just found out they were dating when the invite came."

Margaret is trying to come outside to join us, but Therese grabs her by the arm and announces that they are going back upstairs with Pippi to *bond some more*. Margaret looks stricken and disappears back inside. Apparently Hanna isn't the only one on board with the full-court press. I keep waiting to overhear her dad mention the details of her dowry while Glenn goes for his third bottle of sangria.

Since it is hotter than the surface of the sun out here, the four of us tear ourselves away from the easel and head back inside.

"Ten minutes!" Hanna yells out.

Ruth grabs a bottle of sangria, pointedly removes the tag and ribbons and straw, all of which she drops neatly in the garbage can, and takes a deep swig. Her eyebrows raise. She looks very much like someone who wants to spit. I motion my head towards the counter where Hanna was mixing this elixir, where there is a canister of Crystal Light fruit punch, a bottle of triple sec, and a large jug of Gallo table red. Ruth leaves her denuded still-full bottle on the counter and grabs a can of Diet Coke from the galvanized bucket on the sideboard to wash the taste out.

The caterer comes in with all the food and puts everything in the various chafing dishes. Hanna has a quiet but clearly unhappy conversation with him, he goes running out the front door, and we hear the truck chug to a start.

"She's coming!" Hanna hisses frantically, shuttling us all out to the backyard and thrusting her camera at Ruth and demanding she capture the exciting moment. We're both shocked that she has stopped taking pictures of her own crafty handiwork long enough to remember there is a reason for the event.

Jean turns the corner to enter the backyard. We all yell, "Surprise!" and "Happy birthday!"

The look on Jean's face is that of someone who has indeed been surprised.

By a drive-by rectal exam or an unexpected Amazonian jumping spider in her cornflakes.

"Wow!" she manages to get out. "Look at all this."

Hanna grabs her in a lip-lock that stops just shy of mouth-to-mouth resuscitation, and then allows her to make the rounds to greet the small gathering of family and friends. She thanks us all for coming with a deer-in-headlights look that tells me that perhaps she and Hanna are not quite in the same emotional headspace.

"Go tell Jeanine happy birthday and how much you love her!" Hanna's mom pushes Pippi in Jean's direction. Because nothing is more comfortable for a three-year-old than having to tell some woman she has met four times that she loves her. Pippi begins to cry. Hanna's mom thrusts the soggy child at poor Jean, but Pippi is having none of it and runs for her mother.

"How silly, Pippi. You know you love Jeanine!" Hanna says to the poor thing, who is clutching her leg like it's a life raft. She leans down and picks up Pippi, who now has a charming double trail of thick snot falling over her upper lip. I think about how many times Jean has said that she loves children "well behaved and living at someone else's house" and decide that Ruth and I don't really have to worry, because no sex in the world will be good enough to convert Jean into a suburb-dwelling Pippi-has-two-mommies girl.

"Everything's ready. Everyone make a plate!" Hanna announces, gesturing us all inside to the buffet. We follow her in and help ourselves to the food. The caterer has returned, and he and Hanna have another intense side conversation, and the look on Hanna's face is of deep hatred. We fill our plates and arrange ourselves at the table outside, Gary and Richard sitting across from Ruth and me. We all struggle to untie our beribboned flatware, but I think the hot-glue gun she used to attach the sea-shells and tags may have melted the pieces together. We generally give up, eating mostly with our hands, and Glenn snaps the top off his trapped fork and uses it to eat his pasta salad. Hanna and Pippi are nowhere to be found.

"Where'd she go?" Gary asks twenty minutes later when they haven't reappeared. Most of us are done with our first plates and heading back to the buffet for seconds, more out of boredom than actual hunger.

"I think she went to go scrapbook this precious moment before she forgot a detail," Ruth mutters. Richard snorts sangria up his nose. Hanna's parents share a charming story about bringing Hanna's brother into the family business and then firing him, and imply there are reasons he was not invited to this gathering. Guess that whole "Siblings are precious and family is everything" motto has some loopholes. Jean, trapped at the end of the table next to Hanna's empty chair and flanked by Therese and Hanna's dad, Nick, is trying to look like she doesn't want to crawl into a hole.

Eventually Hanna returns, having put Pippi down for a nap. The sand-covered boxes appear to be the favors. Ruth opens hers to find that it is full of peanut butter cups, which are all completely liquefied as a result of having been outside in the heat for several hours baking in their boxes. She eats one with the half a broken spoon Gary is finally able to wrestle out of its ribbons.

Hanna's parents regale the table with how much they hate Pippi's dad, whose name is either "that son of a bitch" or "you know who," and how much they love Jeanine. These two things seem very connected for them.

"This is the best play I've been to all year," Richard says dreamily.

"I think I'm going to pitch *Guess Who's Coming to Dinner* for next season," Gary says.

"Where are we going to drink when we leave here?" Ruth asks.

"My house," I say. "Bubbles is going to need details while they're fresh."

"Done. Her martinis are the best anyway," Ruth says, nodding.

After lunch, Hanna makes a big show of presenting Jean with her framed poem print. Jean looks it over quickly and then says she wants to focus on it later, privately.

Probably after she gets home and determines if there is a dead bunny in the pot on her stove.

The cake is served, and we are all relieved to see that it does not have a tiny little bride and bride on top. Although we can't be sure of what was originally planned, since apparently all the frantic whispering in corners with the caterer earlier was because he forgot to pick up the specially ordered cake from the bakery.

There was no time to go into the city to get it, so he ran out to fetch a basic one from the Jewel instead. Only Hanna seems upset at this. At a birthday party? In this heat? Jewel cake is just the ticket. I'm deeply grateful she didn't ask me to bake one.

After dessert, Ruth gives me the "I can't take much more" signal, and we get ready to make a quick retreat. I stop in the bathroom, where I am confronted with a huge wall stencil informing me that "Laughter is the light we sprinkle about the world." Super. I get up, turn to flush, and am taken aback by what appears to be a small blue jellyfish attached to the inside of the bowl. Momentarily I wonder exactly what horrible disease of my girl parts would result in my peeing tiny, slimy sea creatures, but on closer inspection I realize it is some sort of disinfecting gel-pod thing. Whew.

Ruth and I make the rounds, giving Jean big, deep hugs and asking her to call us later, and Jean plasters on the kind of smile you save for smelly aunts who give wet kisses, says that of course she will, and thanks us so much for coming to share this special day. Gary and Richard invite us to join them for alcoholic slushies at Sidetrack, but we take a rain check. Margaret and Glenn hug us both and promise to call next time they are coming downtown.

"Thank you both so much. I've just always wanted sisters, and it means the world to me that you are that for Jeanine, and I'm just feeling so happy to have you in our lives," Hanna says. Because, *cuckoo for Cocoa Puffs!*

"What the fuckety fuck was that?" Ruth asks as soon as we get in the car.

"That was simply the best story we will ever be able to tell about Jean when she introduces us to her next rational girlfriend."

"God, I hope so," Ruth says, peeling out like the bad guys

are chasing us. "I hope that insane woman doesn't have some surprise beach wedding planned for next weekend."

"Even Jean wouldn't let herself get trapped into a spontaneous wedding."

"I know. I know," Ruth says. "The table . . ." She drifts off and we start to giggle, and if laughter is the light we sprinkle about the world, then we did some serious light sprinkling all the way home. And in the Nook, with plenty of emotion, we made Bubbles sprinkle so hard she had to run to the bathroom before she peed her pants, and I discovered that if you snort ice-cold martini up your nose while laughing, it gives you brain freeze, but in a good way.

⁓

By the time we finish our martini-fueled giggle fest, it is after six, and Ruth heads for home to salvage her evening. I'm suddenly ravenous.

"Do we need grilled cheese?" I ask Bubbles.

Her face becomes slightly sheepish. "So sorry, schnookie. I've got dinner plans."

"That's nice. Who with?"

She looks around, not meeting my eyes. "Just a friend, dear. My goodness, I should be getting ready as we speak!" And quick as a flash, she's off upstairs to change. Very cagey.

"Well, looks like it's just you and me and the TV, old Snatcheroo," I say to the dog, who glances up from gnawing his paw just long enough to register complete indifference, and then returns to his ablutions.

I grab the nonstick skillet, put it on the stove, and fetch four slices of bread from the breadbox. I've been playing with a new bread recipe, a cross between sourdough and English muffin, baked in a sliceable loaf. Makes fantastic toast, and I've been craving grilled cheese with it since I brought it home yesterday.

I liberally butter all four slices all the way to each edge, place them butter-side down in the skillet, and top each with a thick slice of American cheese. Then I turn the skillet on. Starting the sandwiches in a cold pan is my secret to perfect grilled cheese. That way, as the pan slowly heats up, the cheese starts to melt, and by the time the outsides are crunchy and crispy, the cheese is a goo-fest, and nothing gets burnt. And I always make two, because one grilled cheese sandwich is never enough.

I grab a bag of chips from the pantry and the jar of pickles out of the fridge, and put both on the table in the Nook. I pause. What the hell. I also grab the tub of French onion dip I made two nights ago when I got home to an empty house and a note from Bubbles saying that she was out at the movies. I didn't have the energy for much of a meal, so I grabbed the onion soup mix and a container of sour cream and spent the evening dipping just about anything I could find into it.

I slide the perfectly cooked sandwiches onto the cutting board and let them sit for just a minute before I cut them, so all the cheese doesn't ooze out. While I'm waiting, I run upstairs and grab my laptop. I can eat and catch up on Wedding Girl emails with one eye on TCM.

When I get back down the stairs, Bubbles is putting on lipstick in the front hall mirror.

"Have a wonderful dinner." I kiss her, noticing that her usual scent, the Arpège she's always worn, has been replaced by something new, something different. "You smell good. New perfume?" It smells familiar, but I can't place it.

She blushes prettily. "Do you like it? I had an urge to try something new."

"You smell delicious." Which she does. And I suddenly wonder about the "friend" she's having dinner with. To my knowledge, she's not dated at all since my grandfather passed away, but that doesn't mean she couldn't start.

I open up my email and write a brief answer to my dad, telling him to be patient, that even the best of women get a little crazy about weddings, and encouraging him to only push back on stuff that he really cares about. Then I tell him he should enlist his daughter to help manage her mother, and see if the tag team doesn't work. If nothing else, I'm just really hoping he will call me and ask me in person for advice and not write Wedding Girl ever again.

I'm just finishing up when I get an email notification.

Sunny—

I cannot thank you enough for your help with the bachelor party. The frat boy brothers went out of their way to say that it was the best bachelor party they had ever been to, and by the end of the night, were calling my buddy their "brother from another mother," and saying he might be too good for their sister. A rollicking success, with no sloppy drunkenness, no naked women, and no glitter. And none of them were hungover for the wedding. I'm eternally grateful. You are a genius and don't let anyone tell you differently. The wedding was beautiful, and now I'm just packing for the big trip to London Monday. I keep meaning to ask, is the advice site your full time job or do you do something else?

Jake

I start to write and then realize that in many ways, I'm verging on breaking my own rules. I vowed not to say anything in my notes to him that could in any way reveal my true identity. He doesn't know any details about me personally, and I need to keep it that way. If I let anything slip that is specific enough that he could use it to figure out who I am, I'd be sunk.

It's really hard to be Batman.

And it isn't lost on me that the same seems to be true on his end. As much as I've been enjoying our correspondence, he's certainly kept his cards close to the vest, which I respect. First thing he gives me that hints at being searchable, and I will be stalking him all over the interwebs. So I can only expect the same from him, and lord knows, I'm eminently Google-able. And none of it is flattering. Which is why the anonymity is so soothing. In email I'm smart and funny and charming and attractive, or I can try to be. In real life I am sad and broke and dumpy and embarrassed. Fallen from grace is not a good look on me.

I'm going to have to lie. Like, really *lie*.

This seems worse than lying by omission or not sharing, especially since he's a total stranger who is clearly doing the same thing. But it does make me a little bit sad. Because once a real lie is out there, it has to be managed; it has to be maintained. Lies are like fussy houseplants; they need the proper care and feeding or they drop leaves all over the living room and start to smell of rot.

I sit back. It would be so nice to be able to talk to someone about the whole Herman situation, but if I'm going to do that, it is going to be a work of carefully crafted fiction. I have to express that I work for someone who is elderly, that the business was something of a throwback that we've invested a lot of time updating, that there is a new business coming in that could close it all down. But it has to be something so far from the real thing that he can't put two and two together. It has to be in a different part of the city, to start; it can't be in any way connected to baking or food. But it has to be something I know something about so that I sound plausible. I think about law or psychology, since I know about those from my folks, but reject those ideas. I don't really know what Jake does; he has only ever referenced "business meetings" and "clients," so it could be anything. If I go with something broad like law he could turn out to be a lawyer, and then I'd be screwed. It has to be some sort of random little narrow-niche business, because then the odds of him being in that business are limited, but not so narrow that he would think of starting to look into it.

What do I know besides food and weddings?

Out of the corner of my eye I catch the Cake Goddess article, which is sitting on my desk. I can't seem to throw the hateful thing away. Because I keep adding extra details to the picture. MarySue currently has three of her precious teeth blacked out and two turned into fangs dripping blood. She is sporting devil horns, a huge hairy cheek mole, and a double chin. And a jaunty fedora. I'm a really good doodler. I think about her moving into that beautiful apartment that Anneke designed and built. And the restaurant that almost was, the details we discussed, the finishes and fixtures, all those bits and bobs that I was so excited about. I need a small business that can be pushed out by a big-box store. A lightbulb goes on. I do a quick Google search on home improvement stores opening in Chicago and boom. There it is. Home Depot is about to open a new store on the South Side, in Brighton Park. An old-school enclave of Polish, Lithuanian, and Italian immigrants—similar to my neighborhood except Catholic instead of Jewish—which has in the past fifteen years seen a massive influx of Latinos. So the local profile is similar enough: The older generation is still there but outnumbered by new, younger families that don't fit the same profile or needs. More searching reveals that there are still three old-school family-owned little hardware stores in the neighborhood, all of which must be scared about the big orange monster coming in. This is perfect.

Jake—

For the moment I work part-time for my uncle at his hardware store. The business has been in the family for generations. But he is old, and the place isn't exactly completely up on the times, despite best efforts. His inventory is limited to items he considers proper quality, so not always the cheapest options or biggest selection. And now there is a Home Depot coming in a little too close for comfort. He has enlisted me to help him update and modernize so that he can compete, and I'm not sure if I'm doing it right. Or even if we should be trying. Any advice?

Sunny

This feels specific enough that if he does his own bit of research, he will find the general neighborhood; what he might do with that information I have no idea. But at least it will keep him away from the truth, which is all I can think about right now. I hit Send.

It doesn't take long for him to reply.

Sunny—

You must help your uncle fight, of course you must. Full stop. And I'll help you, if I can. None of the women in all of these movies you have recommended to me would sit back and let something special die on the vine. If you fight and lose, you can still stand tall. But if you give up you'll never stop wondering. Just think about the different elements of the problem as if it were a wedding you need to take from horrible to perfect! And take the problems one at a time, or it will be overwhelming.

If you get stuck or need to bounce specific ideas off someone, send them my way!

Jake

– – – – – – – – – – – – – –

Jake—

Thank you. Fight it is. This is good advice. I owe you $4.99.

Sunny

Sunny—

You don't owe me a thing, but I'm glad you think it is useful. Keep me posted. I expect that by the time I return that little hardware store is going to be the hottest place in the city to buy a hammer. I really think you'll turn it around. I wouldn't know a washer from a nut, I do not come from a handy people, the joke around my family was always that we liked to make sure that the local handymen really earned their keep, so anytime there was a small problem, we would turn it into a big problem trying to fix it ourselves, so that when the trained professionals came, it was really worth their while!

Jake

This is a relief; if he isn't handy, he'll have no need to try and support my "uncle's" store with his business.

Jake—

We all have different skills. Luckily I don't need you for home repair advice. Now go finish packing! And safe safe travels.

Sunny

- - - - - - - - - - - - - -

Sunny—

Thank you. I'll send a report from Merry Olde England when I can.

Jake

I'm suddenly pumped with energy and ready to really kick it into high gear to help Herman. I feel like I got a halftime pep talk from Ditka himself, and my heart says that the efforts we are making are worth it, the choice to stay and fight is right. For the first time since I can't remember when, I feel strong and confident. The way I used to. And it feels really, really good.

The Bachelor and the Bobby-Soxer
(1947)

You know I'd die for you, only sometimes it's so hard living with you.
• MYRNA LOY AS MARGARET TURNER •

I'm just filling the last of the tart shells with pistachio pastry cream when Herman floats into the kitchen. After my rah-rah email session with Jake, I realized that if we are going to survive, we have to find the magic eureka moment, that Cronut® thing, that totally perfect, drive-the-foodies-insane item that will keep our doors open beyond Halloween. We either need a single genius item that people will line up for or a generic basic thing that everyone in the neighborhood will want to come grab every single day. Now if only I knew what that was.

"Good morning, sweet girl. What are you working on there?" he asks as I top each tart with a flower of sliced fresh figs.

"Fig tarts with pistachio cream."

"That sounds wonderful. I do love figs." He reaches over and pops one of my unsliced figs into his mouth whole. I swat at him with my side towel.

"Cut that out!"

He giggles like a little boy. I swear the man has gotten younger these past weeks. There is practically a skip in his step, and he is smiling all the time. I consider that perhaps dementia is beginning to set in; after all, business is decent, but still not anywhere near compete-with-Cake-Goddess great. Then again, if I knew the actual date of my death, I wonder if I wouldn't just find as much joy as I could between now and then. For sure I'd eat more pie.

"Okay, you look like the canary that swallowed the cat. What gives?"

"My dear, your talents are about to be tested. Your *real* talents, the ones that have languished since your arrival."

"Herman, did you get into the schnapps this morning?"

"No, my dear, although that is a good idea! We should drink a toast!"

"*Herman!* We are not drinking schnapps at six thirty in the morning. What on earth is going on with you?"

"Oh, just this." He slides an envelope over to me. The return address is from the French Pastry School of Chicago. Inside is a letter.

Dear Mr. Langer—

We are delighted to inform you that your application to compete in the first annual Chicago Cake Competition has been accepted. Your team will be one of just five local teams who will be joining us for this exciting event benefitting our scholarship foundation.

Your information packet will arrive next week with all of the information you need, but for the time being, we would like for you to save the weekend of September 19th. There will be a VIP cocktail kickoff reception on Friday night with

all of the teams; the competition will take place on Saturday,
with a celebration dinner Saturday night.

Congratulations again, there were over 100 teams apply-
ing for this competition, and we are thrilled that you are one
of the lucky five!

Look forward to seeing you in September,
Jacquy Pfeiffer and Sebastien Canonne
Co-Founders French Pastry School of Chicago

My stomach sinks. "Herman. What did you do?"

"We're competing! A citywide competition, best cake maker in Chicago! When we win, there will be wonderful press, and we will get lots of new customers. I saw the application on the book of faces when I was looking at our page, so I applied for us."

"Herman, this is insane. How on earth could we possibly compete at this level?" This is crazypants. Any cake competition run by my alma mater is going to be much more like a world pastry competition than some Food Network special.

"Sophie, my pet, you are one of the finest pastry chefs in the city of Chicago; just because you're currently making more cookies than croquembouches doesn't change that. You *can* compete at this level, and more importantly, you *should* be competing at this level." He comes around and reaches up to take my face in his strong, warm hands. "If we win, maybe I stay open. But even if we lose, when you compete, your options will blow right open."

And I suddenly realize that he did this for me, not for himself. All of this, keeping the bakery fighting, pushing back, this is all for me. Which I really should have known in my heart of hearts. He believes in me. And now there's no way I can let him down.

"Old man, you'll be the death of me. Do you have any idea what we will be expected to do?"

"Not yet. But I think it is just a cake, one cake, that we make together."

Little does he know. That cake, whatever it is, will have to adhere to a theme, will have restrictions about what components can be included, will probably require chocolate work at the minimum and, god forbid, sugar work at the maximum. I count on my fingers. We have precisely seven weeks till this debacle goes down. Last time Georg and I entered a competition together, we practiced for four months. But we won. We did win. So weirder things could happen.

"Herman, you're an insane person, but I'll follow you anywhere. Promise me you'll tell me the moment the information packet arrives?" I wish I could thank Jake. Before our conversation, the idea of going anywhere near a competition like this would have been off the table. But something about his simple belief in me, though he doesn't even know me, is giving me a bit of gumption.

"I promise," he says, reaching over and grabbing a fig tart.

"Hey, that's not glazed yet!"

He grins and takes a huge bite. "But it's already delicious!" He mumbles around a mouthful of crust crumbs and cream, and heads out to open the doors for the seven a.m. on-the-way-to-work crowd. I turn to grab the warm glaze I've made by straining melted fig jam, focus on applying a thin layer to seal in the freshness of the figs, and try very hard not to think at all about what it will mean to be at Herman's side for this competition.

⁓

"I think it's terrific, sweetheart. What a wonderful thing for the two of you to do together," my mom says, when I return her calls from earlier. I spent the whole day baking ahead for the weekend; weekdays are still slow enough that I can stockpile the walk-in with prepped batters and doughs and components to keep up with the weekend crowds. Herman managed up front, except when he went upstairs for his lunch, at which point I ignored no fewer than six calls from my mother, who has taken the overseeing of the renovation of their new loft and the planning of their wedding as a unique opportunity to go completely off the rails.

"Thanks. It makes him happy, and considering we're just three months off from the big Cake Goddess opening, anything I can do to keep him happy is sort of my duty."

"You're a good egg, Miss Sophie."

"I come by that right. So, sorry for missing all the calls today. Lay it on me; what do we have to decide?"

"I'm thinking about Café Brauer."

"For what?"

"For the wedding."

I gulp. "Mom, that is a *very* expensive venue. And it is really designed for big weddings, like two hundred and fifty to three hundred."

"Well, the list is getting a bit bigger . . . After all, we're only doing this once, and there are all of our colleagues and clients to consider."

Oy, no wonder my dad is emailing Wedding Girl. She's gone completely off her nut.

"Mom, you aren't really going to want clients at the wedding, you know? Don't you want separation of church and state for this thing? Isn't that some sort of breach of ethics or something?"

"They're people, Sophie; they may not be sophisticated, fancy people, but they certainly don't deserve to be left out. I thought it would be a very nice thing to include them."

"Okay, but since they are not sophisticated, fancy people, why would you want to do a sophisticated, fancy party? If you want to include them, and no one will disbar Dad or take your license for doing it, why not a simpler event? Besides, I thought something small and intimate and casual was what you and Dad were talking about?"

"One would think that *you* of *all people* would appreciate this, Sophie. Weren't all these sorts of special and expensive touches exactly what you couldn't live without when you planned *your* wedding?"

I take a deep breath. "Yep, and look how that turned out."

"That's not funny, Sophie."

"No, it certainly isn't. Is Dad on board with any of this? It sounds like not at all his style."

"He said as long as at the end we say 'I do' to each other, the rest is whatever I want, just tell him where to be and what to wear."

Way to take my advice, Dad; not only has he not reached out to me for help, but clearly he hasn't done anything to even gently try to rein her in. "That sounds like Dad. But this doesn't sound like you."

"I know you like to think of me as some barefoot peasant in a field, young lady, but I will have you know that I am just as entitled to an elegant, sophisticated event as any woman." It sounds like she is convincing herself as much as she is convincing me, and I wonder what pressure she may have gotten from her family about getting married back in the day. It's almost like the minute she embraced the conventionality of actually getting married, she began reverting to the conservative upbringing that she always has rebelled against. Like some sort of weird muscle memory. But suspecting this doesn't make her behavior less annoying.

"I don't disagree; you are absolutely entitled to all the elegance

and sophistication you want, but then again, I return to not inviting a couple hundred juvenile delinquents and low-level criminals
to the event."

"You're the worst kind of snob, Sophie Bernstein; if you
didn't have my nose, I'd wonder if there was a mix-up at the
hospital." And then, she hangs up.

She hung up on me. On purpose. Holy shit. I'm so stunned I
don't know what to do. I just sit staring at the phone. Then it
rings, and the caller ID is my parents' house. I pick it up, expecting to hear my mom apologizing, but instead it is my dad, hiss-
ing into the phone.

"What did you say to your mother? She's throwing books
into boxes over here with a force that makes a tsunami look
tame."

"I just suggested that perhaps a smaller event at a less
expensive venue might be a good idea for the wedding, and that
inviting all of your combined current clients might not be the
best idea, and she questioned my parentage."

My dad sighs deeply. "Sophie, what do I do? She's going nuts.
She has lists upon lists all over the house; she's met with a dozen
different photographers, none of whom are good enough. I came
home the other day and heard her yelling on the phone to someone about letterpress invitations. I hate to say it, but it's like her
mother's ghost is doing a demonic possession."

"Did you tell her you don't want any of this? Ask her to
reconsider?"

"Of course not! I'm not insane, Sunshine. I don't want her to
stab me in my sleep."

I giggle. "Dad, you have to be honest with her." I hear some
slamming sounds in the background. "But maybe tomorrow?"

"I love you, kiddo. But if you don't hear from me by tomorrow night, send in the National Guard."

"Will do. Tell her I love her, and that I'm sorry and I'd love to have lunch or something with her this week to talk face-to-face about the wedding stuff."

"Okay, honey. How's Bubbles?"

"You know your mother; she's out on the town for the third night this week. I think at Theater on the Lake this time."

"She always was the social butterfly; it makes me happy she hasn't had to give up that part of her life. So she's doing okay?"

"She's great, Dad; she's doing great."

"It means the world to all of us that you are there with her, you know, but don't feel like it has to be forever. You're doing really well, and when you're ready to be back in your own place, don't worry about leaving her. We'll have it all taken care of, and your little nest egg will be ready for you."

"Thanks, Dad, but for now, there's nowhere else I'd rather be."

"Okay, good." More slamming noises. "I have to go."

"Don't poke the bear."

"I won't. Love you."

My poor dad. I can't imagine what is going on with my mom, and I wish Bubbles were here to talk it through with me. Plus it is a little embarrassing that her social life is so much better than mine. Ruth is out of town for some sort of conference; Jean is on lockdown with her new show and has been avoiding contact since breaking up with Hanna upon their return from Connecticut. Apparently, after the birthday party, Jean tried to go with the flow, but on their trip Hanna pouted more and more every day, and then confessed on the plane ride home that she had thought the trip was for getting engaged, and when no ring appeared, it made her angry. Jean, thank goodness, could smell the crazy, and said she thought they were moving fast even for lesbians and should take a little break. Then she changed her locks. I tried to get her to come over tonight, but she is working on drawings for a design presentation next week. Amelia and Brian are on their honeymoon in Southeast Asia, and Bubbles is either moonlighting as a stripper or definitely has a gentleman caller, because she is out and about every other night, getting home later and later. But she still chats openly with my grandfather's spirit, so I'm not going to quiz her on it. When she is ready, if ever, she will tell me who is squiring her about town. After all, who would I be to judge about keeping a secret or two?

I make myself dinner and watch the *Kings of Pastry* documentary on Netflix, figuring I had better start boning up on some of my competition knowledge if Herman and I are actually going to not make idiots of ourselves.

After the movie, feeling even more certain of our embarrassment than before, I head upstairs to answer some Wedding Girl emails, and there is a note from Jake.

Sunny—

Cheerio and tiddly pip! I'm here in the land of rain and chill, and have just eaten my fifth dinner in a row with roasted meats and Yorkshire pudding. I believe these people think gravy is a beverage. I've settled in a bit to work, and while there is quite the mountain to climb over here, I can see the path pretty clearly, so I'm tentatively optimistic that I'll be able to do what my company needs me to within the three month time frame. I'm not sure my liver will last that long, and I may be about to set a landspeed record for fastest cholesterol jump, but what can one do?

How are things over there in the colonies? I'm dying for news.

Jake

Jake—

You're certainly up early, is it the jet lag, or are you a morning person? Glad things are off to a good start. Here's the best story I can think to share . . .

I write the *Reader's Digest* condensed version of the surprise party debacle, which is a story that just gets better the more you tell it, and then tell him about the subsequent breakup.

Sunny—

Jet lag for sure, I'm not much of a morning person as a rule. And I'm assuming you aren't either?

That is the funniest, scariest surprise party I ever heard of. Thank god your friend broke up with the crazy lady. Did she do it on the plane?

Jake

- - - - - - - - - - - - - -

Jake—

Nope. In the cab on the way back from the airport. And no, not a morning person.

Sunny

- - - - - - - - - - - - - -

S—

Oh, that is fantastic! You have to promise to tell me the unabridged version of that story when I'm back. I bet you are leaving out tons of juicy details.

J

I have to say that it does make me feel a bit warm and fuzzy
for him to mention our future date so offhand.

J—

Yes, well, we shall see if you are worthy of such a wonderful
story. You might have to earn it a bit.

S

This is about the most blatant flirting I've done, and I hope
it lands okay.

S—

Duly noted. How's your uncle doing at the store, things okay
there?

J

- - - - - - - - - - - - - -

J—

He's good, thanks for asking. Things have been picking
up a little bit, some of our efforts seem to be bearing fruit,
I don't know if we can save it, but we're giving it the old college try.

S

- - - - - - - - - - - - - -

S—

Good for you! That's the spirit. Anything fun in the world of
wedding advice?

J

J—

Nope just the usual stuff, family disasters, too many people RSVPing yes, stretching budgets, why are flowers so expensive, the basics.

S

- - - - - - - - - - - - -

S—

So I'm still your best and favorite client.

J

I laugh.

J—

Well, so far. But it's early yet.

S

- - - - - - - - - - - - -

S—

Ouch. Well on that note, I have to get ready to go to work, and by my clock you should be off to sleep soon. Goodnight.

J

- - - - - - - - - - - - -

J—

And good morning ☺ Have a good day at work and try to eat some vegetables!

S

I hear the door downstairs unlock and look over at the clock. It is after eleven. I head downstairs and catch Bubbles attaching Snatch's leash.

"Hello, dear. I hope I didn't wake you."

"Of course not. You taking the dog out?"

"Just a quick walkies; it's a beautiful night."

"Want me to join you?"

"I'd love it."

I slip into my work clogs, which are by the door, and grab my keys. We head out and the night is indeed beautiful—warm but not humid, and with enough of a breeze to keep things moving. We walk down the block, letting the dog snuffle his way and stop to pee on every tree.

"How was your evening?" I ask, trying to be conversational but not prying.

"Lovely; thank you for asking. How was yours?"

"Eventful." I fill her in on my parents.

She laughs. "Give your mother a break. Can you imagine the upheaval? In one fell swoop she is giving up the home she's been in for over four decades, trying to figure out how to make a new place feel like home and function for her future, and planning a wedding that she never ever expected to be planning. And all of this while you are still seeking your own balance."

"What do I have to do with it?"

"Sweet girl. A parent is only as happy as their unhappiest child. And I don't mean to imply that you are unhappy; you seem to be heading in a very good direction. But your whole life exploded, and that is hard for all of us who love you to watch. You've given up on your old dreams without really appearing to be pursuing new ones. So while your mother knows you aren't miserable, you aren't really quite happy yet, and until you are, she can't be. I think she thought the wedding would be something you could do together, but she doesn't know how to relate to you on those things. So on the one hand, she wants to do the kind of event you will be proud of, the kind you would want for her, but she also feels like a lot of her decisions lately go sort of against her personal politics, so she's battling with herself. Imagine, all these years of their 1960s sensibilities, the choices they've always made, and suddenly they're overnight millionaires and getting married to boot? And what is worse, they like it; they like the nice things, and the financial security, and I think they even like the conventional parts of it. And that must be very scary for your poor mom to swallow, to face about herself. Plus, I don't need to tell you, she's at a complicated and difficult age, hormonally speaking, which I'm sure is exacerbating the whole megillah."

I hadn't thought of any of this. "Aren't you the insightful one? So how do I handle it?"

"Be kind, have a sense of humor, and at the end of the day, use all of these plans as a way to let her in. Share with her where you are in your life; confess some of your fears. Let her go into mommy mode a bit."

I reach over and link my arm through hers. "You are very wise, my bubbly Bubbles. Thank you."

"That's what grandmothers are for. That and good snacks. Speaking of which, what do we have in the kitchen? I confess to being somewhat peckish. This night air does it."

"Hmm. Carbonara?" There is nothing more soul satisfying at the end of a long night than a pan of creamy, salty, bacony pasta.

"Just the thing. Oh, Snatch." She looks down at the dog, who is happily rolling in a patch of dirt. He gets up, shakes his girth, and dust flies everywhere, making him sneeze four times in quick succession.

"He's quite the dog, isn't he?"

"Don't knock it; every girl should have a dog. It's good for us."

"Yeah, well, I always wanted one, but with my career? Not good for having pets."

"Oh, honey. That is an enormous load of bullshit. Your career—whatever it was, is, or will be—will have room for a man, children, dogs, whatever you choose. And if you claim otherwise, you are lying to yourself."

"Careful, old woman. If you get too sassy, I'm going to put extra black pepper in the carbonara." Bubbles is not a fan of black pepper, and I use it very judiciously where she is concerned.

"I surrender," she says as we climb the stoop.

And the three of us head towards the kitchen, where everything is easily controlled.

Without Love

(1945)

You never want love in your life again, and I never want it in mine. But our reasons are as different as the sun is from the moon. You don't want it because you've had all the worst of it. I don't want it because I've had all the best.

* KATHARINE HEPBURN AS JAMIE ROWAN *

I reread the sheet for the eleventh time, while eating cold leftover lasagna for breakfast.

2016 CHICAGO CAKE COMPETITION INFORMATION

Cakes are to reach a minimum of four feet in height with a minimum of three tiers. Internal dowels are allowed for tiers, but cakes should be a minimum of 95% edible. These cakes will be served to the crowds post-judging.

Cakes should have a strong Chicago theme visually.

Cakes must have a minimum of three different flavor profiles represented, one of which must be chocolate. At least one tier must incorporate a dacquoise component. Decoration can incorporate fondant, gum paste, chocolate, and sugar work, all decoration must be edible. There are no specific requirements regarding the use of these techniques, but the scorecards add points for number of techniques executed well.

Judging criteria are as follows, a full sheet of judging points to be earned is attached.

Taste: 50%

Chicago Theme and Visual Impact: 20%

Execution: 15%

Technique: 15%

Judges will be judging the actual display cakes; you will not be able to make smaller versions for the taste category. We are looking to promote your large-scale event cake work, so it is that cake that will be tasted.

Cake layers, dacquoise layers, fillings, buttercream, and pre-colored base fondant may be prepared ahead of time and delivered to the venue. All assembly and decoration work must happen on site, including the modeling of any figures, all sugar and chocolate work, and fondant rolling. A list of equipment that each team will have at their disposal is attached, if there is other specialty equipment you require, it must get pre-approved by the committee. You will have six hours to assemble and decorate your cake, during which time you will also have press and photographers coming by, as well as members of the public. These people will know that they are not to speak to you or ask questions.

Judges will also be coming around, and they do have leeway to ask questions, taste components, and observe your working style.

Your team can consist of one lead baker and one assistant. You are allowed to take two 30-minute breaks for meals and rest; your team members can decide if they want to take their breaks together or separately.

If you have any questions that are not answered here,

or in the attachments, don't hesitate to reach out to us! We'll be in touch closer to the competition date to arrange for delivery of prep items and other details.

It's not as bad as it could have been. Clearly they have learned that the public doesn't want to watch people mix batter and wait for cakes to cool, so the amount of prep that can be done ahead is really fantastic and allows for great quality control. That just means that the focus the day of is all about assembly and decoration, which is the fussiest work. I'm not worried about our flavors; I know we can knock the delicious part out of the park. But we have to figure out a great theme and execute well. I'm really worried about Herman and his endurance for such a physically demanding day. I don't see us doing much sugar work—too time-consuming and complicated—but I do think we can do some interesting things with chocolate and fondant and gum paste, once we have the right design.

The design will be everything, and I haven't the foggiest clue what we should do. I need to knead something. Bread work, the act of bringing together the dough under my hands, is like meditation for me. I think about what ingredients I have in the house; I don't want to have to go out and get anything. I've been unsuccessfully trying so hard to find that one amazing thing for the bakery, but I've hit a wall. I've given up on finding the next hot hybrid; the world doesn't need more cruffins or sconssants or any other Frankenpastry. The world needs something simple, comforting, versatile, and addictive. The kind of thing that never goes stale, because it never lasts long enough. The kind of thing that you buy two of, because you'll eat half of the first one in the car on the way home.

And then it hits me like a bolt.

Milk bread.

Dexter and I went to Charlotte a couple of years ago for their Wine & Food Weekend. Turned out to be our last trip together. But it was a good one. We snuck off to eat dinner at a brand-new place in Davidson called Kindred. As soon as we sat at the table, they brought over an enameled metal bowl, which had four huge rolls baked into it, golden brown and glistening, sprinkled with large shards of crunchy salt. It turned out to be milk bread, a simple yeast bread of Japanese origin, which has a tender and elastic crumb, a soft crust, and a slightly sweet flavor. We demolished the whole thing in minutes. After our dinner, we introduced ourselves to the team, and I got chatting with the pastry chef, bonding the way we do. We traded info; doing the usual dance about reaching out if either of us were in the other's city, yadda yadda. We haven't stayed in touch.

I grab my phone and check my contacts. There she is, Stephanie Detweiler, pastry chef at Kindred. I hit Dial.

"Hello, this is Stephanie."

"Stephanie, not sure if you remember me. This is Sophie Bernstein; we met last year. I used to be at Salé et Sucré in Chicago."

"Jesus, Sophie, of course I remember you. You poor thing. I totally wanted to reach out after that whole thing; it was just so shitty what happened. But . . . you know."

"That is very sweet of you. Ancient history and a large bullet dodged."

"Good for you! Are you coming to town? I'd love to see you again!"

"I'm not, at least not soon, but I was wondering if I could ask a massive favor."

"Of course, what do you need?"

I explain, best as I can, about Herman and Langer's and Cake Goddess and the whole debacle. I tell her that I'm trying to find that one specialty item that no one else has, to try and keep the doors open. And that I thought milk bread was just the ticket, but that I didn't have time to do all the recipe testing to make my own version and wanted to just steal hers wholesale.

"We'll call it Stephanie's Kindred Milk Bread; and on all of our social media stuff, we will link to you guys and say that if people are going to Charlotte, this is just a small taste of what they will find at your place. I know it's a long shot, but I figure since we are so far away, it isn't direct competition, and we can promote you while totally using your recipe for our own gain. I want to start with your plain version, and then do some daily variations so that people keep coming in to see the different versions."

There is a pause, and for a moment I think that I'm about to spend long hours trying to reinvent the wheel. "I love it."

"You do?"

"Sure. Look, it's not like I invented milk bread, after all. Just tweaked a recipe till I liked it. And we published the home version of the recipe a while back in *Bon Appétit*. It's not hard; you'd have figured it out really quickly. But I'm happy to share the large-batch recipe we are using. I love what you're doing there. There was a bakery like that in my hometown, probably the reason I do what I do, so if I can help you try and save one? I'm in. Is your email the same?"

"It is."

"It's coming your way. My batch makes a dozen of those four-roll pans, which are about the equivalent of one small loaf per. But it multiplies up pretty easily."

"You're a lifesaver."

"I'm touched and honored, and I hope it does what you want it to do."

"Thanks so much. If there is anything you ever need from me, you've got it!"

"All I want is that you have to keep me updated on the variations. I want to know what you do with it!"

"Of course!"

"Oh, and to be honest, I could really use a great recipe for chocolate babka."

I laugh. "I've got just the thing. You'll love it. When I get your email, I'll attach it to the reply."

"Perfect. And, Sophie, I'm really glad you called, and I'm really glad you're doing okay. Keep in touch."

"Will do. And thank you again; it means the world."

"Hey, us baking girls have to stick together!"

I finish the last bite of lasagna and drop my plate into the dishwasher, then run upstairs to check my computer. I scroll past dozens of new Wedding Girl emails, and there it is, subject line "Milk Bread." I read over the recipe. It really is simple. A basic yeast dough enriched with heavy cream and butter, an egg, some honey, and an interesting combination of cake flour and bread flour. Even better, it does a one-hour initial proof, then kneading and forming, and then a second proof before baking. Which makes it perfect for something you have to bake every day, unlike some of our other breads, which require two full risings before forming. It's the kind of recipe Herman can manage easily on his own if need be, which is also important. And the soft, sweet dough should lend itself beautifully to additions like dried fruits, so if Herman supports the idea, we can hopefully get people addicted to the original, and then after the cake competition we can roll out a daily new variation, just so people don't get bored.

I reply to the email, attaching the chocolate babka recipe, and tell Stephanie again how much I really appreciate her generosity. Then I check my watch. I have about an hour before I have to go to the bakery, so I figure I should work on some Wedding Girl emails while I can. I get through half a dozen before I see it.

Dear Wedding Girl—

I keep seeing your site when researching my wedding online, and so I thought I would reach out for some advice. I'm having some problems with my wedding planning, and I hope you can help. I'm in my early sixties and about to marry the man I've been with for over forty years. The problem is that our only child, my daughter, seems to disagree with many of my ideas. I am trying to be very understanding about her attitudes. We have very different styles and aesthetics, and it is difficult to find common ground. When I try and suggest things I think are more in line with her likes, she is dismissive of them as incongruous with her perception of who I am. And I'm afraid to even broach certain ideas, since I know that while she loves us, the lifestyle her dad and I have always chosen is at odds with her own desires. As much as I'm tempted to just bag the whole thing and elope, there is a part of me that really does want to mark this new chapter of my life with a wonderful memorable event. But not to the detriment of my relationship with her. Any advice on how to bridge the gap?

First time bride, longtime mom

For the love of all that is holy. It is bad enough that I have to even do this whole wedding advice thing. But with the money I've earned from it plus my dad's bonus check, I've been able to pay down nearly 15 percent of the principal on my stupid debt, so I do know that it's worth it. If only I could keep my freaking parents from writing in, it would be so much better. I close the email, not remotely in a place to think about how to answer her, and print out the milk bread recipe. I grab it, along with my folder for the cake competition, and head for the bakery, where I can think about cookies and bread and other things that are far less stressful.

I'm just pulling the first batch of milk bread out of the oven when my cell phone pings. Instead of baking the bread as four roundish rolls in a deep round tin, I portioned it as four rectangular mini-loaves in a rectangular dish. They are the perfect size for one large roll for dinner or breakfast, but still usable for sandwiches if someone was so inclined. Like Stephanie, I did a light egg wash and then sprinkled them with flaky sea salt crystals, so the tops are burnished and shiny. I put the pans on racks to cool, and grab my phone out of my pocket. I have a text from Amelia.

> Brian and I are back, having dinner tonight with pal from college who recently moved to town, and would love to know more locals besides the two of us. I know it's last minute but are you available? Would love to have you join us. Just going for casual Italian over at Buona Terra. 8pm?

The bakery closes at seven, so I should have time to go home quickly to change, and I know that Bubbles is attending the symphony tonight. Plus I love that Amelia is so kind; I know if I moved here and didn't know many people, I would totally want what few friends I did have to introduce me to their circle. I'm really flattered she would think of me, and even though part of me feels like I should go home and knock out Wedding Girl replies, I didn't have any red exclamation points in the inbox. And if I do answer emails, I'll have to think about how to

reply to my mother, which is pretty much the last thing I want
to deal with, either online or in person. I'm just about to accept
the invite when my phone pings again.

Also, he's single and cute, so that can't hurt, right? ;)

Hell to the no. A fix-up double date? Out of the blue? With
less than an hour after work to pull myself together? Thank god
I hadn't finished typing my reply. I delete the part I had written
about meeting them there, and instead decline as politely as
I can.

So sorry, tonight not good. But thanks for thinking of me!
We'll make plans soon . . . Ruth wants to do a girls night to celebrate Jean's new freedom.

Looks like it's going to be the computer and me tonight after
all, but here's what I know: I'm in a far better headspace to deal
with my mother than with a date.

Damn, but worth a try. And I'm not giving up on this one, he's
a good guy, and I think you'll like him, so be prepared for my
cashing a rain check. Girls night sounds good. Talk soon.

Bless her little meddling heart.

Herman comes through the door to the kitchen, wiping his
hands on his apron. "What is that smell?"

I gesture to the pans cooling on the racks. "Milk bread.
Hopefully our new signature bring-them-in-by-the-hundreds,
can't-live-without-it offering."

"That's a lot of pressure on some rolls."

"Yep."

He peers at them over the tops of his glasses. He pokes one
gently. "May I?"

"They're still too hot. Give them fifteen minutes."

"Okay. How are we looking on the cake? Did you read the packet?"

"Yeah, I did. I think we'll be good; we just need to start with the theme. Did you have any ideas?"

"You know me. I want a cake to look like a cake."

"Well, then forget how you want it to look; how do you want it to represent us?"

"By being delicious!"

I laugh. "That's a given. But what are our best qualities? What are we trying to convey?"

He considers this for a moment. "I think it should just represent who we actually are. A neighborhood bakery, serving the people in our community, making simple things that are wonderful and bring joy to people."

"Okay. And how are we specifically Chicago?"

"Chicago is a city of neighborhoods. We aren't trying to be all things to all people; we just want to be good neighbors. What's more Chicago than that?"

"You make a good point. Now we just have to figure that out visually."

"I know you can do it!"

"Your faith is admirable." How on earth am I going to visually depict Chicago's neighborhood feel?

Herman reaches for a side towel and the nearest pan, which he flips over deftly, releasing the four conjoined rolls onto the rack. I'm delighted to see how easily they came out of the pan, and that they are golden and crusty on the bottoms. He pulls one roll off the set, releasing a cloud of steam. I can see how the interior stretches, little shreds pulling apart, very elastic and tender. That's a good sign. Herman breaks off a piece and blows on it gently before putting it in his mouth. And then his eyes close. He chews and swallows, and when he opens his eyes, they are moist with tears.

"My mother's bread," he says simply. I reach for a roll and pull off a bite, savoring the slight sweetness, the softness, the pop of salt on the top, and I know what he means. Whatever the recipe, the emotion behind this simple bread is home cooking; it's Thanksgiving, it's Sunday supper. It's the bread of our mothers and grandmothers and favorite aunts. It's home. I can feel my eyes well up a bit myself. Herman puts an arm around me, and we finish our rolls in damp silence.

I take a swig of my gin and tonic, and face the computer.

Dear First Time Bride—

Congratulations on your upcoming nuptials, and I'm sorry for the complications that it is presenting.

I think first and foremost, you should have the day YOU want. And you can't worry about whether your daughter thinks it is wonderful or awful, it isn't her day. The best advice I can give about weddings in general is that what other people think of you is none of your business. The only opinions that matter are yours and your husband to be. If you start planning a wedding based on public perception, or crowdsourcing details, you'll end up with an event that isn't you, and the memories won't be what you want them to be.

For starters, I will say what I say to any bride who isn't 25. Only put the people in the room who you love most, who you most want to witness you saying those vows. This is not the time for old acquaintances, casual colleagues, or everyone in the Rolodex. If you've waited this long to marry this man, you want the day to be about the two of you and the family and friends around you who are the most important to the life you've built together. That might be 20 people or it might be 200, but you should only fill the space with the people that mean the most. My rule of thumb is if it is someone you would pick up a phone and call directly to share important breaking news, good or bad, then they make the list.

As far as your daughter is concerned, I'd just tell her that you love her and that you would love for her to support you as you plan your wedding, in whatever way she feels comfortable. I think the clearer idea you have about the type of event you want, the easier it will be for everyone to communicate about it.

And there is nothing wrong with eloping if you and your fiancé decide it is the most "you." You can always just plan a simpler party to celebrate after!

Best of luck,
Wedding Girl

I say a little prayer that the elopement message sinks in. It would be a load off everyone's mind and, I think, the best thing they could do, but even if we are still going full-bore wedding, hopefully she'll tone it down a little bit. For all of our sanity's sake.

It Happened One Night

(1934)

I want to see what love looks like when it's trium-
phant. I haven't had a good laugh in a week.

• CLARK GABLE AS PETER WARNE •

S—

Tonight I ate something called Spotted Dick. And it was delicious. I'm now wondering if I may be questioning my whole
identity. I would give my left arm for a char dog or an Italian
beef. I find myself dreaming of the crispy almost burnt cheese
edges on a Pequod's pizza. How are things with the sassy old
lady?

J

I love when I get to wake up to his emails. He tends to shoot off
some little missive every third day or so. Just silly stuff usually, but
sometimes he goes a little deeper. And slowly I'm revealing myself,
as much as I can. I fessed up to living with my grandmother, but
just said I had made some bad decisions career-wise and real estate
investment—wise and was regrouping a bit. He was very kind and
supportive, said I was smart to get out from under the condo before
I ended up with something like a foreclosure or bankruptcy on my

record, and thinks it is sweet that I have such a close relationship with Bubbles. He assumes the Wedding Girl site is to build back up my savings and create a nest egg. I still have not been able to tell him my real name or job, or that I'm forty grand in debt on a wedding that didn't happen; he thinks I'm over at the hardware store helping good old Uncle Earl.

Considering his reaction to my being semi-unemployed and living with Bubbles, I probably should have just let the whole thing out, but it is still too tender, and now I like him too much to jeopardize it. I think it warrants a face-to-face conversation. I even thought briefly about suggesting Skype or FaceTime or one of those things, but then I tried it with Kenzie, my pal from culinary school who is doing a stage in Rome, and saw how I looked on the screen: pale, hair frizzed out. And the computer-camera angle does nothing for either of my current chins. Besides, our schedules are totally opposite. He is keeping insane hours at work, wanting the assignment to end sooner rather than later, and he spends at least half his week traveling to his company's holdings all over England. That and the time difference make anything but email a moot point. I'm at the bakery nearly round the clock, working up recipes for the competition cake after hours in addition to managing my usual load. I'm getting close to feeling good about the flavor combinations, which means I really need to amp it up in terms of the look. I still have no idea what our theme should be.

So when I saw his email this morning before I left for work, and read about how much he was missing some classic Chicago foods, it made me wonder.

J—

The old lady is a dynamo. I should have half her energy. I think a man who can order spotted dick without irony and enjoy it thoroughly does not have anything to worry about in terms of his, um, inclinations. ☺ But I do have a question for you. Since you are missing Chicago, if I were going to take a picture of something here, what do you think would be iconically Chicago, something that in one fell swoop would give you that sense of home that the city evokes in us?

S

While Herman went to some doctor's appointments, I spent the whole day at the bakery alone, playing with some new milk bread variations, dealing with just enough customers to keep me hopping. After closing, I stayed till nine doing prep for tomorrow, and with Jake's email in my head, I picked up a drippy Italian beef sandwich and fries from Al's and ate them in the den while watching the second half of *Lady with a Past*, which has one of my favorite movie lines ever:

"People who live in glass houses shouldn't live in glass houses."

"They don't make them like that anymore, Snatch," I say to the pup, giving him a belly rub. He wiggles in delight and then makes a little snorting noise. I've almost forgiven him for snarfing up the last quarter of my sandwich while I was in the bathroom. His stolen treat resulted in some truly horrific flatulence during the credits of the film, and a very scary deposit in the backyard, which I have every intention of letting Bubbles deal with when she gets home. When I go up to bed, I have a reply from Jake.

S—

This is going to maybe sound weird, I know most homesick guys would want a great picture of the skyline, or Navy Pier all lit up with the fireworks behind the ferris wheel, or a picture of the 1985 Super Bowl Bears or something like that. But I think if you were going to take a single picture to make me feel *home*, it would be a picture of one of those classic old graystone three flats, like in Logan Square or one of those turn of the century neighborhoods, you know the ones that have the Chicago flag proudly on the porch instead of the American flag, and a Cub's W sign in the window. Maybe on a block party day, where the old people are sitting on the stoop gossiping about the neighbors, and someone is grilling Vienna Beef five to the pounds on a Weber in the front yard. That's quintessential Chicago to me, you know?

But you can also send me a picture of a pizza. I'm not picky.

J

And just like that the lightning bolt goes off in my head.

J—

You don't know it, but you are a genius.

S

I jump up from my bed and strip off my sweats, pull on jeans and a T-shirt, and twist my hair into a more secure bun. It's so weird. Mark's birthday was last week and he was in California, and Herman asked me to help him freeze and ship a Pequod's pizza for him as a birthday treat. He also mentioned something about Mark going to an old friend's wedding a couple of weeks ago. If I didn't know better, I'd almost be tempted to think that Mark and Jake are one and the same. You know, if Mark weren't the total opposite of Jake in every possible way. It's kind of sad, really. Mark could be an actual decent human being with just a little effort. I make a mental note to suggest Jake do his own website of advice for guys to make them likeable.

I hop down the stairs, toss a treat to Snatch, and scribble a quick note to tell Bubbles that I'm at the bakery and not to worry when she gets home and finds me gone, and that I've already walked the dog. I head out into the muggy night and jump in my car. I drive two blocks over and three blocks up, and there it is. A house Bubbles and I have walked by a million times in my life. The house where Bubbles grew up.

She's a beauty, a three-story graystone, one of those typical limestone mini-castles that are all over our fair city, with a turret and a wide stone porch, a Juliet balcony on the second level, and a little red tile roof. I take my phone out and snap a bunch of pictures, hoping the homeowners don't catch me.

Then I get back in my car and head for the bakery. I unlock the door quiet as can be, reach up to silence the bells, and relock it behind me. I walk through the dark store and back into the kitchen. I turn on the lights and wince as the bright fluorescents blare to life, reflecting off the steel worktables and white tile walls. I grab the big drawing pad that Herman and I have been using to sketch out ideas, and start to do a rough line drawing of Bubbles's old house. Once I have the basic structure down, with some key features, I start adding details. The Chicago flag on the porch. That Cubs W sign hanging off the balcony railing, and a Chicago Bears logo in the little third-floor window. I give it a front yard, with a guy in a "Hawks Fans Don't Give a Puck" apron manning a Weber kettle grill, and a table off to the side filled with the toppings for classic Chicago hot dogs, just like Jake said. My pencil is flying over the page. I put in some stick figures on the front stoop. A tall black iron fence with an orange "No Parking/Block Party" sign tied to it. A bag toss game set up in the front yard. I start to laugh. It's perfect. A three-flat, so each level of the building will be its own tier. I can do some simple sugar work to make all the windows, and chocolate for the tile roof details. The people and other accessories can all be molded from fondant and gum paste and marzipan. We won't have to worry about it toppling over, since it is a huge, solid structure, but we'll have to get the look of the stone just right. I remember a technique I saw for brickwork, where you use slate tiles and a glue gun to actually make a template for rolling fondant into. You take the rough slate, make the brick pattern on it with the glue gun, and then make a silicone mold of the whole thing. Ends up with great texture, and you can roll fondant right over it and pull it off in large sheets. Much easier than trying to texturize flat sheets.

I start making a list of supplies I'll need for us to begin creating the molds and templates for the various components, when suddenly I hear a massive crash upstairs. My heart leaps into my throat. Herman!

I run from the kitchen into the store and grab the key to his secret door from its hiding place behind the counter. I unlock it and take the little rickety staircase two steps at a time, and open the door at the top of the stairs, into Herman's tidy little kitchen. I'm down the hall in a flash and into the bedroom, where I see something I will never be able to unsee.

Kneeling next to Herman, who is lying on the floor, is Bubbles, her hair a wild nest. She is putting a pillow under his head and murmuring to him in a soothing way.

And they are both exceptionally naked.

"The ambulance is on its way," I say to Bubbles once she is in Herman's bathrobe and he is covered with the afghan from the foot of the bed.

"Okay, he's conscious, and his breathing seems fine, so I'm going to get dressed."

"Are you okay?"

"Just a bit shaken, dear; that's all."

"Well, that's to be expected."

"Are you okay?"

"I'm, um, just . . . surprised."

"That makes three of us. Will you go downstairs and wait for the ambulance, honey?"

"Of course."

I head back down the stairs, relocking everything behind me, and go out the front door of the store just as the sirens approach. I meet the paramedics outside and lead them up the front stairs to Herman's apartment. Bubbles is fully dressed, re-coiffed, and Herman is magically wearing a velour tracksuit but is still on the floor. Figuring they don't need me to hear any more detail than I've seen, I wait in the living room while Bubbles explains what happened.

Bubbles and Herman. It is at once the cutest thing imaginable and the most horrifying. I hear the words "was on top" come out of my grandmother's mouth, and decide I cannot stay up here. I head back downstairs. A few neighbors have wandered out to see what is going on, but so far they are all keeping a respectful distance.

There are some loud clumping noises, and pretty soon the paramedics reappear, with Herman in a strange contraption that looks like a chair on a two-wheeler, Bubbles right behind.

"Honey, I'm going to ride with him; we're going to Swedish Covenant. They'll bring him into the emergency room." She hands me a slip of paper. "Can you please call Herman Jr. and have him meet us there?"

"Of course. I'll see you there." I head back into the store, into the kitchen, and dial the number.

"Hello?"

"Mark, it's Sophie."

"Sophie, what's up?"

"Are you in Chicago?"

"Yeah. Why?"

"Um, he's okay, but your dad is on his way to the Swedish Covenant hospital. I think he took a little fall."

"Oh god, is anything broken?"

"Not as far as I know, but he's in the ambulance, and I'm on my way there now, so, um, we'll be in the emergency room."

"I knew something like this would happen," he says in a tone that could either be worry or annoyance. I can't really tell which. Then he sighs. "I'm glad you were there. Thank you, Sophie; I'll be there as soon as I can."

I shut down the lights in the kitchen, and then grab a large box from up front and take it into the walk-in. I fill it with cookies and brownies, figuring everyone will need a little something to nibble on, and I'm a big believer of bribing doctors and nurses for attention. As I'm heading out, I grab a chocolate babka for good measure, and some of the paper plates and napkins and plastic flatware we keep under the counter. Then I lock up and head for the hospital.

By the time I get to the emergency room, Herman is already in a cubicle and Bubbles is at the front desk checking him in. I go to stand beside her as she hands over his insurance card and fills out paperwork.

She winks at me. "Schnookie, why don't you see if you can find us a quiet place to sit, and I'll be over as soon as all this is done?"

"Will do." I spot an empty corner with a couch and some chairs, and go to commandeer it. Bubbles comes over to join me.

"Quite the night, huh?" I say.

"Indeed. But it looks like he will be fine; they don't think it was a heart attack or anything serious like that."

"Thank goodness."

"Yes. Poor fellow. I'm glad you're here, but what on earth were you doing downstairs at this hour?"

"Had an idea for the competition cake and wanted to sketch it and make some notes and lists and things. I guess I don't have to ask what you were doing upstairs at this hour!"

She blushes. "He's mortified, you know? He's wanted to tell you for weeks. What a way for you to find out!"

"Why on earth would you keep it a secret? Did you think I wouldn't approve? I'm delighted for you both."

"It's complicated."

"Seriously?" How complicated could it be?

"Seriously."

"Because you both lost spouses you loved? Does it feel like cheating?"

"Goodness no, it's not that; it's just . . ."

"Bubbles, whatever it is, you know I won't judge you." I wonder if she felt guilty having a romantic life when I have none. Like it would be rubbing my nose in it or something.

She looks me dead in the eye. "Herman and I have been what I believe you kids call 'friends with benefits' for about the last couple of years. Only recently, he admitted that he wanted to explore taking it to a more serious place, and I realized that I too was feeling more for him than I had perhaps allowed myself to admit, but we didn't want to tell anyone until we were sure that we were fully compatible."

Holy shit. My grandmother and Herman were sex buddies.

I try and make my face impassive. "Well, that seems very smart. And do you think you are? Fully compatible, I mean?" I refuse to let this get weird for her.

She smiles. "I think we love each other. Which neither of us had really anticipated."

"I'm happy for you. You deserve that."

"So we do."

There is a warm breeze, and Mark comes flying into the emergency room, wearing jeans and a Chicago Cougars T-shirt. He spots us and comes over, greeting Bubbles with a respectful kiss on the cheek and nodding at me.

"How is he? Can I go in?" he asks.

"Give them some time; they are taking blood and other stuff. The doctor said that they would come out and get us when they were ready."

"But he's fine?"

"He got up from bed too fast, felt a little woozy, may have lost consciousness for a second. Took a fall. They are doing X-rays to be sure, but they don't think he has any broken bones. Looks like just bruising and maybe some things might be slightly out of alignment in his lower back; he's having pain there. But they know it wasn't a heart attack. They are pretty sure it was some sort of vaguevaso something or other, nothing scary, but obviously they will do all the tests for stroke, et cetera. But he was talking and joking with the nurses when I left him, and said he wasn't in terrible pain."

"You were both there?"

"I was upstairs with him. Sophie was downstairs in the store and heard the thump when he fell and came upstairs to help," she says, her face impassive, as if this is the most natural thing in the world. Which in a way, I suppose, it is.

Mark registers all of this information. "I see. Well then." There is the tiniest hint of a kind smile playing around the corners of his mouth. For some reason, I find this strangely endearing. It also makes me feel a little sheepish about some of my stronger opinions of him.

The doctor comes out and finds us in our corner. The long and short of it is that after the exertions of the evening, Herman just got out of bed too fast and fainted. When he went down, he gave himself a bit of a sprained knee, whiplash, a bruised shoulder where he landed on it, and some lower back spasms. They are going to keep him overnight for more tests, to completely rule out any other causes, but at the moment, all the crucial tests have come back negative for anything more frightening. He will need rest and probably some physical and occupational therapy for a bit, and he won't be able to do any heavy lifting for about a month while he heals up. The doctor says we can all go back to see him and keep him company while they wait for him to get admitted to a room.

"You go see your father, dear. We'll wait here till you're done," Bubbles says.

"Thank you. I'll be back," Mark says and follows the doctor back to the patient area.

"I thought I'd better let Herman do the serious talking on this one," Bubbles says.

"Probably best."

"What's in the box?"

I open it and slide it across the table to her. She looks inside and takes a huge brownie.

"Thank goodness. I'm ravenous!"

"I bet you are!" I say, and the two of us burst into laughter.

"So, the two of them are . . . ?" Mark asks me in the hallway. They got Herman into a room, and Bubbles is in there with him saying good night so I can take her home.

"Yep."

"For years, apparently?"

"So it would seem."

"Wow."

"Yeah."

"Sophie . . ."

"Yes?"

"I am really glad you were there; I mean, I know your grandmother is a very capable woman, but it does make me feel better that you were, you know . . ."

"I know. And look, I can manage the store while he's recovering, no worries. But I think we are going to have to drop out of the cake competition."

"You can't. You can't drop out. It'll kill him, and make him feel even worse."

"I can't do it alone. I certainly can't do it alone and run the whole store, and I don't know where I would begin to find help."

"What would you need? To do both, I mean."

I think about this. "In the immediate, I need an assistant for the cake competition, to do the planning and practicing and prep work with me. For the next couple of weeks, that would be it. But then, for the last two weeks before the competition, I would need someone to help at the store, a second baker and maybe even someone to run front of house while I work on final prep, and then to keep things going the actual weekend of competition."

"You've got it. So the assistant can be working with you after store hours and on Mondays when you're closed? And then more help full-time two weeks before the event to free you up completely?"

"That's right."

"When do you need the assistant by?"

I think. "I can get through this weekend but would need them for at least a few hours on Monday."

"Monday by three p.m. okay?"

"Of course."

"Someone will be there."

"Mark, that's . . ."

"Someone will be there."

I sort of hate that my first impulse is to decline. I would

dearly love not to have to do the competition, and I don't know why Mark's generous offer feels so irksome to me. I guess deep down I know he is just worried about his dad. I'd be inclined to be more tolerant of him if only he weren't such a pompous douche canoe all the time.

Bubbles comes out and says to me, "Herman wants to see you, honey."

I go into the room. Herman looks small there in the bed, all his big personality diminished.

"You aren't angry with me?" he asks.

I lean over and kiss his forehead. "Of course not, silly. I'm just so glad you didn't really damage yourself. You and my grandmother are going to have to stop going all Cirque du Bengay up there and be a little more careful." I wink at him, and he smirks.

"What can I say? She's a heck of a woman."

"Yes, she is. You're okay, really?"

"At the moment I'm full of drugs, but I know that the pain is coming. I'm mostly embarrassed."

"Don't be. And don't worry. I've got the store covered, and Mar . . . Herman Jr. is going to get me some help for the cake contest."

"He is?"

"He says he is."

"We still need an idea."

"I think we have one." I fill him in on my brainstorm, the reason I was even there at all tonight.

"I love it. And I especially love that it is Betty's old house for the inspiration. She'll be so happy about that."

"Yes, I think she will. You rest. Sounds like if you are a good boy, they'll release you tomorrow, and I'll come see you."

"Thank you, my dear. And thank you for your blessing; it means everything to me."

"She's been happier recently than I've ever seen her, so I think you are the one that needs thanking. Now you just have to heal quickly."

I head back out into the hall. "He's all yours," I say to Mark.

"Okay."

"You talk to him, but I think you'll agree it's best," Bubbles says to Mark.

"Only if you agree to my terms," he replies cryptically.

"That's between the two of you, dear. You work that out with him."

"She's a tough negotiator, this one," he says to me.

"I wouldn't cross her," I say.

"No. No, I wouldn't either. Thank you both again. I'll see you tomorrow. I'm going to stay here with him tonight, so I'll call in the morning when there is news."

Bubbles and I head for my car.

"What was all that about?"

"I want Herman to come recuperate at our house. We have the guest room all set up on the first floor right next to the bathroom with the walk-in shower, and there's just the five steps up and down at the front door. He shouldn't be doing those stairs at his apartment, and his shower is in the bathtub, which isn't ideal. They said something about a residential rehab facility, but that just seems horrible, especially since he doesn't need such an intense level of care. The home health people can come to the house for his therapies. How would you feel about that?"

"I think it sounds smart. And I hate the idea of him in one of those places. It is lovely of you to want to care for him."

"Mark says only if he can provide some help, cleaning services and other assistance, while Herman is in residence."

"That seems fair and will be welcome."

"You don't mind?"

I reach over and squeeze her hand. "Not at all."

She squeezes back. "Thank you."

I pause. "What are you going to tell my folks?"

"Crap," she says. "I haven't the foggiest. We'll have to figure that out."

"Yeah, that should be interesting."

We get in the car. "Eggs and pancakes?" she asks.

"It's nearly three in the morning," I say. "We'll also need sausage."

"Golden Nugget?" she says.

"On my way."

And we pull out into the night.

The Thin Man

(1934)

WILLIAM POWELL AS NICK CHARLES: Well, I do believe the little woman cares.

MYRNA LOY AS NORA CHARLES: I don't care! It's just that I'm used to you, that's all.

If you've never lived with a pair of octogenarians, let me tell you. It is alternately the most hilarious thing you've ever experienced and the most annoying thing you can imagine.

For starters, as savvy and sassy as they are for their age, Bubbles and Herman are still elderly. In the past three days I've had to explain the *vast* difference between a "butt dial" and a "booty call," I've discovered that without his hearing aids in, Herman's natural speaking voice is just shy of the decibel level of a 1972 Who concert, and I've learned about the private lives of the neighborhood biddies in excruciating detail. On the other hand, they are adorable; fully released into their public romance, they are sweet as can be, and both of them are glowing. If Herman weren't in a reasonable amount of pain, I'd be worried that there is some middle-of-the-night tiptoeing going on. Between the two of them and the fleet of nurses, assistants, cleaning ladies, and therapists who are in and out of the house like it's Union Station, what little time I have at home isn't exactly restful.

I'm trying to sneak a quiet breakfast in the Nook alone when I hear a long, resonant explosion of flatulence coming down the hall.

"Bubbles!"

"Oops. Didn't know you were about at this hour."

"Well, goodness, if I wasn't awake before, I'd certainly be up now to see if the house was coming down!"

She swats at me. "It's your fault. You should know better than to feed an old woman ratatouille."

I wave my hand over my nose. "Well, considering it's now like a monkey house in here, I'll make a note to never do that again!"

She curtseys. "Roses, my dear, my wind is like roses."

"Your wind is like hell itself has belched up six-day-old sausage and onions," says Herman, who has appeared in the kitchen with the help of his new rolling walker. "But in a good way, my love, in a good way!"

She puts her hands on her hips. "Careful, you old thing, or I'll be sure to come to *your* room the next time I'm feeling some pressure in my belly."

"Really? Do I have to listen to all of this?" Their banter isn't exactly William Powell and Myrna Loy, no matter how clever they think they are.

"No, dear, you most certainly do not," Bubbles says.

"Actually, I have an idea about that," Herman says, sitting across from me at the little table.

Bubbles puts on the coffeepot and slides some slices of bread into the toaster. "This is actually a good idea; you listen to Herman."

"I was thinking that all of this tumult around here with me and my entourage must be making your life insane. You have little enough downtime these days with the whole bakery on your shoulders, and goodness knows it will only get worse as you start prepping for the cake contest in earnest. So I thought, why don't you temporarily relocate to my apartment? You'll have peace and quiet. I converted Junior's old room to a very comfortable guest room a few years ago, and no one has ever used it! The bed has never even been slept in, and it has its own bathroom. You could have some privacy for a change, and you can't beat the commute!"

It never would have occurred to me; I haven't even thought about moving out of Bubbles's house at all, let alone now, let alone into Herman's apartment.

"Isn't he brilliant?" Bubbles says, sliding a cup of coffee and a plate with buttered toast in front of Herman.

"Just during my recovery, dear. Just till the contest is over and I'm back to my old self. What do you think? I know our company is fascinating . . ."

"And our wind is so delightful . . ." Bubbles adds.

"*Enough.* You people will be the death of me. Yes, thank you kindly, Herman. I shall take you up on your generous offer and house-sit for you while you are convalescing here." It'll be weird as hell to be in Herman's apartment, but the thought of some time on my own is too good to let me focus on the other parts. And I do like the idea of being able to just live my life for a bit without someone else witnessing my every move. Even though I spent many nights at Dexter's, I still really did live alone, and much as I love Bubbles, I do miss that solitude now and again.

"Good," Herman says.

"I'll pack a few things today and take them over when I go."

"But the bakery is closed today," Bubbles says.

"True, but I've got the week ahead to prep for, and my new assistant is arriving today at three to meet me and go over our plan for the cake contest."

"Do you know anything about them?" Bubbles asks Herman.

"Nope. Junior told me I wasn't to worry about anything except my recovery, and that he had everything in hand, and I'm letting him manage. But, my dear, if you meet this person and it isn't the right person, you need to say so, and we will find someone else." He waggles a finger at me.

I shake my head. "I'm sure it will be fine."

I leave the two of them to their breakfast and head upstairs to pack for the next part of my adventure. My phone rings. It's my dad.

"Hey, sweetheart," he whispers.

"Hi, Dad. Why are you whispering?"

"Your mother is here."

"So?"

"I'm hiding in my office."

"Why, pray tell?"

"She was crying in the bathroom, so I went to comfort her and asked why she was crying and she said she didn't know and I asked if it was about the house and she said no and I asked if it was about you and she said no and I asked if it was about the wedding and she stopped crying and got angry and said that there didn't need to be a reason for a woman to cry, she was just crying, but if I wanted to use her emotions as an excuse to back out of the wedding, she would really appreciate it if I would tell her as soon as possible before she writes any nonrefundable deposit checks. I assured her I would never back out of the wedding, and she said fine, then I should just let her have a healthy cry without trying to be all Mr. Fix It about it, so I left before I said anything else wrong, and now I'm hiding in my office."

"Jesus, Dad, has it ever been this bad before? I mean, I remember a couple weird meltdowns over the years. Was it just that I didn't see it?"

"Nope, it has never been this bad."

"Do you think you should . . . ?"

"Crap!" he interrupts me. "I hear footsteps. Gotta go." And then he hangs up.

❧

I let myself into Herman's place and drop my bags in the living room. It's clear that Herman's late wife, Rose, decorated the place and that he hasn't really changed a thing. There is a decidedly feminine feel to it. The sofa is a subtle floral; the pillows have fringe and tassels. I give him credit, though; Herman keeps it pretty impeccably clean. I go down the hallway, trying not to think about the other night and all that was witnessed, and head right instead of left at the end. The guest room is actually quite charming, with an old brass queen-sized bed covered in a handmade quilt, the kind that is silky soft from years of use and washing. There is a small desk, a tall dresser, and a little kidney-shaped settee. One door leads to a tiny closet, the other to the en suite bathroom, with a claw-foot tub and pedestal sink. I go get my bags and unpack quickly, putting work clothes and underwear in the dresser, toiletries in the bathroom, earplugs on the nightstand. I set my computer up in the den, where the television is, and log in to be sure the Wi-Fi is working. Thank goodness Herman is a modern man; he, like Bubbles, has a decent smart TV and fast Internet, so for the hour a day I am both awake and not working, I'll have entertainment, and I'll be able to hopefully not get too far behind on Wedding Girl emails.

A quick check of the kitchen and cupboards reveals for the first time that the place is inhabited by a bachelor of a certain age. Plenty of canned and frozen prepared foods, lots of cereals, most with a hefty bran component. The fridge is a wasteland of condiments, olives and pickles, plus a bag of desiccated baby carrots, some various sliced cheeses, and a couple of beers. With so much to do today, I'm not really up for a run to the store, so I log in to our Instacart account and place a grocery delivery order for some staples. Bubbles has got plenty of spunk, but errands like grocery shopping can sometimes take it out of her, so I taught her how to use the online delivery service, and she loves it. I've added my debit card as one of the payment options, so once I enter Herman's address, I've got groceries headed my way within the next two hours. I check my watch. It's just after eleven, so I have plenty of time to get everything sorted here and prep for meeting my new assistant downstairs at three.

Herman and I have been doing a lot of talking about the cake the past couple of days, and we think we have a good plan for the three tiers. The bottom tier will be the chocolate tier and incorporate the dacquoise component, since that will all provide a good strong structural base. We are doing an homage to the Frango mint, that classic Chicago chocolate that was originally produced at the Marshall Field's department store downtown. We're going to make a deep rich chocolate cake, which will be soaked in fresh-mint simple syrup. The dacquoise will be cocoa based with ground almonds for structure, and will be sandwiched between two layers of a bittersweet chocolate mint ganache, and the whole tier will be enrobed in a mint buttercream.

The second tier is an homage to Margie's Candies, an iconic local ice cream parlor famous for its massive sundaes, especially their banana splits. It will be one layer of vanilla cake and one of banana cake, smeared with a thin layer of caramelized pineapple jam and filled with fresh strawberry mousse. We'll cover it in chocolate ganache and then in sweet cream buttercream that will have chopped Luxardo cherries in it for the maraschino-cherry-on-top element.

The final layer will be a nod to our own neighborhood, pulling from the traditional flavors that make up classical Jewish baking. The cake will be a walnut cake with hints of cinnamon, and we will do a soaking syrup infused with a little bit of sweet sherry. A thin layer of the thick poppy seed filling we use in our rugelach and hamantaschen, and then a layer of honey-roasted whole apricots and vanilla pastry cream. This will get covered in vanilla buttercream.

We figure this gives us a chocolate layer, one that is fruit forward, and one that is more nut based, so something for everyone. The focus will be on getting the tiers, all of them rectangular and the same size, stacked on one another and then covered in the stonework fondant in a base color of gray. Gray is the hardest color to achieve with fondant—it can go blue or lavender really quickly—but I have a secret formula for it, so hopefully that will be fine. Once the thing is built, we'll go back and do shading and details with powdered food colors for depth and realism. All of the extra structural components attached to the building, like the porch, balcony, and roof detail, will be made of Rice Krispies treats and then covered in fondant. They're easy to cut into blocks and shapes, or mold free-form, and if you leave them uncovered, they firm up pretty well. And they are lightweight, so hopefully they won't fall off even when they're covered in fondant.

We'll do the tiles for the roof out of tuile cookie batter cooled on a special template to give them the form, and then will glue them on with chocolate. All of the carved stonework for the columns, the urn on the front staircase, and the detail work on the roof will be molded and carved chocolate sprayed with white chocolate colored gray. The windows will be panes of clear sugar mounted in chocolate window frames made to look like wood, the wooden front door will be composed of chocolate with sugar windows embedded, and the transom and sidelights will be made of designs baked in cookie dough and filled with colored sugar to create edible stained glass. And all of the other details, the people, etc., will be made of fondant or gum paste or marzipan.

It is a lot of very exacting work, and I really hope that whoever is coming today will have some artistic skills to offer. I'm really good at all the fussy bits, but I won't be able to manage it all alone, not in six hours. At the very least, I hope my new right hand can handle the big fondant sheeting work, and the roof tiles and structural details, so that I can deal with the small stuff, some of which will likely get screwed up and need to be redone.

I make a list of every individual component, determining which ones can be prepped ahead and delivered to the contest venue completed, and which will have to be managed on-site. I created a calendar of when each component can be made, working backwards from the contest to figure out what can be done when.

All of this is making me hungry, and my groceries are still at least an hour out. I go to the computer and log in to Philly's Best, order myself a large cheesesteak and onion rings, and then hunker down to deal with as many Wedding Girl emails as I possibly can before I have to go downstairs. I'm just eating the last onion ring when my groceries show up, and I stock Herman's fridge and cabinets with everything I'm going to need for the next few days. I still have over an hour before I have to be downstairs, and that claw-foot tub is calling my name. I run the water as hot as I will be able to stand it, and strip, grateful that this tub is deep and wide. The tub at Bubbles's is on the small side, and not really terrific for getting a good soaking. But this one is almost oversized, and when I get in, the water covers my shoulders, and I sink in gratefully. The quiet is amazing, and I realize I haven't really been alone like this since I moved into Bubbles's house.

This might need some tunes.

I have a killer 1980s playlist in my phone, and suddenly all I want is to be soaking in this lovely hot bath and singing along to some serious New Romantic pop music.

I get out of the tub, the cool air feeling amazing on my skin. I skip the towel and scamper out in my wet altogether to the living room to get my phone from the charger.

"Aaaaaaaaaaahhhhhhhhhhh!!!!!!!!!" I scream and fling myself behind the couch.

"Um, hi," says Mark.

An afghan comes flying over the top of the couch and lands on me. I awkwardly wrap it around myself and stand up.

"What. The. *Fuck*," I say. "Don't you *knock*? Or ring a bell? Or announce your presence when you come into a place? What are you doing here anyway?" The afghan feeling prickly against my damp skin.

"I had no idea anyone was here; my dad is at your house, and the store is closed today, and I was early, so I thought I should come upstairs and see what sort of state the place was in. What are *you* doing here?"

"Your dad said I should stay here while he is at my grandmother's place, since it is a little nuts over there."

"Oh, well, that makes a lot of sense, really," Mark says.

"Will you give me a moment? I'm going to go get dressed." I sidle out of the living room, and once I'm in the semi-protected space of the hallway, I run to the bathroom, pull the plug on the drain, and grab a towel to finish the job the afghan couldn't handle. I get dressed, throw my wet hair into a bun, and head back into the front room.

"Make yourself at home," I say, looking at Mark, who has one hand in my bag of Fritos and is eating a massive sandwich made with my freshly procured provisions.

He holds the bag out to me, and I wave it off.

"So, did you want to talk up here or downstairs?" he asks, plucking a piece of salami from the side of the sandwich and popping it in his mouth.

"About what?"

"About the contest."

Great. Now he's going to be all involved. Super. I check my watch; it's twenty to three. "The assistant won't be here for another twenty minutes. I think we should wait."

He grins at me, with a bit of mustard in the corner of his mouth. "The assistant is here."

"Downstairs?"

"Right here, baby." He winks at me and grins like a game show host.

This has got to be a nightmare. "You?"

"Yep. I have made arrangements to leave work early every Monday, and you can have me three other nights per week after the store closes, and I'm taking vacation time for the Thursday and Friday of the competition weekend. Will that be enough?"

My head is spinning. "But . . . you . . . can't . . ." I sputter. If I didn't have high blood pressure before, I do now. In fact, this might be sending me right into atrial fib.

He nods. "I thought you might feel that way. I brought my bona fides."

He gets up, walks over to the door, and picks something out of his briefcase. He comes back and hands me a couple of papers. I shuffle through them.

"You went to culinary school," I say.

He looks smug. "Yeah."

"At the freaking CIA."

"True."

I look back down. "You did the intensive pastry session at Ferrandi in Paris."

"Yup."

"You fucking staged with Jacques Torres."

"Uh-huh. And, you know, also with my dad, since, um, birth. Will I be good enough?" he says, sarcasm dripping with every word.

"I don't understand."

"What's that?"

"You have better credentials than I do. Why are you . . . ?"

His face changes from self-satisfied to resigned. "Not baking for a living? Because I never wanted it. None of it. I had shitty grades in high school; culinary school was an easy choice. There was a business waiting for me. I did what I was supposed to do, finished the program, went to Paris, did the course there, staged around, came home. Only took a month of working with my dad to realize I hadn't ever thought about whether it would make me happy. But I hated it. I figured I'd get used to it—it was just work; everyone has to work. It didn't occur to me it should be fun or fulfilling. And then Noah died. Added that whole 'life is short' element to my general discomfit. Dad said I didn't have to stay, I could go do the fine-dining thing, but that wasn't it. I have aptitude but no passion. Technique but no soul. I'm really good at the technical side, the problem solving, the chemistry and math of it, and I have a good palate. But it doesn't feed me. So I applied to business school, and they liked that my background was different, and let me in. And that was that."

I don't know what to say. "Your dad never mentioned it."

Mark shrugs. "I don't know if he feels more guilty that I went through all the baking rigmarole essentially for him, that those years were a bit lost and wasted for me, because I wanted to please him, or disappointed that I had all the right background and still couldn't love what he loves. It was a long time ago. We don't speak of it."

"But you are coming out of retirement for this?"

He looks me in the eye. "I'm a Langer. This may not be my dream, but it's my dad's whole life, and you and I both know that this is the last hurrah. I haven't been able to give him much, but this is something I can do, a gift I can offer. To help you make sure that Langer's goes down fighting."

For the tiniest moment, I can see Mark's heart in his eyes, and the love he has for Herman, and it touches me.

His voice becomes softer. "For what it's worth, Sophie, I know I've given you a hard time, and I still wish that things had gone differently, but I'm glad he has had these months with you, and I am grateful for all you've done."

"Thank you."

"So, want to take me through the game plan for this insane project?"

I nod. "Buckle up, buttercup."

Mark laughs, and we get down to work.

Made for Each Other

(1939)

LOUISE BEAVERS AS LILY THE COOK: Never let the seeds stop you from enjoying the watermelon.

CAROLE LOMBARD AS JANE MASON: That's alright if you've got a watermelon.

I don't know that I've ever been more exhausted. Life was tiring enough when I was full-time at the bakery and managing Wedding Girl responses. But with Herman gone and the whole business on my shoulders, plus cake practice four days a week, the Wedding Girl backlog getting bigger than I care to think about, and helping my parents deal with both their construction project and wedding planning? I'm hanging by a thread so thin that I'm beginning to worry I may not make it through the week, let alone the next month—three weeks till the cake contest.

My one saving grace has been Jake. We've fallen into a pretty solid routine: He still emails me every few days or so. Our communications remain fun and friendly: He might mention whatever new black-and-white movie he's watched, or the television shows he has turned me on to that I've been checking out on Netflix while answering Wedding Girl emails. Did I know that I would fall in love with totally modern and super-dark series? Nope. But I am now officially a *Luther/Justified/Sons of Anarchy* girl, thanks to Jake, and he is absolutely hooked on the old classic films. We still seem to be keeping information mostly limited to the surface stuff, which is fine by me. I've given up feeling guilty about the parts of my emails that are supporting the web of lies I've created around my identity, and I wonder if he, like me, wants to wait for some of the deeper stuff until we are face-to-face. I do feel like I know a bit about his morals, his ethics, the nature of his governing personal code. I trust his kindness, and his humor. We've hinted at exes, but just in a funny way, enough for us both to have the comfort of knowing that we've had serious relationships in the past and understand what that is about. Often we use the movies or TV shows to express bigger thoughts, keeping that safety net of the conversations being ostensibly about the media.

I really like him.

And for the first time, I sort of understand some of the courting that I've been watching my whole life in those old movies. The way they show pen pals falling madly in love having never met or seen each other. How you can really feel like you get to know someone in a deep and meaningful way, and can feel attracted to them without even knowing what they look like. I feel a bit at a loss on that end; after all, I have not a clue what Jake looks like. But in my heart? I feel weirdly half in love with him already, and I don't think I care a fig about his appearance. At this point, he could be half troll; if he can make me laugh in person the way he does with his emails, then I'm his.

At least Mark has turned out to be a great help, reluctant as I am to admit it. His skills, while a bit rusty for our first few sessions, are formidable, and we've broken down the cake duties pretty well. He is great at both structure and fondant work, so he will actually be able to assemble all the tiers of premade cakes and fillings, and do the doweling internal structure. We will stack them together for control, and then he will do a crumb coat over the whole thing, and we will get it into the walk-in to chill and firm up while he rolls out the fondant. I will be working on all of the bits and pieces, and he will be doing the bigger architectural details while the cake chills, and then I will help him apply the textured fondant to the building. I'll make the tuile tiles for the roof and do the sugar work while he gets the chocolate and Rice Krispies pieces assembled and attached, and then he will work on the shading for the stone and brick. Once the building is up, he can start installing the smaller pieces that I'm making, and we've created a priority order for those in case we run short on time. Building is most important, with the "landscaping" and Chicago-specific details next. Setting up the people and the activities in the front yard are last, since if we have to skip them, it will still look like a finished piece.

We've officially tweaked the recipes to death, and have three tiers that are ridiculously delicious. Tonight we brought samples over for Bubbles and Herman, and the four of us had a really nice dinner together. Bubbles made smothered skirt steaks with mushroom farfel and a green bean salad, and I supplied some of today's special milk bread rolls, the soft sweet dough rolled with thin slices of caramelized fennel and sprinkled with black sesame seeds. While Bubbles and I are cleaning up, Herman and Mark go into the other room for some sort of serious, hushed conversation.

"The cakes are wonderful, schnookie; you'll win on flavor alone," Bubbles says. She doesn't know we're doing her old house, just that we're doing a classic Chicago building. I really want it to be a surprise for her.

"You're a tiny bit biased, but I have to say, I do think they are really great, and I know we'll have a strong showing in that category. I just also know that the other competitors may be doing some slick things visually that will make ours look a bit homespun," I say, drying a serving bowl and putting it away.

"Don't knock homespun. All comfort food is homespun, and according to you and my cooking magazines, comfort food is the trend. You do what you do, do it as best you can, and if you don't win, at least you know you didn't compromise who you are in an effort to please someone else."

I kiss her temple. "Thank you."

She reaches up and plops a small bit of foam on the tip on my nose with a wink. "You're very welcome. How are your parents?"

"Getting worse by the day."

"I feared as much. We're all going to have breakfast tomorrow and hash this out before things get any worse. I'm the only living parent the two of them have left, and I'll be damned if I'm going to let them behave like idiots. You'll be here."

This is not a request. This is what we call in our family a "command performance."

"Of course. What time and what can I bring?" Tomorrow is Monday so the bakery is closed, and Mark isn't coming till late afternoon. I'd prefer to sleep in a tiny bit, but I'm also very curious to see how Bubbles handles my folks.

"Bring yourself and a chocolate babka for your mother. Nine o'clock. I'll take care of the rest."

Oy. That is much earlier than I would have hoped, but she did say breakfast and not brunch. "What about Herman?"

"Herman has follow-up doctor's appointments scheduled all morning."

At this point Mark and Herman reappear, cutting our conversation short. Herman takes over drying duties and shoos me out.

"Go home, Sophie; you've got to get plenty of rest." And tired as I am, I don't argue. Mark walks out with me.

"Everything okay with your dad?" I ask.

He pauses. "Yeah, actually, everything is really good. How about your grandmother?"

"I think she is feeling useful and happy. From all accounts, she was really good at the whole partner thing, at supporting my granddad. They apparently lived easily and well together, with lots of laughter, and I'm seeing that now with your dad, so that's really nice. It's a side of her I've never seen."

"Yeah. He and my mom were like that too. And you're right; I can see that energy in him again. He's really happy."

"Lucky for them both."

"Indeed. Now we just have to take their example!"

"I thought you were practically engaged?" Herman always refers to Mark's invisible girlfriend as "the one we hope gets away," but I've never met her and Mark doesn't mention her.

He waves the idea off like it is some mosquito annoying him. "Not even close. Dad tends not to believe that it is just a casual dating thing, I guess since I'm not seeing anyone here in Chicago. But it has never been a serious relationship. In fact, I'm working on an exit plan."

"An exit plan? As in, you don't want to be with her anymore, but you haven't told her yet?"

"It's complicated."

"Nothing is that complicated. If you are in it, and you shouldn't be, you ball up and have a difficult conversation, and everyone gets out with dignity."

"There are some moving pieces that need to be handled delicately."

"That smells like bullshit."

"Well, you'll forgive me if I point out that relationship advice might not actually be something you should be doling out." His tone is friendly, lighthearted and ball-busting, but it stings, especially since I'm headed home to do at least three hours of Wedding Girl responses.

"Maybe, but I know a little something about getting dumped,

and I can say definitively that a little honest conversation would have been most welcome."

"Fair enough." He pauses as I walk around my car to get in. "I'm sorry. I didn't mean to poke at you like that. It was unfair."

I shrug. I've given up trying to figure out what makes this man tick. "Whatever."

He walks over to my side of the car. "Not whatever. I was kidding, but it was rude. Forgive me?" Something in his face softens my heart.

"Okay."

"Nightcap?" he asks.

I look at my watch. I'd really rather just go home and work on email, but for some reason I feel like I have to say yes.

"Maybe just one."

"I know where my dad keeps the good single malt."

"Well, how can I say no to that?"

"I'll meet you there."

I'm not going to turn down a good scotch.

I open one eye and see that the room is lightening, and the clock, which conveniently projects the time onto the ceiling for easy viewing, says 4:47. I stretch a bit and look up. Mark is walking towards the bathroom, with one earplug stuck to his right buttock. I can feel myself blush deeply in the dark. The night, what I can remember, comes in flashes . . . There was scotch, and then more scotch. And some laughter and some cake. And then some photo albums and more laughing. And then more scotch. And then there was kissing and undressing, and there was the couch, and then the floor, and then the bed, and then dark.

I hear the toilet flush and the water running in the sink. I'm reasonably sure he is about to do a runner, for which I'm enormously

grateful, and now I have to make an important decision. Fake sleep, or say good-bye? Fake sleep is very tempting, since I'm completely mortified. I've just had sex with my boss's son. Three times. Really good sex. I'm still not even sure I like him as a person, but I do know I don't like him the way I like Jake, and I suddenly feel like a cheater, even though Jake and I aren't technically dating. I can't take the coward's way out; I have to face him.

The door opens, and Mark comes back out into the room. I try not to look at his nakedness as he approaches. He sits on the bed beside me.

"Morning," he says, without a hint of either regret or remorse.

"Morning."

"Here, you might want these." He hands me a pair of Tylenol and a large glass of water. I accept them gratefully and down the pills with the water, draining the glass.

"Thank you."

"So . . ."

"This was lovely and unexpected, Mark." I interrupt him before he can say anything that makes me feel worse than I already feel. "But I think we both know that it was more about the scotch and the circumstances than about either of us. You have to get your house in order, serious or not, and I obviously have some stuff I'm dealing with, so perhaps we can just chalk this up to one of those things that sometimes happens between friends, and let it be a nice memory." This comes out in a flood.

Mark pauses, as if he is mulling this over. "If that is what you think is best, then that seems smart." There is no discernible emotion in his voice.

"I mean, you do still have a girlfriend, or whatever, and I have someone in my life that I want to give a real shot to, and you and me are working together and have to be able to focus, and then there is the whole 'your dad, my grandmother' thing, and . . ."

"Sophie, I get it. It's fine. We're grown-ups. We had a nice

night together, and it doesn't have to mean more than that. No worries."

Whew. "So we're good?"

He smiles. "We're good."

"And we can just not talk about it?"

"Well, if you will stop talking about it, I can get dressed and leave, and then when I come back this afternoon we can very specifically not talk about it." He smirks.

I smack him on the shoulder. "Get dressed and go before it gets weirder."

"Well, I think if we're not going to talk about it, then you shouldn't watch me all naked."

"Such a delicate flower. Like if I see you naked, what? I'm just going to jump you all over again?"

"You might, if memory serves, and with good reason."

"Augh!" I throw the blanket over my head. I hear him moving around the room.

"Have to say, I never got to do that in here when I was growing up, so thanks for making an adolescent fantasy come true." His voice is muffled by the blanket.

"You're welcome," I say, not really sure how else to respond.

Suddenly the blanket is pulled away from my head.

"I'll see you at three thirty, boss lady. I'm bringing the people who will be helping out for the next couple of weeks as things heat up. I mean, as we get busy. I mean . . ." He is stammering, but it is fake; he's doing it on purpose, and his eyes are twinkling in a wicked way.

"Seriously?"

"Seriously. Thank you for a lovely night, Miss Sophie. One for the record books." And he leans over and kisses me softly on the mouth, and despite my firm resolve that this was all kinds of a huge mistake, and my clearheadedness that it should never happen again, my body, which apparently didn't get the message,

cries out to grab him and pull him back into bed. "I'll see you later." And then, thank goodness, he is gone.

⁓

My phone peals on the nightstand, the alarm ringer set for maximum "get my ass out of bed" volume. I grab it and shut it off, then press my fingers into my throbbing temples and go to the bathroom for more Tylenol and more water and an endless pee. My body feels all of the aftermath of a night of passion, and just the flashes of memory that are attacking my brain are enough to mortify me.

I'm weak. I have succumbed to my basest primal desires and slept with the wrongest of men for the wrongest of reasons. All I can do is pray that he sticks to the plan and that we don't ever speak of it again. I get into the shower and scrub hard, wanting to remove all evidence of the previous night, and I find only one earplug, tidily tucked behind my left ear. I get dressed, zip downstairs, and grab a chocolate babka and a loaf of rye bread, just in case, and head over to Bubbles's. My parents' cars are both parked in front, which means they are both heading straight to work from here. My headache is down to a dull roar, and I know that breakfast will help.

"Hello?" I call out as I come through the door. Snatch snuffles his way over to see who is here and if they have treats, and I lean down to rub his head. He's wearing a very jaunty argyle sweater in shades of mint green and Tiffany blue, with a knitted-in bow tie. I toss him one of the biscuits from the bowl on the foyer console and hang up my jacket on the coatrack.

"We're in here," my mom calls from the dining room.

I make the rounds, kissing everyone, before sitting next to Bubbles at the place she has left for me between her and my mom. I set the babka and the rye on the table. Bubbles has put

out a lovely spread. I fill my glass with orange juice, drain it quickly, and then fill it again. For a few minutes, everyone passes around the dishes, filling our plates, taking first bites, and praising Bubbles for the grub.

"As nice as it is to have us all together, I do have an ulterior motive," Bubbles says, patting her lips with her napkin. "As the titular matriarch of this family, I think there are a few things that we should discuss with some frankness as we look to get through the next few weeks."

"What's going on, Mom?" my dad asks around a mouthful of spinach and cheese strata.

"Is everything okay?" My mom spreads marmalade thickly on a half of an English muffin that she has already lavished with butter.

"I think everything will be fine, but we do need to address the elephants in the room." Bubbles chews a piece of bacon thoughtfully. "I think the best way I can put this is to say that I love you both very much, and I appreciate that you are currently doing many things at once which are terribly stressful; however, I also think that you both are in danger of behaving in ways that you will be embarrassed about later, and would like to help you avoid that if I can. After all, I know that my children are not assholes, and would prefer that everyone around them not be put in a position to question it."

Damn. I cannot *wait* until I'm eightysomething and can just say whatever comes into my brain with no filter.

"*Mom!*" my dad says, not sure if he should be insulted or amused.

"Really," my mom says, her eyes narrowing in a way that makes me quite sure she is now looking at Bubbles with a clinical eye and wondering if this is the first stage of dementia. I take another piece of strata and dig in, the rich combination of eggs,

bread, spinach, onion, and cheese filling the hole in my stomach, and settling the remnants of the previous evening's bacchanal.

"Really, indeed, my loves. Robert? You have turned, these past weeks, into some cowering milquetoast who has lost his voice, and I'm not really sure why you are allowing yourself to be bullied by the love of your life for the first time since you met."

My dad's mouth drops open.

"And, Diane, my darling daughter-in-love, you have become a demanding, shrewish bridezilla, which I know is the opposite of who you are and what you want."

My mom stops mid-chew, and her lovely violet eyes fill with tears.

"I don't want to hurt either one of you. This is purely from a place of concern, but I do have to be honest. So I would like for the four of us to talk about your upcoming move, and the wedding, and all of the things that are sending you both into personality chaos, so that we can help in any way that we can."

"Am I so awful?" my mom asks, her chin quivery, though she's not quite crying yet.

I reach over and squeeze her arm. "We think you are going through so much all at once that it is making you really super stressed-out, and we just feel like you aren't having any fun with any of it. This is so amazing for you guys, moving, doing the new place, getting married . . . It should be full of joy and excitement and fun, and you both just seem miserable and frustrated."

"It has been a little bit . . . complicated," my dad says, looking at his lap.

"I'm not really sure how to . . ." my mom starts and then trails off.

"Here is what I think," Bubbles says, matter-of-factly. "You are a little bit at odds with the life you are about to embark upon and the personal politics and lifestyle that have preceded it, and how to reconcile those things."

My mom nods, the analyst in her processing this. "I think that is very astute, and could certainly add a layer of emotional complexity to everything."

"Haven't you both always said that the most important part of living a good life is to be true to yourself as long as it doesn't cause harm to others?" I ask.

"Of course," my dad says firmly.

"And, Mom, don't you always say that people are ever evolving, and that change is both possible and healthy as we continue to grow in our lives, that embracing those changes is positive and a sign of a strong person?"

"That's true," my mom says, reaching for the babka and ripping off a chunk.

"Okay, then you should both know that there is nothing wrong with wanting nice things or a secure future. There is nothing fundamentally wrong with wanting to stand in front of the people you love and vow to continue to love and support each other as you move forward in your life. There is nothing that hurts anyone else about your having financial security and a lovely place to live and a legal expression of the love you have always shared."

My mom blushes, and my dad reaches for her hand.

"Your daughter is very astute," Bubbles says. "You both need to get over whatever weird guilt you are feeling about your newfound wealth and about having a home that functions well and is comfortable. And, for goodness' sake, you cannot be strange about getting married; it is the most natural thing in the world!"

"And for what it's worth, you can't feel at all weird or bad about me and my wedding that wasn't or what happened after. I'm really happy for you guys, about every bit of it, and I want to help in any way you want me to."

"Thank you, honey; that means a lot," my mom says with a sheepish smile.

"And I promise I'll participate in making the decisions instead of abdicating," my dad says, getting up to come around and wrap his long arms around me and my mom in a big hug. "And thanks, Mom, for the kick in the britches."

"Good," says Bubbles. "Now let's make some plans . . ." And the four of us, our strange little family, sit and eat, and start to hash out how to get my parents married properly without anyone ending up in a padded room. And for the first time since I became Wedding Girl, I actually have fun offering some wedding advice, because the one thing that is the most important about any wedding is love, and however weird my clan is, we've got that in spades.

By the time we've finished plotting out a wedding that will make sense for my folks, it is nearly eleven thirty, and I head back to Herman's to take a nap. They have decided to do a simple late-afternoon ceremony the first weekend in November, followed by a casual party at their old house. The place will be empty, since they will have moved out the week previous, and they can set up tables and chairs all over the first level, with the buffet in the dining room. They can put up a heated tent in my mom's garden for the ceremony, and have a DJ for dancing in there. They called the developer on the spot, and he said immediately that he couldn't think of a nicer way for them to say good-bye to their old home, and agreed that they could have the house for the extra week so that it could happen. Not surprising since he has been so tolerant of the ever-changing target that has been their actual move-out date. They'll invite just friends and family and colleagues with whom they socialize. About one hundred people total. And, of course, I'm making the cake.

I sleep like the dead for about two hours, full of strange sex dreams starring Mark, and wake groggy and not feeling rested

at all. I drink two cans of Coke, eat a slice of leftover Lou Malnati's sausage pizza from two days ago, and head down to the bakery to meet my new team.

"Hey, Sophie, good to see you." I'm shocked to see Jason standing in the kitchen with Mark. "This is my girlfriend, Annabel." He gestures to a slight redhead, who I recognize as the hostess from Café Nizza.

"Hi. What are you guys doing here?"

"They're your backup team," Mark says.

"Wait, what?"

"Mark told me what was going down over here, and that you needed help for a couple of weeks, and our place is running pretty well. We're talking about wanting to open a second location, which means we need to know if it can run without us, so we figured taking a couple of weeks off to help you here will tell us a lot about how things will shake out over there, without us being too far away in case of emergency," Jason says, very matter of fact and implying that it is no big deal, even though I know that the sacrifice of two weeks of time when you own a place like his is *huge*.

"I don't know what to say, that is above and beyond."

"Nah, I'm here to steal all your secrets. You were always way above me," Jason says with a wink.

"And I'm here to assist him, and do front of house," Annabel says. "I love this place. My grandparents lived here when I was growing up. I've been eating Langer's stuff since I was born."

"I'm so, so thankful, to you both, really."

"Okay, I'm totally useless here for all of this," Mark says, "so I'm going to take off. I've been told I have some serious housecleaning I need to take care of most urgently." He winks at me, and I can feel my face go red. I suppose when I said we shouldn't speak of it, I should have also said we shouldn't reference it or intimate it or wink at it in any way.

"Okay, then, good luck with that," I say, knowing that he can't leave soon enough for my tastes.

"Will do, I leave you all to it. Sophie, I'll see you Wednesday night at the usual time."

"Yep, sounds good." At least I have two days before I have to see him again. Hopefully he will have figured out how to be cool about the whole thing by then.

"Yeah, well, stop with the endless good-byes, then, and take us through the week and show me the recipes. I want to study up so that I can hit the ground running for you next week," Jason says, and I reach for the recipe bible and start to tell him what Langer's is all about, as Mark slips out of the kitchen.

I Love You Again

(1940)

"Okay, are you ready?" Ruth says from her perch on a stool at
the door between the kitchen and the store, armed with a copy
of our list of components.

I look over at Mark, who nods at me. "Yes, I think we are
ready."

"I have the official clock," Amelia says, finger ready to punch
the countdown timer she has set up on an iPad mini and
mounted to the wall with duct tape.

"And I've got the judging points list," says Jean, who has a
clipboard with all of the various points and criteria that will be
used on Saturday for the competition. I've annotated it for her,
along with a list of questions she should ask and some things we
need her to do while we are working, including coming around
and getting into our work space, tasting components as we work
with them, and generally being both a nuisance and distracting
presence at key moments.

"I think we are good to go. Let's get this party started!"

Mark says companionably. Since our little naked adventure he
has been as good as his word and has not brought it up, teased
me about it, or in any way indicated that it even happened. I
wish I could say that it was fully a relief, but working so closely
together for all of these hours in a hot kitchen, touching hands
as we mold fondant, feeding each other tastes of this and that, or
feeling his whole front pressed tight against my back, like we're
spooning, while I stabilize the base of the cake as he puts the
final tier on over my head—it has an effect. I keep getting
flashes of him grabbing me movie-style, sweeping all of the
equipment off the prep table and making passionate love to me
in the debris field. Of course these images also haunt me anytime I start to get the least bit flirtatious in my emails to Jake,
making me feel even worse. I know intellectually that I've done
nothing at all wrong, but it still feels like I've betrayed him. I
know that if I found out that he was sleeping with someone in
London that my feelings would be hurt, as if it would be some
sort of indication of lack of faith or hope in this weird whatever-
it-is we have started.

Then again, it was an itch that clearly needed scratching, so
I suppose I have to just be glad that Mark was there, that he was
really good and fun in bed, and that he hasn't turned it into a
whole thing between us.

"Alright, team. Let's do it!" I give Amelia the thumbs-up
and she sets our countdown clock in motion. We have six hours
to finish the cake, and it will be our final practice before the
competition. This week Jason and Annabel will run the bakery,
using the kitchen at the café for everything except the challahs,
which have to be done here. Mark and I will spend the week
making all of the cake layers, filling components, fondants,
Rice Krispies treats, and other elements that are allowed to be
prepped ahead, so that we can deliver them to the Astor Place
Hotel on Friday. The hot new boutique hotel is hosting both the

VIP cocktail party Friday night and the competition Saturday. I've heard nothing but good things about the space, a high-end, all-suite, five-star hotel that offers a very personalized level of service. There is a wonderful new fine-dining Italian restaurant on the first floor that is getting raves, and they have been focused on donating their event spaces and services to various local charities, all of which have gotten them good coverage. They are focused on a "one-stop shopping" sort of approach to events—in-house catering, floral design, event production—the perfect place to have an event if you don't have time or the inclination to shop around for each individual element. The buzz is that they are seriously going after the destination wedding market, and hoping to become the place in Chicago for weddings in general, and gay weddings in particular.

Mark heads for the left side of the table and begins assembling the chocolate tier of the cake, spreading the first layer of cake with a layer of ganache, then the big piece of crunchy dacquoise, another layer of ganache, and then the second layer of cake. He is working quickly and efficiently, getting the cake into the walk-in to chill and firm up, and bringing out the cakes and fillings for the second tier. I'm using a stiff chocolate gingerbread dough to make the templates for all of the windows and doors. I called in a small favor from Anneke, who has been stuck home with the twins for nearly six months, and was more than grateful to turn my photos of Bubbles's old house into some simple AutoCad drawings, and then print them to scale for the cake, so that we can lay parchment paper over them and build the different elements right over the drawings for precision.

I get all of the sheets of windows and doorframes into the oven to bake, and turn my attention to the tuiles for the tile portion of the roof. As I'm pulling the first sheet out of the oven and quickly laying the pliable sheet into the form I've built so that it can cool in the right shape, Jean appears at my elbow.

"So what is that made of?"

I explain the contents of the tuile batter, and the decision to color the dough itself a terra-cotta color instead of risking breakage by trying to paint it with colored chocolate after assembly. She makes some notes on her clipboard, and heads over to talk to Mark, and I realize that while I was answering her, I stopped working, and my other cookie has now hardened on the sheet and will have to be re-baked. I make a note to myself that my hands and mouth have to be able to work at the same time, or I will get behind. I toss the now-useless cookie onto the small table for the girls to snack on, and pull a new piece of parchment, smearing the thin tuile batter over the template, and getting the sheet back in the oven.

Jean is getting in Mark's way, tasting all of the various fillings for the second tier, and chatting with him about the inspiration for that layer, and unlike me, he manages to talk with her easily while still spreading the pineapple jam over the first layer of cake. Whatever other ups and downs and complications Mark has presented in my life these past months, I have to give him total credit. He is a very skilled baker, and a godsend on this project. With him by my side I can believe that we will not embarrass ourselves, and I cannot say the same of Herman.

I get the second tuile safely into the form, and move them aside to cool completely and be out of the way till we need them.

"One hour gone," Amelia says cheerily. That flew by, and I know that the day of the contest will be even worse, since the adrenaline will really kick in.

Ruth walks over and hands first Mark and then me bottles of water, which we both open and down in one go, and then get back to work. I pull the gingerbread out of the oven and set the sheets on racks to cool. I have to wait to fill the larger window sections with clear sugar caramel, and they have to be completely cooled, since they will shrink a bit as they cool, and we

want the windows to be a tight fit. The stained glass pieces will get colored sugars sprinkled in the various sections and then will get torched to melt them. I've given myself enough time to do the windows twice, just in case of cracking.

Mark gets the second completed tier into the walk-in and pulls out the components for the top tier. I turn my attention to making some of the smaller, more intricate carved details for the house out of gum paste, so that they will have plenty of time to dry and harden before we have to attach them. As with the fondant, I've pre-colored the gum paste gray so that it has a good base, and once everything is assembled, we'll soften the edges with gray and black and white powdered food colors.

Mark gets the third tier into the walk-in, pulling out the first tier, now firmed up and ready for its buttercream coating. Jean comes back around.

"So, Sophie, how are you feeling about your time-management on this?"

"Pretty good," I say, being sure not to look up or stop what I'm doing, carefully crafting the capitals for the columns that will hold up the balcony. The columns themselves are already made of formed chocolate set around a large dowel, but the capitals and plinths have to be done the day of since they are a more decorative element.

"Mark, are you feeling good about your time management as well?" Jean asks.

Mark finishes spreading the thin layer of mint buttercream over the top of the cake, smoothing it easily with a large offset spatula, and hefts it up to take it back to the walk-in. "Seems okay so far," he says.

"Looking good, Billy Ray," I call out to him.

"Feeling good, Louis," he calls back, and we all giggle except for Amelia, who is apparently too young to get a decent *Trading Places* reference when she hears one.

"Two hours," Amelia says.

And so it goes. We check things off the list; we deal with problems as they arise. The first batch of stained glass windows went too-dark-caramel with the blowtorch, losing the colors, so I tried the second batch in the oven under the broiler instead, and they are gorgeous, the colors clear and bright, and when you hold them to the light, they are absolutely stained glass. Mark, being handy, has set us up with a small battery-operated lighting system, with tiny LED bulbs that will go into the little vestibule to backlight the stained glass transom, and sidelights to show off that we will have done that entry to perfection: the mosaic tiled floor, the intricate crown molding, the William Morris–style wallpaper printed on edible sheets of rice paper.

By the time we hit the final hour, the house is up and both Mark and I are working on details. He focuses on the landscaping details, trees and shrubs and plants created with green cotton candy and chocolate and frosting, and I work on the people, fun little roly-poly characters sitting on the porch, a toddler in a little Cubs sunhat splashing in a kiddie pool that I've lined with crumpled tinfoil before filling it with blue melted sugar, to make it look like the sun is catching on the water. A Weber grill covered in tiny hot dogs and burgers with even tinier grill marks. When the bell rings, we are sweaty, muscles cramping, and bleary-eyed, but with the exception of a couple of the planned party guests, and some of the smaller details we had designed, like the green hose curled on the side of the house, the classic Chicago black garbage cans and blue recycling cans in the alley, and all of the animals we had thought of, the Labradors in the yard, the squirrels in the tree, the little nest of robins in the eaves of the house, the important stuff all got done.

"You guys," Amelia says, handing us bottles of water as we collapse onto stools to sit for the first time in six hours. "It is *amazeballs.*"

"Really, it is just spectacular. You are totally going to win this thing," Jean says.

"Have to admit, it's very impressive," Ruth says. "I hope this means we can all show up for just the last hour on Saturday, though, no one needs to sit through the whole thing twice, you know?"

Jean smacks her on the arm. I laugh. "Of course you can come at the end. I can't imagine how boring it will be to watch it again."

"It's not boring, though; it's fascinating," Amelia says. "I was riveted."

"Yeah, it was fine. But I don't need to see it again. What I do need is sustenance. Are we going out for dinner?" Ruth asks.

"Hell yes, I'm starving," Jean says.

"I'm in for sure," Amelia says.

"I love you guys, but I'm barely going to make it up those stairs, and I'm not in any condition to change and make myself presentable to go out. You go and eat, thank you all again for helping us out today, and we'll see you Saturday."

"Okay, then. Let's go, troops," Ruth says and herds them away, Mark following to let them out the front and then relock the door.

When he comes back, we work in companionable silence, getting everything cleaned up.

"She looks good," he says, giving the beast a once-over. "Damn good."

"Yeah. True enough. Thank you."

"No thanks necessary."

"Well, necessary or not, I could not have done it without you. You are doing your dad very proud."

I look over and see that Mark's eyes are extra sparkly, and it touches my heart to see him getting a little emotional about his dad.

We finish cleaning up and shut down the lights in the kitchen, leaving the cake standing on the prep table. When

Jason and Annabel get here tomorrow we will do a full tasting of the three tiers, just to make sure that no one has any notes on flavors that might need tweaking.

"Want a beer?" I ask Mark as we head into the store.

"That would be really good," he says, following me through the secret door and up the stairs. I really hope he isn't looking too critically at the wide expanse of my ass.

"Beer's in the fridge, I'm just going to change really fast," I say, heading for my room to get out of my sticky work clothes. I forgo a shower, figuring once Mark leaves I'll take a long hot bath, and just give myself a fresh layer of deodorant and pull on some black leggings and an oversized gray long-sleeved T-shirt.

Mark is standing at the stove. Something smells delicious.

"What are you making?" I ask, as I grab a beer out of the fridge, open it, and take a long pull at the cold, bitter brew.

"Dinner. We need to replenish what we lost," he says. And I don't blame him; all we ate for six hours were protein bars, which are great for speed, but don't really sustain for long.

I go over to the stove and peer into the pot, where a thick, creamy mixture of rice is forming. "Are you making risotto?" I ask, as he pours chicken stock from the box at his side into the pot, never stopping stirring.

"Yes, a quick and somewhat bastardized version, but you had the rice and an onion and stock, and I saw some rotisserie chicken in the fridge, and a package of baby spinach, so I figured we could make do."

"I think this is more than just making do. What can I do?"

"You want to shred the chicken? Maybe grate some of that chunk of Parm I spotted in the cheese drawer? Chop some of that parsley you have over there?"

"You got it." I pull the chicken out of the fridge, only missing one breast from my dinner last night, and remove the rest of the meat from the carcass, shredding it into bite-sized pieces as Mark

continues to stir. Without even thinking, when I remove the first oyster from the back, I reach over and offer it to him, and he eats it from my fingers as if it is the most natural thing in the world, which shoots tingles right up my arm and into my loins. I'm glad he can't see me flush. Suddenly I wonder why I was always so annoyed by the whole cooking with someone thing. It's kind of nice.

I put the shredded meat into a bowl and hand it to him, and he adds it to the pot with more stock, while I attack the wedge of Parmesan with a Microplane, creating a huge mound of fluffy cheese snow. I rip off a fistful of parsley from the bunch I have in a glass of water on the counter and give it a rough chop. Mark tastes the rice, and then throws a couple of handfuls of baby spinach in, with the last of the stock, giving it another good stir. He drops the stock box into the garbage, pulls the butter out of the fridge, cuts a large knob off the stick, and drops it into the pan, stirring with one hand and beginning to add fistfuls of grated cheese with the other. The smell is intoxicating. He drains the last of his beer, and without a word, I go to the fridge and open him another. He winks his thanks at me, pulls two large bowls from the cabinet, and spoons up a generous helping into each one, sprinkling more cheese over the top and adding a quick swirl of olive oil for garnish. He hesitates, then takes a lemon from the bowl on the counter, and my discarded Microplane, and showers a light bit of zest over each one. I give both bowls a hefty scattering of parsley, and we each grab our bowls and a fork from the drawer and head to the kitchen table with our beers.

The risotto may not be fancy, might not have the homemade stock or delicate saffron or special ingredients, but it is fucking delicious. Hot, savory, salty, cheesy, with the pop of acid from the lemon zest and the bright greenness of the parsley and spinach, and despite the fact that he made enough for what looked like six people, we devour our first helpings, and refill both bowls even more full than the first time and demolish those as well.

"I think we'll do fine," he says after dumping the empty bowls in the sink and getting us each a third beer.

"I agree. I think we should be in good shape to not make a laughingstock of ourselves." I grab the beer he proffers and take a deep swig as he walks around to join me on the couch.

He does the same, letting out a huge, resonant belch.

"Really?" I say.

"To-tal-ly." He belches out.

What the hell. If you can't beat 'em, join 'em. *"Bbbbrrrr-raaaaaap."* I let the full force of the built-up pressure explode out of my face with unapologetic vigor.

Mark starts to laugh, and then so do I, and pretty soon we are both wiping tears and making dolphin noises. There is something to be said for that punch-drunk laughter that only happens in strange situations. When we get control over ourselves, Mark says, "You're a heck of a talent, Sophie Bernstein. What are you going to do when all this ends?" He waves a hand around the building.

"I have no idea," I say, not bothering to argue with him. I've seen the books. Our little uptick with the relaunch and social media blitz would have been enough to give me hope for the future, but not with Cake Goddess opening her doors in less than six weeks. We have not increased revenue nearly enough to withstand the kind of hit we are going to take, and even if some miracle happened and we win this contest on Saturday, there is not enough time for newfound event-cake business to kick in and save our bacon.

"What do you want to do?"

I think about this. "I wish I knew. I'm in limbo, a bit. I think I've changed too much to want to go back to what I had before, the pressure of that fine-dining tasting-menu place, chasing stars. But I also know that this"—I repeat his gesture—"this isn't really enough, not for the long haul. I thought what I wanted

was a restaurant, something in the middle, serious food, but unfussy atmosphere, less pressure, but still challenging creatively."

"But not now."

I think of my dream, currently being fully realized and lauded without me. "Not now."

"You'll figure it out." He reaches out and squeezes my shoulder.

"Yeah. I will. Thank you." And then, not being able to stop myself, I lean forward and kiss him gently on the mouth.

He kisses me back for a moment, and then buries his hands in my hair, pulling my face away from his.

"Um, I sort of haven't full finished that whole, um, housekeeping issue."

What an ass. This one sentence sends the fluttery excitement that was building in my girl parts right into remission. "Seriously?"

He blushes. "It's, um . . ."

"Yeah, complicated."

"And you've got your guy . . ."

I think about poor Jake, and wonder if "my guy" will ever be anything more than theoretical. And if he wasn't, if I would even be remotely interested in pursuing something purposeful with Mark. I think back to my brief thought of them being the same person, and wonder if I'm just trying to mentally Frankenstein the perfect guy. Mark's looks and skills in bed, Jake's intelligence and sense of humor and kindness. Or worse, if I just kind of wish it were Mark emailing me instead of Jake, and what would that mean? Really don't even want to think about this right now. "Exactly. No worries, I'm just overtired and a little buzzed, and as impulses go, it was probably a spectacularly bad idea."

"I should go," he says, not disagreeing with me.

"Yeah, you should."

"Okay. See you tomorrow?"

"Yes, you will."

"Okay, then."

"Mark?"

"Yeah?"

"Thanks for dinner. For what it's worth, when you do find the sack to break it off with the wrong girl, you will make the right girl a really good wife." I grin at him.

He smiles and belches one more time for good measure, and bows, taking his leave. I shake my head, glad that he has saved us both from making a second, more serious mistake, and head back inside to run a hot bath, and hopefully fall into a dreamless sleep.

Wife vs. Secretary

(1936)

Gosh, all the fighting and worrying people do, it
always seems to be about one thing. They don't
seem to trust each other. Well, I've found this
out. Don't look for trouble where there isn't any,
because if you don't find it, you'll make it. Just
believe in someone.

· JAMES STEWART AS DAVE ·

Friday morning, Jason and Annabel help me load up the van
with all of our prepped materials. We have all of the cake layers, the dacquoise, sheets of Rice Krispies treats. The pre-molded
chocolate columns, a whole bucket of gray fondant, and a rain-
bow of other pre-colored fondants and gum pastes. All of the
fillings and ingredients, as well as our structural supports, templates, and preapproved specialty equipment. I check everything off my list, while Jason does the same, and before we lock
the van, we compare lists to be sure they match. Mark has some
work stuff to deal with today, so he is just going to meet me at
the hotel for the reception tonight. Annabel is going to hold
down the fort while Jason helps me make the delivery and get
our station set up for tomorrow before heading back to the bakery. The two of them have been an absolute godsend, and I have
to figure out the proper way to thank them when this is all over.

"Have fun storming the castle!" Annabel says, waving at us,

in a fairly good Carol Kane impersonation as Jason and I get into the van.

"I'll have him back as soon as I can," I say out the window of the passenger seat, as Jason pulls away and we head downtown.

The Astor Place is nestled on a fairly quiet street in the Gold Coast neighborhood, but still walking distance to all of the hustle and bustle of the Magnificent Mile. Just eight stories tall, but taking up nearly a full block, the Italianate architecture is stately, and the new deep navy blue awnings and shutters really look terrific. Jason pulls down the alley, and into the loading dock, where another van is already parked.

"Well, well, my other sister Sophie," I hear as I get out of the van. I turn to see Sophie Goodman, owner of Bakehouse, behind me. "I thought you were dead, woman." She walks over and grabs me in a hug. Sophie is a few years younger than me, but we met when I was doing a workshop at the French Pastry School while she was studying there, and for a week we were "Sophie Squared" or "The Sophies," and we kept threatening to start a band. She took over at Bakehouse a few years ago, and has been knocking it out of the park with her impeccable takes on French classic pastry work.

"Not dead, just laying low," I say. "I was very happy to see you on the list for this thing, it's one thing to come to probably lose, but at least I can lose to someone I like."

She smacks me on the arm playfully. "Whatever, you'll kick my ass for sure. I'm just glad we're both here, it's a freaking sausage fest in there. But I had no idea you were competing, you weren't on the list. I thought I was the only girl."

I laugh. "I know, right? You'd think with all the girls killing it these days that we would have had all five slots. But the lead on this was supposed to be my boss, he owns the bakery, but he got sick so I'm taking the lead." I never contacted the organizers about the change. I figured Mark's real name is still technically

Herman Langer, there wasn't a need to make any changes. Chicago pastry, especially for fine dining, is heavily weighted with women, and they are absolutely moving the industry in exciting directions. But the other three teams are all men; Thomas Beckman is a pastry instructor at Le Cordon Bleu Chicago, and the other two, Dimitri Fayard and Scott Gerken, are hotel guys, Dimitri at the Peninsula and Scott at the Four Seasons. Just some of the most amazing and talented pastry chefs we're lucky to have in Chicago.

"Hey, Soph, I know I probably should have called or, or something . . . you know, when it all went down . . ." She looks a little sheepish.

"Why? It was a shit show, and totally not remotely up to you to reach out. The phone dials two ways, and I didn't call you either."

"Well, you could have. You still can. If you want to, I mean, after I kick your ass tomorrow." She winks at me, that bubbly personality shining through.

"Sounds like a plan. I will call you to take you for a consolation cocktail after I wipe the floor with you."

She gives me another hug and whispers, "Fuck it, let's tie. The Sophies, together again."

"Deal."

"You broads want to start a book club or have a mani-pedi over there, or should we unload these vans?" Jason says, walking up behind me and greeting Sophie with a hug.

"You gonna let him talk to the boss like that?" Sophie asks, laughing.

"It makes him feel important, which gets his man-juices all riled up, and then he does more of the heavy lifting." I shrug, like it's all part of my master plan.

She laughs, and we all head to our vans to carefully unload our wares.

"You look beautiful, Sophie," Mark says, handing me a glass of champagne.

"Thanks," I say, accepting it gratefully. I'm standing in the corner of the beautiful ballroom at the Astor, having a small panic attack. The room is full of my former colleagues and peers. A good fifty people here were actually in attendance at the wedding that wasn't. I was feeling okay when I left the house, almost happy. It had been a good day, setting up, reconnecting with Sophie. The other contestants I only ever knew peripherally, so there was a formal respectful friendliness there, but I didn't feel awkward with them, and all of their team partners were younger sous chefs and assistants who I didn't know at all. Jason and I got everything set up and did another full checklist and everything was in good shape. I went home, visited with Herman and Bubbles, and had a sweet email from Jake, who said he was going camping with some work friends for the weekend, but would write Monday night. I got into my new outfit, a simple black pencil skirt with a drapey charcoal gray top that hides my multitudes of flaws, and even got my hair to behave. I was sort of happy.

And then I got here, looked around the room, and my stomach turned over. I found a dark corner and kept my head down, my hair hiding my face in shadows, until Mark found me.

"You okay?" he asks. "You look a little pale."

"Yeah. Just not really my crowd."

"I get it. Don't worry, we won't stay a minute longer than we have to."

I know he knows most of my secret shame, so when he says this, I believe him. We stay where we are, a few people stop by to say hello, a couple of journalists find me and ask some ques-

tions, it's mostly a blur. We eat some passed hors d'oeuvres, all of which are excellent.

"Hey, Mark, good to see you." A guy in a very smart suit comes over and claps Mark on the back. "Very excited for tomorrow, man, good luck. Is this the famous Sophie?"

"That it is. Sophie Bernstein, David Francisco. Dave is the GM, and part owner here at the hotel."

"Very nice to meet you, the place is just beautiful."

"Thank you," Dave says. "It's a labor of love."

The two of them talk companionably, and Dave asks me tons of questions about our cake and my connection to Langer's, and the two of them put me very much at ease. I have a second glass of champagne, and some more nibbles, and my shoulders start to unclench. And then Jacquy gets up to the podium.

He welcomes the group, reminds us all that this is for a good cause, for their scholarship program, and announces the five teams. We all get polite applause.

"And finally, it is my pleasure to announce the judges. You know that we have kept their identities a secret, so that there could be no sneaky bribing or influencing!" The crowd laughs. "But we are very delighted to have them here, and we know that they will have a very hard time making decisions tomorrow! Will you please join me in welcoming our panel of judges. First, she is one of our city's shining stars, the fabulous Mindy Segal!" The place goes wild, we love her, and I'm glad she is one of the judges. "She is new to our fair city, but we know she will be a welcome addition, you know her as the Cake Goddess, but she wants us all to just call her MarySue! MarySue Adams!" Oy. I hadn't even considered that as a possibility, but the PR angle makes sense. "The fabulous Greg Mosko!" Jacquy says, another solid choice. "And finally, a dynamic duo, whose new restaurant is already becoming a mainstay, Dexter and Cookie Kelley!"

Mark catches me as I start to swoon, and he and Dave each take an arm, and wind me through the crowd and out a door into the hall. Dave leads us through another door, and into a small anteroom, where they set me down on a couch, and Dave goes to get me some water.

"Well, that is shittier than we anticipated," Mark says.

"I can't. I can't do it. I can't . . ."

Mark takes my shoulders firmly in his hands and looks into my eyes. "You can, and you will. Because you are smart and strong and amazing, and enormously talented. And you will not let that crapweasel and his bony wife take you down. You will be loose and funny and snarky tomorrow, and more important, you will win this whole thing. Because they are only two votes, and you'll get the other three because you deserve them. And when you win, you'll be gracious and clever and you'll ride off into the sunset in your white hat, and they will have to wake up every day of their lives and be *them*. Can you imagine anything worse than that?"

"Mark, that all sounds . . ."

"True. It sounds true."

"But I . . ."

"Look at me, Sophie. I'm only going to say this once. You are spectacular and a shining star and you are finished hiding in my dad's store and your own shadow. You're too good, too talented, and too smart to let what that asshole did to you and what happened after be the defining elements of your life. So I'm going to sneak you out of here and take you home, and tomorrow morning I'm going to pick you up, and we are going to eat a huge breakfast, and then we are going to come here and wipe the floor with everyone."

I nod, as much because I'm overwhelmed at what he has said as I am by finding out that tomorrow I'm going to be face-to-face with Dexter and Cookie. I drain the water bottle Dave brings

back to me, and let Mark lead me by the hand through a series of back hallways and out into the night air. Mark takes me to his car, tucks me into the passenger side, and drives me home. When we get there, he opens my door, and gently takes my hand and leads me to Herman's apartment.

"Can you eat something?" he asks after I've shimmied out of my fancy new outfit and into some seriously mangy loungewear.

"I'm okay, Mark, really."

"That's not what I asked."

I shrug.

"Grilled cheese and soup?" he asks, having foraged in my kitchen and found the makings.

"Probably," I admit. I'm a lot of things, but I'm not one of those girls who loses her appetite when she gets sad. Just the opposite.

"Here." He hands me an ice-cold Coke from the fridge. "Keep your blood sugar up."

He makes a bunch of noise in the kitchen, and I return to my notes, going over everything for tomorrow, trying to ignore the new reality. My cell phone rings.

"Sophie? It's Sebastien." Great, now I'm probably in trouble for leaving the party early.

"Hi."

"Sophie, we are so sorry. Your name—it wasn't listed on the paperwork for Mr. Langer; we did not even know you were involved until Sophie and the other contestants told us. Please know that if we had known, we never would have offered the judging positions to the Kelleys."

So, not in trouble, but totally outed. Then I think about what Mark said, and look over at him, making me soup and grilled cheese in his dad's little kitchen, and I can feel my shoulders pull back. "Oh, Sebastien, don't think twice, they're a great choice, and you know, that is such ancient history!" I put as

much ease and light into my voice as I can. "It's sweet of you to worry, but please don't. I've been consulting with Mr. Langer, and when he took ill his son asked me to continue to work on the contest as his partner. I didn't want to take his name off of the team; after all, it will be his vision we are executing in his absence. You couldn't have known, and I couldn't care less."

"I'm relieved to hear it. When we didn't see you after the announcements . . ."

"Strategy, silly man. A bit of psychology. Once I heard, I thought I could use it to my advantage, slip away and come home to prepare and rest up while my competition stayed to wine and dine and think that I'm going to be nervous and no competition at all tomorrow!"

Sebastien laughs. "A smart thing, to be both underestimated and well rested. Brava. Well then I leave you to it, and I will see you tomorrow morning. *Bonne nuit.*"

"Thanks for calling, Sebastien. If I had actually been upset, it would have been a relief to hear that you would have had my back."

"We do try to take care of our alums when we can. Good luck tomorrow. I for one cannot wait to see what you do."

I hang up and Mark comes out of the kitchen, handing me a bowl of chicken noodle soup, and putting a platter of grilled cheese sandwiches, cut in neat triangles, on the coffee table. He returns to the kitchen to get his own soup, and I grab a sandwich and dunk it in my bowl, devouring it.

"Who was that?"

"One of the contest organizers, the dean of my old school. Apologizing for the Dexter and Cookie thing, they didn't know I was even involved in the contest."

"That was nice of him. You handled him like a champ. I like the spin of psyching out the competition."

I reach for a second sandwich. "Fake it till I make it."

"You're a lot of things, Sophie, but fake is not one of them."

We finish our soup and all of the sandwiches, as well as a pile of cookies that Mark slips downstairs into the bakery to fetch us, and talk through our game plan. Just before ten, he checks his watch and gets up.

"We're going to kill it," he says.

"Of course we are."

"We have to be there at ten, so I'll pick you up at eight thirty. We'll hit Tempo for breakfast to power up?"

"Sounds good. And, Mark . . ."

He puts a hand up to stop my gratitude from spilling out. "It's what friends are for."

"Are we friends?" I ask before I can stop myself.

His face goes serious. "I certainly hope so, Sophie. I certainly hope so."

It takes all of my strength not to ask him to stay.

⟨⟩

Despite the inner turmoil in my head, I manage to get a good night's sleep, thanks to a hot bath and an Ambien. Mark picks me up promptly, and after massive breakfasts of omelets and pancakes, we head over to the hotel. Our station is fully set up, and we do one last check of materials and equipment, setting up our separate tables with what we will need once the clock starts. The room is buzzing with people who have come to watch, as well as organizers, press, and across the room, the judges, in a huddle with Sebastien and Jacquy, presumably getting final instructions.

When the buzzer sounds, we know we'll have a full hour to work before judges are allowed to come pester us, and my plan is to use that hour to get so in the groove that when they begin to come around, I'll be head-down and focused and can just answer questions while I keep working. And in six hours, it will all be over.

Once we are set up, we head for the stew room, where we will

take our allotted breaks, and wait for judging to be over. We greet the rest of the teams, grab bottles of water, snag protein bars for our pockets. Mark and I have agreed to limit our breaks to just quick runs to the bathroom if needed, and to eat the bars on the fly if we are feeling hungry. We are going to need every minute if we are going to be a contender in this thing.

Sebastien comes to the room and gives us the nod, and we follow him out, into the competition space, to the sound of applause. Mark reaches for my hand and gives it a squeeze and we are off.

The day flies. Mark is as on it as he has ever been, getting the tiers layered and chilled in no time, and prepping the architectural elements like a champ. I get the windows and doors baked off and the sugar work done with no issues. We're working like a well-oiled machine, the pieces coming together smoothly, and when we lay the top tier on the cake, we get a bit of applause. The judges begin to come over around the hour and a half mark, one at a time. Mindy tastes everything, and is really kind. Greg is effusive about our basic premise, and cautions us that the devil is in the details and not to skimp on the little bits and pieces, they'll make all the difference.

MarySue comes by full of praise, and says that while she can't guarantee anything, her heart is on my side, us being neighbors and all. I'm awfully proud of myself for not stabbing her in the eye with my long-handled tweezers.

Mark and I have just finished putting the primary fondant layer over the building when Dexter and Cookie, attached at the hip, come over.

"Hello, Sophie," he says.

"Hey, Dex, good to see you. You too Cookie. Congrats on the place, the buzz is tremendous, sorry I haven't been able to get

there yet." I smile like my life depends on it, and keep assembling the Weber Grill.

"That's very kind," Cookie says, sounding a little shocked.

"You'd be welcome anytime, as our guest, just let us know," Dexter says in a pained way.

"That's sweet, thanks."

"So, we didn't know you'd be competing today, actually didn't know if you were still even baking," Cookie says pointedly, with that faux concern that always smacks of condescension and pity.

"My fault, I'm afraid," Mark says, coming up behind me and putting an arm around my shoulder. "Her grandmother and my dad are close friends. I knew her ambitions went beyond the restaurant industry, and convinced her to leave Salé et Sucré to consult with my dad in hopes of rebranding the family business. Made her promise to work with us on the down low, since I knew she'd be in such demand if people knew what she was doing that I'd lose her for sure." He is smooth and confident, and it comes out so naturally that I almost believe him.

"How lucky for you that she was willing," Dexter says.

"And available," Cookie says.

"Yes, indeed. She wasn't supposed to be here. I was going to assist my dad for the competition, but he had a small health crisis, and you know Sophie, she's best in a crisis, and immediately jumped in to take the lead and make sure that we were going to be able to execute my dad's vision on his behalf. She's a goddamned saint, this one." He leans over and kisses my temple. "Sorry to cut it short folks, but I need Sophie to help me get the balcony attached to this baby if we're going to stay on track." And before they can say a word, he gently pulls me over to his station, where the columns are all set up.

"You know you don't need my help for this," I say. "It's made out of Rice Krispies treats for lord's sake."

"I'm feeling weak," he says, gesturing for me to take one end of the balcony to help move it to the top of the support columns. "There's too much asshole in the air, it's affecting my oxygen levels." I giggle a bit, and we put on a good show for the audience, slowly lifting the piece, and getting it settled into place, and then high-fiving like we've done something important.

"Go Langer's!" we hear, and look out into the crowd, where we see that there is a whole row of supporters there for us. Herman and Bubbles, my parents, Amelia and Brian, Ruth and Jean.

"Looks great, baby!" says a blonde with killer cheekbones, who is sitting on the other side of Herman. Mark blanches, but waves. She blows him a kiss.

"How's that housekeeping coming?" I ask, brushing my hands on my pants.

He shakes his head. "Not in a way that is making me proud. I told her we needed to have a face-to-face, I think she misunderstood." He grits his teeth.

I look him in the eye. "Head down, do the work. Doughs before hoes."

He snorts with laughter, and we both get back to work, ignoring the various and sundry people in the room with whom we have complicated history, and just focus on making something beautiful.

⁂

"You guys, that thing is *insane*," Dimitri says when we are all in the stew room, waiting for the points to be tallied.

"Seriously, amazing. I want to rent a unit in that building," Sophie G. says.

"Yeah, well, you guys didn't exactly bring your B games," I say. And they didn't. Sophie's cake is a full-on representation of the Bean sculpture with Taste of Chicago happening all around

it. The sheer volume of little food stands with tiny people eating is shocking, I have no idea how she did it. Dimitri did an abstraction of the skyline, with tons of sugar and chocolate work that is a true piece of art. Scott's got the Picasso, all dolled up in a Walter Payton jersey and Bears helmet. And Thomas did a winter version of the old Marshall Field's at Christmas, the windows full of holiday scenes, and the trees outside ablaze with tiny lights. Truly, it's anyone's game, and will come down to tiny margins, especially since I know all of these people will have brought it with the flavors.

The door opens. "They're ready for you," says Jacquy's assistant, who leads us all out and back into the ballroom, and up onstage.

"We are so proud of all of these teams, who have done such amazing work today," Jacquy says.

"We could not have asked for a better showing, and you are all setting the bar very high for next year's competitors," Sebastien says.

"But there can only be one winner," Jacquy continues.

"So, without further ado . . . a tie for fourth place, with Thomas Beckman and Scott Gerken!" Everyone applauds, and Mark elbows me. We both had said that as long as we weren't last, we would be happy.

"In third place, Dimitri Fayard."

I can't believe it; his was spectacular. Sophie winks at me, and mouths the word "tie." And grins.

"It should be no surprise to anyone that these two talented women are standing here. And we want you to know that the margin was less than three points."

My blood pressure is through the roof. We could actually win this thing.

"And finally, the winner of the first annual Chicago Cake Competition is . . . Sophie . . ." I hold my breath. "Goodman!"

And I exhale. Sophie takes her trophy, and then comes over to me and we hug deeply.

"I'm so glad it was you!" I say in her ear as she is whispering, "It should have been you," in my ear.

"It's all good," I say. And it is. We came in a close second, and beat out three of the best pastry chefs in the city. Not bad for the team from a little neighborhood bakery on the decline.

"I'm really proud of you," Mark says, hugging me hard.

"I'm proud of us," I say, just as I'm being elbowed aside by the blonde.

"You did great, baby, really great," she says, snuggling at him with her razor-sharp cheekbones.

"Thanks, Ella, didn't know you'd be here."

"My meeting got cancelled, so I came to support you."

Mark looks equal parts annoyed and resigned. "This is Sophie. Sophie, this is Ella."

"His girlfriend," she says pointedly, narrowing her eyes at me, and extending a hand with impossibly long fingers.

"Nice to meet you, Ella," I say, just as I'm swarmed by my family and friends, blissfully pulling me into a safe zone of love and happy.

"You stop my heart, sweet girl," Bubbles says with tears in her eyes. "You got every brick of that building just right, it was like looking into my past."

"I'm so glad you like it, we wanted it to be a happy surprise."

"And so it is."

"You did great, kiddo, just great. Your mom and I have decided we want you to replicate it for the wedding!" my dad says with a twinkle in his eye.

"Yeah, fuck you," I say, and my mom pretends to be shocked.

"We might want you to do that Frango mint combo, though; that was delicious," Mom says.

"I dunno, Diane, I thought the walnut one was pretty spectacular . . ." my dad says.

"They were all amazing," Herman says. "You make me so proud, both of you."

"You didn't tell us about the judges," Ruth says. "You okay?"

"We couldn't believe it when we saw," Jean says.

"You seem totally good," Amelia says. "Are you?"

"Yeah, I'm fine. It was fine. But I'm ready to break it down and get out of here."

"Everyone is coming back to my house for a little celebration, I have a lot of champagne and we're ordering pizza!" Bubbles says. "You kids get organized as quickly as you can, and we will meet you there."

"Will do. Thanks for being here." I kiss her soft cheek, and then Herman's.

"Sorry, we'll have to pass," Ella says, turning to Mark. "Surprise! I got us a room here for the night, and we have a date with room service. I even packed a bag for you. You all understand."

Herman looks sad and disappointed, the girls look irritated, and Bubbles looks positively gassy. Mark just looks defeated.

"Well, that is very lovely, dear. I'm sure you'll have a wonderful night," Herman says. "Junior, thank you again." He pulls Mark into a deep hug. Mark claps him on the back and whispers something in his ear, and Herman pats the side of his face gently before turning with his walker to follow Bubbles and the rest of the gang towards the door.

Ella hands Mark a keycard. "Penthouse Suite, love, 810. See you when you're done. Nice to meet you, Sophie, you did really well, considering."

"Considering?" I ask.

"Ella," Mark says, almost a warning.

"Well, considering that not only were you up against some

of the best pastry chefs in the city, but you were being judged by your ex *and* his new wife *and* your competition? I'd say second place is a gift, wouldn't you?"

Suddenly every bit of guilt I've been feeling about having slept with Mark disappears completely. This woman is a raging bitch. Of course, she could only know those things if Mark told her, so he isn't exactly on the top of my list right now either.

"Ella, Sophie is also one of the best pastry chefs in the city, and she earned every point we got today. We have to clean up; I'll meet you in the room."

"She's a doll," I say after Ella leaves. "I can see how it would be so hard to extricate yourself."

"Alright, no need to go all sarcastabitch on me. I didn't know she was coming, she's been traveling a lot for business. She was supposed to be in New York."

"Yep. She must look amazing from nine hundred miles away."

"It's . . ."

"Yeah, Junior, I know, it's complicated. Let's just get it packed in so I can go celebrate with our friends and families." I don't know why I'm so pissed off, so hurt. I know that he didn't plan this, but I can't help being disappointed. I wanted to celebrate with him; today's showing was as much him as me, and we deserved to be with our people tonight.

Mark just nods and doesn't reply, and for the next half hour we break down our station in silence, the companionability of the day lost, the closeness we had started to feel, gone. And the near win, the almost had it, the strong showing, marred by the day ending on such a sour note. I know that I'm acting like a petulant child, and I'm sure my pouting must seem like jealousy to him. But all I can think about is him and that tall, skinny, mean girl, with her sheaf of shiny bone-straight hair, and her designer suit hanging perfectly on her pelvic bones, lying in bed talking about

the sad little roly-poly girl his dad has taken in like some urchin, ruining all his plans and making a general nuisance of herself. The girl who was so unlovable her fiancé couldn't be bothered to even tell her he didn't want her, and simply didn't show up at the wedding. The poor little baker girl who became completely unraveled by her breakup, and ended up broke and hiding out at her grandmother's house. I bet she laughed, I bet he made me sound like quite the joke.

We finish packing up everything into our tubs and carts, and seal it all up with plastic wrap so that they can't be tampered with, and I use a Sharpie to sign my name on them.

"Since I'll be here anyway, I'll get this stuff back to the store tomorrow, no need for you to schlep all the way down here," Mark says.

"Yeah, fine. Just text me when you are on your way and I'll meet you in the alley to unload."

"Okay. Have a good night, Sophie, a good celebration. You've earned it."

"I will. And same to you."

"See you tomorrow, then," he says, and walks away. And as much as I want to call after him, to apologize for being brusque, to tell him it was an amazing day and an amazing few weeks, and that it would always be a cherished memory, I can't seem to move my feet or open my mouth. And I stay frozen until I see his back disappear through the people who are still milling about, the other teams who are packing their stations up, the hotel staff beginning to clean. And slowly, regaining the power of movement, I take a deep breath, and shake it off. I can't think about Mark or his girlfriend or anything else, not tonight. Tonight I need to go home, and be with my family and my friends and eat a tremendous volume of pizza and drink a sea of champagne, and try, best as I can, to remember that today, despite all of the odds that were stacked against me, I did better

than just make it through. I was amazing. I haven't been amazing in a very long time, long enough that I had almost forgotten what it feels like. And whatever ick I feel about how I've just left things with Mark, it can't take away the part of me that is really, really happy to be back, even just for a day.

Goodbye Again

(1933)

RUTH DONNELLY AS THE MAID: Is he ill?

JOAN BLONDELL AS ANNE ROGERS: No, he's *nuts*!

I look in the mirror, taking in the full effect. My face is painted gray, with a false pink nose and whiskers; my hair is slicked back, with a pair of pink-lined gray ears on a headband. I'm wearing charcoal gray sweatpants, and a gray long-sleeved T-shirt, with matching gray gloves. I've got a white apron tied around my waist and a long, tapering pink tail is attached to the apron belt and hangs jauntily nearly to the floor.

I look fucking ridiculous.

"You are so adorable," Bubbles says, standing in the doorway of my room.

"I look like a deranged opossum."

"Nonsense, you look exactly like Remy from *Ratatouille*! It's wonderful! And more importantly, the kids will love it."

"Seriously?"

She narrows her eyes at me. "I think you are fantastic, and when you are standing next to Herman, with him all dressed like Chef Gusteau, the store all decorated with my copper pots

and pans, and all those little helper rats perched about, everyone will get it."

Herman insisted we go all out for Halloween, especially
since it is the Cake Goddess's grand opening, and she is having a
full day of events . . . there will be "make your own monster
cookie" decorating in her event space all day, and she's debuting
a line of new cupcake flavors inspired by traditional candy bars.
There are going to be free caramel popcorn balls for the kids,
and displays of "dessert sushi" for the adults—thick rice pudding spread onto kiwi fruit leather, and topped with Swedish
Fish or other gummi offerings. And apparently, with every purchase of ten dollars or more, there's an entry into a raffle to win
one of five iPad minis with custom Cake Goddess covers. And
"special celebrity guest stars" popping in all day, all of which
will be endlessly promoted on her social media channels.

Langer's is fighting back best as we can. We've installed a
television, and will be showing *Ratatouille* on an endless loop,
and will be giving out traditional Halloween candies to any
trick-or-treater who stops by, regardless of purchase. There will
be a cauldron of spiced hot cider, and pumpkin shortbread fingers with caramel and fudge dipping sauces as our freebies, and
I've done plenty of special spooky treats. Ladies' fingers, butter
cookies in the shape of gnarled fingers with almond fingernails
and red food coloring on the stump end. I've got meringue
ghosts and cups of "graveyard pudding," a dark chocolate pudding layered with dark Oreo cookie crumbs, strewn with
gummi worms, and topped with a cookie tombstone. There are
chocolate tarantulas, with mini cupcake bodies and legs made
out of licorice whips, sitting on spun cotton candy nests. The
Pop-Tart flavors of the day are chocolate peanut butter, and
pumpkin spice. The chocolate ones are in the shape of bats, and
the pumpkin ones in the shape of giant candy corn with orange,

yellow, and white icing. And yesterday, after finding a stash of tiny walnut-sized lady apples at the market, I made a huge batch of mini caramel apples.

"You'll have fun," Bubbles says. "The weather is supposed to be beautiful for a change."

"Well, that is something." It's been a little strange since I moved back home last week. Herman is up and about and back to his usual self, so we swapped places once again. It's lovely to be back with Bubbles, but also a little strange. It's amazing how quickly one can get used to privacy and quiet and solitude; I'm a little unsettled being back here. And while we did have a hectic couple of weeks right after the cake competition, and a heavy uptick in our likes and follows, last week the weather was really crappy, and we were back to our usual level of business. I had a pretty hefty backlog of Wedding Girl emails to get through, having slacked off a bit in the weeks leading up to the competition. Despite the positive publicity of our second-place showing at the contest, we haven't gotten any event-cake orders coming up except for my parents' wedding cake for next weekend.

"I'll be by to bring you both some lunch," Bubbles says, smiling, and I smile back, trying to put a good face on things. "Is Mark coming by?"

"I'm not sure, I think so. I know Herman invited him." I haven't really seen much of Mark since the day of the contest. He of course was back to business as usual at work, back and forth to California, and there wasn't much of a need for him to come by the store. He came last week to help Herman move back upstairs, but I only saw him for a couple of minutes and it was a bit awkward. Whatever. I have bigger things to worry about than my brief friendship with even briefer benefits with Herman Mark Langer Jr. And bigger things to look forward to.

Jake comes home in a couple of weeks, and we have an official date planned. I got the email a couple of days after the contest.

S—

Good news! I've finally got a firm re-entry plan. In a few weeks I'll be wrapping things up here, and will be home the first week of November. Which means I have a request. Will you be my date to the Juvenile Diabetes Research Foundation gala the second Saturday in November? I know, boring fundraising gala dinner is not exactly the thing that comes to mind for a first date, but hear me out. My company bought a table, and have asked me to attend. I can't think of anyone I would rather sit next to and be snarky with than you. Plus I figure after all these months, meeting me when I'm in my tuxedo and at my most Cary Grant has to be my best shot. We'll bid on silly stuff at the silent auction, and pick at the rubber chicken, and quietly make fun of some of the more ridiculous dance moves, and then we'll sneak out and pick up hotdogs, and go sit somewhere we can see the skyline. What do you say?

J

He's been wonderful with emailing, and we have been sharing more and more about our deeper thoughts and feelings. It's so strange. I know his politics, and his thoughts on love and marriage and children and pets and friendships. I know the foods he likes, the wines he drinks, the way he takes his coffee. I know all about his favorite books and television shows and movies and music. I know the horror stories of some of his previous relationships, the details of his best and worst vacations and dates and birthdays. But I don't know his last name, or any-

thing about his family or where he grew up or where he went to school.

And the same is still true for me. I still hide what I need to hide, lie when I need to lie. Part of me thinks that he will come pick me up for the gala and then slam the door right in my face. I don't ever really think that I might be the one to want to slam the door, unless of course he turns out to be married, in which case not only will I slam the door, I'll slam some available part of his anatomy in it. But for now, I'm allowing myself to be tentatively optimistic.

J—

Well of course I would be delighted to accompany you. But mostly for the hot dogs. I'm glad things are finishing well for you, and look forward to seeing you in a few weeks.

S

"Well, scoot, or you'll be late." Bubbles pinches my tush, and heads out of the room. I can hear her down the hallway, talking in her loving voice to the dog, who she has dressed up in a little Stay Puft Marshmallow Man costume, complete with the little hat, to accentuate his pudgy rolls. "Who's a fat Snatch? Who's a great big fat Snatch?"

And on that note, I head downstairs, hoping that I can make it to my car before anyone sees me looking so ridiculous.

⁂

"It'll pick up after lunch, for sure," Herman says with false bravado. "None of those mommies want to start the day with sugar, the kids won't survive."

"Of course it will," I say, not believing a word. We've been

slow since we opened, and while everyone who comes in has been excited about the freebies, the specialty Halloween treats aren't exactly flying off the shelves. We've sold precisely three Pop-Tarts, one pudding, half a dozen caramel apples, and a pair of ghost meringues, but that is it. Everything else is the usual breads and pastries, typical of a Saturday morning. We've seen a couple of costumes, and once we explain who we are, people get it, but we're not exactly being asked to take pictures with the kids. I don't know what else we could have done; we are certainly giving it our all. But at least three of our customers mentioned that they were here because the "lines over at Cake Goddess were just more than I could deal with," which doesn't bode well. When I can, I check their Twitter, which is full of postings of pictures of long lines, of kids making cookies, of the cast of *Chicago Fire* signing autographs and handing out cupcakes. It breaks my heart.

"Sophie, since it's quiet, and before your grandmother gets here, I want to ask you two important questions."

"Shoot."

"First, I want to know if you would give me your blessing to ask for her hand in marriage. I know it probably seems fast, but we are at a place in life where waiting seems silly. I would very much like to be her husband, if you would be okay with that."

I grab Herman around his belly, hugging him with all my heart. It isn't like it's surprising, the two of them are so terrific together, but I love that he thought to ask me. "Of course, you old bear, I can't think of anything that would make me happier. You absolutely have all of my blessings and encouragement."

He hugs me tight. "Thank you, my sweet girl, that is very wonderful to hear."

"Of course! And I get to make your wedding cake."

"Naturally. Speaking of which, that is the second question I have for you. I know that it is time for me to retire. My little

incident tells me that I should slow down and enjoy and not keep working."

In a way, I'm glad he is coming to this realization of his own accord and not because Cake Goddess is putting us out of business, which, without a miracle, like her accidentally killing someone's kid with a cupcake, she certainly will, and if today is an indication, sooner rather than later.

"But this is a good place. A special place. So I wonder if you might want it."

Uh-oh. "Um, Herman . . ."

"Not to keep Langer's as Langer's. But the space, the building. You could make it anything you want. I know that once we are married, I will go live in your grandmother's house, I could never ask her to leave it. And that will be less than an ideal situation for you. If you transformed this space, into whatever you want it to be, a different sort of bakery, or a small restaurant, or just an event-cake location, you could live upstairs . . ." He trails off a bit. "I could be a silent partner and landlord till you are in a position to buy it out. If you wanted."

"That is so lovely and so generous. But what does Ma . . . Herman Jr. say?"

"It was his idea."

This floors me. "It was?"

He smiles. "It was."

Well holy crap. "It is a lot to think about. Can I have some time to see if it makes sense?"

"Of course, my dear, of course. And if it doesn't make sense, it doesn't. If it doesn't further your dreams and you have to say no, you will not hurt my feelings. I'm ready to let go of this place, truly. But if it can be what you want, what you need, I want you to know that I believe in you and want to help if I can."

Tears prick my eyes. It is maybe the kindest thing anyone

has ever said to me. "Thank you, Herman, it's the most amazing offer, and I promise, I will give it long and careful consideration."

He reaches for me and we hug again.

"What's all this then?" says an unmistakable voice behind us.

"Junior! You are here." Herman lets me go, and walks around the front of the counter to hug Mark. "And you got my instructions," he says.

"Yeah, I sure did," Mark says, waving his arm over his body. He is dressed like Linguini from *Ratatouille*, with a curly red wig under a tall paper chef's toque, full set of whites, and a whisk tucked into his apron. "What can I do?"

"At the moment, very little," Herman says, gesturing to the empty store.

"Perfect. I'm eminently qualified to do very little," Mark says, perusing the case. "These are some truly inspired holiday treats. I may have to do some tasting, just to be sure they aren't poisonous." He walks around the counter and grabs a pumpkin Pop-Tart. "Hi." He looks me up and down, and then smirks, talking at me out of the side of his mouth.

"Hi yourself," I say.

"Interesting costume choice," he says. "I would have pegged you to go for Colette. But Remy, that is a good one."

I'm stunned that he knows the movie that well, and feel like an idiot that it didn't occur to me to just dress like the female lead. All I would have needed was a sleek black bob wig and my chef's whites. I shrug. "Well, you know how I love to be the star."

"Remy is sort of perfect when you think of it, all the talent, but still needs someone else to be the public face. Kind of apropos."

I can't tell if this is a dig, but he seems to be in something of a good mood, and he does get major points for showing up here in full regalia to support his dad. I wonder if he too knows how

dire things are about to get. "Yep. That's me. Plus I do like the idea of being able to make you my puppet."

This comes out somewhat more double entendre-y than I intended, and Mark raises an eyebrow at me, and then winks and purses his lips. I can feel myself blush, but I also can't help laughing.

"What a merry sight this is!" Bubbles says, blowing through the door on a gust of autumn wind, carrying her large cooler bag with both hands.

"Let me take that from you, my dear." Herman rushes to her side, kisses her tenderly, and takes the burden from her. They are so adorable I could just spit.

"Herman Jr., how lovely to see you. You look wonderful."

"My love, I hate for you to pick up my bad habits, he really does prefer Mark," Herman says, nodding at his son, who looks first surprised, and then sheepishly happy. I know that feeling, and I'm glad for Mark that his dad is honoring his wishes. I get the sense that with everything that has happened, the two of them have found more common ground, and seem to be closer. It makes me happy for them both.

"Mark it is, then. Mark, I hope you haven't had lunch, I've brought plenty," Bubbles says.

"As a matter of fact, I have not. Someone warned me you might be stopping by with delectables, why do you think I'm in this ridiculous get-up? I believe in singing for my supper if necessary."

"Wicked boy," she says happily. "He's a good one, your son," she says to Herman.

"He's the very best one," Herman says, and Mark actually blushes.

"Okay, since someone has to mind the store, and we are moments away from high noon, and we know how the two of you love to keep to your schedules, why don't you lovebirds go

have a quiet lunch à deux upstairs, and when you're done, you can come relieve Mark and I and we can eat whatever you haven't snarfed up," I say.

"A good plan, my dear, a very good plan." Herman hoists the cooler bag and heads for the private door, Bubbles and Snatch close on his heels.

"I do feel so special, getting to use the secret entrance like this." She giggles. "Behind the magic curtain, or off to Narnia or some such thing." The three of them disappear up the stairs and the door clicks shut behind them.

"He hasn't been this happy since Mom died," Mark says. "Your grandmother is a godsend."

"She has that effect on people. For what it's worth, while I've never thought of her as unhappy, and I never saw her with my granddad, I know I've never seen her so glowy as she's been these past months."

"Did you know the whole time, that they were . . ."

"Intimate pals?" He nods. "Nope. She fessed up when I busted in on them when your dad fell."

"Yeah, he told me in the hospital."

"Shocking, but kind of funny."

"I'd say surprising more than shocking. I was really kind of relieved to know he hadn't just been fully alone all these years."

"Yeah, that's how I felt for her. More 'You go girl!' and not too much 'Ewwww.'"

"He wants to marry her, you know," Mark says.

"I know. He asked for my blessing."

"Me too. He wants to give her his mother's ring. I have my mom's engagement ring, he didn't get the other one till my grandmother passed, so it wouldn't be the same one. He wanted to make sure I was okay with it."

"And are you?"

"Of course. Although . . ."

"Although?"

"Well, it would make you my step-relative."

"Indeed. Sorry, it appears you'll be stuck with me."

Mark looks me in the eye. "I can think of many worse things."

And before I can suss out his meaning, the door opens, and a gaggle of tiny Elsas and Annas and Minions fly in yelling "trick or treat," with parents in tow and, hopefully, hearty appetites.

⁘

"He offered me the store," I say to Mark as we are cleaning up our lunch plates. Bubbles didn't disappoint, with a hearty lasagna, which she makes with what she calls a "cheat," layering large cooked cheese ravioli with homemade thick Bolognese sauce in lieu of dealing with the pasta and cheese separately. Mark and I devoured nearly half the pan, with some of the Caesar salad she had also made, and the sourdough baguette Herman had snagged on his way upstairs.

"Yeah, he and I talked about that too."

"He said it was your idea."

"Well, he won't need the same kind of equity that he would have now that he is just moving into your grandmother's place instead of into a retirement community. I know it might not be the right fit, but I figured it might be worth offering."

"That is very kind."

"Not really. I mean, if you think it would be good, great. In the meantime, the neighborhood keeps improving, the property value could increase significantly if he keeps it for a few more years, and goodness knows we couldn't ask for a better tenant. Are you going to take it?"

"I have no idea. He said he wanted to offer, in case it would help me forward my dreams. Which is so wonderful of him. If only I knew what my dreams were, I would know if this would be helpful."

"Well, your options, since I presume you are planning on staying in the baking biz, seem sort of clear. You can go back into super high-end fine-dining pastry work. You can work at a mid-range restaurant. You can open your own restaurant. You can have a little bakery. You can specialize in event cakes and not run a retail operation at all. Or you can go work for some catering operation or hotel or something. Or you can teach . . ."

"Slow your roll, there, Sparky. I know my options; I just don't know what I want, what I need."

"Well, you should maybe figure that out, no?"

"I know. I think . . . I think maybe after everything that happened last year, after everything that was leading up to what I always thought was my dream fell apart—my dream job and my dream guy and my dream life—I just don't know if I have it in me to dream that big again. If that makes sense."

I've never said this out loud, never even wanted to admit it to myself, but when I hear the words, I know they are true. Why would I look for a whole new set of dreams when my last dreams did nothing but hurt me? Why else would I get so attached to Jake, who is still mostly theoretical, and let's be honest, unlikely to be everything I've built him up to be in my head, instead of pursuing something real, something tangible?

"Of course you do. No one knows that better than me. I watched you plan that cake, execute, do what you did here with my dad, for my dad. You have dreams in you, Sophie Bernstein. And I think it's high time you let yourself want them to come true."

"Thank you, for the faith in me. It's duly noted."

"Look, when you figure out what is in your heart, I hope you'll call me."

I look over at him putting our plates in the drying rack, my heart beginning to race. He smiles at me.

"After all, I am pretty good at the whole business plan thing, so whether or not you intend to take my dad up on his offer, I

can at least help you go over the numbers, see if we can figure out the best way to get you where you want to be."

I wish I knew why I'm disappointed that this is just about my business future.

"I thank you for that, and once I know, I'll be sure to let you know."

"Good," he says, drying his hands on a towel.

"Hey, how's Ella?"

"She's back in California. And I assume she is doing fine." This sentence tells me everything I need to know. Good for him. "How about your Snuffleupagus guy that no one has ever met. Will he be in later?"

"He's away on business." And before this can go any further, I add, "We should get back to work."

"After you," he says.

S—

I'm sorry to hear that things at your uncle's store are not looking good. I know it must be difficult to imagine shutting it down. But if, as you say, you are fighting a losing battle, sometimes the better part of valor is knowing when to surrender. And you both know that you gave it your all, went down fighting, all of those horrible clichés. There is no shame in fighting a losing battle, just in not fighting at all. And if, as you say, he'll be okay financially, then I would recommend just ripping off the bandaid quickly, so that he protects as much of what he has saved as possible, and doesn't keep throwing good money after bad trying to save it.

Regardless, you know that what you did for him was a gift, and you should be very proud of yourself for the efforts you put in. If it doesn't sound too weird, I'm proud of you for it!

J

J—

Thanks for your good thoughts, and support, it means a lot.
Now if only I really knew what my next step should be . . .

S

If only indeed.

Double Wedding

(1937)

Women don't like noble, self-sacrificing men.
Women are not civilized like we are. They like
bloodshed. They like forceful men, like me.

• WILLIAM POWELL AS CHARLES LODGE •

I love being here at the bakery at night. Herman is over at Bubbles's, having dinner and watching a movie, but I begged off to stay and work on Mom and Dad's cake. The wedding is this Saturday, and thankfully, I think it will be both beautiful and very much them. Dad's best pal, Russell, has gotten ordained on the Internet to perform the secular ceremony, and my mom's cousin Seth, who is a reform rabbi, will do the few parts of the traditional Jewish ceremony that are important to them. They are having a Middle Eastern feast, all buffet, with plenty of vegetarian options for the myriad aging hippies who are flocking to Chicago from all areas of the country to watch the vows and eat their weight in falafel and hummus. They've hired an old-school DJ who promises that he owns all of the Motown, psychedelic oldies, and classic disco that they will be able to handle. Mom is doing the flowers herself—being the gardener extraordinaire, she loves to arrange simple bundles of colorful blooms—and she's enlisted one of her former clients who is now a florist to help her out.

Bubbles and I took her shopping, and found her a lovely simple dress of antiqued lace embroidered all over with tiny colorful flowers, worn over an ivory sheath. It has more than a hint of California boho chic, but she looks like an elegant lady in it, and not like a Bonnaroo attendee. I even talked her into a pair of Stuart Weitzman pumps, since some of the new styles have a solid chunky lower-height heel that will be comfortable for dancing. She's never spent that much money on shoes before, but I caught a little glint in her eye, and I do think I might convince her that the occasional designer splurge is good for the soul. She bought me a lovely new dress in a beautiful blush pink with a hint of gray in it, and Bubbles got a snappy suit in dove gray, with a kicky peplum.

The cake is pretty simple; they didn't want anything too fancy. Two tiers. The bottom is the Frango mint tier from the cake contest, but the top is a new one. An almond cake with a whipped honey caramel filling and a layer of thinly sliced spiced poached pears, with vanilla buttercream. The whole cake will get a smooth white fondant coating, and then a detailed lace pattern hand-piped with white royal icing. They've opted out of toppers, so I've made some simple wildflowers out of gum paste, colored with the powdered food colors to look incredibly real.

Tonight I'm working on the cake layers, so that I can do fillings and frostings tomorrow, assemble tiers and put on the fondant on Thursday, and then decorate it on Friday. Mark offered to help, but I declined. I also declined Herman's generous offer of the store. I thought about it endlessly, but I know that I'm just not feeling like I want the pressure of launching something on my own. The more I think about it, the more I believe that I need to work with challenges that are strictly pastry related, and the pressure of managing every aspect of a business is just not for me, as much as I love the creative freedom. I'm not sure what I'll do, but I know it can't be here. Herman totally understood,

and said that he would be putting the place on the market, but not closing the business until it sells. So I could be out of a job next week or next year, depending.

I get the first chocolate layers in the oven, and sneak up front to grab a brownie. You'd think I'd get sick of my own baking, but I never get tired of sweet treats to keep my energy up. I'm stuffing half the brownie into my maw when there is a knock on the door. I look up, prepared to tell whichever hipster with munchies is trying to get in that we are closed, but I see Mary-Sue Adams waving at me through the window.

"Sophie, how are you, sugar?" she asks when I let her in, locking the door back up behind her.

"I'm good, MarySue, how about you?"

"Busier than a one-armed paper-hanger, as you can imagine. I was leaving the store and saw you through the window, what are you doing here so late?"

"Working on my parents' wedding cake for this weekend."

"That is so sweet; is it a big anniversary that made them want to do a vow renewal?"

"Nope, they've been living in sin for over forty years and figured they were finally sure it was gonna stick."

She looks perplexed, but bounces back quickly. "That is just darling! Good for them."

"Congrats on the opening, looks like you've got a huge hit on your hands."

She smiles, blinding me with her huge choppers. "Thank you, it's been a labor of love, heavy on the labor, but really worth it. It's actually why I thought I would pop in, since you were here. I've been wanting to talk to you."

"Really?"

"Really. Ever since I was in here and tasted all of your goodies, and then your cake at that competition . . . Really, Sophie, you are just so talented."

I'm taken aback a bit by the sincerity of this statement. "Thanks, MarySue. That means a lot."

"I'm here to make you an offer. I know you are committed to this place." She waves her hand around. "But you also must know, deep down, that you can and should be doing so much more. And I'd like you to do it with me."

"What?"

"I'm offering you a job. Creative Director of the new store. Once it's up on its feet, I need to step away and let it live without me, and while I do love and trust the team I have there now, there isn't a ton of oomph in the forward-thinking department. I want to bring in someone who can really make the place more than just an outpost of what I've always done, someone who can work with the existing brand, but keep things fresh and exciting. You'd be perfect, and you and I both know that this place, as darling as it is, will not likely survive very long. I'm sorry, I know that Mr. Langer is your dear friend, and I think he is the cat's pajamas, but it can't really be helped."

I can't decide if I'm hating her or respecting her right now.

"You don't have to decide right now. But I know you'd be great, and I'd be lucky to get you."

"MarySue, that is very unexpected and truly wonderful of you to even think of me, I just don't know where my head is with the idea of moving on. Herman and I are both aware that this community will not be able to sustain us both, but I won't leave him until he is ready to close, and my best guess is that he will not do that before he is able to sell this building. He lives here as well, so he is going to have to make sure that he comes out with a decent deal, and I don't know how long that might take."

She looks me in the eye. "He's going to sell the building and the business or just the building?"

I can smell what she's thinking, and suddenly have a brain

wave. "Well, the place is zoned properly, so even if someone doesn't want to keep it as a bakery, they could do a small café or other food-related business here, so he would be looking to sell the building with the downstairs space priced to acknowledge that. Especially in this neighborhood, which is so up-and-coming, and could use some more food destinations."

"I see. And is the property listed yet?"

"His son, Mark, will be handling the sale, I'm happy to give you his info if you think you know someone who might be interested . . ."

She nods, and I reach for my phone and give her Mark's information. Hell, she's got plenty of money, and her fiancé is a billionaire. Let her buy this place and turn it into some peaches and cream café or cupcake outlet store for all I care. I'd love to get Herman out smooth and with a nest egg. After all, he's going to have to take good care of Bubbles.

"Can I put together an offer memo for you?" she asks, and then looks at me with eyes full of savvy. "Or do you need to have your head clear? I can wait till after you have an official store closing date."

I smile. "I do think that waiting would be better. Who knows how long a sale might take, or who else you might find in the meantime while I'm still encumbered over here?"

She nods. "You're a smart girl, Sophie, a very smart girl. I'll be back in touch soon. For what it's worth, I thought you and your boyfriend should've won that cake competition. And I think if Dexter and Cookie hadn't been there, you would have, by a landslide."

"He's not my boyfriend, and we were proud of second place."

"Really? I watched you both all day, you have such a great energy between you, I would have sworn you were a happy couple. Oh well. Anyway. We'll talk again soon. You have a great night."

"Will do. And MarySue?"

"Yes, sugar?"

"Thank you. I don't have any idea where I will land once all of this goes away, but it really does mean a lot to me that you would think of me and want me in such a key position in your new store, and whatever happens, I'll always be grateful for the interest."

"Don't be thankful, honey. I'm a coldhearted business-woman these days, and I only do things that I think will make me money. I smell success on you, and I'd rather have it in my house than competing with me in someone else's house." She winks, and heads out the door. I lock up after her and head back into the kitchen to get the cakes out of the oven, and to call Mark to warn him that he might be getting a call about buying the building, and to keep the price as high as he can.

⌒⌒⌒

"Diane and I want to thank everyone so very much for sharing this special day with us. It is a day we never really thought would happen, but now that it has, we couldn't be happier or more in love or more thrilled to have you all with us."

My dad is beaming, with his arm around my mom, their new wedding bands glowing on their fingers, surrounded by family, and decades' worth of friends, the tent warm with the heat of nearly a hundred people who have been dancing up a storm.

"And now, we have a special surprise." He says, "Mom, will you come up here, please?"

Bubbles walks over to my parents, and kisses them both on the cheeks. She and Herman have been cutting a rug together, sort of standing and swaying to the beat in each other's arms, and Jean keeps elbowing me to point them out, while Ruth rolls

her eyes and says that we get it, they're really cute old people in love.

Suddenly Herman appears at Bubbles's side, and takes the microphone from my dad.

"You all don't know me, but I'm Herman Langer, and I am a friend of this beautiful lady."

Bubbles smiles at him, and takes his hand. He turns to look at her.

"And I want to take this opportunity to say that it seems only appropriate as we all celebrate this wedding that was so beautiful, to be moved to say to my love that she has changed my life for the better, and made me happier than I ever thought I could be again. They say that it is never too late, and I believe that. So I hope that you will do me the great honor of becoming my wife. I'd get on one knee, but I fear I'd never get up . . ."

Bubbles claps her hands, and nods yes, overcome by emotion. The place goes nuts. Herman pulls the ring out of his pocket and puts it on her finger, and we all go crazy again. I head across the dance floor to meet them, and we end up in a giant family hug. When we pull apart, the DJ is playing "At Last," and the two couples, newlyweds and newly engaged, take to the floor.

"Shall we?" Mark says at my elbow, opening his arms to me.

"Of course." I curtsy, and let him pull me into his embrace. He's a shockingly good dancer, a strong lead, and I let myself just float around the floor where he moves me.

"Those crazy kids, think they'll make it?" he asks.

"Which ones?"

He laughs. "All four, I guess. It does make you believe in love a bit, though."

"Didn't you believe in love before?"

"It always seemed like a good idea. But often better in theory than in practice."

"Yeah, I know what you mean. But still, one can hope."

"And your Invisible Man, do you think he is your great hope?"

I think about this. "I don't know. I think I can hope that he is kind and caring, and that if he isn't my great hope, that he at least is enough to let me hope for a greater hope."

"He's a lucky guy, for what it's worth."

"Yes, yes he is." And for the first time in a very long time, this is not just bravado. I'm a catch, I'm a good person. The shit I've been through doesn't define me, but how I've handled it does, and whatever insecurities I may have about my current living situation, or lack of career focus, or the debt I'm still carrying, despite having made some really nice big payments from my Wedding Girl money, he is lucky. Or will be. When I meet him.

"Pumpkin time for me," Mark says, when the song ends, and the DJ shifts into "Disco Inferno."

"Thanks for coming tonight, I know it meant a lot to my folks and your dad and Bubbles that you were here."

"Wouldn't have missed it for the world."

"Well, it was nice for you to be here for a bit. Hot date to get to?" I tease him.

He winks at me. "Nope. Just me, and some popcorn, and a good old movie."

And with that, he turns and leaves, and it takes me a moment to realize what he just said. A good old movie. It couldn't possibly be, right? I'm a crazy person. Mark is not Jake. That is patently ridiculous. I've definitely had too much champagne. And I shake it off as I catch sight of my parents heading for the cake table, and walk over to watch them dig into the best gift I could give them: sweetness.

"Okay, this shit is insane, you should bake for a living or something," Ruth says, digging into her second helping of cake.

"So. Good," Jean says, well into her third, each more generously portioned than the last.

"You think I have a future?"

"In cake, absolutely," Ruth says.

"Now if only I had a job."

"You'll get a job as soon as you don't have a job," Jean says.

"Right. Like last time."

"It's nothing like last time. Look, you already have one offer, or at least the promise of one. And once you are officially done at Herman's place, your focus won't be split, and you'll find the right thing. Or you'll find the wrong thing that will be a placeholder while you find the right thing," Ruth says, licking caramel off her finger.

"Exactly," Jean says.

"Hell, you might even find a guy," Ruth pipes in.

"Funny you should mention that, I have a date. Two weeks from tonight."

"Mazel tov. Who is he?" Jean asks.

"Just a guy I met online, might be nothing, but I'm looking forward to it." Bubbles might not be computer savvy enough to question my meeting someone online and go poking around for my profile, but there was no way to tell the girls the same thing, they would have totally gone snooping.

"Ugh, better you than me with the online dating thing, I can't do it. But it works for a lot of people, so fingers crossed!" Ruth says. "Which site? I wanna see your profile." Exactly.

"I'm so proud of you," Jean says. She probably wouldn't be so proud if she knew the specifics, but I'm leaving those out.

"JDate." Ruth reaches for her phone. "But I took my profile down. This guy seems interesting enough, but the process felt weird and unnatural." Which is going to be a heck of a thing to explain to them if Jake turns out to be nothing and I do have to do the online thing for real someday.

All of a sudden, Jean and Ruth both stop. "It's our song, bitches," Ruth says, as the opening bars of Gloria Gaynor's "I Will Survive" begin. And Jean jumps up and drags us both by the hand to the dance floor, and we dance in a group, my parents and even Bubbles and Herman joining our circle, and we sing at the tops of our voices that we will survive, and I know that I believe it.

Bringing Up Baby

(1938)

KATHARINE HEPBURN AS SUSAN VANCE: You're angry, aren't you?

CARY GRANT AS DAVID HUXLEY: Yes, I am!

KATHARINE HEPBURN AS SUSAN VANCE: Mm-hmm. The love impulse in man frequently reveals itself in terms of conflict.

Bubbles walks into the kitchen and finds me sitting in the Nook.

"Are you all right, sweetheart?"

"Yep."

"You look a little pale."

"I'm just a little bit shocked."

"By what?"

"By the call I just got."

I've just hung up from a call with David Francisco. He has a job for me. The Astor Place Hotel wants to bring in a head event pastry chef, since the current pastry chef has his hands full enough with the needs of the restaurant and room service. Since the events job is so site-intensive and long hours, and they are anticipating doing a heavy-duty event business, the offer, which has a competitive salary and excellent benefits, also comes with

a small one-bedroom apartment in the wing of the hotel that is set up for long-term stays, should I want it. It isn't required that I live on-site if I don't want to, as long as I know what sort of hours are expected of me. It was all I could do to not jump at it right there, but I managed to keep my composure enough to thank him profusely and tell him that I would get back to him by the end of the week with my answer.

I fill Bubbles in on the development, and she weirdly doesn't seem surprised.

"I'm delighted for you, sweetheart, do you think that is something that would make you happy?"

"I do, at least I think I do. I've always thought that hotel work would be a good place for me, and I really loved that hotel, and David was a very nice guy. It certainly seems like the kind of job I could really get into. And the fact that it comes with housing is certainly a perk! When Herman moves in, you two are going to want some privacy!"

"You know you always have a home here."

I shake my head. "I'll always have a room here, but I need to make a home somewhere else. With occasional movie-night sleepovers."

"Fair enough. I think it's a wonderful opportunity, and I'm very glad that it is coming before you had to think about working for that woman with the teeth."

"Hey, that woman with the teeth may be providing you and Herman with a tidy little nest egg, so don't knock her too hard."

"Humph. We'll see about that. I'm not mixing the martinis till I see a check."

I laugh. Mark and MarySue's attorney apparently had a decent first conversation the other day about her company purchasing the building and business, and while they are hashing

out some details, I do think that ultimately it will work itself out. Whatever her adopted business persona might be, deep down, there is still a little bit of a soft creamy center, and I think she probably feels a bit badly about knocking Herman into retirement, and is making it right . . . albeit with a savvy real estate investment, so not exactly charity.

"Alright, well, we are going to need to have a small celebration. I have one little errand to run, but when I get back, champagne?"

"Absolutely."

"I'll be back in about an hour."

Bubbles heads out the door. "What do you think, Snatch, should I go live in a grand hotel like Eloise?"

Snatch licks my shoe.

"That seems good enough for me." And I toss him a treat, and head upstairs to work on Wedding Girl emails. With my new salary, and the fact that my housing is included, my days as Dear Abby to the Wedding Set are officially numbered. I should be able to pay off the remainder of my debt within the next four months or so. That will be a huge relief—as much as it isn't terribly difficult, and I've had a lot of people tell me that my advice was hugely helpful, it definitely isn't my dream to continue. The more I answer those emails the more I realize that what I like about weddings is the personal touch. Meeting the clients and caring about their details. One of the things that most excited me about Dave's offer was the thought of getting back to that. I think about meeting Amelia and how much fun it was to assist her, the joy of watching my parents taking their vows, Bubbles and Herman planning their sweet little nuptials. Maybe even someday one of my own. If I'm going to be involved, I want to be *involved*. Doling out pat answers to the same questions over and over might be lucrative, but it isn't in my soul. I've made up my mind to use it to

finish paying off my debt, and then see if Beth over at SineQua-Non wants to buy the site from me. She'll be a much better Wedding Girl than I ever was.

Nearly an hour and a half later, I hear Snatch barking his fool head off, which is very unusual; he almost never barks in the house. I can hear Herman and Bubbles, talking in hushed tones, and I head downstairs to see what the ruckus is about.

"What's going on down here?" I ask as I get to the bottom of the stairs.

"We have a little surprise for you. A present," Bubbles says.

"Oh, I do love presents, as you know."

"Well, I wanted to do something special, to thank you for everything you've done for me," Herman says.

"And when he said he wanted to make you a present, I knew just the thing," Bubbles says.

Snatch barks loudly as Bubbles and Herman lead me into the dining room. The place is covered in bags and boxes, and on the dining room table is what looks like a large basket made of rope. Then I hear the squeaking.

I walk over and look in the basket, where a tiny little pug puppy is chewing on a corner of a blanket and squeaking and scratching his ear all at once.

"You did not!" I say.

Herman puts his arm around Bubbles and they both look at me with faces full of love. "We did indeed," Herman says, and Bubbles winks. "I always told you a girl needs a dog."

I reach for the wiggly little piglet of a puppy, and he snuggles into my arms, immediately grabbing the end of my ponytail.

"He's a little muncher," Herman says.

"*Oooh*, that's a good name for him." Bubbles gets excited. "Munch!"

Oh lord. "Bubbles . . ."

"It's perfect," Herman says. And I know I can't fight it.

"Munch it is," I say, extricating my hair from his mouth. Sigh. At least I can just tell people I named him after the *Homicide: Life on the Street* Richard Belzer character. He turns his attention to the shoulder of my shirt, and I can feel his sharp little puppy teeth shredding the fabric already. I wrest the shirt out of his mouth and put him down on the floor, where he attacks Snatch, latching on to his tail, and the two of them yip at each other happily. I go to hug Herman and Bubbles. "Thank you both, so much, I love him. He's perfect."

"He's perfectly peeing on the floor at the moment," Bubbles observes.

"Oh, *Munch*!" I say, picking him up before he can walk through the puddle.

"You take the dogs out, ladies, I'll clean the floor and get the champagne ready," Herman says, and Bubbles hands me a small leash to attach to Munch's collar.

"Snatch! Now you're all wet!" she says to the dog, who is happily rolling in the puppy puddle. Herman looks at me with a glance that says that he, unlike Bubbles, is fully aware of the implications of the dog's name, and finds it just as charming as I do. We finally get both dogs out of the house and into the brisk autumn air.

"You're amazing, you know that," I say.

"Well, I do what I can. You are happy about him, aren't you? I know they say you should never give a pet as a present, but when Snatch's breeder called to say that she had a litter with one unclaimed, and she knew that Snatch was getting up in years, and wondered if maybe I was thinking I would want another, it just felt right for you."

"I adore him already. And you're right, it will be good for me to have him. I can't keep waiting for every aspect of life to be

settled before doing things for myself. So he'll be my partner in crime, whatever is coming down the pike. The perfect man for the next chapter of my life."

"Well, dear, he's a dog, not a man, and I don't recommend you confuse them. A girl still needs a little two-legged loving, if you know what I mean."

"Yes, I do, and also, *ewwww*!"

She shrugs. "Just telling it like I see it. Herman and I got you everything you'll need for this little guy, including a meeting tomorrow morning with a trainer. He is already crate trained, so you have a little crate to set up next to your bed, and it has a blanket in it from the crate the breeder was using, so the smell will soothe him. Herman and I are going out for the evening, and then we'll stay at his house with Snatch tonight, so the two of you can get a bit settled. Plus if I know your girls, they are going to head over as soon as you call them to come meet him."

She's right about that. "Thank you, Bubbles, it's all just so amazing."

"*Munch!* Snatch is not food; you cannot munch on Snatch!" She *tsks* at the puppy, and quickly hands me a treat to distract him from attacking the older dog, who is looking at us with a world-weary face. I snicker to myself, and pull my new best buddy off, and the four of us continue our walk around the block.

"He's so stinking cute," Jean says, reaching for another chip, and looking over at Munch, who is curled up asleep in Amelia's lap.

"Seriously. I could rethink my no pet policy," Ruth says.

"I kinda want to eat him," Amelia says, poking gently at the pup's ear just to watch it twitch.

"I can't believe it, and lord knows I would have said no if she'd asked, but I'm glad she did it. I love him already. Remind me of that when it's forty below windchill and I'm waiting for him to poop."

"I want to hear more about this date," Ruth says.

"Oooh. A date! I didn't know you had a date. Who with?" Amelia asks.

"Some guy she met online," Jean says.

"Not Best Man?" Amelia says. I had bragged a bit about my influence after Jake sent me the full report on the success of the bachelor party, including that the frat boy brothers went out of their way to say that it was the best bachelor party they had ever been to.

I pause, and smile a little.

"Wait, Best Man? What does she know?" Ruth says.

"Didn't you tell them about the site?" Amelia asks.

"What site?" Ruth says, clearly annoyed that Amelia knows something she doesn't.

"The advice site I did for Sophie."

You can practically hear the needle scratching across the record. Crap. Well, what the hell. They're my best friends, what's the worst that can happen.

"I've got a sort of event advice site that I've been doing on the side."

"Event advice," Jean says.

"Yeah, you know, sort of event-specific ideas or how to handle challenges sort of thing. Like Martha Stewart meets Dear Abby," I say.

"Just for the hell of it?" Ruth says. "Or is this some kind of blog or something that you think can turn into money?"

"It's a paid site," Amelia says. "She gets paid to answer their questions."

"What's it called? I want to see!" Jean says, pulling out her iPad.

Here we go. "WeddingGirl.com," I say.

"Not really," Ruth says, looking at me with incredulity.

"No, really, it's right here!" Jean says, handing the tablet to Ruth, who looks it over.

"This is you?" she asks.

"Yeah," I say.

"Some girl in my office was raving about it, something about saving her whole bridesmaid situation. She made it sound like you were some famous person," Ruth says. "She literally said it was the best money she spent on her whole wedding."

"That's so nice!" Amelia says loudly, waking Munch, who yips a bit, turns around, and then resettles and goes right back to sleep.

"This is so cool, why didn't you tell us?" Jean says.

"I was embarrassed."

"Why on earth would you be embarrassed?" Ruth asks. "You're not stripping or hooking, which also would not be embarrassing, by the way, as long as you were being safe."

I take a deep breath. "Because I'm doing it for money on the side because I have some debt I need to pay down, and the bakery was not enough money to do much more than make interest payments."

"Oh, honey," Jean says. "I had no idea you took such a bath on your place! I thought you sold it, did it get foreclosed?"

"Not that kind of debt. Credit card debt."

"From the wedding, right?" Ruth asks, narrowing her eyes. "From that amazing wedding that asshole didn't show up for. He didn't pay for any of it, did he?"

"Nope."

"But you didn't do it the way you could afford, or with the money your folks gave you, you just did it all," she continues.

"Yep. Did it all. Put it all on the credit cards and figured

Dexter would pay it off for me once his trust kicked in. So stupid, in love and in finance."

Ruth gets up from her chair and walks over to me. She puts her hands on my shoulders and looks deep into my eyes. "I'm really fucking proud of you, and I'm really sorry you didn't think you could tell us, and I'm really glad that it all happened because this past year you are more the you I remember from us growing up than you've been in a long time, and I missed her." And then she kisses me, and musses my hair. "And you." She turns to Amelia. "Thanks for doing that for her, for helping her out. You're a good one, and you may stay." Having made this proclamation, she returns to her seat.

"So then, who is Best Man?"

I fill them in on Jake, the whole thing, and that I'm his date for the gala next weekend, and I still don't know what to wear, and I'm totally petrified that when I fess up to all of the lying that he'll hate me.

"Well, I can't do anything about the other stuff, but I can take care of the costuming," Jean says. "Is your wedding dress upstairs?"

I nod. "Yep, in the closet."

"Do you trust me?" she asks.

"Are you going to go all *Pretty in Pink* on me?"

"Sort of. But not cheesy." She smiles broadly.

"Have at it," I say, not at all sure what she plans to do, but knowing that whatever it was, the dress is now just fabric, and if it can become something remotely useful, it will be a good thing.

Jean runs up the stairs, and returns with the garment bag with my dress. "Okay, if she needs this for a week from Saturday, I need to get going."

"I've got the job in the morning," Ruth says.

"I'll walk you guys out, I have to take the dog for one more walk before bed."

"I'm sorry, did I mess up?" Amelia whispers in my ear as I pluck the sleepy puppy from her lap.

"Nah. It was time for me to own it. Once again, you did me a favor."

"Whew!" She gives me a hug.

"That's the thing about girlfriends. Even when you mess up, they're still there for you."

And the four of us head out into the brisk night air, to walk a puppy who is suddenly all kinds of awake and playful.

Munch, despite his purported crate training, does not seem to be particularly interested in either getting into the crate, or settling down to sleep once I plunk him in there. I grab the sheaf of papers that the trainer who is coming in the morning left with Bubbles for me, and start to read, while Munch whines at me. The papers say to shut out the lights, but to talk a bit so the puppy knows you're still there, and if you have to, put the crate on the bed with you, or sleep on the floor next to the crate. If the dog really gets upset the first few nights, you can let it sleep in the bed with you. But I've never been a dog in the bed person, that always sounded intrusive to me, so I'm hoping the talking thing will work.

I turn out the light, cooing at the dog.

"Good boy, that's a good Munch. Time for beddy-bye."

At this point he begins to howl in a way that sounds practically like screaming. Someone is going to call the police, it's like I'm killing a baby in here. And so piercingly loud I fear for my eardrums, and I've literally got rock star earplugs in. Then it is weirdly quiet. And then the smell hits me.

I turn on the light, and look down. There is Munch, completely covered in his own poop, as is his blanket, the toys, and pretty much everything inside the crate, as well as many of the lower half of the crate bars themselves. I cannot believe such a

tiny little dog has produced this much crap, with such a powerful odor.

"Good lord, dog, we're going to need to not make this a habit, okay?"

He looks up and me, and I swear he smiles. The fact that he has his own poop on top of his head like a little fecal yarmulke does not take away from the cute. I go to the bathroom and grab an old towel, and come back to grab him, dumping him right in the bathtub for a good scrub. I make a note to check downstairs later to see if they bought doggie shampoo, since bathing him in my pricy extra-moisturizing shampoo for curly hair will be egregiously expensive. I plop the now-clean and weirdly citrusy-smelling dog in the middle of my bed with a chew toy, and grab the crate. I put everything that was inside in the washing machine in the hallway, and dump the crate itself in the tub, and hit it with the hand-held shower sprayer. Once it's clean, I leave it there to dry, making a mental note to Ajax the hell out of the tub in the morning. Then I go back to see the dog, looking innocent as can be, sitting on my pillow.

"C'mon, buddy, we're going to do another walk." Although I can't imagine there is anything at all still left in his tiny body, maybe another walk will wear him out. There is a neighbor coming towards us with his dog. I stop and have Munch sit down, waiting for the beagle to approach, and after a very polite butt sniffing, and some hopping, we make our good-byes, and head for home.

Whatever crate problem he was having, Munch curls up between my feet without a peep and falls right to sleep, with the cutest little bit of a snuffly snore that you've ever heard. And before long, I follow suit.

It Had to Be You

(1947)

CORNEL WILDE AS GEORGE McKESSON, KISSING VICTO-
RIA: How!

GINGER ROGERS AS VICTORIA STAFFORD, POST-KISS:
And how!

～～～

The licking wakes me. I open one eye to see Munch, standing on my chest, shockingly heavy for such a little guy, breathing his puppy breath in my face, smiling like a lunatic.

"Good morning, silly little man. Are you ready for a very big day?" I say, plucking a wayward earplug off of his left buttock. Apparently I'm a "let the dog sleep in the bed" kind of girl after all. I'm certainly learning a lot about myself these days, and I wonder if I'll ever really know me completely.

Today is moving day. After a decent twenty-four-hour interval, and confirming that my furry little dependent would be welcome in my new apartment, I accepted the Astor Place job. I went in for a meeting the next day, met with the executive pastry chef and some of the other key culinary staff. I'll be able to hire my own assistants once I get up to speed. We signed contracts, and Dave took me to see my new place. The apartment is everything I need, about one thousand square feet, with a decent-sized bedroom, a small living room/dining room, a well-appointed galley kitchen, and an en-suite bathroom in the bedroom and a small

powder room near the entrance. Since the apartments are designed for long-term business housing, they are furnished, which is a huge relief, since I don't own a stick of furniture. Dave said if at any point I wanted to swap anything out, I can just notify housekeeping and they will remove the hotel's stuff to make room for mine, but I can't think about that anytime soon.

The last two days I've gradually loaded in most of my boxes and belongings—between buttoning things up at the bakery and at home, and the constant attention a new puppy requires, my mind and body have been well occupied. Which is good, because if not, I'd be completely obsessing about tonight.

Jake emailed last night to confirm that he is indeed back in Chicago full-time, if jet-lagged, and that he would be picking me up for the gala at five thirty this evening. It felt really great to give him the address of the hotel, and when he replied asking why I was staying at a hotel, I said all would be revealed later. Jean dropped off the dress earlier today with the hotel, and is coming by around six thirty once I'm gone to puppy-sit, with Ruth bringing her dinner. I know that they are claiming they just want to be sure the little guy is okay his first night in the new place, but I also know that they could have stopped by to walk him and play for a bit; the whole waiting-for-me thing is about wanting to be there if the night goes south, or is amazing.

"Good morning," Bubbles says as I come into the kitchen, Munch immediately running to pounce on poor Snatch, who is resting on the floor under the table.

"Good morning to you. What's all this?"

Bubbles has clearly been cooking up a storm. She's made her famous muffins, there is a pile of eggs that she has scrambled with chives, and a platter of grilled salami, cut half an inch thick and seared on both sides to crispy goodness. There is a dish of her hash brown casserole, the thinly shredded potatoes mixed with cream cheese, cheddar cheese, and sour cream, and

baked with a crunchy buttered breadcrumb topping. A basket of toasted rye bread, a bowl of strawberries, and a plate with a chocolate babka already sliced up. There is a pitcher of orange juice, freshly squeezed, and a bottle of champagne at the ready.

"It's your last morning, and your folks are back from their honeymoon, so we're having a family breakfast to celebrate!"

She barely gets the words out when we hear voices at the front door. Munch and Snatch take off as fast as their short little bowlegs will take them, Munch losing his footing on the hardwood floors making the turn and sliding right into Snatch's butt face-first.

"Well goodness, such a welcoming committee!" says my mom, scooping up the puppy in her arms and receiving his face-licking welcome most happily.

"Yes, we're happy to see you too, old man," my dad says, leaning down to rub Snatch's head and slip him a treat from the bowl on the table by the door.

"Who are you calling 'old man'?" Herman says, coming up the front stairs behind them, carrying a white box.

There are kisses and hugs and welcomes all around, and we help Bubbles bring the feast into the dining room, where we start to make hearty plates while she and Herman make mimosas for us all. I toss both of the dogs bully sticks to keep them busy.

"How was the vacation?" Bubbles asks, when we are all seated and tucking into the amazing food.

"Glorious," my mom says. They did ten days in Berkeley, Napa, and Sonoma, plenty of hiking and wine tasting and eating, and two days at a funky spa in Calistoga with mud baths and mineral pools and couples massages.

"Really fun. But we're both exhausted. You know honeymooners . . ." my dad says with a lascivious look.

"Gross, dad, we're eating here."

"Really, Bobby, not breakfast conversation."

"Yes," Herman says. "Save sex for lunch."

"Well, for an hour after lunch, like swimming, you don't want a cramp," Bubbles says.

"*Hey!* Horny old people. I'm *eating!*" Seriously, I don't know what they are all putting in their Metamucil, but they are some randy seniors.

"Forget our X-rated honeymoon, I want to hear about the job," my mom says.

"Well, I'll be in charge of all special-event baking. So specialty cakes, but also any pastries or breads connected to events, from weddings and parties to corporate events. And when the main restaurant does their own special menus for holidays, I'll be brought in to assist with those as well. Once I get up to speed in the next week or so, I'll be able to hire a pastry sous chef as well as a full-time assistant, so I'll be managing a team of three to start, and as the event business expands, maybe more. They've set aside a separate baking kitchen for me, and it is amazing. Huge walk-in, all the equipment imaginable."

"And the apartment is good?" my dad asks, picking up a round of salami in his fingers and taking a big bite.

"It's pretty cute. I mean, it looks like a nice hotel suite, with a kitchen. All in shades of gray, so it's sort of calm and soothing."

"You don't worry about essentially living at work? How will you separate?" my mom asks.

"I thought about it, and for this first year at least, I think being there will make my life easier, especially for the larger, more complicated events. If I'm doing the wedding on Saturday night with the midnight snack buffet and the brunch on Sunday, not having to go far will work in my favor. Once things are up and running, and I have staff I trust, I might look to move off campus, but for now, it is easy, and free!"

"And the daily housekeeping service with in-house laundry and dry cleaning probably doesn't hurt," Bubbles says.

"No, it certainly doesn't. And I've never lived right downtown like that, so it might be fun. It will certainly be good for Munch to be so close to the park."

"I think the whole thing is terrific," my dad says. "Good for you!"

"Hear, hear," says Herman.

"And we understand you may have a buyer for the building?" my dad asks him.

"Juni . . . Mark is working on it. He won't tell me details, says to just do what I do until he brings me an offer he thinks is the right one, but I do know there is someone interested, and he seems hopeful they might come to acceptable terms."

"And what about a wedding date for you two?" my mom asks. "I have to say, as long as you keep your stress in check, it really is a wonderful thing to do!"

We all laugh.

"We were thinking maybe Valentine's Day," Bubbles says. "You know, we're elderly, so we figured we'd better pick a date we could remember."

"I think that sounds wonderfully romantic," my mom says. "A dreamy winter wedding."

"Would you want to do it at the hotel?" I ask. "Dave says that I get a forty-percent discount on events that I book for family and friends for the first year while we are building the business."

"That sounds lovely, dear, thank you for the offer. When we figure out what we are really talking about, we will let you know," Bubbles says.

"Well, regardless . . ."

"We know, you'll do the cake!" Herman says, and the group breaks up again, and digs back into seconds and thirds.

After we clean up and visit a little more, my folks head home and I go back upstairs to finish packing up the last load of stuff that I'm taking to the hotel. I weirdly wish that Mark had been there; he's been mostly in California lately, according to Her-

man. Our little blended family seems somehow incomplete without him around. I called him yesterday and left a message, thanking him for the introduction to Dave, and what I presume was his influence in my well-timed new job offer. He called back and said that he was delighted for me, but that he had nothing to do with the job. Dave had just really been impressed with me from the cake competition, and had apparently sent some secret diners to the bakery to bring him samples of my other work over the course of a couple of weeks right after, and then sent his sister with her kids on Halloween to bring him all the specialty items, and that locked the offer in.

"But something tells me that the interest in my dad's building might have something to do with you," he said.

"Only if it has a great outcome. If it doesn't, I had nothing to do with it."

"Duly noted. But thank you, regardless."

"You know, Dave says I get to hire my own staff . . . any chance you want to leave the world of high-stakes business and get back into baking? You have some skills."

He laughed. "I think that contest was my last baking hurrah, except for the occasional banana bread. I do make a superior banana bread."

"You'll have to make it for me sometime." This comes out flirtier than I mean it.

"Maybe I will."

"Well, thanks again, at least for the intro to Dave. You might not have put me up for the job, but I doubt I would have gotten it without that connection, so I just wanted you to know that I appreciate it."

"Hey, what is family for!?" he says with a wicked tone in his voice.

"Ugh. You seriously are going to have to cut that out. The whole family thing gives me the willies."

"Why? Didn't you always want a step-cousin-brother or whatever we will be?"

"Um, no, and particularly not one that I've . . ."

"Seen naked?"

"*Really?* You promised we'd not speak of that. It's all too *Flowers in the Attic*. I was going to say not one that I've come to think of as a friend."

"Awww. That's so sweet. And I haven't spoken of it at all. But speaking of it, how's your absentee boyfriend? Still hiding from you?"

"Actually, we have a date tomorrow night."

"Wow. Well, where are you going? You know, maybe I should come in case he doesn't show up again."

"I'm not worried. He's taking me to a gala."

"An event expert headed to a fancy event. Seems appropriate."

"What does that mean?" How would he know about Wedding Girl?

"I mean, don't you make wedding cakes and special-occasion cakes? Didn't you help plan your parents' wedding to perfection? Won't you be helping my dad and Bubbles?"

Whew. I've got very little time left to give my advice to the wedding challenged, and since Mark has decided to play the teasing friend role with me, I don't need him to have any more ammunition than he already does. "Yep, that's me, wedding expert at your service."

"Maybe someday you'll help me plan mine." I don't know why this stung, but it did.

"If you're lucky."

"Indeed. Congrats on the job, Sophie, you'll be amazing. But you were always going to land on your feet. They're lucky to get you, be sure you don't forget that."

I look down at Munch, who is defiling a sock he plucked out

of my suitcase. "Dog, you ready to go home?" He hops up and does a happy little spin. "Okay, let's do it!" And I grab my bags, and turn out the lights, and we take those first steps together.

I get Munch all settled, filling his water bowl and setting up his toys in a corner of the living room, and leave him to play while I unpack the rest of my stuff. I know that the place is going to feel like a hotel for a while, but I tell myself that there are worse things than being on permanent vacation. And Bubbles isn't wrong—the amenities are pretty sweet. I always hated making a bed. I make a mental note to warn the housekeeping staff about the earplugs.

I open the closet, and there is the hanging bag. I pull it out and open it up and my breath stops. My former wedding dress is transformed. The silk under-dress is now a deep slate blue, and the gossamer over-dress is a pale violet gray, so the effect is just spectacular. I know how hard it is to dye fabrics like these; Jean is a master. There is a little note tucked in the bottom of the bag.

You'll be stunning, and he's going to thank his lucky stars. Have a beautiful night!

XO jean

PS Figured these colors will still work with the shoes.

She's amazing. And she's right, the opaline Dior pumps, the heel fixed better than new by the cobbler, will be stunning with it. I check my watch. I've got a three o'clock appointment with the salon downstairs for hair and makeup.

"C'mon Munch, let's take a walk and check out the new hood."

I snap on his leash and take the elevator down to the lobby, where Munch is immediately swarmed by people who want to meet him. He prances around, is generally charming, and I can tell that this hotel living is going to suit him awfully well. We take a nice long walk and meet some neighborhood dogs, and Munch rewards me with ample marking of territory and a good solid poop, so I'm feeling okay about Jean coming later to manage him.

We get back home, and I toss him a chew toy, put up the gate to keep him in the kitchen, where even if he has an accident it will be on tile floor, and head downstairs.

The salon is buzzing, being a Saturday night, but Amber, the stylist, is very excited to play with my hair. She talks me into a deep conditioning treatment, and then gives me a quick cut, and pulls it into a sort of messy chignon, with a zillion bobby pins. I had no idea that all those hairdos that look so effortless and slightly undone are actually harder to do than sleek smooth ones. Amber hands me off to Gigi, who asks a few questions about my dress, and then attacks my face. When she's done she spins me around to face the mirror. My skin looks flawless, and my eyes are the deepest blue they've ever been, my lashes are long and dark, and my lips are in a perfect shade of nude pink, with the slightest shimmer.

"Here you go." Gigi hands me a lipstick, liner, and gloss. "For touch-ups. Bring 'em back tomorrow."

"Thank you!" I check out, once again loving the employee discount, and tip them both generously. Then I head back up to my new place. Munch has turned the chew toy into a pile of tiny bits, but hasn't had an accident. I clean up the pieces and head in to get dressed. Jean has changed the dress construction to incorporate the corseting into the underdress so that I don't have to have a separate foundation garment. I pull on a pair of brand-new Spanx, and a bra, and then get into the dress. The inner corseting hooks up my back and it definitely flattens out the

tummy and pulls in the waist, but somehow is still letting me breathe. I slip into my pumps, and then close the bedroom door to check the full-length mirror on the back.

As much as I momentarily felt like a princess on my almost-wedding day is nothing compared to how beautiful I feel right now. The way the gray moves over the blue underdress as I turn my hips is glorious, and almost looks like water. My curves might be on the very generous side, but they are sassy and sexy in this dress. The words "brick house" are coming to mind. And for the first time, I'm not at all worried about meeting Jake. Because my life is not something to be embarrassed about, nor are my looks. If he can't see me in this dress and hear my confession about who I am and where I come from and forgive and forget, then he will not be worth my time.

I'm just finishing putting my borrowed lipstick and some Kleenex into my silver beaded clutch when there is a knock on the door. Munch starts yipping excitedly and I take a deep breath and open the door.

"Hi," says the man in the tuxedo outside my door. I try not to be disappointed. He looks perfectly nice. Shorter and balder than I had anticipated, or maybe hoped for, but he has kind eyes. And I think back to our emails and how much I enjoy the way his brain works, and straighten my spine. And receive the bottle of champagne he proffers.

"Hi there. It's so nice to finally meet you," I say, taking the bottle and setting it on the little console table beside the door.

"And you," he says, shaking my hand. I use it to pull him in and kiss him on the cheek. I'm determined to give Jake every chance in the world.

"Oh, my," he says, looking puzzled. Munch yips happily. "And who is this fellow?"

That's weird. I emailed him about the puppy the day he arrived. "That's Munch. My puppy? I told you about him?"

"You did? But we've just met." Just met?

"I'm sorry, Jake?"

"No, I'm Wallace. The head maître d' downstairs? I wanted to sneak up before service tonight to welcome you, and say that my team and I are all very much looking forward to working with you."

Oh, my. "I'm sorry, I was expecting someone else."

"I can see that. You look lovely. I'll get out of your hair, we can meet in a couple of days, just wanted to welcome you on behalf of the front-of-house staff."

"Sorry for the mix-up."

"Not a problem in the least. Have a wonderful evening. You too, little man." And he turns to go. I'm just closing the door when there is a light knock on it.

"Hi," says Mark, looking very Cary Grant in a tuxedo with a shawl collar and an ivory silk scarf. Apparently my evening is going to be a farce of tuxedoed men.

"What are you doing here? My date will be here any minute," I say as Mark boldly walks right in and scoops Munch up in his arms. "Careful, you'll get dog hair all over your beautiful tuxedo," I say, as Mark hands me a small bag.

"For you," he says. "Banana bread. As promised. To welcome you to your new home. And a squeaky toy for the beastie."

"Thank you, really lovely, and now you really have to . . . go . . . Why are you wearing a tuxedo?" My heart stops.

"Ahem. Um, Sunny? Very nice to meet you. I'm Jake."

"You. Are. Not," I say, but I don't mean it, and as confused as I am, I'm also suddenly feeling really, really happy.

"Yeah. A nickname from high school, apparently some girls thought I looked like a Jewish Jake Ryan and it sort of stuck as a joke with my high school pals. Are you horribly disappointed?"

My voice catches. "I really wanted it to be you. I didn't believe, but sometimes I thought maybe, but you, and then, and we, but then you . . ." I cannot find words.

"Look. We've got the rest of our lives to apologize to each other for stuff, and explain what needs explaining, but for the moment, we look pretty gorgeous, and my company is going to need me to show up to schmooze the clients at the table, so what do you say we pretend that this is what it should always have been, a really special first date that is very long overdue. We'll go, and we'll be quietly snarky about bad outfits and boring speeches, and we'll charm the pants off the people at our table and dance a lot and drink champagne and then we'll go for our hot dogs and look at our city and in the morning, we'll eat banana bread and figure out the rest."

"Well, um, I mean . . ."

"The word is yes, darling. Let me see if this helps loosen your tongue." And Herman Mark "Jake" Langer Jr. pulls me into his arms and kisses me very, very deeply, and exceedingly well, and then Munch leans in and starts licking the tears off my cheeks where I hadn't even felt them falling, and nothing else in the world matters.

~~The End~~

~~The Beginning~~

~~Happily~~ Hopefully Ever After

Wedding Girl Recipes

Sophie might not share these delectables with the Cake Goddess, but she knows she can trust you with her secrets.

HERMAN'S CHOCOLATE BABKA

Adapted from Breads Bakery

MAKES 3 BABKAS

Herman might be old-school, but this chocolate babka is still everyone's favorite. Made a little bit easier now since Hershey's sells an easy-to-use jarred chocolate spread. You can up the ante a bit by swapping it out for Nutella; Sophie won't tell Herman.

FOR THE SYRUP:

½ cup sugar

⅔ cup water

FOR THE DOUGH:

¾ cup whole milk

1½ packets (10 grams) active dry yeast

2½ cups bread flour, sifted, plus more for dusting
    work surface

2½ cups pastry flour, sifted

2 large eggs

½ cup and 1 tablespoon sugar

1 teaspoon vanilla

¼ teaspoon kosher salt

1 stick unsalted butter, at room temperature

FOR THE CHOCOLATE FILLING:

30 ounces Hershey's chocolate spread

1 cup semisweet chocolate chips

Make the syrup: Add sugar and water to a pot set over medium-high heat and bring to a boil. Reduce heat and let simmer until sugar dissolves, 2 minutes. Remove from heat and let cool. Cooled syrup can be stored, refrigerated, in an airtight container up to 1 month.

Make the dough: Pour milk into a bowl. Activate yeast according to instructions on packet, then add to milk. Add the following ingredients to milk-yeast mixture in this order: flours, eggs, sugar, vanilla, salt, and half the butter. Using your hands, or an electric mixer with a dough hook set on the lowest speed, blend until combined, 3 to 4 minutes. Continue blending, increasing speed to medium if using a mixer, and slowly add remaining butter in small chunks until combined, about 4 minutes.

Place dough on a work surface lightly dusted with flour and knead by hand until dough starts to feel inflexible, 2 minutes. Shape dough into a square. Place on a tray, cover with plastic wrap, and refrigerate 8 to 12 hours.

Make the babka: Place dough on a work surface lightly dusted with flour. Using a rolling pin, shape dough into a 10 x 28-inch rectangle about ⅕-inch thick. Slather chocolate spread evenly over dough, then sprinkle dough with chocolate chips. Roll dough tightly like a jelly roll and lay seam-side down. Use a serrated knife to cut roll into thirds, then cut each segment in half lengthwise.

Lay two dough pieces on a work surface so they form an X shape. Twist each end once or twice, so babka resembles a simple braid. Repeat with remaining dough pieces, so you have 3 babka loaves in all. Transfer each to an 8 x 3-inch loaf pan, tucking ends of dough under.

Cover pans with a dry towel and let rise until loaves double in volume, about 60 minutes. For best results, place a bowl of warm water at the bottom of an oven that hasn't been turned on, then place loaves inside oven and shut the door.

Set oven to convection mode and preheat to 350°F. Bake loaves 25 minutes. (If not using convection mode, bake an additional 5 minutes.) Check babkas after 20 minutes. If they are starting to turn dark brown and are still not cooked through, cover with parchment or aluminum foil to prevent tops from burning. Once baked, remove babkas from oven and brush immediately with a generous amount of syrup.

⟅⟊⟆

BUBBLES'S LEMON MUFFINS WITH BLUEBERRIES AND STREUSEL
MAKES 12 MUFFINS

Sophie isn't the only talented cook in the family; much of her love of baking she found at Bubbles's knee. These are Bubbles's signature lemon-blueberry muffins. No one will blink if you decide to drizzle them with a little lemon icing.

FOR THE MUFFINS:

1½ cups all-purpose flour

½ cup sugar

2½ teaspoons baking powder

½ teaspoon salt

½ teaspoon cinnamon

1 teaspoon lemon zest

⅔ cup plain yogurt

4 tablespoons unsalted butter, melted and cooled

3 tablespoons buttermilk

1 egg, lightly beaten

¼ cup freshly squeezed lemon juice

¼ teaspoon pure vanilla

2 cups fresh blueberries, washed and tossed with 1
tablespoon of flour to coat

FOR THE STREUSEL:

½ cup butter, softened

½ cup granulated sugar

½ cup firmly packed light brown sugar

⅔ cup all-purpose flour

1 teaspoon ground cinnamon

½ teaspoon ground nutmeg

¼ teaspoon lemon zest

Preheat oven to 375°F. Line 12-cup muffin tin with muffin/cupcake liners.

In one large bowl, whisk together the flour, sugar, baking powder, salt, cinnamon, and lemon zest. In another large bowl, whisk together the yogurt, butter, buttermilk, egg, lemon juice, and vanilla. Fold the wet ingredients into the dry ingredients, mixing just until combined. Fold in blueberries gently.

Fill each of the 12 muffin liners about ⅔ full. Mix all the streusel ingredients in a bowl until it resembles wet sand. Sprinkle the mixture evenly on top of the 12 muffins.

Bake 17 to 19 minutes, until puffed and golden. Transfer to a wire rack to cool.

LAMB SHAWARMA WITH TAHINI SAUCE AND GREEN SAUCE
SERVES 8

When your husband or boyfriend has a simple palate, you need your girlfriends to eat the adventurous stuff with you! Sophie knows that her new pal Amelia would never get to have this richly spiced Middle Eastern dish at home, so she's more than happy to accommodate her. This makes for a wonderful dinner party dish; just put out pita and lavash breads and all the toppings for people to make their own sandwiches. Sophie serves it with a cucumber yogurt salad and a freekeh and lentil pilaf.

FOR THE LAMB:

2 lemons, juiced

½ cup plus 1 tablespoon olive oil

6 cloves garlic, peeled, smashed, and minced

1 teaspoon kosher salt

2 teaspoons freshly ground black pepper

2 teaspoons ground cumin

2 teaspoons paprika

½ teaspoon turmeric

pinch of ground cinnamon

red pepper flakes, to taste

2 pounds lamb shoulder, cut into 2 x ½-inch strips

1 large red onion, peeled and quartered

2 tablespoons fresh parsley, chopped

Combine the lemon juice, ½ cup olive oil, garlic, salt, pepper, cumin, paprika, turmeric, cinnamon, and red pepper flakes in a large bowl, then whisk to combine. Add the lamb and toss well to coat. Cover and store in refrigerator for at least 1 hour and up to 12 hours.

When ready to cook, preheat oven to 425°F. Use the remaining tablespoon of olive oil to grease a rimmed sheet pan. Add the quartered onion to the lamb and marinade and toss once to combine. Remove the lamb and onion from the marinade and place on the pan, spreading everything evenly across it.

Put the lamb in the oven and roast until it is browned, crisp at the edges, and cooked to medium, about 30 minutes. Remove it from the oven and allow to rest 2 minutes. (To make the lamb even crispier, set a large pan over high heat, add a tablespoon of olive oil to the pan, then the lamb, and sauté until it curls tight in the heat.) Scatter the parsley over the top and serve with tomatoes, cucumbers, pita, white sauce, hot sauce, olives, fried eggplant, feta, or rice—really anything you desire.

TAHINI SAUCE

½ cup tahini

1½ tablespoon lemon juice

water

pinch of cumin

salt and pepper, to taste

Mix tahini with lemon juice and add enough water to make it the consistency of heavy cream. It should be a liquid sauce. Add cumin and season to taste with salt and pepper.

GREEN SAUCE

1 serrano chili pepper

½ cup parsley

½ cup mint

2 garlic cloves

4 tablespoons vegetable oil

1 tablespoon water

1 teaspoon lemon juice

¼ teaspoon cumin

½ teaspoon red pepper flakes

¼ teaspoon salt

Put all ingredients in a blender or food processor or use your immersion blender to make a smooth sauce.

SOPHIE'S MOM'S FAMOUS NOODLE KUGEL
SERVES 12

In Sophie's family, they know that difficult news goes down better with delicious food. This classic Jewish brunch dish may seem strange if you've never had it, but trust Sophie, it is delicious. Whatever bombshell someone might drop on you.

16 ounces broad egg noodles

4 tablespoons butter, melted

1 pound cottage cheese

1 pound sour cream

4 eggs, beaten

½ cup sugar

2 teaspoons vanilla extract

1 cup crushed cornflakes

1 teaspoon cinnamon

¼ cup demerara sugar (or you can substitute light
    brown sugar)

Preheat oven to 350°F. Cook noodles to al dente in boiling salted water according to package directions. Drain and rinse with cold water. In a large bowl, mix the melted butter, cottage cheese, sour cream, eggs, sugar, and vanilla, and then fold in the cooked noodles. Pour into a greased 9 x 13-inch pan. In a separate bowl, mix the cornflakes, cinnamon, and sugar. Sprinkle the cornflake mixture on top of the noodle mixture. Bake for about 1 hour until the top is brown and a knife inserted in the center comes out clean.

You can also make this in muffin tins for attractive individual portions; if doing so, reduce the cooking time by about half and then start checking for doneness.

CHOCOLATE PUDDING

Adapted from the *New York Times*

SERVES 6

Sophie's dad is a man of simple tastes and pleasures, and this classic chocolate pudding is nostalgia at its finest.

2¼ cups half-and-half, divided

6 tablespoons sugar, divided

2 tablespoons cocoa

2 tablespoons cornstarch

¼ teaspoon salt

1 large egg

2 large egg yolks

5 ounces bittersweet chocolate, melted and still
   warm

2 tablespoons unsalted butter, at room temperature
   and cut into 4 pieces

1 teaspoon vanilla extract

Bring 2 cups of the half-and-half and 3 tablespoons of the sugar
to a boil in a saucepan. While the half-and-half is heating, toss
the cocoa, cornstarch, and salt into the work bowl of a food processor and pulse to blend; turn the ingredients out onto a sheet
of wax paper. Place the egg, egg yolks, and remaining 3 tablespoons sugar in the work bowl and process for 1 minute. Scrape
down the sides of the bowl and add the remaining ¼ cup half-
and-half. Process for a few seconds. Return the dry ingredients
to the bowl and pulse just until blended.

With the machine running, slowly pour in the hot half-and-
half, processing to blend. The mixture will be foamy, but the
bubbles will disappear when the pudding is cooked. Pour the
mixture into the saucepan and cook over medium-high heat,
stirring continuously, for about 2 minutes, or until the pudding
thickens. (The pudding should not boil.) Scrape the pudding
into the processor, add the chocolate, butter, and vanilla extract,
and pulse until they are evenly blended.

Pour the pudding into 6 4-ounce bowls or 1 large bowl. Chill
for at least 4 hours. Serve plain or topped with heavy cream,
whipped or not.

FIG TARTS WITH PISTACHIO CREAM
MAKES 6 TARTS

Sophie helps Herman expand the bakery's offerings, and this tart is one new recipe he absolutely approves of! It's actually really easy to make, and a showstopper for dinner parties.

FOR THE PASTRY:
1½ cups all-purpose flour
½ cup yellow cornmeal
1 teaspoon salt
1 tablespoon sugar
12 tablespoons unsalted butter
4 tablespoons ice water

FOR THE FILLING:
2 tablespoons flour
2 tablespoons sugar
¼ teaspoon cinnamon
3 dozen small mission figs, stemmed and quartered
¼ cup honey

Blend all pastry ingredients except water in food processor and pulse to form coarse meal. Add in ice water until the dough comes together. Divide dough in half and wrap halves in plastic. Chill 1 hour. Divide each piece of dough into thirds and roll into rough 7-inch circles. Preheat oven to 350 degrees.

For the filling: stir together flour, sugar, and cinnamon. Sprinkle 2 teaspoons of mixture onto dough rounds, leaving 1-inch border. Arrange fig pieces, cut-side up, in concentric circles. Fold in borders over figs. Transfer to greased baking sheets.

Bake until crust is lightly browned, about 20 minutes. Drizzle honey over figs and bake 5 more minutes. Serve with pistachio cream.

PISTACHIO CREAM

1 cup heavy cream
1 teaspoon sugar
¼ cup pistachio paste (homemade or canned)

Whip the cream to soft peaks with the sugar. Then mix in the pistachio paste and taste for sweetness and flavor. It shouldn't be too sweet, but should have nice pistachio flavor. Add more pistachio paste or sugar to taste.

ᕮᘏᕬ

MILK BREAD

MAKES 6 ROLLS, 1 (9X5) LOAF, OR 12 SPLIT-TOP BUNS

This recipe is being reprinted gratefully with permission from Kindred Restaurant in Davidson, North Carolina. And while you should absolutely make it yourself, especially for holidays, if you ever find yourself in the greater Charlotte area, go eat at the restaurant. Because, delicious. *It's no wonder that when Sophie needs to find the perfect thing to try to save Langer's, she calls Stephanie for this recipe.*

5⅓ cups bread flour, divided, plus more for surface
1 cup plus 1 teaspoon water
1 cup heavy cream
⅓ cup mild honey (such as wildflower or alfalfa)
3 tablespoons nonfat dry milk powder

2 tablespoons active dry yeast (from about 3
    envelopes)
2 tablespoons kosher salt
3 large eggs, divided
4 tablespoons (½ stick) unsalted butter, at room
    temperature and cut into pieces
nonstick vegetable oil spray
flaky sea salt (optional)

Cook ⅓ cup flour and 1 cup water in a small saucepan over medium heat, whisking constantly, until a thick paste forms (almost like a roux but looser), about 5 minutes. Add cream and honey, and cook, whisking to blend, until honey dissolves. Transfer mixture to the bowl of a stand mixer fitted with a dough hook and add milk powder, yeast, kosher salt, 2 eggs, and 5 cups flour. Knead on medium speed until dough is smooth, about 5 minutes. Add butter, a piece at a time, fully incorporating into dough before adding the next piece, until dough is smooth, shiny, and elastic, about 4 minutes.

Coat a large bowl with nonstick spray and transfer dough to bowl, turning to coat. Cover with plastic wrap and let rise in a warm, draft-free place until doubled in size, about 1 hour.

If making rolls, lightly coat a 6-cup jumbo muffin pan with nonstick spray. Turn out dough onto a floured surface and divide into 6 pieces. Divide each piece into 4 smaller pieces (you should have 24 total). They don't need to be exact; just eyeball it. Place 4 pieces of dough side by side in each muffin cup.

If making a loaf, lightly coat a 9 x 5-inch loaf pan with non-stick spray. Turn out dough onto a floured surface and divide into 6 pieces. Nestle pieces side by side to create 2 rows down length of the pan.

If making split-top buns, lightly coat two 13 x 9-inch baking dishes with nonstick spray. Divide dough into 12 pieces and

shape each into a 4-inch-long log. Place 6 logs in a row down length of each dish.

Let shaped dough rise in a warm, draft-free place until doubled in size (dough should be just puffing over top of pan), about 1 hour.

Preheat oven to 375°F. Beat remaining egg with 1 teaspoon water in a small bowl to blend. Brush top of dough with egg wash and sprinkle with sea salt, if desired. Bake, rotating pan halfway through, until bread is deep golden brown, starting to pull away from the sides of the pan, and is baked through, 25 to 35 minutes for rolls, 50 to 60 minutes for loaf, or 30 to 40 minutes for buns. If making buns, slice each bun down the middle deep enough to create a split top. Let milk bread cool slightly in pan on a wire rack before turning out; let cool completely.

WALNUT CAKE WITH POPPY SEED FILLING AND HONEY-ROASTED APRICOTS

SERVES 12

For the cake competition, Sophie needs one of her tiers to nod to the history of the neighborhood. This moist walnut cake, with a bit of poppy seed filling and roasted apricot halves, pulls inspiration from Herman's classic rugelach fillings.

1 cup cake flour
2 teaspoons baking powder
1 teaspoon kosher salt
4 tablespoons canola oil
4 tablespoons maple syrup
½ cup milk

8 ounces walnuts, lightly toasted

8 ounces unsalted butter, at room temperature

1 cup light brown sugar

1 vanilla bean

4 large eggs, at room temperature

1 cup canned poppy seed filling

honey-roasted apricots (recipe follows)

vanilla buttercream frosting (recipe follows)

Preheat oven to 350°F. Butter 2 8-inch round cake pans and line with parchment paper. Set aside.

In a medium bowl, whisk together the flour, baking powder, and salt, and set aside.

In a small bowl, whisk together the canola oil, maple syrup, and milk, and set aside.

Place the toasted walnuts in a food processor and grind until they are the size of bread crumbs. Be careful not to grind them into a paste!

Place the butter and brown sugar in the bowl of a stand mixer. Scrape the seeds from the vanilla bean and add them and the pod to the bowl of the stand mixer. Using the paddle attachment, cream the mixture on medium speed until pale and fluffy, about 3 minutes. Remove the vanilla bean pod and discard. Add the eggs, one at a time, mixing thoroughly after each addition. Scrape down the bowl as needed. Once all the eggs are added, beat for another minute. Reduce the speed of the mixer to low, and add the ground walnuts. Mix to combine.

With the mixer running on low, add ⅓ of the flour mixture. Mix until just combined and then add ½ of the milk mixture. Repeat with another ⅓ of the flour, then with the rest of the milk mixture, ending with the last of the flour mixture.

Pour the batter into the prepared cake pans and smooth the tops. Bake until done, about 25 to 30 minutes. The baked surface

will spring back slightly when touched in the center, the sides will begin to contract from the pan, and a toothpick inserted into the center of the cake will come out clean. Remove the cake from the oven and let cool completely before removing from the pan.

To assemble, spread the poppy seed filling thinly over the bottom layer of the cake. Pipe a ½-inch ring of frosting around the edge of the cake, on top of the poppy seed. Place this in the freezer for 15 to 30 minutes, so that the piped frosting is firm. You just want to be able to put the apricots in and top the cake without everything squirting out the sides.

Arrange enough apricot halves inside the ring of frosting to cover the poppy seed filling in one layer, and then put the top cake layer on. Frost the rest of the cake.

HONEY-ROASTED APRICOTS

1 pound fresh apricots, halved and pitted
1 tablespoon honey (warmed slightly so that it is
    liquid)

Preheat oven to 350°F. Place apricots cut-side up on a parchment-lined rimmed baking sheet and drizzle with honey. Roast 30 minutes and let cool completely.

VANILLA BUTTERCREAM FROSTING

6 to 8 cups confectioners' sugar, divided
2 sticks unsalted butter, softened
½ cup whole milk
2 teaspoons vanilla

Mix 4 cups sugar and butter in large mixing bowl. Add milk and vanilla. Beat with electric mixer till smooth and creamy, about 3

to 5 minutes. Gradually add remaining sugar 1 cup at a time, beating for about 2 minutes after each addition, until the icing is thick enough for your purposes. You may not need all the sugar. Use and store icing at room temperature. It can be stored in an airtight container for up to 3 days. This may make more frosting than you need for this cake, but better too much than too little!

~⁓~

SPINACH AND CHEESE BREAKFAST STRATA
SERVES 6 TO 8

Bubbles makes this breakfast casserole whenever she needs to feed a crowd first thing in the morning. You make it the night before and then just pop it in the oven when you wake.

1½ cups finely chopped onion

3 tablespoons unsalted butter

1 teaspoon salt, divided

½ teaspoon black pepper, divided

¼ teaspoon freshly grated nutmeg

1 10-ounce package frozen spinach, thawed, squeezed of all excess liquid, and chopped

8 cups French or Italian bread, cut into 1-inch cubes (about ½ pound)

6 ounces (2 cups) coarsely grated Gruyère cheese

2 ounces (1 cup) finely grated Parmesan

9 large eggs

2¾ cups milk

2 tablespoons Dijon mustard

Sauté onion in butter in a large, heavy skillet over medium heat until soft, about 5 minutes. Add ½ teaspoon salt, ¼ teaspoon pepper, and nutmeg, and continue cooking for 1 minute. Stir in spinach, remove from heat, and set aside.

Spread ⅓ of the bread cubes in a well-buttered 3-quart gratin dish or other ceramic baking dish. Top with ⅓ of bread cubes, ⅓ of spinach mixture, and ⅓ of each cheese. Repeat layering twice with remaining bread, spinach, and cheese.

Whisk eggs, milk, mustard, and remaining ½ teaspoon salt and ¼ teaspoon pepper together in a large bowl and pour evenly over strata. Cover with plastic wrap and chill strata for at least 8 hours or up to 1 day.

The next day, let it stand at room temperature for 30 minutes while preheating the oven to 350°F. Bake strata, uncovered, in middle of oven until puffed, golden brown, and cooked through, 45 to 55 minutes. Let stand 5 minutes before serving.

~~~

MARK'S BANANA BREAD
MAKES 1 (9X5) LOAF

Mark has some secret skills in the baking arena, but it is this simple and homey banana bread, full of nuts and chocolate chips, that is the gift he brings to Sophie for their first date. It's the perfect thing to eat in bed with your beloved!

½ cup butter, softened

1 cup sugar

2 eggs

3 very ripe bananas, mashed (Mark lets his go
     brown and speckled, and pops them in the
     freezer as is. If yours are frozen, thaw on the

countertop, snip one end off with kitchen
scissors, and let the banana and liquid slide out
into a colander to drain the liquid. If you try to
peel them, you will have a mess!)

1¼ cups flour

½ teaspoon salt

1 teaspoon baking soda

ADD-INS:

½ cup toasted nuts of your choice, chopped if large

½ cup chocolate chips or chunks

Preheat oven to 350°F. Grease a 9x5 loaf pan.

Cream softened butter and sugar with a hand mixer or in a stand mixer on medium speed until light and fluffy.

In a separate bowl, beat eggs until smooth. Add mashed bananas to eggs, blending quickly, then add the mixture into the butter and sugar and stir together.

Sift flour, salt, and baking soda, and fold into wet mixture. Fold in any add-ins. Pour into greased loaf pan and bake 45 to 55 minutes until a skewer comes out clean.

Cool on a rack.

Bring to the one you love.

Wedding Girl

READERS GUIDE

Discussion Questions

1. Sophie is bound and determined to have her dream wedding, even though she knows it goes beyond the scope of her means and requires that she hide the expenses from her fiancé. What do you think about someone who is that committed to a type of event that she will put herself in financial straits in order to make it happen?

2. Sophie is very determined to keep herself hidden away after her public embarrassment. Would you have handled it the same way? What is the most publicly embarrassing thing that has happened to you?

3. Bubbles gives Sophie a safe place to land when her life falls apart. Why do you think Sophie chooses to move in with her instead of with her parents? Who would you move in with in a similar scenario?

4. Sophie adores the movies of the 1930s and 1940s. How can you see those movies influencing her life, good or bad? What do you think it says about her that she is so much more drawn to those old films than to contemporary movies?

5. Do you think that Sophie should be giving out wedding advice for money? Do you like or agree with the advice she gives? If you needed a second source of income, what sort of advice website would you launch?

6. WeddingGirl.com brings Jake into Sophie's life. Why do you think she is drawn to him? Were you excited for her or concerned that he was going to be trouble? Have you ever met someone randomly online and ended up knowing them in real life?

7. Cake Goddess's arrival in the neighborhood means trouble for the already-troubled Langer's and puts Sophie in the awkward position of wanting to help the failing business, without really being committed to it for the long run. Mark calls her out on getting Herman's hopes up. Do you agree with his side of things, or do you think it was right for Herman and Sophie to fight for the business?

8. The cake competition was bound to put Sophie back in the public eye, even if she was only assisting Herman. Do you think she was ready? If you were going to make a cake based on your hometown, what elements would it have?

9. Were you surprised to discover Mark is such an accomplished cook? Did it alter your opinion of him?

10. Were you glad that "Jake" turned out to be Mark? Do you think that he and Sophie are a good match? What do you think their wedding will be like? And who will bake the cake?